VITA NUOVA

Dante Alighieri

VITA NUOVA

ITALIAN TEXT

with

FACING ENGLISH TRANSLATION

by

DINO S. CERVIGNI

&

EDWARD VASTA

The University of Notre Dame Press

Notre Dame   London

Library of Congress-in-Publication Data

Dante Alighieri, 1265-1321.
  [Vita nuova. English & Italian]
  Vita nuova / Dante Alighieri; Italian text with facing English translation
  by Dino S. Cervigni & Edward Vasta.
    v. cm.
  Includes index.
  ISBN 0-268-01925-8 (cloth)   ISBN 0-268-01926-6 (paper)
  I. Cervigni, Dino S. II. Vasta, Edwaud, 1928-   . III. Title.
  PQ4315.58.C47   1995   v. 1
  851'. 1—dc 20   95-2300
                                                             CIP

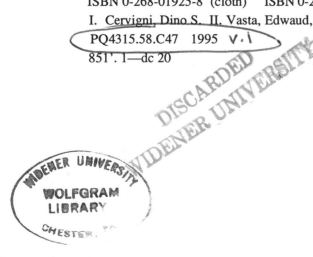

Contents

Preface

Each of these two volumes on Dante's *Vita nuova*, the first centering on text, the second on commentary, has two objectives: to render the original Italian text accessible faithfully and fully to English readers, and to open text and translation meticulously and comprehensively to study by a wide audience. Thus, volume one's introduction reviews Dante's life and his *libello* with sufficient clarity and comprehensiveness to familiarize Dante's or the *Vita nuova*'s first time reader, and also explains the translation's governing theory and data to the Dante scholar. The Italian original reprints Michele Barbi's 1932 international edition, but with two important modifications: it no longer divides the structure of Dante's text into chapters nor interrupts the text with numbered divisions; it thereby restores the text as faithfully as possible to its original manuscript culture. Similarly, the English translation breaks free from the romantic tone and vocabulary evident in English translations thus far and seeks instead to translate Dante's text faithfully in spirit as well as in letter. The index of the English translation and the concordance with glossary of the Italian original, together with appendices, strive to serve scholarship by providing tools for complete and careful access to both texts. The commentary in volume two, finally, provides information and observations intended to serve reading and scholarship both particularly and broadly.

These objectives and the means of their implementation, it must be added, were not fully foreseen at the initiation of these volumes; they did not bring us, the volumes' two curators, both medievalists, readers of both Italian and English, one a specialist in Italian literature and the other in English literature, to the task; we discovered the necessity of these objectives and their implementation as we proceeded. Our original objective centered on making available, for the first time since the Temple Classics edition of 1906 and the King's Classics edition of 1908, both long out of print, a facing page English translation of Dante's *Vita nuova*. The first draft of our translation, however, instigated between us, in our determination to be faithful to the original, a penetrating give-and-take that released us from the romantic orientation established by the translations of the nineteenth century: those by Garrow

1843, Emerson 1847, Norton 1859, Martin 1861, Rossetti 1861, and Boswell 1895: the first translations produced in English and never fully left behind. Fidelity required the translation not only of the narrator-protagonist's words but also his rational spirit and the precise and clear intellectual and spiritual understanding that, as he reflects upon his memories, control his youthful passions, however intense.

Simultaneously, fidelity's continuous revisions and refinements of the translation exposed the degree to which the medieval culture of oral communication governed Dante's expression along with that of written composition. A faithful translation of the original text came to require the preservation of its oral address and locutions as well as its literate meanings, forms, and effects. We had to translate the narrator-protagonist's voice together with his mind, and we had to translate it from his poetry, by free verse rather than English iambics and rhyme, as well as from his prose. Our revisions of the translation in regard to its orality, rationality, and literacy have continued to the last moment before submission to the press, and the result is a translation that reads and sounds, at least to us, quite different from those available. This translation may invite a revision of the English-only reader's expectation and understanding regarding the substance and style of Dante's text.

Fidelity's ultimate challenge became, however, that of translating Dante's text not only in light of itself but in light of the manuscript culture that produced it. This requirement confronted the print culture format and numbering that became universal in Dante studies after Barbi's 1907/1932 edition succeeded editions by his nineteenth-century forerunners: Torri 1843, Witte 1876, and Casini 1885. All of these print culture editions obliterated important manuscript culture qualities of the work, and to this day they affect and control, to an extent that scholars more and more appreciate, how today's readers, English or Italian, experience, understand, and study Dante's text. After detailed examination of both Barbi's report and available manuscript evidence regarding textual format and divisions, and in light of today's understanding of narrativity, particularly narrative's verbal representation of temporal structure, we have removed from the text the unjustified concept of chapters, replaced unjustified paragraph divisions with divisions that are strictly justified by the text's internal structure, and lifted Barbi's canonized numbering from the text by placing them, to preserve scholarly continuity, in the margins. In accord with manuscript practices, we have marked and decorated the beginning of prose paragraphs with drop letters, and in place of line numbers and indentations that indicate the prosodic divisions of the poetry, we have marked these divisions with bold letters. We have avoided fragmenting the text, finally, in the original and in translation, by the intrusion and distraction of footnotes, whose contents are instead incorporated in the second volume. Employing print culture technology, then, as well as philology, we have sought within reasonable limits to enhance our presentation's fidelity to Dante's original.

The years required to produce these volumes also produced papers that explored the data and principles that ultimately laid the groundwork for the volumes' form and objectives. The sequence of these presentations reflects the progress of our labors and records the sources of discussion included in our introduction and commentary. In all, we have presented six papers that confront the issues resolved in the present volumes. The first paper, "It takes Two to Be Faithful: Translating Dante's *Vita nuova*," was written by Edward Vasta and presented by him at the American Association of Italian Studies conference held on April 9-12, 1992, at the University of North Carolina, Chapel Hill. Then followed "Against Dividing the *Vita nuova*: Philology, Literacy, and Orality," composed jointly and presented by Dino Cervigni on November 23, 1992, at the University of Wisconsin, Madison. At the meeting of the Modern Language Association in New York, December 27-30, 1992, Dino Cervigni presented the jointly composed paper, "Revising Editorial Practices and Rereading Dante's *Vita nuova*." In the following year, at the symposium entitled Dante Now: Conference on Current Trends in Dante Studies, University of Notre Dame, October 29-30, 1993, we jointly presented a paper jointly composed: "Restoring Orality to Dante's *Vita nuova*." Cervigni then composed and presented a plenary address, "From the Manuscript Tradition to a New Edition of the *Vita nuova*: Time and Narrativity in Dante's *libello*," to the Dante Society of America, a meeting held in Toronto in conjunction with the Modern Language Association, December 27-30, 1993. Finally, a revision of the jointly written and jointly presented Notre Dame conference paper, entitled "From Manuscript to Print: The Case of Dante's *Vita nuova*," appears in *Dante Now: Current Trends in Dante Studies* (Notre Dame: U of Notre Dame P, 1995).

In the course of this work and these presentations, we have also engaged the attention of colleagues and acquaintances who, in varying degrees, offered advice and encouragement. Among these, our students, graduate and undergraduate, at the University of North Carolina, Chapel Hill, and the University of Notre Dame deserve our first acknowledgment. At least four different drafts of our translation have constituted four different classroom texts, and in each case we have taken serious note of our students' textual experiences, reactions, and suggestions.

After expressing our thanks to our students, we are happy to acknowledge interaction with colleagues: Teodolinda Barolini of Columbia University, Aldo Bernardo of SUNY- Binghamton, Paolo Cherchi of the University of Chicago, James Cook of Albion College, John Fleming of Princeton University, Britton Harwood at Miami University of Ohio, Allen Mandelbaum of Wake Forest University, Giuseppe Mazzotta of Yale University, Lee Patterson of Yale University, and Richard A. Shoaf of the University of Florida.

We extend our thanks as well to colleagues in Italy: Luciano Bottoni and Andrea Battistini of the University of Bologna, Domenico De Robertis of the University of Florence, Aldo Vallone of the University of Naples, and especially to Mario Marti of the University of Lecce, whose voice of encouragement has always been with us.

A special thanks also to John Ehman, Administrative Director of the Notre Dame Press, who not only guided publication of our work before his retirement but whose awareness of the unavailability of an Italian-English facing page translation of Dante's *Vita nuova* makes him the very first cause of our interest in this project.

We invite other colleagues and readers, finally, to join us in the continuing effort to enhance our understanding of Dante's *libello* and to assist these volumes, presented as tools for reading and research, by calling attention to details we have overlooked, mistakes we have made, or achievements that may be improved.

Dino S. Cervigni
Edward Vasta

Introduction

1. Dante Alighieri

Readers familiar with Dante's life and works find striking in the Florentine setting of the *Vita nuova* the absence of political and economic turmoil. So erratic and violent was Florentine life from the mid-eleventh to the late fourteenth centuries, as the city grew from a feudal village to a free commune, that in Dante's time (1265-1321) history's vicissitudes might easily have prevented the young man's fulfillment as a poet, or even have destroyed the man himself, as it did his best friend and fellow poet, Guido Cavalcanti (ca. 1250-1300). Dante lived and grew, physically, intellectually, and poetically, during the period of Florence's growing pains, the death-dealing politics that drove him into exile from family, friends, and city, and from the centers of Italian art and learning. His *Divine Comedy*, generally accounted the greatest of all poetic masterpieces by the greatest of all philosophical poets, vividly and vehemently records the anguish he suffered in exile, where his only recourse was to eat another man's bread at another man's table (*Par.* 17:58-60).

Yet, contrary to what we see in the mature work of the *Divine Comedy,* the autobiographical *Vita nuova* tells of a youthful poet who exhibits no sign of entanglement in the harsh vicissitudes of Florentine life. Rather, the *Vita nuova*'s intense and reflective protagonist struggles with a love that governs him from childhood to young adulthood in an ambience of self-conscious poetic cultivation, a love that ultimately directs him beyond that ambience's poetic frontiers. The protagonist, who never identifies himself by name, moves in a society of courteous ladies and a few courtly gentlemen, all elegant youths who constitute an elite of learned and sensitive mutual acquaintances. In Dante's account, they occupy themselves, the ladies in particular, with strolling along the streets in their finest finery and gathering at church services, weddings, and funerals, where they pause in asides to gossip about the poet's romantic strategies and to pursue subtle critiques of his poetry.

During Dante's entire lifetime, however, the fortunes of his person, his
family, and his city were tossed between the violent hands of the politico-
economic factions of Guelphs and Ghibellines, and Blacks and Whites. The
two older factions, Guelphs and Ghibellines, took their names from two
German castles, Welf and Weibling, in which resided two German Emperors,
Otto IV of Brunswick (c.1175-1218) at Welf and Frederick II (1194-1250),
great grandson of Barbarossa (Frederick I), at Weibling. In the early 1200s,
these two emperors divided German loyalties between them, and they divided
the citizens of Florence and of northern Italy as well. The basic issues were
already centuries old, centering on the Church's struggle for freedom from the
authority of secular feudal power: that is, on the issue of investiture, the
question of whether clerics would be appointed to ecclesiastical positions and
perquisites by the Pope or by the Holy Roman Emperor. In the mid-11th
century, during the reigns of Pope Gregory VII and Emperor Henry IV of
Germany, Florence's struggle for independence from the commercial and
political control of the surrounding feudal landed aristocracy became attached
to the Church's struggle for freedom of investiture. Thus Florence, a
commune surviving on the group loyalties of wealthy magnates, religious
and ecclesiastics in convents, monasteries, and churches, professional and
artisan guilds, and citizen laborers and farmers, stood with the Church to
promote economic expansion and political and religious freedom. They
fought against the German imperial powers and the feudal nobility, who
crammed Florence with fortified tower houses in order to maintain for their
use the leverage of citizenship within the Commune. In the 12th century, a
two-year civil war (1177-78) for control of the city pitted the urbanized feudal
nobles and their commoner dependents and serfs in bloody street battles
against Florentine citizens and their communal oligarchical governors.
Dante's beloved and much lamented Florence became a city of two clear-cut
factions. In 1216, when a personal insult by a Florentine citizen family
against a family of resident feudal nobility failed to be resolved first through
argument, then through an attempted inter-marriage, and finally through a
vengeful murder perpetrated on Easter morning, the guilty nobles claimed
immunity from communal law by aligning themselves with the Ghibelline
Emperor Frederick II. Their position left the Florentine citizens no choice but
to align themselves with the rival Guelph Emperor Otto IV. Dante, whose
family claimed descent from the original Romans who founded Florence as a

military camp under the aegis of Mars, god of war, was born into a family of Guelphs in a period when Florence was governed by the Ghibellines.

Despite the family's ancient communal origins, and therefore its Guelph affiliation, Dante's father, unlike Dante himself, stayed clear of politics and wars. The elder Alighiero's twelfth-century progenitor and the poet's great-great grandfather, Cacciaguida, whom Dante memorializes in the *Paradiso*, had died, according to the elder spirit's own words (*Par*. 15: 139-48), on the second crusade in the Holy Land, but Dante's father served in no public office and fought in no campaigns. He did his best to earn an unempowering but respectable income from small land holdings and modest money lending. He married Bella of the Abati family, who sometime between May 14 and June 13 in the year 1265 gave birth to Dante, their only son.

Facts about Dante's life from birth to young manhood are scattered. He lived in the parish of San Martino del Vescovo, where he was baptized on Holy Saturday, March 26, 1266, along with all the other parish children born during the previous year. It is possible, but uncertain, that a sister was born to Dante some four or five years after his own birth. Sometime between 1270 and 1273, when Dante could have been as young as four or as old as eight, he lost his mother and saw his father remarried to Lapa Cialuffi. His stepmother eventually gave Dante a stepsister and three stepbrothers. In 1274, the ninth year of life for both Dante and Beatrice, according to the *Vita nuova* (*VN* 1), these future protagonists of the poet's first major work met for the first time. Less than three years later, at age 11, on January 9, 1277, Dante was betrothed by contract to Gemma Donati, bound thereby under the second and most irrevocable of the three steps in the typical medieval arranged marriage; the first step, the bestowal of the ring with the promise of marriage, must have already taken place, and the third and final step, the taking of the hand in the official ceremony, would take place by contractual necessity, as it did around 1285. Meanwhile, Dante studied Latin grammar, which normally required analysis of works by such authors as Cicero, Virgil, Cato, and Aesop, with one of Florence's many learned humanist teachers, a private tutor who practiced near the Alighieri home.

Sometime between 1281 and early 1283, when he endured the death of his father, Dante assumed the eldest son's responsibilities as head of his sizable family. In the face of economic hardship and political strife (the Guelphs were now in power, and the Ghibelline leaders had been banished from the city), Dante's first requirement was to sell, for 21 *lire*, his father's modest credit accounts, thus ending the family's money lending resources.

In the next few years, from ages 18 to 20, Dante met Beatrice again (1283), married Gemma Donati (likely in 1285), served on a military campaign near Siena (Poggio Santa Cecilia, 1285), involved himself in public affairs, and wrote his first known poetic compositions. In the next five years (1285-90), Dante became both a family man when his wife gave birth to their first child (1287) and a Florentine citizen with close political and intellectual acquaintances; in politics his important acquaintances were Nino Visconti and Guido da Polenta, the latter of whom became mayor (*podestà*) in 1290; in literature and learning, Guido Cavalcanti and Brunetto Latini (1220-1295). In different ways, Cavalcanti and Latini stimulated Dante's already intense interest in Latin classics and in the French vernacular poetry of the previous half century, and they fostered in Dante patriotic ambitions for Florentine and Tuscan culture. In 1287, Dante traveled to Bologna to pursue further studies. There he was exposed to Bolognese lyrics that would influence his own productions, but he resided in Bologna less than a year, probably only a few months. In 1289 (June 11) he served on a military campaign at Campaldino against the Ghibelline city of Arezzo and shortly after (August 16) at Caprona against the Ghibelline city of Pisa.

Dante's intellectual formation and poetic development went hand in hand with his military and political involvement. Although the exact configurations of experiences and acquaintances during this period (1283-1290) cannot be ascertained in detail, clearly they impelled Dante's education beyond grammar and rhetoric and deeply into philosophy and poetry. It is now generally accepted that in these years Dante worked on two poetic compositions: the *Fiore*, a sequence of 232 sonnets recounting the story of the French *Roman de la Rose*, and the *Detto d'Amore*, an unfinished narrative of 480 seven-syllable verses. He also added to his lyrics (*Rime*), which would eventually reach 89 in number, including the 31 poems in the *Vita nuova* and the 3 canzoni in the *Convivio*. Some twenty-six additional poems are attributed to Dante with some hesitation (*Rime dubbie*).

In 1287, Beatrice married Simone dei Bardi. In 1290, most likely on the 8th of June, in the weeks surrounding Dante's 25th birthday, Beatrice died. Between 1292 and 1295, Dante completed the *Vita nuova*. He also took up, and continued for some years, studies in philosophy and theology in

Florence's religious schools. He frequented studies and debates among the Franciscans at Santa Croce and the Dominicans at Santa Maria Novella. These pursuits enriched and perfected Dante's rhetorical interests and steeped him in scholasticism, Averroism, and the works of such theologians as Albertus Magnus, Thomas Aquinas, and Bonaventure.

At this point in Dante's life, another division developed in the roiled history of Florentine factions: the division of the Guelphs into Blacks and Whites. At the vortices of this division were two mutually envious private citizens of Dante's parish, Corso Donati (no immediate relation to Dante's wife) and Vieri de' Cerchi. Both were wealthy magnates and rivals in real estate ventures. The Florentine citizens, especially the populace, liked Cerchi for his amiable generosity and his *nouveau riche* financial success, and they respected Donati as the fortunate beneficiary of old money, although he was much less wealthy than his rival and overbearing in his boldness and cleverness. At that time, Corso Donati lost his first wife, from the Cerchi family, who suspected him of having poisoned her, and passed on to his second matrimony. At one point during the Calendimaggio (May Day) of 1300, a public springtime festival held in the square before Florence's church of S. Trinità, the two families and their friends stirred up a brawl that left a member of the Cerchi seriously wounded. Factions emerged; as in the past, Donati found supporters among the city's patrician magnates; Cerchi, among the populace and the guilds. In the same year, the politics of a nearby town, Pistoia, where a single family had generated two political parties, the Blacks and the Whites, infected Florence when the city harbored Pistoia's two exiled party leaders. Donati threw his faction's support to the Blacks: Cerchi's faction gave protection and hospitality to the leader of the Whites. Among the Whites was Dante's best friend, the wealthy young magnate, soldier, scholar, and poet, Guido Cavalcanti.

Disorders continued to erupt, forcing the government, finally, to bring up infantry to keep peace in the city, until Cavalcanti himself provoked an attack that brought him a heavy fine and exile and sent Donati, whose ambition and trickery made him a serious threat to orderly government in the Florentine republic, into exile as well. Thereupon the clever Donati mounted a propaganda campaign that identified himself as a super-Guelph and denounced Cerchi and the Whites to Pope Boniface VIII as tainted with Ghibellinism. Donati's campaign succeeded; in time, the Whites, Dante included, came to feel the deep distrust and dislike directed at them by Pope Boniface, especially during those periods when the Whites controlled the Florentine government.

Although not himself a magnate or nobleman, Dante continued to gain trust and regard among Florentine citizens. The family of Gemma and Dante grew to four children, and they lived mainly on mortgage payments from the sale of family property and on loans guaranteed by Gemma's father. To render himself eligible for political office, Dante enrolled as a non-practicer, customary at the time, in the Guild of Physicians and Apothecarians. At age 30, in 1295, Dante became a member of one of the Florentine commune's governing organizations, the Capitano del Popolo. From November 1295 to April 1296, he served in one more restricted civic structure of the commune as a member of the Consiglio dei Cento. On June 15, 1300, Dante took office for two months of service as one of the six chief counsellors of the commune (Priore of the Signoria). His many duties as Priore included superintending public works and administering public funds. He was probably in Rome in 1300 for the Jubilee and almost certainly again in 1301 with other special legates of the Florentine commune. Their mission: to reconcile Pope Boniface VIII to the Florentine Whites. While Dante was in Rome, however, the Whites in Florence lost power to the Blacks, who at the beginning of 1302 accused Dante and his fellow Whites of corruption in office, including, in Dante's case, charges (never substantiated) of conflict of interest and embezzlement. Further, the Blacks ordered Dante and his colleagues banished from the city and their houses destroyed, had they failed to return to the city to pay substantial monetary amends. Dante did not return to Florence but fled directly into exile, leaving his family at home. On March 10, 1302, the Blacks imposed the death sentence on fifteen previously elected Florentine officials, including Dante. The poet, already economically as well as politically ruined, never returned to Florence during the remainder of his life.

Moving in exile among the communes in Tuscany, Dante at first continued to fight the cause of the Whites, militarily as well as politically. A succession of defeats soon joined the White cause to that of the previously expelled Ghibellines. After the White Guelphs and the Ghibellines failed in a joint assault on Florence itself in 1304, Dante, disconsolate, left Tuscany for Northern Italy. From the fall of 1302 to 1309 he moved from court to court (Forlì, Verona, Padua, and others); he also returned to Tuscany, and according to Villani and Boccaccio, whose statements can neither be confirmed nor disproved through other sources, between 1309 and 1310 Dante may have spent some time in Paris. For one lord after another, Dante carried on social, secretarial, and ambassadorial duties, which restricted both his free movements and his free time, and which gradually distanced him from Florentine politics.

The change in Dante's concerns are reflected in his works, which he continued to write despite obstructive conditions. During his first eight years in exile, 1302-1310, he produced additional lyrics, wrote but left incomplete both the *De vulgari eloquentia* (ca. 1303-1304), a Latin treatise in two books on the vernacular languages, and the *Convivio* (ca. 1304-1307), a philosophical narrative in four books, and composed the entire *Inferno* (1304-1309), the first canticle of the *Divine Comedy*. The sequence of these works reflects the movement of Dante's preoccupations from the purely literary, albeit morally and religiously complex, issues of the *Vita nuova* to increasing preoccupation with the historical and spiritual issues of the works that followed.

Between 1310 and 1316, Dante wrote the *Purgatorio*. Between 1310 and 1313 Dante's hopes of returning to Florence were raised by the presence in Italy of the German Henry VII, Count of Luxembourg, who was on his way to Rome to be crowned Holy Roman Emperor. Although during this period Dante returned in the *Purgatorio* to his idealized conception of Beatrice and wrote in a spirit of worldly detachment and of great distance from the temporal problems of Florence, he placed his hopes in the German Emperor as the power able to reconcile Florence to its citizens in exile and restore both parties to a just and orderly home. The Emperor was crowned in Rome on June 29, 1312, but he died in the following year (August 24, 1313) on his return to Germany. The death of Henry VII sent Dante to Verona, to the court of Can Grande della Scala, who had taken up the Ghibelline cause. Dante remained there until 1318 and during that time made public the first two canticles of the *Divine Comedy* and undertook work on the third. At Verona, Dante most likely also wrote his *De Monarchia*, a treatise in Latin on church-state relations, addressing the issues at the basis of Florentine, and indeed European, political strife. He also wrote here the last three of his Latin epistles, making thirteen in all, and all thirteen written in exile.

With the death of Henry VII, political strife in Florence abated before a

growing desire for reconciliation and peace. In 1315, the Florentine
government offered amnesty to exiles in return for payment of a modest fine
rendered in a ceremony of obeisance. Dante regarded the offer as infamous and
refused on principle to acquiesce (*Ep.* 12). The mood of peace continued to
grow in Florence, however, and by the end of the year the republic's internal
problems were substantially resolved. Despite his indignation, Dante shared
that peaceful mood, which is reflected in the softened resentments and the
nostalgic tone of the *Paradiso*, his poetic composition at the time.

In 1318 Dante moved to Ravenna, where he spent the remainder of his
life. He may have been joined there by his wife and his daughter Antonia,
who entered religious life at Ravenna, perhaps under the name of Sister
Beatrice, at the monastery of St. Stephen of the Olives, and who was
eventually buried in that city next to her father. Dante's last years seem
somewhat fulfilled, or at least secure; Ravenna brought him physically closer
to Florence than he had been, and he was able to make the last revisions of
the *Paradiso*, which he had begun by 1316 and completed by 1321. He also
wrote his two Latin *Eclogues* (1319-20), elegantly versified allegorical
bucolics that, in classical fashion, defend his poetic interests and practices,
and the Latin *Quaestio de Aqua et Terra*, a treatise on natural philosophy that
defends his poetic depictions of the physical universe. In 1321 he was sent to
Venice on a mission of peace, to dispel the specter of war between Ravenna
and San Marco. In the course of his embassy he fell seriously ill and
ultimately returned to Ravenna in grave condition. On either the night of the
13th or the morning of the 14th of September, 1321, at age 56, Dante died.

2. The *Vita nuova*

Dante's dedication to the political and ethical well-being of his people was
lifelong, but his dedication to letters was for all time. He became versed in
the medieval arts and sciences, subjects taught in the *trivium* (grammar,
rhetoric, logic) and the *quadrivium* (music, arithmetic, geometry, astronomy);
he also became a scholar of both classical and vernacular language and
literature and of scholastic philosophy and theology. At an early point in his
poetic career, Dante set as his goal the task of integrating the highest
qualities and aspirations of medieval intellectual and artistic traditions into a

new literary excellence, a refined poetry that would bring the Florentine vernacular to an elevated perfection and would address not only Florentines and the literary elite of Europe but all humanity. The *Vita nuova*, Dante's first major work, records the experiences that brought him to the first achievement toward this comprehensive goal, and it is itself that first achievement.

Exactly when Dante began the serious writing of vernacular poetry is unknown (formal education at Dante's time addressed Latin language and literature, not the vernacular), but the earliest poems selected for the *Vita nuova* were written, quite expectedly, in 1283, the year when the eighteen-year-old poet re-encountered the almost eighteen-year-old Beatrice. It is known, however, that his earliest models and immediate predecessors were the Sicilian poets, the Florentine poet Guido Cavalcanti, and the Bolognese poet Guido Guinizelli. From them Dante learned rational conceptualization as the substance of poetry, rhetorical and prosodic refinement as its form, and the search for an appropriate vernacular.

Dante's sojourn in Bologna, to which he traveled in 1287, exposed him to the sweet style and benign romantic conceptions of the Bolognese love poet Guido Guinizzelli (ca. 1235-1276). However brief, Dante's Bolognese experience moved him away from earlier influence and toward the Bolognese Stilnuovo ("New Style"). This movement was buttressed by the vernacular works of Provençal, French, and Sicilian "makers" that were captivating Florentine poets, among whom Guido Cavalcanti (ca. 1250-1300) came to be recognized as the finest and most authoritative poet in the vernacular tradition. Cavalcanti became Dante's "first friend" (*VN* 3.14), and in interaction with him and with other local poets, Dante opened himself further to vernacular experiments. Ultimately, however, Guinizzelli's poetry moved Dante beyond the influence even of Cavalcanti and toward a development of his own "sweet new style" (*Purg.* 24:57). While Guido Cavalcanti wrote of love's contradictions and sufferings, and its tensions with social, moral, and spiritual ideals, Dante found in Guinizzelli's lyrics a sweeter temperament than in Cavalcanti's, and celebrations of love's joys and perfections rather than lamentations over its sorrows and deficiencies. Dante found himself less inspired by Cavalcanti's complaints of love than by Guinizzelli's praises.

In the year of his trip to Bologna, Beatrice married, and three years later, in 1290, Beatrice died. In those three years, and for some two years after

Beatrice's death, Dante came to see the praising of Beatrice as the ennobling objective of a "new life," an objective that required a moral, philosophical, theological, and even mystical elevation in thought and disposition as well as a corresponding elevation in poetic language, subject matter, and form. To Love, which had come to him through Beatrice, Dante assigned the empowerment of all his new ability toward that visionary end. His response to Beatrice, an historical personage whom Dante mythologized as his guiding mediatrix to the highest conceivable Christian life and work, brought him to a conception of love that far surpassed that of Guinizelli and of any love poet before or since. His love of Beatrice also brought him to a style whose personal sincerity, human authenticity, and poetic sweetness surpassed that of his contemporaries. To open his experience and his achievement not only to fellow Florentines but to the world, and to commit himself publicly to even higher poetic achievements in the future, Dante began writing the *Vita nuova* around 1292, at age 27, as he completed the third nine-year period of his life. He included in the work poems that Beatrice had earlier inspired him to compose, and he worked on the "little book" (*libello*) for some three years.

The subject matter of the *Vita nuova* arises autobiographically from Dante's eleven remembered encounters with the lady Beatrice. Looking back at the astronomical moment in which they began and the frequency of their governance by the spiritually symbolic number nine, he saw these encounters as arranged in the created universe providentially. Six of these encounters were real: direct, overt, and the seeming result, at the time they occurred, of chance; they took place unexpectedly in streets, houses, and churches of the city in which Dante and Beatrice lived. The remaining five encounters were either oneiric, fantastic, or mystical: interior and private responses caused in Dante either by the overt encounters with Beatrice or, ultimately, as he saw upon reflection, by some mysterious and supernatural intervention. The latter encounters comprise one dream of Beatrice (*VN* 3), a delirious, illness-provoked fantasy in which Beatrice dies and ascends into heaven (*VN* 23), one imagined experience (*VN* 39), and two quasi-mystical visions of Beatrice after her death (*VN* 41; 42). These eleven encounters of various kinds motivated the composition of thirty-one lyrics, comprising twenty-three sonnets, two double sonnets, a ballade, two parts of canzoni, and three complete canzoni. Thus Dante's remembered exterior and interior experiences with the lady Beatrice, together with the poetic compositions they inspired, constitute the memories and documents that generated for the poet the material of his first great work.

This concrete material is elaborated, as already suggested, not in an historical but in almost a-historical directions: that is, not toward local circumstances or personal backgrounds but toward the immaterial and transcendent realities that disclosed to the poet the meaning and significance whereby the materials became worthy of preservation in his "book of memory" and worthy of public record in the "little book" transcribed from memory. We know, for example, that the encounters and experiences of the *Vita nuova* belong to a period covering some seventeen years, from 1274 to approximately 1291, but Dante gives no dates except that of Beatrice's death, and this in allegorical form (*VN* 29). Rather, he measures time and space primarily with the accurately applied but spiritually symbolic and divinely transcendent number nine. We know from Boccaccio's biography of Dante that Beatrice was Bice Portinari, daughter of Folco Portinari and a member of one of Florence's honored families, but Dante provides no identifying information other than her first name, which he inscribes in the *Vita nuova* 31 times while otherwise refering to Beatrice by epithets, such as "that most gentle one." Indeed, Dante allows the male protagonist to speak Beatrice's name only once in direct discourse, and then fragmentarily, when the bedridden youth, during a nine-day illness, strives to call out his lady's name while emerging from the delirious fantasies of a dream (*VN* 23). We are told of the death of Beatrice's father (*VN* 22), but in Dante's carefully a-historical vein the poet refers to the gentleman, and even eulogizes him, without inscribing his or his family's name. Similarly, through extra-textual sources we can identify other characters in the *Vita nuova* to whom Dante refers: members of his or Beatrice's family, or their relatives and friends, but Dante refers to none of these by an historical name. Further still, research has revealed something of Dante's activities and preoccupations during this period in his life, but in the *Vita nuova* the author specifies for himself no other occupation than poetry, and he connects himself professionally to no other personages than his anonymous circle of poetically sophisticated youths. This Dantean society, furthermore, meets only on occasions elicited by universally understandable social customs, such as weddings, funerals, church services, and the communal strolls that are still part of Italian daily life. The city itself of Florence is never identified by name, nor does the author record

his own name in the text. In these ways, history in the *Vita nuova* is pared
down rather than elaborated: it is distilled to essential circumstances and
condensed to the fewest details necessary to make remembered experiences and
their poetic record intelligible to any reader.

While the record of Dante's personal experiences eschews historical
details, it incorporates a broad range of materials from the intelligible
universe: that is, from the universe as known through human reason and
Christian faith. Medieval physical science, physiognomy, and astronomy, for
example, are drawn into the foreground of certain personal experiences in
order to expose the roots and origins of those experiences as ultimately in the
deeper realities of a divinely created and rationally known universe, and to
place the experiences into harmony with universal order. Biblical paraphrases
and borrowings explicitly and implicitly authenticate personal experiences by
according them with scriptural wisdom and the mysteries of faith. The
Christian understanding of divine history, including Christian eschatology,
gives Dante's personal experiences their direction and power, while Christian
ethics and morals measure their quality and value. At one point , for example,
when the protagonist sees Beatrice come preceded by the lady Giovanna, he
posits an analogy between Beatrice and Jesus, whose coming was preceded by
a forerunner of the same name (Giovanni), John the Baptist (*VN* 24).
Mystical concepts and spirituality, finally, empower the young poet's
aspirations as he moves toward a poetic destiny that, in the end, he can
conceive but cannot yet fulfill.

For all such material in the *Vita nuova*, memory is fundamental and
generative, because memory brings up Dante's past in Augustinian fashion:
that is, memory, as in Augustine's *Confessions*, not only brings the past
forward but submits it to analysis and reflection in light of present
knowledge. Further, by subjecting the past to rational penetration in pursuit
of the deepest understanding of its ultimate meaning and present significance,
memory reconstitutes Dante's character and spirit and redirects Dante's will
toward its proper future. Thus while the historical Dante is present in the
Vita nuova as the remembered and transcribed poet-protagonist whose love of
Beatrice changed his moral and spiritual understanding and brought him
progressively to the creation of a new kind of poetry, the later analytical and
reflective Dante is also present. This Dante, the narrator, comments upon and
illumines the historical past in light of current perceptions. His explications

include, for example, a formal delineation for the present audience of the rhetorical and conceptual organization of each lyric written by him in the past, and a formal discourse upon, and defense of, his historically and theoretically founded dedication to writing poetry in the Italian vernacular (*VN* 25). It also includes a lengthy discourse (*VN* 28-29) on the number nine as entailed in Beatrice's life.

And finally, the *Vita nuova* presents not only the past and present Dante but the future Dante as well, as the visionary poet whose dedication to poetry is so deepened and illumined by his love for the divinely elected Beatrice that he commits himself to a self-willed future in which he will create a vernacular poetry still more noble than he or anyone else had thus far achieved, more noble even than the text we are reading. In his life time, Dante did in fact fulfill his own poetically willed destiny; from the *Vita nuova* to the *Divine Comedy*, the persistence of Dante's visionary temper is evident, and so too is Beatrice's power as the integrating force of Dante's uninterrupted moral, spiritual, and poetic calling. Dante's last poetic work and enduring masterpiece, the *Divine Comedy*, is indeed a poetry of such unsurpassed dignity as to be worthy of service in praise of his miraculous Lady.

Out of this broad range of deepening and expansive content, Dante brought an inevitable form. His autobiographical work is first of all rooted in both oral and literate conventions of style and genre typical of the manuscript culture of Europe's "high middle ages," when the technology of the written word had already called up abstract and intellectualized models that were changing the individual's internal experiences, interpretations, and judgments, and when the art of the spoken word, despite the growing importance of literacy, still governed human relations and communicative expression. As does all autobiography, spoken or written, the *Vita nuova* self-consciously defines both Dante's location in a cultural community and his individuality and independence in that community. The work thus roots itself in a memory of selected past experiences, which it expresses through skills, habits, and sensitivities learned in the past but simultaneously reshaped according to meanings, generalizations, and judgments drawn in the present. As in all autobiography, therefore, present reconsideration of the past creates a disjunction between the past's protagonist and the present's narrator. The latter's rhetorical strategies of verisimilitude revise memories away from strict historical accuracy. The narrator of any autobiography bases the pattern of recorded experiences not on strict history or abstract logic but on autobiographical turning points, on those moments in the narrator's life when interior changes emerged. The *Vita nuova* thus turns Dante's "new life" into a text, into something more than a transcription from memory, into a version of remembered life that is subject to alternatives of understanding and interpretation. As autobiography, in short, the *Vita nuova* has the shape of a self-accounting that gives meaning, coherence, direction, and style to influences in Dante's past and thereby allows the formulation and projection of a "new life" for the future.

Although rooted in autobiography's generic conventions, and in the literary convention of combining prose and poetry in a single narrative account, the *Vita nuova* moves uniquely and definitively beyond these conventions. This departure begins with the structural movement away from not only strict history but also from everyday time and space. Dante's experiences are not linked by a unified structure of realistic causes and effects. Most exterior events in the *Vita nuova* are occasional and self-contained; the work's unifying action is interior and moves by the logic of moral, intellectual, and artistic growth, the logic of increasing self-awareness and of responsible self-understanding regarding the world of Christian poets and poetry and the disposition and effort required for greatness in that world. The poet is brought, through Beatrice, to a knowledge of perfect love, all the physical passion of which is presented as interior and unilateral: that is, on the side of the poet. Subtly playing his passion off against courtly conventions of love literature, Dante brings his passionate love to gradual refinement by subjecting it, under Beatrice's influence, to the order of reason and the wisdom of faith. Then the poet learns to move beyond self-awareness and self-understanding to full and praising witness of love taken in itself and in light of its heavenly sources and powers, which are perfectly manifest in his lady (*VN* 18;19). Finally, after the death of his lady (*VN* 28) and the consequent threat of a displacing worldly love of another lady (*VN* 35-38), the poet's visions of Beatrice sustain him in crisis and inspire in him a commitment to the highest possible ideal of love and poetry.

This story of Dante's interior growth is simultaneously the story of his poetic production. The lyrics of the *Vita nuova* come directly from his experience, and his interior development progressively alters the kind of poetry he writes and the sort of poets and readers he looks to for confirmation of his intended effects. This sequence of alterations informs the *Vita nuova* with another structural basis. The pattern of Dante's poetic development moves him clearly from his initial studies to his interaction with other contemporary Tuscan poets, then to a new poetry that addresses particularly the ladies of Beatrice's circle of friends, and finally, after Beatrice's death, draws him beyond the poetic circles of his day and toward his personally conceived poetic ideal. The sequence and distribution of the *Vita nuova*'s lyrics therefore provide another textual access to the work's structure. But while the lyrical forms, subject matter, style, and sequence invite any number of schemas, such patterns are invariably governed by the three completed canzoni. The sequence of the *Vita Nuova*'s three greatest lyrics mark the stages of Dante's interior growth as well as his growth toward artistic independence and poetic responsibility.

The themes, language, and metrics of the first canzone, "Ladies who have understanding of love ("Donne ch'avete intelleto d'amore" 19: 4), mark the change from Dante's youthful, purely Florentine style to a new style, the style of praise ("lo stilo de la loda"), which in the *Divine Comedy* (*Purg* 24: 57) will be redescribed as "the sweet new style" ("dolce stil novo"). In this canzone Dante turns away from such rhetorically self-conscious ornaments and techniques as verbal puns, systematic metrics, and equivocal rhymes, and such conventional language and motifs as Provençal love formulas and Cavalcantian amorous laments. Beginning with this canzone, Dante seeks a sincere and essential expression of true feeling and expansive understanding of Beatrice and Love, both idealized according to their own natures, expressed in language and metrics unequivocally appropriate for the canzone's ennobled subject and sensibility, a style in which the written word is the pure sign of the perceived ideal.

Through the lyrics that follow the first canzone, and that surround and include the two remaining canzoni, Dante extends the range of conceptions and of language possible in this new praising style and develops his poetic powers in accordance with the phases of his heightened personal experiences. He achieves a kind of climax in dealing with the imagined death and heavenly ascent of Beatrice in the second canzone, and then her actual death in the third. The third canzone, however, follows an attempt at a previous third canzone whose composition Beatrice's sudden death interrupts. Dante emphasizes the shock of this personal and poetic interruption by abruptly cutting off the original third canzone with a Latin lament from Scripture (*VN* 28:1). After a settling diversion, he replaces the sweet praises of Love that were the subject of the aborted canzone with a new and completed third canzone that laments the protagonist's loss and celebrates his lady's assumption by the angels.

This disruption of the original third canzone becomes portentous, for personal and compositional disruptions and distractions follow hereafter. After composing the complete third canzone, Dante writes another lament disguised as speaking not for himself but for a friend, actually Beatrice's brother (*VN* 32), but then considers this disguised lament too poor a service for such a friend. He thus writes two stanzas of another canzone, which remains incomplete. One year after Beatrice's death, Dante writes an anniversary sonnet with two beginnings, both of which he records (*VN* 34). He then labors through the distractions of a compassionate lady, distractions that make reason itself his adversary (*VN* 39:1), until one day, at about the ninth hour, he is brought to repentance by a "powerful imagining" ("forte imaginazione") of Beatrice as she first appeared in her ninth year of life. Then the appearance of traveling pilgrims disrupts his whole sense of audience, which he now sees as a potential extending far beyond his Florentine circle (*VN* 40). After writing still another sonnet for two ladies (*VN* 41), he finally stops writing at all, vowing to labor toward a poetic power and expression that he can conceive but neither achieve nor explain.

The narrative of the *Vita nuova,* however, is expressed in prose; while the integration of prose and poetry was not new in Western literature (see, for example, Boethius, *The Consolation of Philosophy*), Dante's achievement in his use of prose also represents a literary landmark. While Dante's prose is composed in the service of memory, order, and meaning educed from the vicissitudes of seemingly random experiences, and of a search for universal and exemplary truth, his prose is also in the service of his poetry, and therefore of language and style. Through a prose style that communicates truth directly and without embellishment, a style that is rational and lucid in its simple elegance, Dante authenticates his poetry as the just expression of the truth of his experience. Through a prose account wherein the significance and effect of Beatrice's earthly presence, unfathomable at the time he wrote his poetry, is illuminated as a providential appearance and a celestial departure, and wherein the perfection of his love for Beatrice is discovered to lie in the confirmation in him of harmony and integrity, Dante's prose also authenticates his poetic myth of Beatrice. Like his poetry, finally, Dante's prose is also drawn forward by the poet's search for effective Florentine vernacular and a fluent, unembellished, and sincere expression.

The style and themes of the *Vita nuova* passed into the works of other writers in Dante's time. As Dante had, other Florentine poets turned to Guido Guinizzelli as their predecessor, thus giving rise to what is now called, following Dante's own suggestion in *Purgatorio* 24:57, the school of *dolce stil novo*. Besides Dante, to this informal school belong Guido Cavalcanti, Cino da Pistoia, Lapo Gianni, Gianni Alfani, Dino Frescobaldi, and others. Beyond the generation of *stilnuovisti*, Dante's particular love themes, such as the lover's exalted praise of the lady, his veneration of the dead beloved, his imaginings, dreams, and visions of her, his fidelity to the beloved's memory, and his sensitivity to the moral and spiritual dimensions of love's bond — these themes and motifs entered by diverse and seminal ways into the new kind of poetry to be developed by Dante's immediate successors, primarily Francesco Petrarca (1304-1374) but also Giovanni Boccaccio (1313-1375), and through them passed into the literature of Renaissance Europe.

As a self-contained work, however, the *Vita Nuova*'s direct connection, through Beatrice, to Dante's *Divine Comedy* caused the early work to be overshadowed by the later masterpiece. Thus the *Vita nuova* received relatively scant publication and translation until the nineteenth century, when outside Italy the work was "rediscovered" and admired by the romantic writers of England and America: Coleridge, Shelly, Landor, Robert Browning, Longfellow, and Emerson. Editions and translations multiplied, culminating with the enduring 1861 translation, available to this day, by Dante Gabriele Rossetti. Enthusiasm for the work continued into the twentieth century, particularly, again, in England and America. It has commanded the attention of such notables as Ezra Pound, T. S. Eliot, and Bernard Shaw.

The *Vita nuova* today comes under broad-ranging study of its historical context, cultural elements, and literary components.[1] The work invites

---

[1] For a fundamental understanding of the *Vita nuova*, we recommend several studies, for which full citations can be found in the volume's bibliography. For an overall study of Dante: Vallone, *Dante*; in English, although at times controversial, Anderson. For a study of Dante within the context of the *dolce stil nuovo*: Marti, *Storia dello stil nuovo*. For a reading of the *Vita nuova* within the

inquiry into the many facets of life and literature that Dante's youthful work integrates into a single entity. It renews traditions of love literature by integrating them into a single love story whose shape and import derive from a spiritual life ultimately informed by the lives of Christ and the saints.[2] It renews poetic experience in light of Dante's theories of literature and language, with its philosophical and theological dimensions, and by his integration of poetry into the ethical and philosophical life. The work's textual self-consciousness gives minute attention to its own techniques and inventions and to the way in which its inventions and techniques lead to mystical understanding. It draws on Love as the spring of knowledge, and on a lady who is both physical and spiritual, and who is the real, rational, and miraculous guide to Love and ultimately to God. The *Vita nuova* unites, in short, Love, poetry, knowledge, wisdom, and faith into a single harmonious text that depicts a life and love in harmony with the universe.[3]

---

tradition of Romance literature: De Robertis, *Il libro della* Vita nuova, and Picone. For the development of Dante's relationship to poetry and poets: Barolini, *Dante's Poets*. For a contemporary reading of the *Vita nuova*, especially in relation to Dante's immediate predecessors and followers: Harrison. Concerning dreams, imaginings, and visions: Cervigni. Additional general bibliography is available in the articles of the *Enciclopedia dantesca,* the various essays on Dante in *La letteratura italiana,* ed. A. A. Rosa, in several volumes, and bibliographical works by Giovannetti and Esposito.

[2] Proposing a reading of the *Vita nuova* as a story of "Saint Beatrice," Branca writes: "It is a very clear and evident itinerary . . . from love seen as a passion to love seen as caritas, from the contemplation of the senses to the ultraterrestrial contemplation in the 'book of memory'" (qtd. & trans. Cervigni, *Dante's Poetry* 60-62). Singleton's reading, proposed in *An Essay on the* Vita nuova, can be situated within such a spiritualized interpretation of the *libello*. Although Beatrice in the *Vita nuova* is not an allegory of Christ (as she may be viewed in the *Divine Comedy*), her "resemblance" to Christ can be "called both an analogy and a metaphor" (Singleton 112). For an attempt to situate the *Vita nuova* within the context of allegoresis see Picone; Charity.

[3] The discussion to this point has been aided by information garnered from articles in *Enciclopedia dantesca* by Marti; Pampaloni; Petrocchi; Pazzaglia; Vallone, and *Appendice* 55-112; also works by Bargellini; Bruner and Weisser; Cervigni; and Took.

3. Text and Translation

The Italian original of Dante's *Vita nuova* is that edited by Michele Barbi, whose edition is recognized as the international standard. Our text differs from Barbi's in one fundamental aspect, to be discussed below: a complete restructuring of Barbi's canonized division of the text into chapters and paragraphs. Based on manuscript evidence and narrative theory, and freed from the "scholars' needs" proposed by Barbi (1932: CCCIX), such a restructuring opens up the text to new readings, so pervasively that the Italian text presented here may justifiably be considered a "revised" or even "new" edition of the Barbi text.[4]

The facing-page translation is the joint effort of this volume's two curators. Through the many considerations that translators face, they have been guided by one overriding objective, that of providing a translation that serves Dante's original. For the English/Italian reader who may wish to work with both languages, and whose work therefore may be facilitated by an easy movement between the translation and the original, the translation strives to reproduce not only the sense of Dante's words but the register of his vocabulary, his syntactical constructions, and his word order. For the reader who may depend wholly upon the English translation, the editors have sought to reproduce as well the tone and energy of Dante's narrator, his rhetorical effects, and his auctorial voice. Above all, the curators have sought to restore, for contemporary English readers, the narrator's meticulous and objective intellectual control over his material as he addresses his reader, a quality that affective, romanticizing translations since the nineteenth century have diminished and sometimes obliterated. Technical terms, for example, abound in the narrator's vocabulary, not only such obviously philosophical terms as *substance, accident, potentiality,* and *act,* but also such often loosely translated terms as *subject, cause, operation, quality, end,* and *beatitude.* Again, Dante's narrator persistently and self-consciously objectifies his own

---

[4] In a recent essay, Gorni criticizes some of the most fundamental principles at the basis of Barbi's edition of the *Vita nuova* ("Per il testo della *Vita nuova*"). However, together with virtually all Italian critics except Marti ("'l'una appresso'"), Gorni fails to object in any way to Barbi's canonized division of the text into chapters and paragraphs — a division that according to Barbi himself does not belong to the manuscript tradition.

subjectivity; he speaks of himself in the first person yet stands back from the self, particularly the self of his past, as an exterior observer of his own interior life. He thus uses such circumlocutions as "I said within myself," and often uses the grammatically passive instead of active voice. Further still, the narrator addresses personal as well as general audiences, listeners as well as readers, to whom he speaks as well as writes, thus giving himself a complex and changing presence and voice that come in various respects from both his oral and literate cultures. These and other effects of the narrator's orientation toward subject matter, text, and audience have also governed, along with meaning and style, the curators' translation.

These objectives, finally, have required the curators to forsake the prosodic form of Dante's poetry and to free Dante's prose text, both the Italian and the English, from the chapter divisions, paragraphs, and sentence numbering imposed rather superficially and arbitrarily by Michele Barbi 's 1907 and 1932 editions of the *Vita nuova*. The curators have translated Dante's lyrics neither into prose nor into modern imitations of his stanza forms, line lengths, and rhymes, but into line-by-line free verse that seeks, despite metrical differences, to reproduce Dante's lyrical complexities of meaning, form, and style. As to Barbi's divisional numbering: because they have become, as Barbi intended,[5] the canonical and uniform reference system for editions, concordances, dictionaries, scholarship, and criticism, the curators have preserved these but have removed them from the text, where they never belonged, and placed them outside the text and in the margins, clearly to show that they are not the poet's work but the philologist's.

The curators have also sought to restore the narrative integrity of Dante's account, not merely by continuing but marginalizing Barbi's useful numbering, but by extricating the narrative itself from the nineteenth-century print culture textual divisions and format that Barbi introduced — continuing the attempts of his predecessors Torri in 1843, Witte in 1876, and Casini in 1885 — and established as canonical. Textual divisions into chapters have no basis in either the *Vita nuova*'s manuscript tradition or in its auctorial intention; Dante nowhere in his *libello* speaks of chapters.[6] Dante does speak

---

[5] Barbi's intentions are explained in the 1932 edition ("Introduzione" CCCIX).

[6] Dante does explicitly refer to his prose as involving paragraphs, and he speaks of some paragraphs as "greater" than others (*Vita nuova* 2:10). In medieval manuscripts, according to Ong, paragraphs are signified not by a break, space, and

of paragraphs, but paragraph divisions must be determined on some justifiable basis consistent not with extant manuscripts, of which no more than eight of the forty-one most likely go back to the fourteenth century, and none of which is a holograph, but with the manuscript culture itself. According to Barbi, who examined meticulously all manuscripts containing Dante's *Vita nuova*, most of which date to the fifteenth and sixteenth centuries, and who reported his findings in his 1907 and 1932 editions ("Introduzione" XVIII), paragraph signs and lead sentences are not lacking here and there among the manuscripts, but no clear pattern of divisions exists.[7]

---

new line, but by the paragraph mark within the line. These paragraph marks, Ong insists, do not signify a unit of discourse; they merely provide an aid to visual location (124). Barbi remained reluctant to introduce an extraneous element like chapter divisions, but he succumbed to such nineteenth-century scholarly concerns "pel comodo delle citazioni": for the ease of citations.

[7] Whether Barbi considers these forty-two divisions of the text of the *Vita nuova* paragraphs or chapters seems uncertain, for his phraseology shifts. Torri proposed the concept of "paragraph" on the basis (accurate, in our view) of the presence of such a term in *Vita nuova* 2:10: "Da questo passo scorgesi che l'Autore dettò in paragrafi distinti la presente opera; ed è per ciò che noi credemmo ben fatto apporre ai medesimi il numero progressivo; col quale metodo, e coll'aver anche numerate le poesie che vi sono comprese, rendonsi più facili i riscontri, stante la precisione delle citazioni" (Torri 3n34). Witte objects to such a term (and concept): "Le altre sottodivisioni s'intenderanno facilmente dalla nostra tavola. L'infima di esse non è indicata nei testi a penna che per capoversi. Il primo a distinguerle per numeri apposti fu il Torri. Applicandovi l'ultimo detto della prima di queste sottodivisioni ('quelle parole, le quali sono scritte nella mia memoria sotto maggiori *paragrafi*') egli cercò dover chiamarle 'Paragrafi'. Non mi sembra però che questo nome corrisponda alle intenzioni dell'autore. Nelle altre sue opere, come nella *Monarchia*, nel *Convivio* ecc. Dante stesso chiamò 'Capitoli' le sottodivisioni dei libri ossia dei trattati. Capitoli ancora da non pochi antichi sono detti li Canti della *Commedia*, e non si vede perché l'autore dovesse aver scelto pel presente libretto, il più semplice di tutti i suoi componimenti, un altro termine, termine che ricorda un po' troppo la pedanteria degli Scolastici. Questi 'maggiori paragrafi', ossia rubriche, non vogliono dir altro, che: oggetti di maggiore importanza a paragone delle altre che infino a quel punto si trovavano registrate nel libro della memoria dell'autore..Si è dunque restituito il nome di "Capitoli" a quello tutto arbitrario di paragrafi" ("Prolegomeni" XVII-XVIII, *La vita nuova*, ed. Witte). We object not only to the division of the *Vita nuova* into chapters but also to the application of the concept of chapter itself to the *Vita nuova*. It is noteworthy that whereas Witte refuses to use the term "paragrafi" even though Dante the author employs it in *Vita nuova* 2:10, he nevertheless takes

The effects of imposed chapter divisions are subtle but not insignificant. Such divisions, executed by a print culture code and a graphic arrangement, add to the *Vita nuova* technological concerns absent from the original and diminish the orality that Dante's writing preserves and uses. The degree of that orality's loss increases sight dominance and diminishes reading dominance, so that we see divisions of ideas more as visual units and less as units of thought and internal structure. We look at the work more and listen to it less, in other words, and consequently the distance between us and Dante — his life, experiences, objectives, intentions — is increased. Simultaneously, chapter divisions complete the print culture's textualizing of Dante's work; they draw the work out from Dante's own manuscript culture and into our print culture, thereby assimilating it, further than otherwise, into modern thought and consciousness.[8]

The result diminishes auctorial control and increases reader control. Chapter divisions add not merely internal junctures, as do paragraphs, but internal closures. These closures subdivide the work into units of discourse and thereby render the text not only easier for the modern reader to cite but easier to read; they render the text, in other words, more "consumer oriented." In subjecting the work more to the reader's consciousness and less to the author's, chapter divisions have the further effect of imposing on the reader's consciousness a significant degree of control. They organize the thought content of the text, structure it, rigidify its sequence, lock up thought into pre-determined divisions, and control it through an imposed format. They thereby limit, if not proscribe, the freedom and inducement to reconsider and discuss the microstructures of Dante's discourse.

The grid that distributes the author's meaning by imposing spaces and numbers that divide the text into chapters, paragraphs, and sentence clusters

---

literally another term used in the text, "proemio" (*Vita nuova* 28:2), in order to view the opening (*VN* 1, according to the Torri and Barbi edition) as a proem to the *libello* ("Prolegomena" XVII).

[8] In the twentieth century Barbi thus implements in Dante's *Vita nuova* what scholars of the twelfth and thirteenth centuries did to many texts, as Rouse and Rouse document: "By the end of the twelfth century, then, we might assume that the needs for a 'finding technique' for classroom use were being met by the development of the clearly displayed text, with its chapter lists, running headlines, and marginal apparatus" (209). Rouse and Rouse, however, do not concern themselves with what those texts might have lost (i.e., in terms of narrativity) as a consequence of this "new" page layout.

(*commi*), is not the author's grid, furthermore, but that of editors, who have thereby perpetuated editorial control through imposing a single conception of unity on given segments of text and therefore on the narrative as a whole. Although Torri, Witte, Casini, and Barbi may not have thought in these terms, they held competing conceptions of the *Vita nuova*'s structural unity, until Barbi succeeded, through his academic standing and personal pleading, in gaining acceptance of his conception.[9] We thus read the text through Barbi's consciousness, and to an extent we have since been more loyal to Barbi in these respects than to Dante. Because spaces and numbers separate meaning and structure into the editor's grid, and not the author's, such editorial interferences affecting the relations between the elements and parts of the text represent control by a kind of cultural ruling class, the class composed of editors, publishers, and scholars who insist on staying within the structural lines laid down by Barbi's national standard edition.

More importantly, print-culture features such as format, divisions, spacing, numbering, punctuation, even the visual presentation on the printed page, affect how readers read, experience, and understand a text. Since Barbi's time, linguistics, literary criticism, semiotics, anthropology, psychology, and social and cultural studies in general have taught us that our print culture techniques produce literary, psychological, social, and political effects not produced in a manuscript culture. Such effects are further complicated and extended by today's electronic culture; the consciousness of today's reader is affected by speech, writing, print, radio, film, television, and computers, all operating simultaneously from their particular areas of utility and dominance, and all interacting with each other. Barbi could not have foreseen the consequent reconsideration today's scholars must therefore bring to modern editions of medieval works.[10] Such reconsideration, this edition's curators

---

[9] Segre: "I manoscritti sono discordi nelle divisioni, o talora ne sono privi. Quando s'erano ormai imposte le divisioni del Torri (Livorno, Vannini, 1843), venne il Witte a mutarle, e il Casini se ne sentì autorizzato a mutarle ancora. Oggi tutti adottano, col testo, le divisioni del Barbi, e per questo penso utile fornire una tavola di corrispondenza. Eccola: I Torri Barbi = *Proemio* Witte Casini; II Torri Barbi = I Witte Casini; III Torri Barbi = II+III Witte Casini; IV-XXV Torri Witte Casini Barbi; XXVI Casini Barbi = XXVI+XXVII Torri Witte; XXVII-XLII Casini Barbi = XXVIII-XLIII Torri Witte" (Cesare Segre, "Presentazione" XVII n23, in *La vita nuova*, ed. Casini).

[10] For a brief introduction into such issues and their implications for medieval studies, see the six essays, with pertinent bibliography, published in *Speculum*

feel, is mandatory for the *Vita nuova*.[11]

As a poet of Europe's "high middle ages," Dante composed his *libello* in a manuscript culture in which, as Walter Ong has demonstrated,[12] the spoken word governed human relations and communicative expression, written as well as spoken; writing during this period, Ong remarks, functioned largely to reconstitute "the originally oral, spoken word in visual space" (123). At the same time, the spreading technology of the written word, as Brian Stock has shown, presented abstract and intellectualized models of thought and communication that affected the individual's internal experiences, interpretations, and judgments. Inevitably, Dante drew upon both medieval cultures, the oral and the literate, for he drew upon three main sources in which both cultures interacted: his literary knowledge and poetic intentions, his desire to address a real, as well as conceived, audience, and his memories of actual experience.[13]

On the one hand, Dante's work is replete with evidence of oral consciousness. His narrator's personal auctorial voice addresses directly a particular and personal audience, including other poets. The narrator constantly uses the expression "I say that" ("Io dico che"), along with verbs of speaking or saying when referring to poetic writing.[14] These usages suggest that the work

---

65.1 (1990).

[11] On the need of a new edition of the *Vita nuova*, see Cervigni and Vasta, "From Manuscript to Print: The Case of Dante's *Vita nuova*," from which a few passages have been incorporated into this one, and also Gorni (for reasons different from ours), "Per il testo."

[12] Although Ong does not mention Dante's *Vita nuova*, his analysis of orality/literacy is the basis for our observations about the evidence of these two cultures in Dante's work. Other major studies relevant to medieval manuscript culture include: Clanchy; Eisenstein; Foley; Kelber; McLuhan; McLuhan and Fiore; Nelson; Steiner. In Italian, one may consult several of the essays in vol. 2, *Produzione e consumo*, of *Letteratura italiana*, ed. Rosa.

[13] Ahern ("The Reader") applies to two passages in the *Vita nuova* (14; 18) this distinction of real and conceived audiences, using respectively the designations "social" and "literate." See also Ahern's "The New Life."

[14] The most common verb the poet-protagonist employs in introducing or referring to his poems (or parts of them) is "dissi" ("I said": *Vita nuova* 7:2; 8:3; 14:10; 15:4; 16:1; 16:6; 17:1; 20:2; 21:1; 23:16; 24:6; 26:4; 26:9; 32:3; 33:2; 34:3; 36:3; 37:3; 38:4; 39:6; 40:5; 40:6; 41:1), followed by "propuosi di dire" or "propuosi di dicere" ("I proposed to write [say]": *Vita nuova* 8:2; 14:10; 15:3; 20:2; 22:7; 23:16; 26:4; 26:9; 27:2; 35:4; 40:5). The next most frequent verb to announce a poem's composition is "fare" ("make"), either by itself or in

was written also to be read *viva voce*. His autobiographical purpose draws personal experiences and utterances from memory (*Vita nuova* 1), resulting in a text presented as rooted in the constantly shifting dynamics of remembrances and poetic literary concerns. His narrative line is chronological, additive, aggregative, based on memory as much as, or more than, on a pre-ordained narrative scheme.[15] His account becomes caught up in explanations, and while chronologically controlled, it is governed only to a certain extent by a preeminently self-conscious and teleological design. Indeed, at a crucial point in his writing, which has by necessity become the "conclusion" of the *Vita nuova*, the writer-protagonist interrupts himself because he feels inadequate to perform the task he had set out to accomplish at the beginning of the *libello*: namely, to transcribe what is written in the book of his memory. His narrative presents characters, particularly Beatrice and the protagonist, as strictly defined and ruled by a few powerful features. He offers prose explanations of the poetry, and he self-consciously insists upon the proper internal divisions of the poems into their thought units. His expressions are replete with the additive use of temporal terms such as "after," "then," and "later." All such features exhibit communicative practices that scholarship since Milman Parry (1928) has identified as operative in an oral culture.

On the other hand, Dante simultaneously and self-consciously directed the *Vita nuova* to the thirteenth-century's expansive writing culture. Literacy

---

conjunction with "propuosi di" (*Vita nuova* 12:9; 22:8; 31:1; 32:3; 33:4; 39:6; 40:5; 41:1). The least common expression, finally, includes a verbal form of "scrivere" ("to write": *Vita nuova* 3:9; 7:2; 13:7; 24:6; 34:3). Concerning the usage of the verb "dire" ("to say") in introducing or referring to the poems, one must be aware of the strong links between this verb and the related verb "dittare" (see *Purg*. 24:54), which in its Latin correspondent ("dictare"), as Curtius remarks, "from the time of Augustine . . . acquires the meaning 'to write, to compose,' and particularly 'to write works of poetry'" 76). More recent studies, however, have emphasized, as Murphy writes, that the term ("dictare") "reveals a concern for the oral-written relationship" (195n5). That Dante at times uses within the same context of the *Vita nuova* not only "dire" and "scrivere" (24:6: "propuosi di scrivere per rima' 'I proposed to write in verse'; 34:3: "dissi questo sonetto" 'I wrote this sonnet'), but also "dire" and "fare" (32:3; 33:2-4; 39:6; 40:5-6; 41:1), should not be construed to signify the identity of those three terms, "dire," "scrivere," and "fare."

[15] For issues concerning memory vis-à-vis orality and literacy see Carruthers 10-12, 159-60, 297, etc.; Corti, *Percorsi* 27-50.

and literature, founded on the written word, govern the work's ultimate auctorial project: namely, to raise a specific vernacular Italian, already widely written, to standards of art and expression comparable to those of written Latin poetry (*Vita nuova* 25). The narrator offers not unaltered memories but self-consciously compiled memories; he addresses the entire subject of writing, from narrative to gloss to several poetic forms; and he introduces innovations (in both form and content) into previous traditions and current trends of literary production. The narrator addresses a literary world; he offers literary references, allusions, and borrowings, and he records the production and circulation of particular written poems. Instead of focusing on the externality of his experiences, typical in an oral culture, the narrator focuses on those aspects typical of a writing culture: interior, interpretive, centered in individual self-consciousness; his materials come from a consciousness-raising that he personally experienced in the past and that he now brings forward in order to promote a wider cultural consciousness-raising in the future. In these efforts, the narrator purposely writes in the spoken language of his community, but he writes that language in an elevated, refined mode that is not communal but private: a written language appropriated to his particular style and personal voice as an individual author.[16]

As translators of Dante's *Vita nuova*, this volume's curators have also sought to replace Barbi's print culture textual divisions with divisions more faithful in principle to Dante's manuscript culture. The text itself certainly calls for divisions; Dante's preoccupation with division is explicit, for example, in his *divisioni* of every poem.[17] Significantly, however, Dante's *divisioni* are not the relatively external divisions of prosody but the more interior divisions of thought; they signify not the structural divisions of versification and rhyme that a print culture makes visual through indentations and spacing, but the divisions of thought units that frame meaning and interpretation. His *divisioni* further reveal an auctorial self-consciousness of the poems as written texts, for they indicate that a poem's meaning may

---

[16] For a study of the *Vita nuova*'s language we refer to: Vallone *La prosa*, De Robertis *Il libro*, De Robertis' commentary to the *Vita nuova*, the essays on Dante's language in volume 6 of *Enciclopedia dantesca*, and Colombo's commentary to the *Vita nuova* (1993).

[17] For a recent study of the *Vita nuova*'s divisions, with extensive bibliography, see chs. 2 and 3 of Stillinger; D'Andrea 25-58; Durling and Martinez 53-70.

neither be taken for granted nor be dependent, as in speech, upon oral give-and-take. At the same time, they reveal a manuscript culture's view of meaning as inherent in the text, as opposed to a print culture's view of meaning as the product of an interpretive mind and therefore distinct from the text.

An issue for the curators of this volume, then, has been whether the *Vita nuova* contains an inherent criterion that justifies dividing the text further than the division established by poetry and prose.[18] Such a criterion, we have concluded, must necessarily arise from the unfolding of human time structured in the fashion of a narrative. As Paul Ricoeur writes: "Time becomes human time to the extent that it is organized after the manner of a narrative; narrative, in turn, is meaningful to the extent that it portrays the features of temporal experience" (*Time and Narrative* 1:3). The temporal development that unfolds in the account of the narrator-protagonist's life, we have further concluded, warrants dividing the text not into chapters but into paragraphs, to be indicated typographically as inconspicuously as possible, because paragraphs propose not internal closures but internal junctures.

Temporality, therefore, whose flow is announced textually by specific expressions of time and emphasized narratively by the diversity of events, constitutes in our view the fundamental criterion for dividing the text of the *Vita nuova* further than the divisions established by poetry and prose. Together with the prose-poetry distinction, temporal expressions provide the clearest internal pattern of textual junctures, and the only consistent pattern sufficiently extensive to provide the number of divisions necessary for understanding and interpreting the text. Thus, because the narrative structure of the *Vita nuova* is temporal, and because temporality governs and integrates the sequence of poetic composition with the protagonist's encounters and

---

[18] On the notion and practice of the division of the text (the medieval *divisio textus*) see Stillinger, mainly ch. 3, with references: "To know the division of a text is to know a good deal about it; to divide the text — to identify the true *divisio textus* — is not only a preliminary to further study but also an important act of criticism in itself" (77). Stillinger thus summarizes the function of *divisio*: "*divisio* is: *in malo*, the condition that separates humanity from God; *in bono*, one process by which humanity reaches toward God" (78). Stillinger's synthesis can be applied to the argument we intend to develop: The division of the *Vita nuova*'s text evinces, on the one hand, humankind's fallen nature, and, on the other, the author's attempt at reaching toward the divinity through language itself.

experiences with Beatrice before and after her death, the temporal category combined with the pattern of prose-poetry provides the most integral bases and the clearest sanctions for textual divisions.[19]

4. Temporality and Narrativity

We can here begin a search for new and justified divisions by noting that at the beginning of his writing, the narrator-protagonist proposes only a twofold principle of narrative unity: the first, based on the notion of time as lived, psychological, and individual, is expressed through the term *vita*; the second, based on the concept of writing, is rendered through the term *libro*. These two notions of writing and lived time merge in the topos of the book of memory, bearing directly on the ways in which narrativity can represent human temporality:[20]

---

[19] The narrator's temporal perspective is threefold: a) the time and narrative of things past; b) the time and narrative of things present (1.*Vita nuova* 1: "In quella parte del libro della memoria . . . si trova scritto" 'In that part of the book of my memory. . . . I find written'; 2. the poems' *divisions*); c) the time and narrative of things still to come (*VN* 42). The unity of these three distinct views of time is created by the narrator's awareness, which comes to the fore precisely as he portrays himself in the act of writing. As he recreates present, past, and future through the act of writing, the narrator provides the principle that creates unity out of many events, thereby establishing a notion of time patterned after that of Augustine. Just as Augustine who, through the notion of *extentio animi*, seeks to comprehend — grasp together — present, past, and future, the narrator of the *Vita nuova* sees each life experience he intends to *assemplare* as both distinct and yet part of a whole.

[20] The question Augustine asks after narrating his life story — "quid est enim tempus?" 'What is time?' (*Confessiones* 11:14.17) — never appears in Dante's *libello*; and yet it is paramount in the metaphor of the "book of memory." If time no longer exists but in the book of memory, how is it possible to recover it? The answer is: By means of narrative; and hence the narrator's decision to transcribe from it its *sentenzia* (*Vita nuova* 1). In what we have been used to calling the proem of the *Vita nuova*, we have the beginning of a book in which the narrator states he cannot commence at the very beginning of his life course but at a certain point not too distant from it, a point that he nevertheless calls a beginning: "*Incipit vita nova*" 'Here begins the new life.' Thus the narrator-protagonist must cope with two failures: first, a part of the book is untranscribable — a beginning, however, that does not correspond to the beginning of his life course; second, not everything is transcribable, although, at best, one can describe the *sentenzia*.

In quella parte del libro de la mia memoria dinanzi a la quale poco si potrebbe leggere, si trova una rubrica la quale dice: *Incipit vita nova.* Sotto la quale rubrica io trovo scritte le parole le quali è mio intendimento d'assemplare in questo libello; e se non tutte, almeno la loro sentenzia.

(In that part of the book of my memory before which little could be read, a rubric is found, which says: *Incipit vita nova* [Here begins the new life]. Beneath this rubric I find written the words that it is my intention to transcribe into this little book; if not all of them, at least their substance.)

(Vita nuova 1)

The narrator-protagonist, therefore, intends to refigure, by means of *graphía*, that segment of his human *bios* that he finds written in the book of his memory under the rubric *Incipit vita nova.* It is this lived, individual, and psychological time, both in itself and in its relationship with that of others, that the narrator-protagonist intends to narrate.

Incipit vita. The term *vita* designates the *continuum* of events in one's life viewed as a totality, ranging from the moment of birth until that of death (in other people's lives), or from the moment of birth until the time of writing (in autobiographies). As one moves from the notion of lived time to that of writing, the same term *vita* designates the totality of the narrative that describes the events making up one's life.

Dante's *Vita nuova* incorporates both meanings of the word *vita*: it is a narrative that intends to describe the life of the protagonist, who at the same time is also the narrator of his life events. The qualifier *nuova* restricts the life events to be narrated: the narrative cannot include the totality of the narrator-protagonist's life but only that section of it that in his memory appears written under the rubric *"Incipit vita nova."* Further limiting the

---

Further concerns are: At what point of the temporal category that marks his birth, and in what manner, should the author commence the narration of his life, which can be recounted only from that moment after which forgetfulness no longer holds sway? How is it possible to narrate the end of Beatrice's mortal life when precisely that moment, set in temporality, gives beginning to a mode of life situated in eternity? And how can Dante the author conclude writing about the life of the narrator-protagonist while he is still immersed in temporality and yet aspires to join the female protagonist who has entered eternity?

purpose of his narrative, the narrator-protagonist plans to *assemplare* in the *libello* not all the words written under that rubric but only their *sentenzia*.

On the one hand, therefore, the narrator-protagonist envisions his life as a whole and its narration as a process of totalization; on the other hand, he also sees that his life consists not so much of episodes or distinct moments but rather of interconnected events whose *sentenzia* can be rendered through words. His writing seeks to refigure both the wholeness of his life course and the multiplicity of his lived events.

As the narrator-protagonist embarks upon the task of narrating the *sentenzia* of his *vita nova*, he cannot but insert it within several other and more encompassing time categories of which lived, psychic time necessarily partakes. In fact, the narrator's notion of time as a lived experience characteristically intersects, as in the beginning of the book of Genesis, with cosmological time:[21]

> Nove fiate già appresso lo mio nascimento era tornato lo cielo de la luce quasi a uno medesimo punto, quanto a la sua propria girazione. . . .
>
> (Nine times since my birth had the heaven of light returned to almost the same point in its orbit. . . .)
>
> (*VN* 2:1)

Next, based on both psychic time and cosmic time, calendar or chronicle time makes a third form between them (Ricoeur 3:106), as is implicit in the same passage quoted above ("Nove fiate già appresso lo mio nascimento" *VN* 2:1), and as becomes explicit in the narrative that announces the death of Beatrice (*VN* 29).

Thus, three forms of time — individual, cosmic, and calendar time — constitute the three fundamental temporal categories making up the narrative. An additional, metatemporal category pervades Dante's *Vita nuova* as well: the notion of eternity. While interacting with both cosmic and calendar time, the narrator-protagonist's belief in eternity becomes an essential aspect of his personal understanding and experience of temporality. Implicitly stated at the

---

[21] The author of Genesis begins his narrative with God's creation of light and its separation from darkness, marking the first day in the universe, even before the creation of Adam and Eve: "Appellavitque lucem Diem, et tenebras Noctem: factumque est vespere et mane, dies unus" 'God called the light Day, and the darkness Night: and there was evening and morning, the first day' (Gen. 1:3).

narrative's beginning in the phrase that also links it with the metaphor of the book of memory ("la *gloriosa* donna de la mia mente" 'the *glorious* lady of my mind'), the category of eternity runs through the text and concludes the story ("*qui est per omnia secula benedictus*" *VN* 42:3).[22] Thus, lived time, cosmological time, calendar time, and eternity provide the narrator-protagonist with an all-encompassing perspective situated within his own life experience, one that helps him envision both his existence and the narrative of his existence as a totality. This lived *continuum* could not unfold, however, and thus could not be organized and retold, except according to a series of closely knit and interconnected narrated events.[23]

Let us further examine these categories of time in order better to understand the ways in which they interact in the configuration of the narrative.

4.1. Cosmic Time

The narrative beginning of the *Vita nuova* is situated within cosmic time.

> Nove fiate già appresso lo mio nascimento era tornato lo cielo de la luce quasi a uno medesimo punto, quanto a la sua propria girazione, quando a li miei occhi apparve prima la gloriosa donna de la mia mente, la quale fu chiamata da molti Beatrice li quali non sapeano che si chiamare. Ella era in questa vita stata tanto, che ne lo suo tempo lo cielo stellato era mosso verso la parte d'oriente de le dodici parti d'un grado, sì che quasi

---

[22] The notion of eternity is stated throughout the text by the several references to the "glorious" Beatrice: *VN* 2:1; 31:11, v. 31; 32:1; 33:1; 37:2; 39:1; 42.

[23] On the one hand, the text of the *Vita nuova* displays what, in Paul Ricoeur's terminology, can be called "the chronology of sequence" ("Narrative Time" 169); namely, events are narrated according to a temporal succession that takes the story, and the reader, from the first encounter of both male and female protagonists at approximately nine years of age to the text's final temporal moment before which everything in the story has already taken place and beyond which the narrator can say nothing but in an anticipatory manner. On the other hand, such a "chronology of sequence" is time and again interrupted, and therefore enhanced, by elements in the story that are situated within an atemporal context: that is, all those textual elements, such as a) all the poems' *divisions*; b) the metaliterary expressions "I dico che" 'I say that'; c) all present tenses outside direct discourse. Referring neither to the past nor to the future of the story, such usages seem to escape the illusion of "the chronology of sequence" and are thus grounded on the illusion of the atemporality of the scribe in the act of writing or of the text in the process of being written.

dal principio del suo anno nono apparve a me, ed io la vidi quasi da la
fine del mio nono.

(Nine times since my birth had the heaven of light returned to almost the
same point in its orbit when to my eyes first appeared the glorious lady
of my mind, who was called Beatrice by many who did not know her
given name. She had already been in this life as long as in her time the
heaven of fixed stars had moved toward the East a twelfth part of a
degree, so that at about the beginning of her ninth year did she appear to
me, and I saw her at about the end of my ninth.)

(*Vita nova* 2:1-2)

Accordingly, the narrator-protagonist places within the all-encompassing
category of cosmic time the beginning of both his remembered life and his
autobiographical narrative. Cosmic time is here indicated in a twofold
manner: first, by means of the cyclical and circular movement of the sun;
second, through the revolution of the heaven of the Fixed Stars. Situating the
time of the male and female protagonists' respective birth and first encounter
within such a cosmic perspective also places the narrative's beginning in
reference to two biblical primordial events — the creation of the sun and the
stars, followed by that of humankind's primogenitors — as described in
Genesis 1-2 (*Par.* 29:13-21; Boyde, *Dante Philomythes* 240-45; 358n14).
Thus cosmic time (the movement of the sun and stars) intersects with lived
time (the birth and encounter of the two protagonists) at the very beginning
of the *Vita nuova*. Were the narrative of this encounter situated outside such a
cosmic dimension, it would merely be an episode, one that could be followed
by other similar episodes, none capable of creating a story. By contrast,
situated within a cosmic temporal category harkening back to both the
biblical creation of the universe and of humankind, this encounter of a man
and a woman constitutes the first in a series of events organized into one
meaningful whole.[24]

---

[24] Another connector that links cosmic time with personal time, according to
Ricoeur, is "implied by history's recourse to documents and monuments": namely,
the trace, or "a vestige left by the passage of a human being or of an animal. A
trace is *left*, a trace *remains*. . . . On the first level, the physical, the trace as a
substitute must be a *mark* left by something. . . . As a physical entity, the trace is
something of the present. Traces of the past exist now. . . . On a second level, the
noetic, . . . A trace, then, is a present thing which stands for [*vaut*] an absent past"
(*A Ricoeur Reader* 345). Almost at the end of the narrative, the narrator speaks of

Beginnings are harbingers of life. Accordingly, as we have seen, the narrative beginning of the life story is rendered through the regularity of the cyclical and circular movements of the heaven of the light and by the slow movement of the heaven of the Fixed Stars toward the East. Endings may suggest catastrophes. Overturning the regularity of the cosmic category announced at the beginning of the story, apocalypse marks the nightmarish vision of Beatrice's death by the weakened and sickly male protagonist:

> Così cominciando ad errare la mia fantasia, venni a quello ch'io non sapea ove io mi fosse; e vedere mi parea donne andare scapigliate piangendo per via, maravigliosamente triste; e pareami vedere lo sole oscurare, sì che le stelle si mostravano di colore ch'elle mi faceano giudicare che piangessero; e pareami che li uccelli volando per l'aria cadessero morti, e che fossero grandissimi tremuoti.

> (Thus, my imagination beginning to wander, I reached a point at which I knew not where I was; and I seemed to see women roaming disheveled, crying along the way, wondrously sad; and I seemed to see the sun darken, so that the stars appeared of a color that made me think that they wept; and it seemed to me that birds flying through the air fell dead, and that there were tremendous earthquakes.)

> (*Vita nuova* 23:5)

In the male protagonist's nightmarish imagination of Beatrice's death, which stands at the opposite pole of his first encounter with her, all the cosmic elements marking the story's beginning are overturned: the sun darkens, the stars weep, and the cosmic order is shaken by earthquakes. Likewise on earth, women weep and walk aimlessly on the streets.

The importance should not be lost of the reality of the narrative

---

several pilgrims' journey to Rome to "see that blessed image that Jesus Christ left to us as a likeness of his most beautiful countenance" (*VN* 40:1). The mention of such Christian pilgrimages provides the narrator with the opportunity to link Beatrice's life and death to that of Christ himself. Such a Christological link cannot be but fundamental for that kind of critical reading that sees Beatrice as a *figura Christi*. At the same time, "that blessed image" of "Jesus Christ" is not only a remembrance but also a *monument*. In fact, that cloth or shroud, also called veronica, on which Christ allegedly left the imprint of his face, constitutes the first historical monument (followed immediately by reference to the shrine at Santiago of Compostella) clearly identified in the *Vita nuova*, where no city, no church, and no palace is mentioned and identified by name.

beginning's cosmic temporal order vis-à-vis the unreality of the *vana imaginazione* with its apocalyptic signs. In the *Vita nuova*, cosmic time is never, except in that nightmarish imagination, overturned by apocalypse through the darkening of the sun, falling stars, and powerful earthquakes. Rather, cosmic time, together with individual time, gives way to eternity. The apocalyptic description of *Vita nuova* 23, in fact, *announces but does not mark* Beatrice's leaving behind individual time and her entering into eternity. When the female protagonist actually leaves the present, marked by the revolutions of the sun and the succession of days and nights, it is precisely at that transitional moment that the narrator-protagonist feels compelled, more markedly so than at any other moment of the narrative, to implement another temporal category, that of calendar or historical time.

4.2. Calendar or Historical Time

After having situated lived time within cosmic time, the narrator-protagonist employs calendar or historical time to record the moment when Beatrice leaves behind that temporal category marked by present, past, and future to enter the immutable permanency of eternity:

> Io dico che, secondo l'usanza d'Arabia, l'anima sua nobilissima si partio ne la prima ora del nono giorno del mese; e secondo l'usanza di Siria, ella si partio nel nono mese de l'anno, però che lo primo mese è ivi Tisirin primo, lo quale a noi è Ottobre; e secondo l'usanza nostra, ella si partio in quello anno de la nostra indizione, cioè de li anni Domini, in cui lo perfetto numero nove volte era compiuto in quello centinaio nel quale in questo mondo ella fue posta, ed ella fue de li cristiani del terzodecimo centinaio.

> (I say that, according to the Arabian custom, her most noble soul departed in the first hour of the ninth day of the month; and according to the Syrian custom, she departed in the ninth month of the year, for there the first month is Tixryn the first, which for us is October; and according to our custom, she departed in that year of our indiction, that is, of the years of our Lord, in which the perfect number nine had been completed nine times in that century in which she had come into this world, and she was a Christian of the thirteenth century.)

(VN 29:1)

In hagiographical writings, death is viewed as a second, true birth: the saints' *dies natalis* into eternity. Thus calendar time marks endings and beginnings simultaneously, bridging the gap between the sun's temporal movement and eternity's timeless permanency.

What, then, is calendar time, which sociology and the comparative history of religions tell us is universally widespread, and whose universal constitution makes it a third form of time between individual time and cosmic time (Ricoeur 3:106)? According to Ricoeur, who here relies on Emile Benveniste (*Problèmes de linguistique générale* 2:67-78), three features characterize every calendar:

> 1) A founding event, which marks the beginning of a new era and by which every other event is dated.
>
> 2) The possibility to traverse time in three directions: backward, from the present toward the past; forward, from the past to the present; and also, by anticipation, from the present toward the future.[25]
>
> 3) Finally, the measurability of calendar time according to constant units of gauging based on cosmic phenomena, such as days and nights, months, and years (Ricoeur 3:106-07).[26]

These three distinct features of calendar time, Ricoeur points out with Benveniste, bear an explicit relationship to cosmic time and lived time; but the founding event whereby cosmic and lived time acquire new significance and give rise to "a new course" of events forms the axial moment (Benveniste 71; Ricoeur 3:108). As Ricoeur goes on to say: "The originality that the axial moment confers on calendar time allows us to declare this the form of time 'external' to physical time as well as to lived time. . . . every instant is a possible candidate for the role of the axial moment" (Ricoeur 3:108).

The possibility for every day to be a candidate for the role of the axial

---

[25] Although Ricoeur does not speak of eternity here, he does so in many other instances, primarily 3:136-37; 264-66.

[26] The astronomical basis of calendar time is succeeded by a biological basis: the succession of generations, that is, the "relationship between contemporaries, predecessors, and successors" (Ricoeur 3:109) that are brought about by the everyday experience of birth, aging, and death (Ricoeur 3:110). In the *Vita nuova* such a relationship is present in many ways: the narrator-protagonist's friends who either take him to a wedding or ask to write poems; the faithful of love to whom he addresses the first poem; the ladies who understand love; the first of his friends; the ideal readers; etc.

moment raises the issue of how to identify this axial moment. Such an identification is based on discourse:

> To have a present, as we have learned from Benveniste, someone must speak. The present is then indicated by the coincidence between an event and the discourse that states it. To rejoin lived time starting from chronicle time, therefore, we have to pass through linguistic time, which refers to discourse.
>
> (Ricoeur 3:108-09)

What are then in the *Vita nuova* the axial moments, the discourse stating them, and the narrative ways whereby the narrator determines present, past, and future and the narrative itself is structured?

These inquiries return us to the apocalyptic description of *Vita nuova* 23, which *announces but does not mark* Beatrice's leaving behind individual time and her entering into eternity. The nightmarish "vana imaginazione" announcing Beatrice's death does not constitute an axial moment capable of giving new significance to past, present, and future events in the *Vita nuova*. In fact, after its description in *Vita nuova* 23, the nightmarish dream is mentioned only once, precisely by the syntagm "vana immaginazione," at the beginning of the following paragraph: "Appresso questa vana imaginazione, avvenne uno die" 'After this vain imagining it happened one day' (*VN* 24:1). The nightmarish dream thus constitutes the temporal and narrative point of reference only for the story that comes after it: the male protagonist's sight of Giovanna followed by Beatrice. And yet, even this event, in light of what Amore tells the protagonist, is linked not so much with the nightmarish and apocalyptic scene as with the first encounter narrated in *Vita nuova* 2. Amore says: "Pensa di benedicere lo dì che io ti presi, però che tu lo dei fare" 'Think about blessing the day I took you captive, for you must do so' (*VN* 24:2). The first and fundamental axial moment, therefore, the true founding event of Dante's *libello,* is the narrator-protagonist's first encounter with Beatrice in *Vita nuova* 2.

That lived and individual event framed by the revolutions of the sun and the movement of the stars constitutes the founding event of all other narrated events until the second axial moment takes place, the actual death of Beatrice. This second axial event structures and gives meaning to all the following events until the end of the *libello*. Finally, at the very end of the *libello*, a third axial moment is firmly posited, the notion of eternity, which was implied at the *libello*'s beginning and then powerfully announced in the nightmarish dream of *Vita nuova* 23. Thus cosmic time, calendar time, and eternity variously interact with lived and individual time throughout Dante's *Vita nuova*.

The inquiry may now turn to the narrative ways by which the two fundamental axial moments — namely, the first encounter of the two protagonists and the death of Beatrice — structure and organize the narrative fabric of the *libello*. The results of this inquiry offer answers to the original question: whether and according to what criteria the *Vita nuova* should be divided into paragraphs rather than into chapters.

4.3. Time's Threefold Notion and the Function of Paragraphs

The *libello* in which the narrator-protagonist seeks to "assemplare" ('transcribe') the words he finds written under the rubric "*Incipit vita nova*" is organized around the two axial moments of birth/encounter and death, according to the notion of present, past, and future. Commenting on such a notion, Ricoeur writes: "If we did not have the phenomenological notion of the present, as the 'today' in terms of which there is a 'tomorrow' and a 'yesterday,' we would not be able to make any sense of the idea of a new event that breaks with the previous era, inaugurating a course of events wholly different from what preceded it" (3:107).[27] Our contention, however, is that the narrative structure of the *libello* itself reflects the multiple experience of temporality as lived time, cosmic time, and calendar time: a time that, despite the narrator's resolve to portray it as a unified experience (a *vita nova*), challenges nevertheless all attempts at absolute unification, thus evincing the Augustinian concept of time as discordant concordance (Ricoeur 1:4, 21, 31; 3:139-40).

That time is one, despite the human inability to hold on to the present and transitory moment, is a concept presented at the *libello*'s beginning and

---

[27] The "today" of the *Vita nuova* is the time when the narrator becomes the closest to what the protagonist is at the end of the *Vita nuova*; the "tomorrow" is the time he looks forward to when he will be able to treat of Beatrice more worthily; the "yesterday" is the time that is inscribed in his memory and that he intends to narrate, as he does, in the *libello*: the lived time of the female and male protagonists measured in terms of cosmic time and calendar time, projected toward the future, and structured, following the chronology of succeeding events, around the three axial moments of birth and encounter, death, and future life.

is expressed through the metaphor of the "libro de la memoria" ('the book of memory'). Assuming the role of reader, the narrator finds written in that book "parole" ('words'), a notion based on multiplicity and divisibility. Yet, the metaphor of the "libro de la memoria" undeniably connotes unity because the mental "book" is utterly immaterial and invisible. Vis-à-vis that immaterial and invisible book of memory stands, by contrast, "questo libello," that is, the little book into which the narrator transcribes his memories and which, because every reader of the *Vita nuova* holds the text in his or her hands, is therefore divisible. The narrator himself offers many examples of the text's divisibility: for instance, the *divisioni,* through which the glossator exemplifies how one can divide and dissect a text, and the poems themselves, which time and again exemplify the *Vita nuova*'s divisibility.

Viewed as a unified story representing one person's life, the narrative whole called *libello* consists of smaller narrative units or, following Ricoeur, quasi-plots, which depend on quasi-events.[28] These are *quasi-* rather than actual plots and events because, as Ricoeur notes, "Artisans who work with

---

[28] Just as Ricoeur emphasizes the relationship between time and narrativity, he also underlines that between event and story ("the events themselves receive an intelligibility derived from their contribution to the development of the plot" 1:207). "Thus" — Ricoeur argues — "due to the fact that they are narrated, events are singular *and* typical, contingent *and* expected, deviant *and* dependent on paradigms" (1:208). Relying on Duby's *The Three Orders: Feudal Society Imagined*, Ricoeur writes that "The quasi-plot really commences when the system is put to the test of 'circumstances' (121-66), undergoes a long 'eclipse' (167-268), and then finally reemerges, this 'resurgence' (269-353) culminating in the system's 'adoption' . . . (Ricoeur 1:220). Ricoeur thus comments: "the quasi-events that indicate the critical periods of the ideological system are set within quasi-plots, which assure their narrative status" (1:221); and also: "*all change enters the field of history as a quasi-event*" (1:224); and finally: "By *quasi-event* we signify that the extension of the notion of event, beyond short and brief time, remains correlative to a similar extending of the notions of plot and character. There is a quasi-event wherever we can discern, even if only very indirectly, very obliquely, a quasi-plot and quasi-characters. The event in history corresponds to what Aristotle called a change in fortune — *metabolé* — in his formal theory of emplotment. An event, once again, is not only what contributes to the unfolding of a plot but what gives it the dramatic form of a change in fortune" (1:224-25). Applying Ricoeur's concepts, we read the *Vita nuova* as one single event (that of the new life), consisting of many quasi-events, and thus quasi-stories. Our purpose is to identify each quasi-event on the basis of temporality and narrativity, and to differentiate them typographically without creating divisions according to chapters.

words produce not things but quasi-things: they invent the as-if" (1:45). Through small narrative units, the narrator traverses, by moving backward and forward in time and thus in the story, the narrative whole called *Vita nuova*, precisely as he writes: "Allora cominciai a pensare di lei: e ricordandomi di lei secondo l'ordine del tempo passato" 'I then began to think about her; and remembering her according to the order of time past' (39:2). The narrator-protagonist thus measures these quasi-events and quasi-plots in terms of what precedes and follows them, presenting them separately and yet viewing them as a whole, while always placing them in relationship, according to a chronology of sequence, to one of the two axial moments.

Thus the fundamental criterion that identifies quasi-events and quasi-plots is inherent in the text itself, for this criterion interconnects quasi-events and quasi-stories, linking them into a narrative whole. Such a criterion, based on narrativity, is temporality, by which, according to Ricoeur, existence, through narrativity, reaches language: "Indeed, I take temporality to be that structure of existence that reaches language in narrativity and narrativity to be the language structure that has temporality as its ultimate referent" ("Narrative Time" 169). And as we quoted earlier: "Time becomes human time to the extent that it is organized after the manner of a narrative; narrative, in turn, is meaningful to the extent that it portrays the features of temporal experience" (Ricoeur, *Time and Narrative* 1:3).

The linguistic link between temporal experiences is the "temporal connector," which Ricoeur defines as those "features of temporal experience" "organized after the manner of a narrative," and which, following Mikhail Bakhtin, may be designated the chronotope: that is, those privileged temporal instances situated within a specific spatial setting in which the relationship between two individuals or between an individual and a social group becomes heightened or undergoes a crisis.[29]

---

[29] "We will give the name *chronotope* (literally, 'time space') to the intrinsic connectedness of temporal and spatial relationships that are artistically expressed in literature. . . . In the literary artistic chronotope, spatial and temporal indicators are fused into one carefully thought-out, concrete whole. Time, as it were, thickens, takes on flesh, becomes artistically visible; likewise, space becomes charged and responsive to the movements of time, plot and history. . . . The chronotope in literature has an intrinsic *generic* significance. It can even be said that it is precisely the chronotope that defines genre and generic distinctions, for in literature the primary category in the chronotope is time. The chronotope as

The chronotopes that help us place events in the *Vita nuova* into larger narrative units can be grouped according to four categories, each comprising several chronotopes.

a) The public life chronotopes: the chronotope of birth and first encounter (1); the chronotope of the church (2), the street (3), the open space or square (4), and the road (5); the chronotope of matrimony (6); and finally the chronotope of death (7).

b) The private life chronotope (8), portraying mostly the solitary bedroom.

c) The chronotope of the eternal and glorious life, to which God, Mary, the angels, and Beatrice belong, and to which the narrator-protagonist aspires (9).

d) The metaliterary chronotope (10), in which the narrator either introduces himself in the act of writing poems or comments upon his own writing.[30]

These ten chronotopes sustain the text's highly interconnected fabric of quasi-events and quasi-stories. These chronotopes are in turn linked together by means of clearly identifiable temporal phrases marking most of the paragraph *incipits* in Barbi's edition. These temporal phrases are:

Appresso (*VN* 2:1; 8:1; 9:1; 13:1; 14:1; 15:1; 16:1; 23:1; 24:1; 27:1; 42:1)
Poi che (*VN* 3:1; 17:1; 30:1; 31:1; 32:1; 33:1)
Un giorno (*VN* 5:1)
Avvenne poi (*VN* 19:1; 36:1)
Appresso che (*VN* 20:1)
In quello giorno nel quale si compiea l'anno (*VN* 34:1)
Poi (*VN* 35:1; 41:1)
Un die (*VN* 39:1)
Dopo (*VN* 40:1)

---

a formally constitutive category determines to a significant degree the image of a man in literature as well. The image of man is always intrinsically chronotopic" (*Dialogic Imagination* 84-85).

[30] In Dante's *Vita nuova*, the 'in' in which events occur marks: (1) those moments in which the narrator presents himself in the act of writing in the present; (2) or the act of dividing the poems after or before they are written, as if they were placed outside temporality; and (3) all those textual elements, such as direct discourses, maxims, and aphorisms expressed in the present tense, that seek to escape the boundaries of temporality.

These temporal phrases occur mostly at the beginning of the so-called chapters in Barbi's edition. In fact, these chapter *incipits* can be grouped according to four categories:

1) The opening chapter in Barbi's edition refers figurally to location: that is, to the place in the book of the narrator's memory from which he intends to transcribe the *sentenzia* (*VN* 1).

2) Thirty-one chapters in Barbi's edition begin with either a preposition, a phrase, a conjunction, or an adverb of time.

3) Four chapters in Barbi's edition begin with an introductory formula, such as "Dico che" or "Ora . . . dico che."

4) Six chapters in Barbi's edition begin with one of a miscellany of expressions (*VN* 18; 25; 26; 28; 37; 38).

A closer analysis of the six chapter *incipits* listed under category number four reveals that almost all of these six chapters seem to have no justification, in that they constitute neither a chronotope nor a story different from what precedes them, to which in fact they should be added (Appendix 2-3).

Of the remaining categories of chapter *incipit*, the largest is that of the temporal opening, which, using prepositions, conjunctions, adverbs, or a phrase indicating an undetermined period of time, initiate thirty-one of Barbi's forty-two chapters. These temporal phrases are rather simple and suggest either an indeterminate amount of time or mark the passing of days, months, years. They will also help us in questioning, with the ultimate result of reducing, the forty-two so-called chapters of the *Vita nuova* that have become standard since last century.

These temporal phrases by themselves, however, cannot constitute the absolute yardstick by which one can proceed to divide the text, identifying quasi-events, chronotopes, and quasi-stories. In fact, the passing of time that these temporal phrases mark must be situated within the broader context of quasi-events and quasi-plots and within the perspective of chronotopes. Temporal phrases and chronotopes link the text's interconnected quasi-events and quasi-stories first around the two axial moments of birth and encounter, second around the chronotope of death, third around the chronotope of eternal and glorious life, and finally around the chronotope of the narrator in the act of writing. The chronotopes of life and encounter, death, and eternity look forward and backward to one another throughout the text, although each quasi-event and quasi-story depends primarily on one of them.

4.4. Beyond Time and Language: Eternity

To conclude: the *Vita nuova* narrator stakes out the boundaries of his own narrative by marking the story's beginning in reference to cosmic time and the story's end in reference to eternity. Thus, on one boundary of the narrative, the time of Beatrice's first "apparimento" ('appearance') to the protagonist is indicated through cosmic time measured through the perspective of the birth of the two protagonists. Already announced at the story's beginning through the reference to Beatrice as "la *gloriosa* donna de la mia mente," eternity stakes out the other boundary of the narrative. Between those two boundaries marked by cosmic time and eternity, the narrative seeks to recover and make permanent the protagonist-narrator's present and past time, while projecting itself toward the future, which the narrator-protagonist hopes will coincide with eternity itself.[31] What Ricoeur writes about the insurmountable aporias of narrating time can be applied to the conclusion of the *Vita nuova*: "There comes a moment, in a work devoted to the power of narrative to elevate time to language, where we must admit that narrative is not the whole story and that time can be spoken of in other ways, because, even for narrative, it remains inscrutable" (3:272). Virtually every critic of the *Vita nuova* says that the future, worthier work announced by the narrator-protagonist at the end of the *Vita nuova* cannot but be, or certainly is, the *Divine Comedy*. Would it not be more appropriate to say that the end, or

---

[31] The chronotope of the road and of the pilgrimage provides the narrator-protagonist with an end to his life account. What we have in fact is an interruption of the narrative, since the narrator-protagonist, who was able to imagine an end for Beatrice, now in the glory of heaven, is nevertheless unable to provide an end to his own life account. In interrupting the narrative of his life account, he projects himself toward his future life on earth set in temporality but also toward a future life in heaven outside the category of temporality. Only by projecting himself beyond the category of temporality can the narrator-protagonist avoid the shortcomings inherent in the interruption of the narrative and also view his own life as a whole, something we, human beings, in Kermode's words, "cannot do from our spot of time in the middle" (8). The narrator, therefore, confronts such issues as how to begin and how to end the narrative of a life by its own definition set in temporality. He also confronts the issue of how to link the chronotopes of encounters, matrimony, death, and pilgrimage that connect the narrative's beginning with its end.

rather the interruption of the *Vita nuova,* emphasizes that moment when the narrator, in Ricoeur's words, "must admit that narrative is not the whole story and that time can be spoken of in other ways, because, even for narrative, time is inscrutable" (Ricoeur 3:272)?[32]

Again with Ricoeur, "The mystery of time is not equivalent to a prohibition directed against language" (3:274). The *Vita nuova,* in fact, displays many "other ways" through which time can be addressed: the dialogues within the narrative and especially the thirty-one poems and the poems' *divisioni.* Through these, narrative intersects and becomes interwoven with other aspects of language in a continuous effort to overcome the aporias of time through its configuration and refiguration through writing.

The issue of the thirty-one poems' interweaving with the prose throughout the *Vita nuova* bears directly on the many ways time can be represented. Since Dante wrote many or most of the poems of the *libello* before the prose, one may legitimately ask what made him decide to write the prose at all. "Narrative is a guardian of time," Ricoeur writes (3:241). Accordingly, Dante's decision to write the narrative that links and conjoins the poems of the *Vita nuova* may precisely lie in his awareness that those poems did indeed represent single and distinct moments of life but not life in its totality, and that only narrative could best link all those moments into a unified narrative.[33] The *Vita nuova*'s answer to the aporetics of time, therefore, is addressed in two ways, which confront both content and style: from the viewpoint of content, by means of the interweaving of cosmic time, lived time, and calendar time with the notion of the permanency of the act of writing and of eternity throughout the *libello*'s prose, while from the

---

[32] At the same time, in "the act of making a promise," which we find in the last few lines of the *Vita nuova,* "are fused personal commitment, interpersonal trust, and the tacit or virtual social pact that confers on the dialogical relation itself the cosmopolitan dimension of a public space" (*Time and Narrativity* 3:259).

[33] Ricoeur's definition of temporality and narrativity apparently is not concerned with what, since time immemorial, literary critics call "lyrical time." And yet, Ricoeur's emphasis on the reciprocity of temporality and narrativity cannot but bear on those textual instances in the *Vita nuova* that strike the critic as lyrical, and thus arguably outside the time reference. Thus the reciprocal nature of temporality and narrativity necessarily anchors the text's lyrical instances into that notion of temporality that is essential to the human condition to such an extent that, just as nothing human can possibly escape time, no literary artifact can likewise be rendered outside any temporal sequence.

viewpoint of style and genres, by means of the interweaving of poems, glosses, and prose narrative that has often been likened to that of Boethius's *De consolatione philosophiae* but that harkens back also to that of the Bible: namely, the book that, in many genres and styles, portrays the primordia of humankind and its journey toward apocalypse and eternity.[34]

---

[34] An analogy can thus be established between the various literary forms constituting the *Vita nuova*'s prose and poems with those constituting the prose and poetic compositions of the Bible. Discussing the aporetics of narrative in presenting time, Ricoeur makes important remarks concerning the ways in which the Bible faces temporality (3:272; 3:334n37).

La Vita Nuova
di
Dante Alighieri

1   In quella parte del libro de la mia memoria dinanzi a la quale poco si potrebbe leggere, si trova una rubrica la quale dice: *Incipit vita nova.* Sotto la quale rubrica io trovo scritte le parole le quali è mio intendimento d'assemplare in questo libello; e se non tutte, almeno la loro sentenzia.

2:1   Nove fiate già appresso lo mio nascimento era tornato lo cielo de la luce quasi a uno medesimo punto, quanto a la sua propria girazione, quando a li miei occhi apparve prima la gloriosa donna de la mia mente, la quale fu 2:2 chiamata da molti Beatrice li quali non sapeano che si chiamare. Ella era in questa vita già stata tanto, che ne lo suo tempo lo cielo stellato era mosso verso la parte d'oriente de le dodici parti l'una d'un grado, sì che quasi dal principio del suo anno nono apparve a me, ed io la vidi quasi da la fine del 2:3 mio nono. Apparve vestita di nobilissimo colore, umile e onesto, sanguigno, 2:4 cinta e ornata a la guisa che a la sua giovanissima etade si convenia. In quello punto dico veracemente che lo spirito de la vita, lo quale dimora ne la secretissima camera de lo cuore, cominciò a tremare sì fortemente, che appariа ne li menimi polsi orribilmente; e tremando disse queste parole: "Ecce deus 2:5 fortior me, qui veniens dominabitur michi." In quello punto lo spirito animale, lo quale dimora ne l'alta camera ne la quale tutti li spiriti sensitivi portano le loro percezioni, si cominciò a maravigliare molto, e parlando spezialmente a 2:6 li spiriti del viso, sì disse queste parole: "Apparuit iam beatitudo vestra." In quello punto lo spirito naturale, lo quale dimora in quella parte ove si ministra lo nutrimento nostro, cominciò a piangere, e piangendo disse queste parole:

The New Life

of

Dante Alighieri

In that part of the book of my memory before which little could be read, a 1 rubric is found that says: *Incipit vita nova* [Here begins the new life]. Beneath this rubric I find written the words that it is my intention to transcribe into this little book: if not all of them, at least their substance.

Nine times since my birth had the heaven of light returned to almost the 2:1 same point in its orbit when to my eyes first appeared the glorious lady of my mind, who was called Beatrice by many who did not know her given name. She had already been in this life as long as in her time the heaven of 2:2 fixed stars had moved toward the East a twelfth part of a degree, so that at about the beginning of her ninth year did she appear to me, and I saw her at about the end of my ninth. She appeared humbly and properly dressed in a 2:3 most noble color, crimson, girded and adorned in the manner that befitted her so youthful age. At that moment I say truly that the spirit of life, which 2:4 dwells in the most secret chamber of the heart, began to tremble so strongly that it appeared terrifying in its smallest veins; and trembling it said these words: "Ecce deus fortior me, qui veniens dominabitur michi" ["Behold a god more powerful than I, who comes to rule over me"]. At that point the 2:5 animal spirit, which dwells in the upper chamber to which all the spirits of the senses carry their perceptions, began to marvel greatly, and speaking especially to the spirits of sight, it said these words: "Apparuit iam beatitudo vestra" ["Now has appeared your beatitude"]. At that point the natural spirit, 2:6 which dwells in that part that ministers to our nourishment, began to weep, and weeping said these words: "Heu miser, quia frequenter impeditus ero

2:7 "Heu miser, quia frequenter impeditus ero deinceps!" D'allora innanzi dico
che Amore segnoreggiò la mia anima, la quale fu sì tosto a lui disponsata, e
cominciò a prendere sopra me tanta sicurtade e tanta signoria per la vertù che
li dava la mia imaginazione, che me convenia fare tutti li suoi piaceri
2:8 compiutamente. Elli mi comandava molte volte che io cercasse per vedere
questa angiola giovanissima, onde io ne la mia puerizia molte volte l'andai
cercando, e vedeala di sì nobili e laudabili portamenti, che certo di lei si
potea dire quella parola del poeta Omero: "Ella non parea figliuola d'uomo
2:9 mortale, ma di deo." E avvegna che la sua imagine, la quale continuatamente
meco stava, fosse baldanza d'Amore a segnoreggiare me, tuttavia era di sì
nobilissima vertù, che nulla volta sofferse che Amore mi reggesse sanza lo
fedele consiglio de la ragione in quelle cose là ove cotale consiglio fosse
2:10 utile a udire. E però che soprastare a le passioni e atti di tanta gioventudine
pare alcuno parlare fabuloso, mi partirò da esse; e trapassando molte cose le
quali si potrebbero trarre de l'essemplo onde nascono queste, verrò a quelle
parole le quali sono scritte ne la mia memoria sotto maggiori paragrafi.

3:1 Poi che fuoro passati tanti die, che appunto erano compiuti li nove anni
appresso l'apparimento soprascritto di questa gentilissima, ne l'ultimo
di questi die avvenne che questa mirabile donna apparve a me vestita di colore
bianchissimo, in mezzo a due gentili donne, le quali erano di più lunga etade;
e passando per una via, volse li occhi verso quella parte ov'io era molto
pauroso, e per la sua ineffabile cortesia, la quale è oggi meritata nel grande
secolo, mi salutoe molto virtuosamente, tanto che me parve allora vedere
3:2 tutti li termini de la beatitudine. L'ora che lo suo dolcissimo salutare mi
giunse, era fermamente nona di quello giorno; e però che quella fu la prima
volta che le sue parole si mossero per venire a li miei orecchi, presi tanta
dolcezza, che come inebriato mi partio da le genti, e ricorsi a lo solingo luogo
3:3 d'una mia camera, e puosimi a pensare di questa cortesissima. E pensando
di lei, mi sopragiunse uno soave sonno, ne lo quale m'apparve una
maravigliosa visione: che me parea vedere ne la mia camera una nebula di
colore di fuoco, dentro a la quale io discernea una figura d'uno segnore di
pauroso aspetto a chi la guardasse; e pareami con tanta letizia, quanto a sé,
che mirabile cosa era; e ne le sue parole dicea molte cose, le quali io non
3:4 intendea se non poche; tra le quali intendea queste: "Ego dominus tuus." Ne
le sue braccia mi parea vedere una persona dormire nuda, salvo che involta
mi parea in uno drappo sanguigno leggeramente; la quale io riguardando
molto intentivamente, conobbi ch'era la donna de la salute, la quale m'avea

deinceps!" ["Wretched me, for often hereafter shall I be impeded!"]. I say   2:7
that from that time forward, Love ruled over my soul, which was so early
espoused to him, and he began to assume over me such assurance and such
mastery, through the power that my imagination gave him, that I was obliged
to do all his bidding fully. Many times he commanded that I seek to behold   2:8
this youthful angel; thus many times in my childhood I sought her, and I saw
in her such noble and laudable bearing that of her could certainly be said
those words of the poet Homer: "She seemed no child of mortal man, but of
god." And although her image, which continually stayed with me, gave Love   2:9
its strength to rule over me, it was nevertheless of such noble power that at
no time did it allow Love to rule me without the faithful counsel of reason, in
those things where such counsel was useful to heed. But since dwelling on   2:10
the passions and acts of such a youthful age may seem a fabulous tale, I shall
move away from them; and omitting many things that might be drawn from
the exemplar from which the present ones originate, I shall come to those
words that are written in my memory under the greater paragraphs.

A fter many days had passed, so that precisely nine years were completed   3:1
following the appearance described above of this most gentle lady, it
happened that on the last of these days this marvelous lady appeared to me
dressed in purest white, between two gentle ladies who were of greater years;
and passing along a street, she turned her eyes to that place where I stood in
great fear, and in her ineffable courtesy, which today is rewarded in life everlasting, she greeted me with exceeding virtue, such that I then seemed to see
all the terms of beatitude. The hour in which her most sweet greeting reached   3:2
me was firmly the ninth of that day, and because that was the first time that
her words were moved to come to my ears, I experienced such sweetness that
like one inebriated I left all company and resorted to the solitary place of my
room, and set about thinking upon this most courteous one. And thinking of   3:3
her, I was overcome by a sweet sleep, in which there appeared to me a marvelous vision: I seemed to see in my room a cloud the color of fire, within
which I discerned a figure of a master, of an aspect frightening to whoever
might behold him; and he appeared so happy in himself that it was a wondrous thing; and in his words he spoke of many things, of which I understood
only a few; among his words I understood these: " Ego dominus tuus" ["I am
your Lord"]. I seemed to see in his arms a person asleep, naked except that   3:4
she seemed to me lightly wrapped in a crimson cloth; one whom I, regarding

3:5   lo giorno dinanzi degnato di salutare. E ne l'una de le mani mi parea che
      questi tenesse una cosa la quale ardesse tutta, e pareami che mi dicesse queste
3:6   parole: "Vide cor tuum." E quando elli era stato alquanto, pareami che
      disvegliasse questa che dormia; e tanto si sforzava per suo ingegno, che le
      facea mangiare questa cosa che in mano li ardea, la quale ella mangiava
3:7   dubitosamente. Appresso ciò poco dimorava che la sua letizia si convertia
      in amarissimo pianto; e così piangendo, si ricoglia questa donna ne le sue
      braccia, e con essa mi parea che si ne gisse verso lo cielo; onde io sostenea sì
      grande angoscia, che lo mio deboletto sonno non poteo sostenere, anzi si
3:8   ruppe e fui disvegliato. E mantenente cominciai a pensare, e trovai che l'ora
      ne la quale m'era questa visione apparita, era la quarta de la notte stata; sì che
      appare manifestamente ch'ella fue la prima ora de le nove ultime ore de la
3:9   notte. Pensando io a ciò che m'era apparuto, propuosi di farlo sentire a molti
      li quali erano famosi trovatori in quello tempo: e con ciò fosse cosa che io
      avesse già veduto per me medesimo l'arte del dire parole per rima, propuosi
      di fare uno sonetto, ne lo quale io salutasse tutti li fedeli d'Amore; e pregandoli
      che giudicassero la mia visione, scrissi a loro ciò che io avea nel mio sonno
      veduto. E cominciai allora questo sonetto, lo quale comincia: *A ciascun'alma
      presa.*

3:10   A ciascun'alma presa e gentil core
                 nel cui cospetto ven lo dir presente,
                 in ciò che mi rescrivan suo parvente,
v. 4   salute in lor segnor, cioè Amore.
3:11   Già eran quasi che atterzate l'ore
                 del tempo che onne stella n'è lucente,
                 quando m'apparve Amor subitamente,
v. 8   cui essenza membrar mi dà orrore.
3:12   Allegro mi sembrava Amor tenendo
                 meo core in mano, e ne le braccia avea
                 madonna involta in un drappo dormendo.
v. 12   Poi la svegliava, e d'esto core ardendo
                 lei paventosa umilmente pascea:
                 appresso gir lo ne vedea piangendo.

3:13 Questo sonetto si divide in due parti; che ne la prima parte saluto e domando
      risponsione, ne la seconda significo a che si dee rispondere. La seconda
3:14 parte comincia quivi: *Già eran*. A questo sonetto fue risposto da molti e di

with great attention, recognized as the lady of the salutation, who the day before had deigned to greet me. In one of his hands he appeared to hold _{3:5} something all aflame, and he seemed to say to me these words: "Vide cor tuum" ["Behold your heart"]. And after he had waited awhile, he appeared _{3:6} to waken her who slept; and he so constrained her in his way that he made her eat this thing ablaze in his hand, which she consumed hesitatingly. After _{3:7} that, he abided but little before his happiness converted into most bitter weeping; and thus weeping, he gathered this lady into his arms, and with her he appeared to ascend toward heaven, for which I suffered such great anguish that I could not sustain my fragile sleep, which indeed broke and I awakened. And immediately I began to think, and I found that the hour in which this _{3:8} vision had appeared to me had been the fourth hour of the night; so that it appears manifestly to have been the first of the nine last hours of the night. Thinking upon that which had appeared to me, I resolved to make it known _{3:9} to many who were famous troubadours at that time; and since I myself had already seen to the art of saying words in rhyme, I resolved to compose a sonnet, in which I would greet all the faithful of Love; and requesting them to judge my vision, I wrote to them what I had seen in my sleep. And I then began this sonnet, which begins, *To every captive soul.*

> To every captive soul and gentle heart _{3:10}
> into whose regard shall come the present words,
> so that they in return may inscribe their views,
> greeting in their lord, who is Love. _{v. 4}
> Almost had passed a third of the hours _{3:11}
> of the time in which to us every star shines,
> when to me appeared Love suddenly,
> the memory of whose being gives me terror. _{v. 8}
> Joyous to me seemed Love, holding _{3:12}
> my heart in hand, and in his arms he had
> my lady wrapped in a cloth asleep.
> Then he wakened her, and this burning heart _{v. 12}
> to the frightened one he humbly fed:
> afterward I saw him turn away weeping.

This sonnet divides into two parts; in the first part I greet and ask a re- _{3:13} sponse, in the second I indicate what requires a response. The second part begins: *Almost had.* This sonnet was answered by many and by di- _{3:14}

diverse sentenzie; tra li quali fue risponditore quelli cui io chiamo primo de li miei amici, e disse allora uno sonetto, lo quale comincia: *Vedeste, al mio parere, onne valore.* E questo fue quasi lo principio de l'amistà tra lui e me,

3:15 quando elli seppe che io era quelli che li avea ciò mandato. Lo verace giudicio del detto sogno non fue veduto allora per alcuno ma ora è manifestissimo a li

4:1 più semplici. Da questa visione innanzi cominciò lo mio spirito naturale ad essere impedito ne la sua operazione, però che l'anima era tutta data nel pensare di questa gentilissima; onde io divenni in picciolo tempo poi di sì fraile e debole condizione, che a molti amici pesava de la mia vista; e molti pieni d'invidia già si procacciavano di sapere di me quello che io volea del

4:2 tutto celare ad altrui. Ed io, accorgendomi del malvagio domandare che mi faceano, per la volontade d'Amore, lo quale mi comandava secondo lo consiglio de la ragione, rispondea loro che Amore era quelli che così m'avea governato. Dicea d'Amore, però che io portava nel viso tante de le sue insegne,

4:3 che questo non si potea ricovrire. E quando mi domandavano "Per cui t'ha così distrutto questo Amore?", ed io sorridendo li guardava, e nulla dicea loro.

5:1 Uno giorno avvenne che questa gentilissima sedea in parte ove s'udiano parole de la regina de la gloria, ed io era in luogo dal quale vedea la mia beatitudine; e nel mezzo di lei e di me per la retta linea sedea una gentile donna di molto piacevole aspetto, la quale mi mirava spesse volte,

5:2 maravigliandosi del mio sguardare, che parea che sopra lei terminasse. Onde molti s'accorsero de lo suo mirare; e in tanto vi fue posto mente, che, partendomi da questo luogo, mi sentio dicere appresso di me: "Vedi come cotale donna distrugge la persona di costui"; e nominandola, io intesi che dicea di colei che mezzo era stata ne la linea retta che movea da la gentilissima

5:3 Beatrice e terminava ne li occhi miei. Allora mi confortai molto, assicurandomi che lo mio secreto non era comunicato lo giorno altrui per mia vista. E mantenente pensai di fare di questa gentile donna schermo de la veritade; e tanto ne mostrai in poco tempo, che lo mio secreto fue creduto

5:4 sapere da le più persone che di me ragionavano. Con questa donna mi celai alquanti anni e mesi; e per più fare credente altrui, feci per lei certe cosette per rima, le quali non è mio intendimento di scrivere qui, se non in quanto facesse a trattare di quella gentilissima Beatrice; e però le lascerò tutte, salvo

6:1 che alcuna cosa ne scriverò che pare che sia loda di lei. Dico che in questo tempo che questa donna era schermo di tanto amore, quanto da la mia parte, sì mi venne una volontade di volere ricordare lo nome di quella gentilissima ed accompagnarlo di molti nomi di donne, e spezialmente del nome di questa

verse interpretations; among the respondents was one whom I call first among my friends, who then wrote a sonnet that begins: *You saw, in my opinion, all worth.* And this was almost the beginning of friendship between him and me, when he learned that it was I who had sent it to him. The true meaning of the said dream was not seen by anyone then, but now it is perfectly clear to the simplest. From this vision onwards my natural spirit began to be hindered in its operations, for my soul was wholly given to thoughts of this most gentle lady; hence I soon became of so frail and weak a condition that many friends worried about my appearance; and many who were filled with envy sought at once to know what I wanted wholly to conceal from others. And I, aware of the malicious questioning that they put to me, through the will of Love, who commanded me according to the counsel of reason, replied that Love it was who had so guided me. I spoke of Love because I bore on my face so many of his signs that it could not be concealed. And when they asked, "For whom has this Love so ravaged you?", I regarded them smiling and said nothing.

One day it happened that this most gentle one was seated where one heard words about the queen of glory, and I was in a place from which I beheld my beatitude; and halfway between her and me in the direct line sat a gentle lady of quite pleasing aspect, who stared at me repeatedly, wondering at my gazing, which seemed to rest upon her. Hence many became aware of her staring, and so much attention was paid to it that, leaving this place, I heard it said behind me: "See how that lady devastates that one"; and naming her, it spoke, I understood, of the lady who had been intermediate in the direct line that proceeded from the most gentle Beatrice and ended in my eyes. Then was I greatly comforted, assured that my secret had not been revealed to anyone on that day by my gazing. And immediately I thought of making this gentle lady a screen to the truth; and soon I made such a show of it that my secret was believed known to most of the people who talked about me. Through this lady I concealed myself for some years and months; and to make others more credulous, I made for her certain small things in rhyme, which it is not my purpose to transcribe here, except insofar as it might serve to speak of that most gentle Beatrice; and therefore I shall omit them all, except that I shall write something that will clearly be in praise of her. I say that during that time when that lady was a screen to so much love as came from my part, the desire arose in me to recollect the name of this most gentle one and to accompany it with names of many ladies, and

3:15
4:1

4:2

4:3

5:1

5:2

5:3

5:4

6:1

6:2   gentile donna. E presi li nomi di sessanta le più belle donne de la cittade ove
la mia donna fue posta da l'altissimo sire, e compuosi una pistola sotto forma
di serventese, la quale io non scriverò: e non n'avrei fatto menzione, se non
per dire quello che componendola, maravigliosamente addivenne, cioè che
in alcuno altro numero non sofferse lo nome de la mia donna stare se non in
7:1   su lo nove, tra li nomi di queste donne.   La donna co la quale io avea tanto
tempo celata la mia volontade, convenne che si partisse de la sopradetta cittade
e andasse in paese molto lontano; per che io, quasi sbigottito de la bella difesa
che m'era venuta meno, assai me ne disconfortai, più che io medesimo non
7:2   avrei creduto dinanzi. E pensando che se de la sua partita io non parlasse
alquanto dolorosamente, le persone sarebbero accorte più tosto de lo mio
nascondere, propuosi di farne alcuna lamentanza in uno sonetto; lo quale io
scriverò, acciò che la mia donna fue immediata cagione di certe parole che
ne lo sonetto sono, sì come appare a chi lo intende.   E allora dissi questo
sonetto, che comincia: *O voi che per la via.*

7:3   **O** voi che per la via d'Amor passate,
                   attendete e guardate
                   s'elli è dolore alcun, quanto mio, grave;
v. 4   e prego sol ch'audir mi sofferiate,
                   e poi imaginate
                   s'io son d'ogni tormento ostale e chiave.
7:4   Amor, non già per mia poca bontate,
v. 8   ma per sua nobiltate,
                   mi pose in vita sì dolce e soave,
                   ch'io mi sentia dir dietro spesse fiate:
                   "Deo, per qual dignitate
v. 12   così leggiadro questi lo core have?"
7:5   **Or** ho perduta tutta mia baldanza
                   che si movea d'amoroso tesoro;
                   ond'io pover dimoro,
v. 16   in guisa che di dir mi ven dottanza.
7:6   Sì che volendo far come coloro
                   che per vergogna celan lor mancanza,
                   di fuor mostro allegranza,
v. 20   e dentro da lo core struggo e ploro.

7:7   Questo sonetto ha due parti principali; che ne la prima intendo chiamare li

especially with the name of this gentle lady. And I took the names of sixty of 6:2
the most beautiful ladies of the city where my lady was placed by the most
high Lord, and I composed an epistle in the form of a *serventese*, which I
will not inscribe; and I would not have mentioned it, except to say that which,
as I composed it, wonderfully came to pass, which is that in no other number
would my lady's name stand except in the ninth position among the names of
these ladies. The lady through whom I had for so long concealed my will 7:1
was obliged to leave the aforementioned city and journey to a faraway place;
so that I, rather fearful that my fair defense was being lost, became greatly
disheartened, more than I myself would have previously believed. And think- 7:2
ing that if of her departure I did not write somewhat sorrowfully then people
would soon become aware of my concealment, I resolved to express a lamentation in a sonnet, which I will transcribe, since my lady was the immediate
cause of certain words in the sonnet, as is clear to anyone who understands it.
And I then wrote this sonnet, which begins: *O you who along the way.*

> **O** you who along the way of Love pass by, 7:3
> attend and see
> if there be any grief as heavy as mine;
> and I pray only that you bear to hear me, v. 4
> and then imagine
> if I am every torment's hostel and key.
> Love, certainly not for my little worth 7:4
> but for his nobility, v. 8
> placed me in a life so sweet and serene
> that I heard it often said after me,
> "Lord, for what merit
> has he so lively a heart?" v. 12
> Now I have lost all my boldness, 7:5
> which quickened from Love's treasure;
> hence I abide impoverished,
> in such a way that I fear to speak. v. 16
> Thus, wishing to do as those 7:6
> who out of shame conceal their want,
> outwardly I show joy,
> and inwardly at the heart I waste away and weep. v. 20

This sonnet has two principal parts; in the first I intend to call upon the faith- 7:7

fedeli d'Amore per quelle parole di Geremia profeta che dicono: "O vos omnes qui transitis per viam, attendite et videte si est dolor sicut dolor meus", e pregare che mi sofferino d'audire; ne la seconda narro là ove Amore m'avea posto, con altro intendimento che l'estreme parti del sonetto non mostrano, e dico che io hoe ciò perduto.   La seconda parte comincia quivi: *Amor, non già.*

8:1   Appresso lo partire di questa gentile donna fue piacere del segnore de li angeli di chiamare a la sua gloria una donna giovane e di gentile aspetto molto, la quale fue assai graziosa in questa sopradetta cittade; lo cui corpo io vidi giacere sanza l'anima in mezzo di molte donne, le quali piangeano assai
8:2   pietosamente.   Allora, ricordandomi che già l'avea veduta fare compagnia a quella gentilissima, non poteo sostenere alquante lagrime; anzi piangendo mi propuosi di dicere alquante parole de la sua morte, in guiderdone di ciò
8:3   che alcuna fiata l'avea veduta con la mia donna.   E di ciò toccai alcuna cosa ne l'ultima parte de le parole che io ne dissi, sì come appare manifestamente a chi lo intende.   E dissi allora questi due sonetti, li quali comincia lo primo: *Piangete, amanti*, e lo secondo: *Morte villana.*

8:4   Piangete, amanti, poi che piange Amore,
                udendo qual cagion lui fa plorare.
8:5   Amor sente a Pietà donne chiamare,
v. 4   mostrando amaro duol per li occhi fore,
                perché villana Morte in gentil core
                ha miso il suo crudele adoperare,
                guastando ciò che al mondo è da laudare
v. 8   in gentil donna sovra de l'onore.
8:6   Audite quanto Amor le fece orranza,
                ch'io 'l vidi lamentare in forma vera
                sovra la morta imagine avvenente;
v. 12   e riguardava ver lo ciel sovente,
                ove l'alma gentil già locata era,
                che donna fu di sì gaia sembianza.

8:7   Questo primo sonetto si divide in tre parti: ne la prima chiamo e sollicito li fedeli d'Amore a piangere e dico che lo segnore loro piange, e dico "udendo la cagione per che piange", acciò che s'acconcino più ad ascoltarmi; ne la seconda narro la cagione; ne la terza parlo d'alcuno onore che Amore fece a

ful of Love through the words of Jeremiah the prophet that say: "O vos omnes qui transitis per viam, attendite et videte si est dolor sicut dolor meus" ["O all you who pass by, attend and see if there be a sorrow like my sorrow"], and to pray that they suffer to hear me; in the second part I tell where Love has placed me, with another meaning that the last parts of the sonnet do not manifest, and I say what I have lost. The second part begins: *Love, certainly not.*

A fter the departure of this gentle lady, it was the will of the Lord of   8:1
the angels to call to his glory a lady, young and of quite gentle aspect, who was greatly favored in the city mentioned above; her body I saw lying soulless amid many ladies, who wept piteously. Then, remem-   8:2
bering that I had once seen her accompany that most gentle one, I could not hold back tears; rather, weeping, I resolved to write some words about her death, in recompense for the several occasions on which I had seen her with my lady. And of this I made mention in the last part of the words   8:3
I wrote about it, as is clear to anyone who understands it. And I wrote then these two sonnets, of which the first begins: *Weep, lovers,* and the second: *Death villainous.*

W eep, lovers, since Love weeps,   8:4
as you hear what cause makes him weep.
Love hears ladies invoke Pity,   8:5
showing bitter sorrow through their eyes,   v. 4
because villainous Death in a gentle heart
has set its cruel working,
wasting what in this world must be praised
in a gentle lady besides honor.   v. 8
Hear how much Love paid her honor,   8:6
for I saw him lament in his true form
over the lovely dead image;
and he looked toward heaven again and again   v. 12
where the gentle soul already dwelled,
for a lady she was of so lively aspect.

This first sonnet divides into three parts: in the first I call and urge Love's   8:7
faithful to weep and tell them that their lord weeps, and I say "as you hear what cause makes him weep" to dispose them better to listen to me; in the second I relate the cause; in the third I speak of a certain honor that Love

questa donna. La seconda parte comincia quivi: *Amor sente*; la terza quivi: *Audite*.

8:8

M orte villana, di pietà nemica,
di dolor madre antica,
giudicio incontastabile gravoso,

v. 4

poi che hai data matera al cor doglioso
ond'io vado pensoso,
di te blasmar la lingua s'affatica.

8:9

E s'io di grazia ti voi far mendica,

v. 8

convenesi ch'eo dica
lo tuo fallar d'onni torto tortoso,
non però ch'a la gente sia nascoso,
ma per farne cruccioso

v. 12

chi d'amor per innanzi si notrica.

8:10

Dal secolo hai partita cortesia
e ciò ch'è in donna da pregiar vertute:
in gaia gioventute

v. 16

distrutta hai l'amorosa leggiadria.
Più non voi discovrir qual donna sia
che per le propietà sue canosciute.

8:11

Chi non merta salute

v. 20

non speri mai d'aver sua compagnia.

8:12

Questo sonetto si divide in quattro parti: ne la prima parte chiamo la Morte per certi suoi nomi propri; ne la seconda, parlando a lei, dico la cagione per che io mi muovo a blasimarla; ne la terza la vitupero; ne la quarta mi volgo a parlare a indiffinita persona, avvegna che quanto a lo mio intendimento sia diffinita. La seconda comincia quivi: *poi che hai data*; la terza quivi: *E s'io di grazia*; la quarta quivi: *Chi non merta salute*.

9:1

A ppresso la morte di questa donna alquanti die avvenne cosa per la quale me convenne partire de la sopradetta cittade e ire verso quelle parti dov'era la gentile donna ch'era stata mia difesa, avvegna che non tanto fosse

9:2

lontano lo termine de lo mio andare quanto ella era. E tutto ch'io fosse a la compagnia di molti quanto a la vista, l'andare mi dispiacea sì, che quasi li sospiri non poteano disfogare l'angoscia che lo cuore sentia, però ch'io mi

9:3

dilungava de la mia beatitudine. E però lo dolcissimo segnore, lo quale mi segnoreggiava per la vertù de la gentilissima donna, ne la mia imaginazione

paid this lady. The second part begins: *Love hears*; the third: *Hear.*

Death villainous, pity's foe,	8:8
woe's ancient mother,	
judgment incontestable and heavy,	
since you have given reasons to the grieving heart	v. 4
whereby I pensive go,	
upbraiding you my tongue grows weary.	
And if I want you to beg for mercy,	8:9
I need only tell	v. 8
of your misdeed, of all wrongs wrongful,	
not because it is hidden from people,	
but to make it worrisome	
to whoever shall henceforth be nurtured of love.	v. 12
From this world you have separated courtesy	8:10
and all that in a lady is praiseworthy virtue:	
in sprightly youth	
you have destroyed Love's charm.	v. 16
No further will I disclose which lady she may be	
than through her known qualities.	
Let one who does not merit salvation	8:11
never hope to have her company.	v. 20

This sonnet divides into four parts: in the first part I summon Death through names appropriate to her; in the second, speaking to her, I tell the cause that moves me to chide her; in the third, I upbraid her; in the fourth, I turn to speak to a person undefined, although in my understanding this person is defined. The second begins: *since you have given*; the third: *And if I want you;* the fourth: *Let one who does not merit salvation.*   8:12

A few days after the death of this lady something happened that made it necessary for me to leave the aforementioned city and travel toward those parts where was the gentle lady who had been my defense, although the destination of my journey was not so distant as she was. And although, to all appearances, I kept company with many, the journey so displeased me that my sighs could hardly relieve the anguish that my heart felt, because I was distancing myself from my beatitude. Therefore, the sweetest Lord, who ruled me through the power of the most gentle lady, appeared in my   9:1   9:2   9:3

9:4   apparve come peregrino leggermente vestito e di vili drappi. Elli mi parea disbigottito, e guardava la terra, salvo che talora li suoi occhi mi parea che si volgessero ad uno fiume bello e corrente e chiarissimo, lo quale sen gia lungo
9:5   questo cammino là ov'io era. A me parve che Amore mi chiamasse, e dicessemi queste parole: "Io vegno da quella donna la quale è stata tua lunga difesa, e so che lo suo rivenire non sarà a gran tempi; e però quello cuore che io ti facea avere a lei, io l'ho meco, e portolo a donna la quale sarà tua
9:6   difensione, come questa era." E nominollami per nome, sì che io la conobbi bene. "Ma tuttavia, di queste parole ch'io t'ho ragionate se alcuna cosa ne dicessi, dille nel modo che per loro non si discernesse lo simulato amore che
9:7   tu hai mostrato a questa e che ti converrà mostrare ad altri." E dette queste parole, disparve questa mia imaginazione tutta subitamente per la grandissima parte che mi parve che Amore mi desse di sé; e, quasi cambiato ne la vista mia, cavalcai quel giorno pensoso molto e accompagnato da molti sospiri.
9:8   Appresso lo giorno cominciai di ciò questo sonetto, lo quale comincia: *Cavalcando*.

9:9   Cavalcando l'altr'ier per un cammino
                    pensoso de l'andar che mi sgradia,
                    trovai Amore in mezzo de la via
v. 4   in abito leggier di peregrino.
9:10   Ne la sembianza mi parea meschino,
                    come avesse perduto segnoria;
                    e sospirando pensoso venia,
v. 8   per non veder la gente, a capo chino.
9:11   Quando mi vide, mi chiamò per nome,
                    e disse: "Io vegno di lontana parte,
                    ov'era lo tuo cor per mio volere;
v. 12   e recolo a servir novo piacere."
9:12   Allora presi di lui sì gran parte,
                    ch'elli disparve, e non m'accorsi come.

9:13   Questo sonetto ha tre parti: ne la prima parte dico sì com'io trovai Amore, e quale mi parea; ne la seconda dico quello ch'elli mi disse, avvegna che non compiutamente per tema ch'avea di discovrire lo mio secreto; ne la terza dico com'elli mi disparve. La seconda comincia quivi: *Quando mi vide*; la terza: *Allora presi*.

imagination as a pilgrim dressed meagerly and in simple vestments. He   9:4
seemed to me frightened, and he stared at the ground, except that at times his
eyes seemed to turn toward a river, beautiful and swift and utterly clear, that
flowed along the road there where I was. It seemed that Love called to me   9:5
and said these words: "I come from that lady who has long been your defense, and I know that her return will not take place for a long time; therefore, the heart that I had you owe to her I have with me, and I bring it to a lady
who will be your defense as was this first one." And he called her for me by   9:6
name, so that I recognized her well. "But all the same, of these words that I
have spoken, if you should repeat any, utter them in such a way that one may
not discern the simulated love that you have shown for this first lady and that
you must display to another woman." And these words said, this imagining   9:7
of mine disappeared all suddenly because of the great portion that Love seemed
to give me of himself; and almost transformed in aspect, I rode that day deeply
pensive and accompanied by many sighs. The next day, I began this sonnet   9:8
about the event; it begins: *Riding*.

> **R**iding the other day along a road,   9:9
> musing upon the journey that I disliked,
> I met Love in the middle of the way
> in the meager dress of a pilgrim.   v. 4
> In his aspect he seemed to me poor,   9:10
> as if he had lost his lordship;
> and sighing he came pensively,
> head down in order not to see the people.   v. 8
> When he saw me, he called me by name,   9:11
> and said: "I come from distant parts,
> where your heart was through my will;
> and I bring it to serve a new delight."   v. 12
> Then I took of him so great a part   9:12
> that he disappeared, and I knew not how.

This sonnet has three parts: in the first part I tell how I met Love, and   9:13
how he seemed to me; in the second I tell what he said to me, albeit not
completely for the fear I had of revealing my secret; in the third I tell how
he disappeared. The second part begins: *When he saw me*; the third: *Then
I took*.

10:1   Appresso la mia ritornata mi misi a cercare di questa donna che lo mio segnore m'avea nominata ne lo cammino de li sospiri; e acciò che lo mio parlare sia più brieve, dico che in poco tempo la feci mia difesa tanto, che troppa gente ne ragionava oltre li termini de la cortesia; onde molte fiate

10:2   mi pensava duramente. E per questa cagione, cioè di questa soverchievole voce che parea che m'infamasse viziosamente, quella gentilissima, la quale fue distruggitrice di tutti li vizi e regina de le virtudi, passando per alcuna parte, mi negò lo suo dolcissimo salutare, ne lo quale stava tutta la mia

10:3   beatitudine. E uscendo alquanto del proposito presente, voglio dare a intendere

11:1   quello che lo suo salutare in me vertuosamente operava. Dico che quando ella apparia da parte alcuna, per la speranza de la mirabile salute nullo nemico mi rimanea, anzi mi giugnea una fiamma di caritate, la quale mi facea perdonare a chiunque m'avesse offeso; e chi allora m'avesse domandato di cosa alcuna, la mia risponsione sarebbe stata solamente "Amore", con viso

11:2   vestito d'umilitade. E quando ella fosse alquanto propinqua al salutare, uno spirito d'amore, distruggendo tutti li altri spiriti sensitivi, pingea fuori li deboletti spiriti del viso, e dicea loro: "Andate a onorare la donna vostra"; ed elli si rimanea nel luogo loro. E chi avesse voluto conoscere Amore, fare lo

11:3   potea mirando lo tremare de li occhi miei. E quando questa gentilissima salute salutava, non che Amore fosse tal mezzo che potesse obumbrare a me la intollerabile beatitudine, ma elli quasi per soverchio di dolcezza divenia tale, che lo mio corpo, lo quale era tutto allora sotto lo suo reggimento, molte

11:4   volte si movea come cosa grave inanimata. Sì che appare manifestamente che ne le sue salute abitava la mia beatitudine, la quale molte volte passava e

12:1   redundava la mia capacitade. Ora, tornando al proposito, dico che poi che la mia beatitudine mi fue negata, mi giunse tanto dolore, che, partito me da le

12:2   genti, in solinga parte andai a bagnare la terra d'amarissime lagrime. E poi che alquanto mi fue sollenato questo lagrimare, misimi ne la mia camera, là ov'io potea lamentarmi sanza essere udito; e quivi, chiamando misericordia a la donna de la cortesia, e dicendo "Amore, aiuta lo tuo fedele",

12:3   m'addormentai come un pargoletto battuto lagrimando. Avvenne quasi nel mezzo de lo mio dormire che me parve vedere ne la mia camera lungo me sedere uno giovane vestito di bianchissime vestimenta, e pensando molto quanto a la vista sua, mi riguardava là ov'io giacea; e quando m'avea guardato alquanto, pareami che sospirando mi chiamasse, e diceami queste parole:

12:4   "Fili mi, tempus est ut pretermictantur simulacra nostra." Allora mi parea che io lo conoscesse, però che mi chiamava così come assai fiate ne li miei

After my return I began looking for that lady whom my Lord had **10:1** named on the road of sighs; and to shorten my account, I say that in a brief time I made her my defense to such an extent that too many spoke about it beyond the bounds of courtesy; and this often afflicted me harshly. And for this cause, that is, for these excessive voices that appeared **10:2** to defame me viciously, that most gentle lady, who was destroyer of all vices and queen of virtues, passing by a certain place, denied me her so dear greeting, in which was all my beatitude. And digressing somewhat **10:3** from my present purpose, I want to make clear what her greeting worked in me because of her power. I say that when she appeared from any **11:1** direction, in the hope of her miraculous greeting I was left with no enemy, but rather there arose in me a flame of charity that made me forgive whoever might have offended me; and if anyone had then asked me anything, my answer would have been only "Love," with a countenance clothed in humility. And when she was somewhat on the verge of the **11:2** greeting, a spirit of love, destroying all other spirits of the senses, drove out the feeble spirits of sight, saying to them: "Go and honor your lady," and he remained in their place. And who wanted to know Love could do so by looking at the tremor of my eyes. And when this most gentle **11:3** salutation greeted me, it was not that Love interposed so that he might shade me from the unbearable beatitude, but he for his superabundant sweetness became such that my body, which was then wholly under his rule, often moved like a heavy, inanimate thing. Thus it plainly appears **11:4** that in her greetings lay my beatitude, which often exceeded and overflowed my capacity. Now, returning to my purpose, I say that after **12:1** my beatitude was denied me, so much grief seized me that turning away from the people, I withdrew to a solitary place to bathe the earth with bitterest tears. And after my weeping had somewhat eased, I repaired to **12:2** my room, where I could lament without being heard; and here, asking pity of the lady of courtesy and saying, "Love, help your faithful one," I fell asleep like a beaten child in tears. It happened that almost in the **12:3** middle of my sleep I seemed to see sitting alongside me in my room a young man dressed in whitest garments; and with the aspect of one deep in thought he gazed at me where I lay; and when he had looked at me awhile, he seemed to call me, sighing, and spoke these words: "Fili mi, tempus est ut pretermictantur simulacra nostra" ["My son, it is time to end our fabrications"]. I then seemed to recognize him, for he called me as in my dreams he had **12:4** often called me before; and as I watched him, he seemed to me to be weeping

sonni m'avea già chiamato: e riguardandolo, parvemi che piangesse pietosamente, e parea che attendesse da me alcuna parola; ond'io, assicurandomi, cominciai a parlare così con esso: "Segnore de la nobiltade, e perché piangi tu?" E quelli mi dicea queste parole: "Ego tanquam centrum circuli, cui simili modo se habent circumferentie partes; tu autem non sic."

12:5 Allora, pensando a le sue parole, mi parea che m'avesse parlato molto oscuramente; sì ch'io mi sforzava di parlare, e diceali queste parole: "Che è ciò, segnore, che mi parli con tanta oscuritade?" E quelli mi dicea in parole

12:6 volgari: "Non dimandare più che utile ti sia." E però cominciai allora con lui a ragionare de la salute la quale mi fue negata, e domandailo de la cagione; onde in questa guisa da lui mi fue risposto: "Quella nostra Beatrice udio da certe persone di te ragionando, che la donna la quale io ti nominai nel cammino de li sospiri, ricevea da te alcuna noia; e però questa gentilissima, la quale è contraria di tutte le noie, non degnò salutare la tua persona, temendo non

12:7 fosse noiosa. Onde con ciò sia cosa che veracemente sia conosciuto per lei alquanto lo tuo secreto per lunga consuetudine, voglio che tu dichi certe parole per rima, ne le quali tu comprendi la forza che io tegno sopra te per lei, e come tu fosti suo tostamente da la tua puerizia. E di ciò chiama testimonio colui che lo sa, e come tu prieghi lui che li le dica; ed io, che son quelli, volentieri le ne ragionerò; e per questo sentirà ella la tua volontade, la quale

12:8 sentendo, conoscerà le parole de li ingannati. Queste parole fa che siano quasi un mezzo, sì che tu non parli a lei immediatamente, che non è degno; e no le mandare in parte, sanza me, ove potessero essere intese da lei, ma falle adornare di soave armonia, ne la quale io sarò tutte le volte che farà mestiere."

12:9 E dette queste parole, sì disparve, e lo mio sonno fue rotto. Onde io ricordandomi, trovai che questa visione m'era apparita ne la nona ora del die; e anzi ch'io uscisse di questa camera, propuosi di fare una ballata, ne la quale io seguitasse ciò che lo mio segnore m'avea imposto; e feci poi questa ballata, che comincia: *Ballata, i' voi.*

12:10   **B**allata, i' voi che tu ritrovi Amore,
                  e con lui vade a madonna davante,
                  sì che la scusa mia, la qual tu cante,
v. 4   ragioni poi con lei lo mio segnore.
12:11   Tu vai, ballata, sì cortesemente,
                  che sanza compagnia
                  dovresti avere in tutte parti ardire;
v. 8   ma se tu vuoli andar securamente,

piteously and seemed to await some word from me; hence I, reassuring myself, began to speak thus to him: "Lord of all nobleness, why do you weep?" And he said these words to me: "Ego tanquam centrum circuli, cui simili modo se habent circumferentie partes; tu autem non sic." ["I am like the center of a circle, to which all the points of the circumference bear the same relation; you, however, are not."] Then, thinking upon his words, I thought he had spoken most obscurely; so I strove to speak, and I said to him these words: "Why is it, Lord, that you speak to me with such obscurity?" And he replied in the vernacular: "Ask no more than may be useful to you." Therefore I then began to converse with him about the greeting that was denied me and asked him the cause; and in this manner was I answered: "Our Beatrice heard from certain people who spoke of you that the lady whom I named for you on the road of sighs received from you some disgrace; therefore, this gentlest one, who is the adversary of all infamies, did not deign to greet you, fearing you might cause shame. Hence, although your secret is in truth somewhat known to her by virtue of its long usage, I want you to write certain words in rhyme, in which you make clear the power that I hold over you through her, and how you have been hers ever since childhood. And of this fact call as witness him who knows, and say that you pray him to tell it to her; and I, who am he, will gladly speak to her; and through this she will know your will, and knowing it, she will recognize the words of those who were deceived. Let these words be like an intermediary, so that you do not speak to her directly, which is not fitting; and do not send them without me to any place where she might hear them, but let them be adorned with sweet harmony, in which I will be present whenever it is necessary." And having said these words, he disappeared, and my sleep was broken. Then, thinking back, I realized that this vision had appeared to me at the ninth hour of the day; and before I left my room, I resolved to compose a ballade in which I would carry out what my Lord had enjoined me; I then composed this ballade, which begins: *Ballade, I want.*

12:5

12:6

12:7

12:8

12:9

> Ballade, I want you to seek out Love,
> and with him go before my lady,
> so that my excuse, which you must sing,
> my Lord may then recount to her.
> You must go, ballade, courteously
> so that without accompaniment
> you may be bold in every place;
> but if you want to go securely,

12:10

v. 4

12:11

v. 8

retrova l'Amor pria,

ché forse non è bon sanza lui gire;

però che quella che ti dee audire,

v. 12   sì com'io credo, è ver di me adirata:

se tu di lui non fossi accompagnata,

leggeramente ti faria disnore.

12:12   Con dolze sono, quando se' con lui,

v. 16   comincia este parole,

appresso che averai chesta pietate:

"Madonna, quelli che mi manda a vui,

quando vi piaccia, vole,

v. 20   sed elli ha scusa, che la m'intendiate.

Amore è qui, che per vostra bieltate

lo face, come vol, vista cangiare:

dunque perché li fece altra guardare

v. 24   pensatel voi, da che non mutò 'l core."

12:13   Dille: "Madonna, lo suo core è stato

con sì fermata fede,

che 'n voi servir l'ha 'mpronto onne pensero:

v. 28   tosto fu vostro, e mai non s'è smagato."

Sed ella non ti crede,

dì che domandi Amor, che sa lo vero:

ed a la fine falle umil preghero,

v. 32   lo perdonare se le fosse a noia,

che mi comandi per messo ch'eo moia,

e vedrassi ubidir ben servidore.

12:14   E dì a colui ch'è d'ogni pietà chiave,

v. 36   avante che sdonnei,

che le saprà contar mia ragion bona:

Per grazia de la mia nota soave

reman tu qui con lei,

v. 40   e del tuo servo ciò che vuoi ragiona;

e s'ella per tuo prego li perdona,

fa che li annunzi un bel sembiante pace."

12:15   Gentil ballata mia, quando ti piace,

v. 44   movi in quel punto che tu n'aggie onore.

12:16   Questa ballata in tre parti si divide: ne la prima dico a lei ov'ella vada, e

find Love first,

for perhaps it is not good to go without him;

because she who must hear you,

as I believe, is angry with me: v. 12

if you were not accompanied by him,

likely she may not do you honor.

With sweet melody, when you are with him,   12:12

begin these words,   v. 16

after you have asked for mercy:

"My lady, he who sends me to you,

when it pleases you, desires

that if he has an excuse, you may hear it from me.   v. 20

Love is here, who through your beauty

changes, at will, that one's appearance:

therefore, why Love made him look at another lady

you can now see, since he has not changed his heart."   v. 24

Tell her: "My lady, his heart has attended   12:13

with such steadfast faith

that in your service has he been molded by every thought:

from the first he has been yours, and never has he strayed."   v. 28

If she does not believe you,

tell her to ask Love, who knows the truth;

and at the end offer her a humble prayer,

that if forgiving might cause her displeasure,   v. 32

she may command through a messenger that I die,

and one shall see a good servant obey.

And tell him who is every compassion's key,   12:14

— before he takes leave of her —   v. 36

and who will know how to plead my good cause to her:

"Through the grace of my sweet melody

remain here with her,

and of your servant speak what you will;   v. 40

and if through your prayer she forgives him,

have her fair countenance announce to him peace."

My gentle ballade, when it pleases you,   12:15

go forth at that moment when you may receive honor.   v. 44

This ballade divides into three parts: in the first I tell it where it must go, and   12:16

confortola però che vada più sicura, e dico ne la cui compagnia si metta, se vuole sicuramente andare e sanza pericolo alcuno; ne la seconda dico quello che lei si pertiene di fare intendere; ne la terza la licenzio del gire quando vuole, raccomandando lo suo movimento ne le braccia de la fortuna.   La seconda parte comincia quivi: *Con dolze sono*; la terza quivi: *Gentil ballata*.

12:17   Potrebbe già l'uomo opporre contra me e dicere che non sapesse a cui fosse lo mio parlare in seconda persona, però che la ballata non è altro che queste parole ched io parlo: e però dico che questo dubbio io lo intendo solvere e dichiarare in questo libello ancora in parte più dubbiosa, e allora intenda qui chi qui dubita, o chi qui volesse opporre in questo modo.

13:1   Appresso di questa soprascritta visione, avendo già dette le parole che Amore m'avea imposte a dire, mi cominciaro molti e diversi pensamenti a combattere e a tentare, ciascuno quasi indefensibilemente; tra li quali

13:2   pensamenti quattro mi parea che ingombrassero più lo riposo de la vita. L'uno

13:3   de li quali era questo: buona è la signoria d'Amore, però che trae lo intendimento del suo fedele da tutte le vili cose. L'altro era questo: non buona è la signoria d'Amore, però che quanto lo suo fedele più fede li porta,

13:4   tanto più gravi e dolorosi punti li conviene passare. L'altro era questo: lo nome d'Amore è sì dolce a udire, che impossibile mi pare che la sua propria operazione sia ne le più cose altro che dolce, con ciò sia cosa che li nomi seguitino le nominate cose, sì come è scritto: "Nomina sunt consequentia

13:5   rerum." Lo quarto era questo: la donna per cui Amore ti stringe così, non è

13:6   come l'altre donne, che leggermente si muova del suo cuore.   E ciascuno mi combattea tanto, che mi facea stare quasi come colui che non sa per qual via pigli lo suo cammino, e che vuole andare e non sa onde se ne vada; e se io pensava di volere cercare una comune via di costoro, cioè là ove tutti s'accordassero, questa era via molto inimica verso me, cioè di chiamare e di

13:7   mettermi ne le braccia de la Pietà.   E in questo stato dimorando, mi giunse volontade di scriverne parole rimate; e dissine allora questo sonetto, lo quale comincia: *Tutti li miei penser*.

13:8   Tutti li miei penser parlan d'Amore;
e hanno in lor sì gran varietate,
ch'altro mi fa voler sua potestate,
v. 4   altro folle ragiona il suo valore,
altro sperando m'apporta dolzore,
altro pianger mi fa spesse fiate;

I comfort it so that it goes more securely, and I tell it in whose company to be if it wants to go safely and without any danger; in the second I say what befits it to make known; in the third I give it leave to go when it will, commending its going to the arms of fortune. The second part begins: *With sweet melody*; the third: *My gentle ballade.* One could indeed oppose me and say that it is not understood to whom my words are addressed in the second person, since the ballade is none other than these words that I speak: and therefore I say that this doubt I intend to solve and explain in this little book in a passage still more questionable; and thus let anyone take note who here questions or would wish to object in this manner.

12:17

A fter the vision transcribed above, I having already said the words that Love had commanded me to say, many and diverse thoughts began to assail and try me, each one almost indefensibly; among which thoughts four seemed most to disrupt my life's peace. One of them was: good is the lordship of Love, since he removes the mind of his faithful one from all vile things. The next thought was: the lordship of Love is not good, since the more faith his faithful one bears him, the more heavy and grievous trials must he go through. The next was: the name of Love is so sweet to hear that it seems impossible that in most instances its own operations can be other than sweet, for names are consequent upon the things named, just as it is written: "Nomina sunt consequentia rerum" ["Names are consequent upon things"]. The fourth was: the lady through whom Love binds you so is not like the other ladies to the extent that she may lightly move from her heart's resolve. And each thought assailed me so that it made me stand almost like one who knows not which way to choose for his journey, and who wants to go but knows not where; and if I thought to look for a way common to all of them, that is, where all might coincide, this way was severely hostile to me: namely, to call upon and to throw myself into the arms of Pity. And languishing in this state, I was caught by a desire to set words about it in rhyme, and I then wrote this sonnet, which begins: *All my thoughts.*

13:1

13:2

13:3

13:4

13:5

13:6

13:7

All my thoughts speak of Love,
and they have in them such great diversity
that one makes me desire its power,
another argues its foolish worth,
another, hopeful, brings me sweetness,
another makes me often weep;

13:8

v. 4

e sol s'accordano in cherer pietate,

v. 8 tremando di paura che è nel core.

13:9 **Ond'io** non so da qual matera prenda;

e vorrei dire, e non so ch'io mi dica:

così mi trovo in amorosa erranza!

v. 12 E se con tutti voi fare accordanza,

convenemi chiamar la mia nemica,

madonna la Pietà, che mi difenda.

13:10   Questo sonetto in quattro parti si può dividere: ne la prima dico e soppongo che tutti li miei pensieri sono d'Amore; ne la seconda dico che sono diversi, e narro la loro diversitade; ne la terza dico in che tutti pare che s'accordino; ne la quarta dico che volendo dire d'Amore, non so da qual parte pigli matera, e se la voglio pigliare da tutti, convene che io chiami la mia inimica, madonna la Pietade; e dico "madonna" quasi per disdegnoso modo di parlare. La seconda parte comincia quivi: *e hanno in lor*; la terza quivi: *e sol s'accordano*; la quarta quivi: *Ond'io non so.*

14:1   **A**ppresso la battaglia de li diversi pensieri avvenne che questa gentilissima venne in parte ove molte donne gentili erano adunate; a la qual parte io fui condotto per amica persona, credendosi fare a me grande piacere, in quanto

14:2 mi menava là ove tante donne mostravano le loro bellezze. Onde io, quasi non sappiendo a che io fossi menato, e fidandomi ne la persona la quale uno suo amico a l'estremitade de la vita condotto avea, dissi a lui: "Perché semo noi venuti a queste donne?" Allora quelli mi disse: "Per fare sì ch'elle siano

14:3 degnamente servite." E lo vero è che adunate quivi erano a la compagnia d'una gentile donna che disposata era lo giorno; e però, secondo l'usanza de la sopradetta cittade, convenia che le facessero compagnia nel primo sedere a la mensa che facea ne la magione del suo novello sposo. Sì che io, credendomi fare piacere di questo amico, propuosi di stare al servigio de le

14:4 donne ne la sua compagnia. E nel fine del mio proponimento mi parve sentire uno mirabile tremore incominciare nel mio petto da la sinistra parte e distendersi di subito per tutte le parti del mio corpo. Allora dico che io poggiai la mia persona simulatamente ad una pintura la quale circundava questa magione; e temendo non altri si fosse accorto del mio tremare, levai li

14:5 occhi, e mirando le donne, vidi tra loro la gentilissima Beatrice. Allora fuoro sì distrutti li miei spiriti per la forza che Amore prese veggendosi in tanta propinquitade a la gentilissima donna, che non ne rimasero in vita più

and they accord only in craving pity,

trembling with the fear that is in my heart.   v. 8

Then I know not from which to take my theme,   13:9

and wish to speak but know not what to say:

so I find myself in amorous wanderings!

And if I wish to draw all into accord,   v. 12

I must call upon my enemy,

the lady Pity, that she may defend me.

This sonnet can be divided into four parts: in the first I say and submit that all   13:10
my thoughts are of Love; in the second I say that they are diverse, and I
expound their diversity; in the third I say in what respect they all seem to
accord; in the fourth I say that, desiring to speak of Love, I know not from
which part to take my subject matter; and if I want to take it from all, it is
necessary that I call on my enemy, the lady Pity; and I say "lady" as a scornful way of speaking. The second part begins: *and they have in them*; the
third: *and they accord only in craving pity*; the fourth: *Then I know not*.

After the battle of the diverse thoughts, it happened that this most   14:1
gentle one came where many gentle ladies gathered; to which place
I was taken by a friend, who thought to do me a great favor, since he was
leading me to where many ladies presented their beauties. Hence, not   14:2
knowing to what I was being led, and trusting in a person who had conducted a friend of his to the extremity of life, I said to him: "Why have
we come to these ladies?" He then told me: "To insure that they are worthily served." And the truth is that they were gathered there in the com-   14:3
pany of a gentle lady who had married that day; for according to the custom of the city mentioned above, it was incumbent on them to keep her
company the first time she would sit at the dining table in the house of
her new bridegroom. Thus I, thinking to please this friend, resolved to
serve these ladies in his company. And upon coming to this decision I   14:4
seemed to feel a wondrous tremor commence in my breast's left side and
quickly spread throughout my body. Then, I say that I rested my body, to
disguise my tremor, on a painting that went round the walls of the house;
and fearing lest one might notice my trembling, I raised my eyes, and
beholding the ladies, I saw among them the most gentle Beatrice. At that   14:5
moment my spirits were so destroyed by the power that Love derived
from seeing himself in such close proximity to this most gentle lady that

che li spiriti del viso; e ancora questi rimasero fuori de li loro istrumenti, però che Amore volea stare nel loro nobilissimo luogo per vedere la mirabile

14:6 donna.   E avvegna che io fossi altro che prima, molto mi dolea di questi spiritelli, che si lamentavano forte e diceano: "Se questi non ci infolgorasse così fuori del nostro luogo, noi potremmo stare a vedere la maraviglia di

14:7 questa donna così come stanno li altri nostri pari."   Io dico che molte di queste donne, accorgendosi de la mia trasfigurazione, si cominciaro a maravigliare, e ragionando si gabbavano di me con questa gentilissima; onde lo ingannato amico di buona fede mi prese per la mano, e traendomi fuori de

14:8 la veduta di queste donne, sì mi domandò che io avesse.   Allora io, riposato alquanto, e resurressiti li morti spiriti miei, e li discacciati rivenuti a le loro possessioni, dissi a questo mio amico queste parole: "Io tenni li piedi in quella parte de la vita di là da la quale non si puote ire più per intendimento di

14:9 ritornare."   E partitomi da lui, mi ritornai ne la camera de le lagrime; ne la quale, piangendo e vergognandomi, fra me stesso dicea: "Se questa donna sapesse la mia condizione, io non credo che così gabbasse la mia persona,

14:10 anzi credo che molta pietade le ne verrebbe."   E in questo pianto stando, proposi di dire parole, ne le quali, parlando a lei, significasse la cagione del mio trasfiguramento, e dicesse che io so bene ch'ella non è saputa, e che se fosse saputa, io credo che pietà ne giugnerebbe altrui; e propuosile di dire desiderando che venissero per avventura ne la sua audienza.   E allora dissi questo sonetto, lo quale comincia: *Con l'altre donne.*

14:11   Con l'altre donne mia vista gabbate,
          e non pensate, donna, onde si mova
          ch'io vi rassembri sì figura nova
v. 4   quando riguardo la vostra beltate.
14:12   Se lo saveste, non poria Pietate
          tener più contra me l'usata prova,
          ché Amor, quando sì presso a voi mi trova,
v. 8   prende baldanza e tanta securtate,
          che fere tra' miei spiriti paurosi,
          e quale ancide, e qual pinge di fore,
          sì che solo remane a vedere vui:
v. 12   ond'io mi cangio in figura d'altrui,
          ma non sì ch'io non senta bene allore
          li guai de li scacciati tormentosi.

no spirits remained alive but those of sight; and even these were bereft of their own organs, because Love wanted to stand in their most noble place in order to behold the admirable lady. And although I was other than before, I grieved much for these little spirits, who lamented strongly and said: "If he did not bolt us like lightning out of our place, we could stay and gaze at the wonder of this lady just as do the others of our peers." I say that many of these ladies, noting my transfiguration, began to wonder, and talking about it they mocked me to this most gentle one; hence my deceived friend of good faith took me by the hand, and drawing me from the view of these ladies, asked me what was the matter. Then, having somewhat rested, my dead spirits having resurrected, and the outcasts having returned to their possessions, I said to my friend these words: "I have set my feet in that part of life beyond which one cannot go with the intention of returning." And leaving him, I returned to my room of tears, where weeping and ashamed I said within myself: "If this lady knew my condition, I do not believe that she would thus mock me; rather I believe that she would have great pity." And in my weeping, I resolved to write words in which, addressing her, I would express the cause of my transfiguration and would tell her that I know well that this cause is unknown, for were it known, I believe that compassion would grow in others; and I resolved to write these words in the hope that they would by chance come to her hearing. I then wrote this sonnet, which begins: *With the other ladies*.

14:6

14:7

14:8

14:9

14:10

With the other ladies you mock my aspect,
and you do not think, lady, whence it comes
that I resemble a figure so strange
when I behold your beauty.
If you knew it, Pity could no
longer hold against me her wonted obstinacy,
for Love, when he finds me so near you,
takes on such boldness and confidence
that he smites among my affrighted spirits,
and some he slays and some he drives out,
so that he alone remains to look at you:
whence I change into someone else's semblance,
but then not so much that I do not hear well
the wailings of those tormented outcasts.

14:11

v. 4
14:12

v. 8

v. 12

14:13 Questo sonetto non divido in parti, però che la divisione non si fa se non per aprire la sentenzia de la cosa divisa; onde con ciò sia cosa che per la sua

14:14 ragionata cagione assai sia manifesto, non ha mestiere di divisione. Vero è che tra le parole dove si manifesta la cagione di questo sonetto, si scrivono dubbiose parole, cioè quando dico che Amore uccide tutti li miei spiriti, e li visivi rimangono in vita, salvo che fuori de li strumenti loro. E questo dubbio è impossibile a solvere a chi non fosse in simile grado fedele d'Amore; e a coloro che vi sono è manifesto ciò che solverebbe le dubitose parole: e però non è bene a me di dichiarare cotale dubitazione, acciò che lo mio parlare dichiarando sarebbe indarno, o vero di soperchio.

15:1 Appresso la nuova trasfigurazione mi giunse uno pensamento forte, lo quale poco si partia da me, anzi continuamente mi riprendea, ed era di cotale ragionamento meco: "Poscia che tu pervieni a così dischernevole vista quando tu se' presso di questa donna, perché pur cerchi di vedere lei? Ecco che tu fossi domandato da lei: che avrestù da rispondere, ponendo che tu

15:2 avessi libera ciascuna tua vertude in quanto tu le rispondessi?" E a costui rispondea un altro, umile, pensero, e dicea: "S'io non perdessi le mie vertudi, e fossi libero tanto che io potessi rispondere, io le direi, che sì tosto com'io imagino la sua mirabile bellezza, sì tosto mi giugne uno desiderio di vederla, lo quale è di tanta vertude, che uccide e distrugge ne la mia memoria ciò che contra lui si potesse levare; e però non mi ritraggono le passate passioni da

15:3 cercare la veduta di costei." Onde io, mosso da cotali pensamenti, propuosi di dire certe parole, ne le quali, escusandomi a lei da cotale riprensione, ponesse anche di quello che mi diviene presso di lei; e dissi questo sonetto, lo quale comincia: *Ciò che m'incontra.*

15:4   Ciò che m'incontra, ne la mente more,
      quand'i' vegno a veder voi, bella gioia;
      e quand'io vi son presso, i' sento Amore

v. 4   che dice: "Fuggi, se 'l perir t'è noia."

15:5   Lo viso mostra lo color del core,
      che, tramortendo, ovunque pò s'appoia;
      e per la ebrietà del gran tremore

v. 8   le pietre par che gridin: Moia, moia.

15:6   Peccato face chi allora mi vide,
      se l'alma sbigottita non conforta,
      sol dimostrando che di me li doglia,

This sonnet I do not divide into parts, because division is made only to open up the meaning of the thing divided; hence, given that it is quite evident through its narrated cause, it needs no division. It is true that among the words that expound the cause of this sonnet are written obscure words, such as when I say that Love slays all my spirits, and the visual ones remain alive but outside their own organs. This doubt is impossible to solve for those who in the same degree are not the faithful of Love; and for those who are, the solution to the obscure words is clear: and so it is not fitting that I explain those obscurities, for my written explanations would be in vain, or in truth superfluous.

14:13

14:14

After the strange transfiguration there occurred to me an insistent thought, which hardly left me, indeed continually chided me, and such was its conversation with me: "Since you take on so ridiculous an appearance when you are near this lady, why do you try to see her? Suppose you were questioned by her: what would you reply, assuming you were free to employ all your faculties in responding to her?" And to this thought responded another, a humble thought, and it said: "If I did not lose my faculties, and were free enough to answer her, I would tell her that as soon as I imagine her wondrous beauty, I am immediately overcome by a desire to see her, which is so powerful that it slays and destroys in my memory what might arise against that desire; and so I am not restrained by my former passions from the attempt to see her." Then I, moved by such thoughts, resolved to write certain words in which, asking her to excuse me from such criticism, I would also explain what comes over me near her; and I wrote this sonnet, which begins: *That which befalls me.*

15:1

15:2

15:3

That which befalls me in my memory dies,
when I come to see you, beauteous joy;
and when I am near you, I hear Love
say: "Flee, if death disquiets you."
My face shows the color of my heart,
which, failing, leans wherever it can;
and through the intoxication caused by great trembling
the stones seem to shout: "Die, die."
One sins who then sees me
and does not comfort my affrighted soul,
at least by showing pain for me,

15:4

v. 4
15:5

v. 8
15:6

v. 12

per la pietà, che 'l vostro gabbo ancide,
la qual si cria ne la vista morta
de li occhi, c'hanno di lor morte voglia.

15:7   Questo sonetto si divide in due parti: ne la prima dico la cagione per che non mi tengo di gire presso di questa donna; ne la seconda dico quello che mi diviene per andare presso di lei; e comincia questa parte quivi: *e quand'io vi*

15:8   *son presso.* E anche si divide questa seconda parte in cinque, secondo cinque diverse narrazioni: che ne la prima dico quello che Amore, consigliato da la ragione, mi dice quando le sono presso; ne la seconda manifesto lo stato del cuore per essemplo del viso; ne la terza dico sì come onne sicurtade mi viene meno; ne la quarta dico che pecca quelli che non mostra pietà di me, acciò che mi sarebbe alcuno conforto; ne l'ultima dico perché altri doverebbe avere pietà, e ciò è per la pietosa vista che ne li occhi mi giugne; la quale vista pietosa è distrutta, cioè non pare altrui, per lo gabbare di questa donna, la quale trae a sua simile operazione coloro che forse vederebbono questa pietà.

15:9   La seconda parte comincia quivi: *Lo viso mostra*; la terza quivi: *e per la ebrietà*; la quarta: *Peccato face*; la quinta: *per la pietà.*

16:1   Appresso ciò che io dissi questo sonetto, mi mosse una volontade di dire anche parole, ne le quali io dicessi quattro cose ancora sopra lo mio

16:2   stato, le quali non mi parea che fossero manifestate ancora per me. La prima delle quali si è che molte volte io mi dolea, quando la mia memoria movesse

16:3   la fantasia ad imaginare quale Amore mi facea. La seconda si è che Amore spesse volte di subito m'assalia sì forte, che 'n me non rimanea altro di vita

16:4   se non un pensero che parlava di questa donna. La terza si è che quando questa battaglia d'Amore mi pugnava così, io mi movea quasi discolorito tutto per vedere questa donna, credendo che mi difendesse la sua veduta da questa battaglia, dimenticando quello che per appropinquare a tanta gentilezza

16:5   m'addivenia. La quarta si è come cotale veduta non solamente non mi

16:6   difendea, ma finalmente disconfiggea la mia poca vita. E però dissi questo sonetto, lo quale comincia: *Spesse fiate.*

16:7

Spesse fiate vegnonmi a la mente
le oscure qualità ch'Amor mi dona,
e venmene pietà, sì che sovente

v. 4

io dico: "Lasso!, avviene elli a persona?";

for the pity that your mockery slays,   v. 12
which is reborn in the dying sight
of my eyes, who desire their own death.

This sonnet divides into two parts: in the first I tell why I do not refrain   15:7
from going near this lady; in the second I say what comes over me when
I approach her; and this part begins: *and when I am near you.* This sec-   15:8
ond part also divides into five parts, according to five different accounts:
in the first I say what Love, counseled by reason, tells me when I am near
her; in the second I express the state of my heart through the likeness of
my face; in the third, I say how all confidence leaves me; in the fourth, I
say that they sin who do not show compassion for me, so that I would be
somewhat comforted; in the last I say why one should have compassion,
and that is for the piteous sight that appears in my eyes, whose pitiful
look is destroyed: that is, not seen by others, through the mockery of this
lady, which draws into similar operation those who could perhaps notice
this pity. The second part begins: *My face shows*; the third: *and through*   15:9
the intoxication; the fourth: *One sins*; the fifth: *for the pity.*

After I had written this sonnet, the desire moved me to write additional   16:1
words in which I would express four more things about my condition,
which I felt I had not yet made clear. The first of them is that I often   16:2
grieved when memory moved my fantasy to imagine what Love was doing
to me. The second is that Love often and suddenly assailed me so   16:3
powerfully that in me remained no more life than a single thought that
spoke to me of this lady. The third is that when this battle with Love   16:4
battered me so, I went, almost wholly drained of color, to see this lady,
believing that the sight of her would shield me from this battle, forgetting
what approaching so much gentleness brought on. The fourth is how that   16:5
sight not only failed to shield me but ultimately discomfited my little life.
Therefore I wrote this sonnet, which begins: *Oftentimes.*   16:6

Oftentimes there come to mind   16:7
the dark qualities that Love bestows upon me,
and there comes to me pity, so that often
I say: "Ah! can this happen to someone?";   v. 4

16:8 ch'Amor m'assale subitanamente,
sì che la vita quasi m'abbandona:
campami un spirto vivo solamente,
v. 8 e que' riman, perché di voi ragiona.
16:9 Poscia mi sforzo, ché mi voglio atare;
e così smorto, d'onne valor voto,
vegno a vedervi, credendo guerire:
16:10 e se io levo li occhi per guardare,
nel cor mi si comincia uno tremoto,
che fa de' polsi l'anima partire.

16:11 Questo sonetto si divide in quattro parti, secondo che quattro cose sono in esso narrate; e però che sono di sopra ragionate, non m'intrametto se non di distinguere le parti per li loro cominciamenti: onde dico che la seconda parte comincia quivi: *ch'Amor*; la terza quivi: *Poscia mi sforzo*; la quarta quivi: *e se io levo*.

17:1 Poi che dissi questi tre sonetti, ne li quali parlai a questa donna, però che fuoro narratori di tutto quasi lo mio stato, credendomi tacere e non dire più, però che mi parea di me assai avere manifestato, avvegna che sempre poi tacesse di dire a lei, a me convenne ripigliare matera nuova e più nobile che la passata. E però che la cagione de la nuova matera è dilettevole a udire, la dicerò, quanto potrò più brievemente. Con ciò sia cosa che per la vista mia molte persone avessero compreso lo secreto del mio cuore, certe donne, le quali adunate s'erano dilettandosi l'una ne la compagnia de l'altra, sapeano bene lo mio cuore, però che ciascuna di loro era stata a molte mie sconfitte; e io passando appresso di loro, sì come da la fortuna menato, fui chiamato da una di queste gentili donne. La donna che m'avea chiamato era donna di molto leggiadro parlare; sì che quand'io fui giunto dinanzi da loro, e vidi bene che la mia gentilissima donna non era con esse, rassicurandomi le salutai, e domandai che piacesse loro. Le donne erano molte, tra le quali n'avea certe che si rideano tra loro. Altre v'erano che mi guardavano, aspettando che io dovessi dire. Altre v'erano che parlavano tra loro. De le quali una, volgendo li suoi occhi verso me e chiamandomi per nome, disse queste parole: "A che fine ami tu questa tua donna, poi che tu non puoi sostenere la sua presenza? Dilloci, ché certo lo fine di cotale amore conviene che sia novissimo." E poi che m'ebbe dette queste parole, non solamente ella, ma tutte l'altre cominciaro ad attendere in vista la mia risponsione. Allora dissi queste parole loro: "Madonne, lo fine del mio amore fue già lo saluto di

for Love assails me suddenly,   16:8
so that life almost abandons me:
there survives in me but one live spirit,
and that remains because it speaks of you.   v. 8
Then I struggle, seeking to help myself;   16:9
and all pale, of all valor empty,
I come to see you, thinking to be healed:
and if I raise my eyes to look,   16:10
in my heart arises a tremor
that from my pulses causes the soul to part.

This sonnet divides into four parts, inasmuch as four things are recounted in   16:11
it; and because they are explained above, I do not involve myself here except
to distinguish the parts by their beginnings: thus I say that the second part
begins: *for Love*; the third: *Then I struggle*; the fourth: *and if I raise*.

After I wrote these three sonnets in which I spoke to this lady, for they   17:1
were the narrators of almost everything about my condition, I believed
I should keep silent and write no more, for I seemed to have revealed much
about myself; and even though thereafter I would keep silent in that I would
not speak to her, I felt it necessary to take up new matter, more noble than the
previous. And because the reason for taking up the new matter is delightful   17:2
to hear, I will recount it as briefly as I can. Because through my countenance   18:1
many had known the secret of my heart, certain ladies, who had gathered to
enjoy each other's company, knew my heart well, because each had been
present at many of my defeats; and passing near them, as if guided by fortune, I was addressed by one of these gentle ladies. The lady who had called   18:2
me was of a graceful way of speaking so that when I came before them and
noted well that my most gentle lady was not with them, with assurance I
greeted them and asked their pleasure. The ladies were many, among whom   18:3
were some who laughed among themselves; there were others who watched
me, awaiting what I would say; and there were others who spoke among
themselves. One of them, turning her eyes toward me and calling me by
name, said these words: "To what end do you love this lady of yours, since
you cannot bear her presence? Tell us, for the end of such a love must be
extraordinary." And after she had said to me these words, not only she but all
the others began visibly to await my response. I then spoke these words to   18:4
them: "Ladies, the end of my love was indeed the greeting of this lady, of

questa donna, forse di cui voi intendete, e in quello dimorava la beatitudine, ché era fine di tutti li miei desiderii. Ma poi che le piacque di negarlo a me, lo mio segnore Amore, la sua merzede, ha posto tutta la mia beatitudine in quello che non mi puote venire meno." Allora queste donne cominciaro a parlare tra loro; e sì come talora vedemo cadere l'acqua mischiata di bella neve, così mi parea udire le loro parole uscire mischiate di sospiri. E poi che alquanto ebbero parlato tra loro, anche mi disse questa donna che m'avea prima parlato, queste parole: "Noi ti preghiamo che tu ne dichi ove sta questa tua beatitudine." Ed io, rispondendo lei, dissi cotanto: "In quelle parole che lodano la donna mia." Allora mi rispuose questa che mi parlava: "Se tu ne dicessi vero, quelle parole che tu n'hai dette in notificando la tua condizione, avrestù operate con altro intendimento." Onde io, pensando a queste parole, quasi vergognoso mi partio da loro, e venia dicendo fra me medesimo: "Poi che è tanta beatitudine in quelle parole che lodano la mia donna, perché altro parlare è stato lo mio?" E però propuosi di prendere per matera de lo mio parlare sempre mai quello che fosse loda di questa gentilissima; e pensando molto a ciò, pareami avere impresa troppo alta matera quanto a me, sì che non ardia di cominciare; e così dimorai alquanti dì con desiderio di dire e con paura di cominciare.

Avvenne poi che passando per uno cammino lungo lo quale sen gia uno rivo chiaro molto, a me giunse tanta volontade di dire, che io cominciai a pensare lo modo ch'io tenesse; e pensai che parlare di lei non si convenia che io facesse, se io non parlasse a donne in seconda persona, e non ad ogni donna, ma solamente a coloro che sono gentili e che non sono pure femmine. Allora dico che la mia lingua parlò quasi come per sé stessa mossa, e disse: *Donne ch'avete intelletto d'amore.* Queste parole io ripuosi ne la mente con grande letizia, pensando di prenderle per mio cominciamento; onde poi, ritornato a la sopradetta cittade, pensando alquanti die, cominciai una canzone con questo cominciamento, ordinata nel modo che si vedrà di sotto ne la sua divisione. La canzone comincia: *Donne ch'avete.*

> Donne ch'avete intelletto d'amore,
> i' vo' con voi de la mia donna dire,
> non perch'io creda sua laude finire,
> ma ragionar per isfogar la mente.
> Io dico che pensando il suo valore,
> Amor sì dolce mi si fa sentire,

whom you are perhaps thinking, and in that greeting lay my beatitude, for it was the end of all my desires. But because it pleased her to deny it to me, my Lord Love, in his mercy, has placed all my beatitude in that which cannot fail me." Then these ladies began conversing among themselves; and as when at times we see rain falling mixed with beautiful snow, so I seemed to hear their words come forth mixed with sighs. After they had spoken somewhat among themselves, the lady who had first spoken to me added these words: "We pray you, tell us where this your beatitude lies." And I, in reply, said so much: "In those words that praise my lady." And then replied the one who was speaking to me: "If you were speaking the truth to us, those words that you have said to us in making known your condition you would have used with another purpose." Hence I, thinking about these words, in shame departed from those ladies, saying within myself meanwhile: "Since so much beatitude lies in those words that praise my lady, why have other words been mine?" Therefore I resolved to take as the subject of my speaking always and ever what would be in praise of this most gentle one; and thinking much upon it, I seemed to have taken on a subject too lofty for me, so that I dared not begin; and thus I tarried for some days with the desire to speak and the fear of beginning.

I t then happened that traveling down a road beside which ran a very clear stream, I felt such a strong desire to write that I began to conceive the mode I might follow; and I thought that speaking about her was not appropriate for me to do unless I addressed ladies in the second person, and not every lady, but only those who are gentle and not just women. Then I say that my tongue spoke as if it moved by itself, and said: *Ladies who have understanding of love.* These words I stored in my memory with great delight, thinking to use them for my opening; then later, returning to the city mentioned above, and thinking for some days, I began a canzone with this beginning, ordered in the manner to be seen below in its division. The canzone begins: *Ladies who have.*

> Ladies who have understanding of love,
> I wish to speak with you of my lady,
> not that I believe I may exhaust her praise,
> but to converse to ease my mind.
> I say that as I think of her worth,
> Love so sweet in me makes himself felt,

18:5
18:6
18:7
18:8
18:9

19:1
19:2
19:3
19:4
v. 4
19:5

che s'io allora non perdessi ardire,

v. 8   farei parlando innamorar la gente.

19:6   E io non vo' parlar sì altamente,

ch'io divenisse per temenza vile;

ma tratterò del suo stato gentile

v. 12   a respetto di lei leggeramente,

donne e donzelle amorose, con vui,

ché non è cosa da parlarne altrui.

19:7   Angelo clama in divino intelletto

v. 16   e dice: "Sire, nel mondo si vede

maraviglia ne l'atto che procede

d'un'anima che 'nfin qua su risplende."

Lo cielo, che non have altro difetto

v. 20   che d'aver lei, al suo segnor la chiede,

e ciascun santo ne grida merzede.

19:8   Sola Pietà nostra parte difende,

ché parla Dio, che di madonna intende:

v. 24   "Diletti miei, or sofferite in pace

che vostra spene sia quanto me piace

là 'v' è alcun che perder lei s'attende,

e che dirà ne lo inferno: O mal nati

v. 28   io vidi la speranza de' beati."

19:9   Madonna è disiata in sommo cielo:

or voi di sua virtù farvi savere.

Dico, qual vuol gentil donna parere

v. 32   vada con lei, che quando va per via,

gitta nei cor villani Amore un gelo,

per che onne lor pensero agghiaccia e pere;

e qual soffrisse di starla a vedere

v. 36   diverria nobil cosa, o si morria.

19:10   E quando trova alcun che degno sia

di veder lei, quei prova sua vertute,

ché li avvien, ciò che li dona, in salute,

v. 40   e sì l'umilia, ch'ogni offesa oblia.

Ancor l'ha Dio per maggior grazia dato

che non pò mal finir chi l'ha parlato.

19:11   Dice di lei Amor: "Cosa mortale

v. 44   come esser pò sì adorna e sì pura?"

such that if I then were not to lose heart,

I would through speaking enamor the people.   v. 8

And I do not wish to speak so loftily   19:6

as to become through daring inept;

but I will speak of her gentle estate

with respect for her, discretely,   v. 12

ladies and amorous maidens, with you,

for it is not a subject to address to others.

An angel entreats within the divine mind,   19:7

and says: "Lord, in the world is seen   v. 16

a marvel in the act that comes forth

from a soul that to this very height shines."

Heaven, which has no other defect

but to have her, asks her of its Lord,   v. 20

and every saint cries out for this grace.

Pity alone our cause defends,   19:8

so that God speaks, having my lady in mind:

"My beloved, suffer now in peace,   v. 24

that your hope may be as long as I please

there where one is who expects to lose her,

and will say in hell: O evil born,

I beheld the hope of the blessed."   v. 28

The lady is desired in highest heaven: 19:9

now I wish to have you know of her virtue.

I say, let who wishes to appear a gentle lady

go with her, for when she goes along the way,   v. 32

into villainous hearts Love casts a chill,

whereby all their thoughts freeze and perish;

and who might suffer to stay and behold her

would change into a noble thing, or die.   v. 36

And when she finds someone worthy   19:10

to behold her, he experiences her power,

for what she gives him turns into salvation,

and so humbles him that he forgets every offense.   v. 40

God has given her an even greater grace:

that one cannot end in evil who has spoken to her.

Of her says Love: "A mortal thing,   19:11

how can it be so adorned and pure?"   v. 44

Poi la reguarda, e fra se stesso giura
che Dio ne 'ntenda di far cosa nova.
Color di perle ha quasi, in forma quale

convene a donna aver, non for misura:
ella è quanto de ben pò far natura;
per essemplo di lei bieltà si prova.

De li occhi suoi, come ch'ella li mova,
escono spirti d'amore inflammati,
che feron li occhi a qual che allor la guati,
e passan sì che 'l cor ciascun retrova:
voi le vedete Amor pinto nel viso
là 've non pote alcun mirarla fiso.

Canzone, io so che tu girai parlando
a donne assai, quand'io t'avrò avanzata.
Or t'ammonisco, perch'io t'ho allevata
per figliuola d'Amor giovane e piana,
che là 've giugni tu dichi pregando:
"Insegnatemi gir, ch'io son mandata
a quella di cui laude so' adornata."
E se non vuoli andar sì come vana,
non restare ove sia gente villana:
ingegnati, se puoi, d'esser palese
solo con donne o con omo cortese,
che ti merranno là per via tostana.
Tu troverai Amor con esso lei;
raccomandami a lui come tu dei.

Questa canzone, acciò che sia meglio intesa, la dividerò più artificiosamente
che l'altre cose di sopra. E però prima ne fo tre parti: la prima parte è proemio
de le sequenti parole; la seconda è lo intento trattato; la terza è quasi una
serviziale de le precedenti parole. La seconda comincia quivi: *Angelo clama*;
la terza quivi: *Canzone, io so che*. La prima parte si divide in quattro: ne la
prima dico a cu' io dicer voglio de la mia donna, e perché io voglio dire; ne la
seconda dico quale me pare avere a me stesso quand'io penso lo suo valore,
e com'io direi s'io non perdessi l'ardimento; ne la terza dico come credo dire
di lei, acciò ch'io non sia impedito da viltà; ne la quarta, ridicendo anche a
cui ne intenda dire, dico la cagione per che dico a loro. La seconda comincia
quivi: *Io dico*; la terza quivi: *E io non vo' parlar*; la quarta: *donne e donzelle*.

He then looks at her again, and within himself swears
that God intends to make of her something new.
Color like that of pearls she has, in just the form
as becomes a lady, not beyond measure: v. 48
she is as much good as nature can make;
by her likeness is beauty known.
From her eyes, however she moves them,   19:12
issue spirits of love inflamed,   v. 52
which wound the eyes of whoever then beholds her
and pass through so that each finds the heart:
you see Love depicted in her face,
there where none may behold her steadily.   v. 56
Canzone, I know that you will go forth speaking   19:13
to many ladies, after I will have released you.
I now admonish you, since I have nurtured you
as a daughter of Love young and forthright,   v. 60
that where you arrive you say, beseeching:
"Teach me the way, for I am sent
to her with whose praise I am adorned."
And if you wish not to go like a useless thing,   19:14
do not remain where folk are villainous:
strive, if you can, to open yourself
only to ladies or to men of courtly ways,
who will guide you there by the speedier way.   v. 68
You will find Love abiding with her;
commend me to him as you should.

This canzone, to be better understood, I will divide more subtly than the   19:15
other things above. And so first I will make three parts: the first part is
proem to my subsequent words; the second is the intended treatment; the
third is almost a servant to the preceding words. The second begins: *An
angel entreats*; the third: *Canzone, I know that.* The first part divides into   19:16
four: in the first I say to whom I wish to speak of my lady, and why I wish to
speak; in the second I say what I myself seem to feel when I think upon her
worth, and what I would say if I did not lose heart; in the third I say how I
hope to speak about her, so that I may not be impeded by faint-heartedness;
in the fourth, again saying to whom I wish to speak, I tell the reason for
speaking to them. The second begins: *I say*; the third: *And I do not wish to*

19:17 Poscia quando dico: *Angelo clama*, comincia a trattare di questa donna. E dividesi questa parte in due: ne la prima dico che di lei si comprende in cielo; ne la seconda dico che di lei si comprende in terra, quivi: *Madonna è disiata*.

19:18 Questa seconda parte si divide in due; che ne la prima dico di lei quanto da la parte de la nobilitade de la sua anima, narrando alquanto de le sue vertudi effettive che de la sua anima procedeano; ne la seconda dico di lei quanto da la parte de la nobilitade del suo corpo, narrando alquanto de le sue bellezze,

19:19 quivi: *Dice di lei Amor*. Questa seconda parte si divide in due; che ne la prima dico d'alquante bellezze che sono secondo tutta la persona; ne la seconda dico d'alquante bellezze che sono secondo diterminata parte de la persona,

19:20 quivi: *De li occhi suoi*. Questa seconda parte si divide in due; che ne l'una dico degli occhi, li quali sono principio d'amore; ne la seconda dico de la bocca, la quale è fine d'amore. E acciò che quinci si lievi ogni vizioso pensiero, ricordisi chi ci legge, che di sopra è scritto che lo saluto di questa donna, lo quale era de le operazioni de la bocca sua, fue fine de li miei desiderii

19:21 mentre ch'io lo potei ricevere. Poscia quando dico: *Canzone, io so che tu*, aggiungo una stanza quasi come ancella de l'altre, ne la quale dico quello che di questa mia canzone desidero; e però che questa ultima parte è lieve a

19:22 intendere, non mi travaglio di più divisioni. Dico bene che, a più aprire lo intendimento di questa canzone, si converrebbe usare di più minute divisioni; ma tuttavia chi non è di tanto ingegno che per queste che sono fatte la possa intendere, a me non dispiace se la mi lascia stare, ché certo io temo d'avere a troppi comunicato lo suo intendimento pur per queste divisioni che fatte sono, s'elli avvenisse che molti le potessero audire.

20:1 Appresso che questa canzone fue alquanto divolgata tra le genti, con ciò fosse cosa che alcuno amico l'udisse, volontade lo mosse a pregare me che io li dovesse dire che è Amore, avendo forse per l'udite parole speranza

20:2 di me oltre che degna. Onde io, pensando che appresso di cotale trattato bello era trattare alquanto d'Amore, e pensando che l'amico era da servire, propuosi di dire parole ne le quali io trattassi d'Amore; e allora dissi questo sonetto, lo qual comincia: *Amore e 'l cor gentil*.

20:3   Amore e 'l cor gentil sono una cosa,
           sì come il saggio in suo dittare pone,
           e così esser l'un sanza l'altro osa

v. 4   com'alma razional sanza ragione.

speak; the fourth: *ladies and amorous maidens.* Then when I say: *An angel*   19:17
entreats, I begin to speak about this lady. And this part divides in two: in the
first I say what is understood of her in heaven; in the second I tell what is
understood on earth, with: *The lady is desired.* This second part divides in   19:18
two; for in the first I speak of the nobility of her soul, recounting something
of the effective powers that emanate from her soul; in the second I speak of
the nobility of her body, recounting something of her beauty, with: *Of her*
says Love. This second part divides in two; for in the first I speak of some of   19:19
the beauties with reference to her whole person; in the second I speak of
some beauties with reference to specific parts of her person, with: *From her*
eyes. This second part divides in two: for in one I speak of her eyes, which   19:20
are the source of love; in the second I speak of her mouth, which is the end of
love. And to remove at this point every vicious thought, let whoever reads
here remember that above it is written that this lady's salutation, which belongs to the acts of her mouth, was the end of my desire while I was allowed
to receive it. Later when I say: *Canzone, I know that you*, I add a stanza   19:21
almost as a servant to the others, in which I say what I hope for from this
canzone of mine; and since this last part is easily understood, I will not bela-
bor myself with more divisions. I do say that to open further the meaning of   19:22
this canzone, it would be useful to employ still more minute divisions; nevertheless, those who have not enough wit to understand it through these already made do me no displeasure if they let the matter drop, because in truth
I fear having communicated its meaning to too many people already through
the divisions made, should it come to pass that many were to hear them.

After this canzone was somewhat divulged among the people, and a cer-   20.1
tain friend happened to hear it, desire moved him to entreat me that I
should tell him what Love is, having perhaps, through the words he heard,
more hope in me than I deserved. Hence, thinking that after that discourse it   20.2
would be beautiful to treat Love further, and thinking that the friend should
be served, I proposed to write words in which I would speak of Love; and so
I wrote this sonnet, which begins: *Love and the gentle heart.*

> Love and the gentle heart are one thing,   20:3
> even as the sage affirms in his poem,
> and so one can be without the other
> as much as rational soul without reason.   v. 4

20:4   Falli natura quand'è amorosa,

Amor per sire e 'l cor per sua magione,

dentro la qual dormendo si riposa

v. 8   tal volta poca e tal lunga stagione.

20:5   Bieltate appare in saggia donna pui,

che piace a gli occhi sì, che dentro al core

nasce un disio de la cosa piacente;

v. 12   e tanto dura talora in costui,

che fa svegliar lo spirito d'Amore.

E simil face in donna omo valente.

20:6   Questo sonetto si divide in due parti: ne la prima dico di lui in quanto è in potenzia; ne la seconda dico di lui in quanto di potenzia si riduce in atto. La

20:7   seconda comincia quivi: *Bieltate appare.* La prima si divide in due: ne la prima dico in che suggetto sia questa potenzia; ne la seconda dico sì come questo suggetto e questa potenzia siano produtti in essere, e come l'uno guarda

20:8   l'altro come forma materia. La seconda comincia quivi: *Falli natura.* Poscia quando dico: *Bieltate appare*, dico come questa potenzia si riduce in atto; e prima come si riduce in uomo, poi come si riduce in donna, quivi: *E simil face in donna.*

21:1   Poscia che trattai d'Amore ne la soprascritta rima, vennemi volontade di volere dire anche in loda di questa gentilissima parole, per le quali io mostrasse come per lei si sveglia questo Amore, e come non solamente si sveglia là ove dorme, ma là ove non è in potenzia, ella, mirabilmente operando, lo fa venire. E allora dissi questo sonetto, lo quale comincia: *Ne li occhi porta.*

21:2   Ne li occhi porta la mia donna Amore,

per che si fa gentil ciò ch'ella mira;

ov'ella passa, ogn'om ver lei si gira,

v. 4   e cui saluta fa tremar lo core,

sì che, bassando il viso, tutto smore,

e d'ogni suo difetto allor sospira:

fugge dinanzi a lei superbia ed ira.

v. 8   Aiutatemi, donne, farle onore.

Nature creates them when she is amorous: 20:4
Love as lord and the heart as his mansion,
in which, sleeping, he rests
sometimes a brief and sometimes a long season.   v. 8
Beauty appears in a wise lady, then,   20:5
which so pleases the eyes that in the heart
is born a desire for that which pleases;
and so long it lasts sometimes therein   v. 12
that it wakens the spirit of Love.
And the same to a lady does a worthy man.

This sonnet divides into two parts: in the first I speak of Love insofar as he is   20:6
in potentiality; in the second I speak of him insofar as from potentiality he is
reduced to act. The second begins: *Beauty appears.* The first divides in   20:7
two: in the first I say in what subject lies this potentiality; in the second I say
how this subject and this potentiality are brought into being, and how one
relates to the other as form to matter. The second begins: *Nature creates
them.* Then when I say: *Beauty appears*, I say how this potentiality is re-   20:8
duced to act, first how it is reduced in man; then how it is reduced in woman,
with: *And the same.*

After I treated of Love in the rhyme inscribed above, I felt a desire to say   21:1
some words also in praise of this most gentle one, by which I might
show how through her this Love awakens, and not only how he awakens
where he sleeps, but how she, where he is not in potentiality, works miraculously and brings him forward. So I wrote this sonnet, which begins: *In her
eyes my lady brings.*

In her eyes my lady brings Love,   21:2
whereby is ennobled whatever she looks upon;
where she passes, everyone toward her turns,
and whoever she greets trembles at heart,   v. 4
so that, lowering the eyes, one grows all pale,
and for each fault one then sighs:
before her flee pride and wrath.
Help me, ladies, to do her honor.   v. 8

21:3   Ogne dolcezza, ogne pensero umile
          nasce nel core a chi parlar la sente,
          ond'è laudato chi prima la vide.
21:4   Quel ch'ella par quando un poco sorride,
          non si pò dicer né tenere a mente,
          sì è novo miracolo e gentile.

21:5   Questo sonetto si ha tre parti: ne la prima dico sì come questa donna riduce
       questa potenzia in atto secondo la nobilissima parte de li suoi occhi; e ne la
       terza dico questo medesimo secondo la nobilissima parte de la sua bocca; e
       intra queste due parti è una particella, ch'è quasi domandatrice d'aiuto a la
       precedente parte e a la sequente, e comincia quivi: *Aiutatemi, donne.* La
21:6   terza comincia quivi: *Ogne dolcezza.* La prima si divide in tre; che ne la
       prima parte dico sì come virtuosamente fa gentile tutto ciò che vede, e questo
       è tanto a dire quanto inducere Amore in potenzia là ove non è; ne la seconda
       dico come reduce in atto Amore ne li cuori di tutti coloro cui vede; ne la terza
       dico quello che poi virtuosamente adopera ne' loro cuori. La seconda comincia
21:7   quivi: *ov'ella passa*; la terza quivi: *e cui saluta.* Poscia quando dico: *Aiutatemi,
       donne*, do a intendere a cui la mia intenzione è di parlare, chiamando le donne
21:8   che m'aiutino onorare costei. Poscia quando dico: *Ogne dolcezza*, dico
       quello medesimo che detto è ne la prima parte, secondo due atti de la sua
       bocca; l'uno de li quali è lo suo dolcissimo parlare, e l'altro lo suo mirabile
       riso; salvo che non dico di questo ultimo come adopera ne li cuori altrui, però
       che la memoria non puote ritenere lui né sua operazione.

22:1   Appresso ciò non molti dì passati, sì come piacque al glorioso sire lo
       quale non negoe la morte a sé, colui che era stato genitore di tanta
       maraviglia quanta si vedea ch'era questa nobilissima Beatrice, di questa vita
22:2   uscendo, a la gloria etternale se ne gio veracemente. Onde con ciò sia cosa
       che cotale partire sia doloroso a coloro che rimangono e sono stati amici di
       colui che se ne va; e nulla sia sì intima amistade come da buon padre a buon
       figliuolo e da buon figliuolo a buon padre; e questa donna fosse in altissimo
       grado di bontade, e lo suo padre, sì come da molti si crede e vero è, fosse
       bono in alto grado; manifesto è che questa donna fue amarissimamente piena
22:3   di dolore. E con ciò sia cosa che, secondo l'usanza de la sopradetta cittade,
       donne con donne e uomini con uomini s'adunino a cotale tristizia, molte
       donne s'adunaro colà dove questa Beatrice piangea pietosamente: onde io
       veggendo ritornare alquante donne da lei, udio dicere loro parole di questa

Every sweetness, every humble thought   21:3
is born in the heart of whoever hears her speak,
and one is praised who sees her first.
What she seems when she but smiles   21:4
cannot be described or held in mind,
so much is she a miracle new and gentle.

This sonnet has three parts: in the first I tell how this lady reduces this poten-   21:5
tiality to act in consequence of the very noble part which are her eyes; and in
the third I say the same in consequence of the very noble part which is her
mouth; and between these two is a particle that is a quasi-petitioner of aid for
the previous and subsequent parts, and it begins: *Help me, ladies*. The third
begins: *Every sweetness*. The first divides into three: in the first part I say   21:6
how through her power she makes noble all that she beholds, and this is
tantamount to saying that she brings Love forth into potentiality where he is
not; in the second I say how she brings Love forth into actuality in the hearts
of all those whom she beholds; in the third I say what, by her virtue, she then
effects in their hearts. The second begins: *Where she passes*; the third: *and
whoever she greets*. Then when I say: *Help me, ladies*, I make it known to   21:7
whom I intend to speak, calling upon the ladies to help me honor her. After-   21:8
ward when I say: *Every sweetness*, I say the same as already said in the first
part, according to the two acts of her mouth: one of which is her utterly sweet
speech, and the other, her wonderful smile; except that I do not say of the
latter how it works in the hearts of others, because memory cannot retain her
smile or its operation.

After that, not many days later, as it pleased the Lord of Glory who did   22:1
not negate death for himself, he who had been the parent of so great a
marvel as evidently was this most noble Beatrice, from this life issuing, to
eternal glory passed truly. Because such parting is painful to those who   22:2
remain and who have been friends of the departed; and no friendship is as
intimate as that of a good father to a good child, and of a good child to a good
father; and this lady was in the highest level of goodness, and her father, as
many believe and is true, was good in a high degree; it is manifest that this
lady was most bitterly filled with sorrow. And since, according to the cus-   22:3
tom of the aforementioned city, women with women and men with men assemble for such grief, many ladies gathered where this Beatrice piteously
wept: and I, seeing a number of ladies returning from her house, heard the
words they spoke regarding this most gentle one, how she grieved; among

gentilissima, com'ella si lamentava; tra le quali parole udio che diceano: "Certo

22:4 ella piange sì, che quale la mirasse doverebbe morire di pietade." Allora trapassaro queste donne; e io rimasi in tanta tristizia, che alcuna lagrima talora bagnava la mia faccia, onde io mi ricopria con porre le mani spesso a li miei occhi; e se non fosse ch'io attendea audire anche di lei, però ch'io era in luogo onde se ne giano la maggiore parte di quelle donne che da lei si partiano,

22:5 io mi sarei nascoso incontanente che le lagrime m'aveano assalito. E però dimorando ancora nel medesimo luogo, donne anche passaro presso di me, le quali andavano ragionando tra loro queste parole: "Chi dee mai essere lieta

22:6 di noi, che avemo udita parlare questa donna così pietosamente?" Appresso costoro passaro altre donne, che veniano dicendo: "Questi ch'è qui piange né più né meno come se l'avesse veduta, come noi avemo." Altre dipoi diceano

22:7 di me: "Vedi questi che non pare esso, tal è divenuto!" E così passando queste donne, udio parole di lei e di me in questo modo che detto è. Onde io poi, pensando, proposi di dire parole, acciò che degnamente avea cagione di dire, ne le quali parole io conchiudesse tutto ciò che inteso avea da queste donne; e però che volentieri l'averei domandate se non mi fosse stata riprensione, presi tanta matera di dire come s'io l'avesse domandate ed elle

22:8 m'avessero risposto. E feci due sonetti; che nel primo domando in quello modo che voglia mi giunse di domandare; ne l'altro dico la loro risponsione, pigliando ciò ch'io udio da loro sì come lo mi avessero detto rispondendo. E comincia lo primo: *Voi che portate la sembianza umile*, e l'altro: *Se' tu colui c'hai trattato sovente.*

22:9   Voi che portate la sembianza umile,
       con li occhi bassi, mostrando dolore,
       onde venite che 'l vostro colore
v. 4   par divenuto de pietà simile?
       Vedeste voi nostra donna gentile
       bagnar nel viso suo di pianto Amore?
       Ditelmi, donne, che 'l mi dice il core,
v. 8   perch'io vi veggio andar sanz'atto vile.
22:10   E se venite da tanta pietate,
       piacciavi di restar qui meco alquanto,
       e qual che sia di lei, nol mi celate.
v. 12   Io veggio li occhi vostri c'hanno pianto,
       e veggiovi tornar sì sfigurate,
       che 'l cor mi triema di vederne tanto.

which words I heard them say: "Surely she weeps so, that whoever sees her must die of compassion." Then these ladies passed by, and I was left in such 22:4 sadness that some tears at times bathed my face, so that I covered myself by placing my hands frequently over my eyes; and were it not that I expected to hear more about her, for I was in a place where passed most of the ladies who were leaving her, I would have hidden myself as soon as the tears had assailed me. But as I lingered still in the same place, ladies also passed near me 22:5 who went along saying among themselves these words: "Who can ever be happy among us, having heard this lady speak so piteously?" After these 22:6 came along other ladies, who approached saying: "This one who is here weeps neither more nor less than if he had seen her as we have." Others then said about me: "Look at this one, who does not seem himself, such has he become!" And these ladies thus passing, I heard words about her and about me 22:7 in the manner indicated. Hence I later, thinking, resolved to write words, since I had a worthy reason to speak, in which I would include all I had heard from these ladies; and since I would willingly have questioned them if it would not have been reprehensible, I conceived of this matter as if I had indeed questioned them and they had replied. And I wrote two sonnets; in 22:8 the first I put questions in the manner in which the desire came over me to question; in the other I give their responses, taking what I heard from them as if they had told it to me in reply. The first begins: *You who bear your aspect downcast*, and the other: *Are you he who has often spoken.*

> You who bear your aspect downcast,   22:9
> with eyes lowered, showing sorrow,
> whence do you come that your color
> appears changed into pity's own?   v. 4
> Have you seen our gentle lady
> bathe Love with her eyes' tears?
> Tell me, ladies, for so tells me my heart,
> because I see you go with no mean bearing.   v. 8
> And if you return from so much pity,   22:10
> please linger with me here awhile,
> and what has become of her conceal not from me.
> I see your eyes, which have wept,   v. 12
> and I see you return so disfigured
> that my heart trembles to see so much.

22:11   Questo sonetto si divide in due parti: ne la prima chiamo e domando queste donne se vegnono da lei, dicendo loro che io lo credo, però che tornano quasi ingentilite; ne la seconda le prego che mi dicano di lei. La seconda comincia

22:12   quivi: *E se venite*. Qui appresso è l'altro sonetto, sì come dinanzi avemo narrato.

22:13
> **Se'** tu colui c'hai trattato sovente
> di nostra donna, sol parlando a nui?
> Tu risomigli a la voce ben lui,

v. 4
> ma la figura ne par d'altra gente.

22:14
> E perché piangi tu sì coralmente,
> che fai di te pietà venire altrui?
> Vedestù pianger lei, che tu non pui

v. 8
> punto celar la dolorosa mente?

22:15
> Lascia piangere noi e triste andare
> (e fa peccato chi mai ne conforta),
> che nel suo pianto l'udimmo parlare.

22:16
> Ell'ha nel viso la pietà sì scorta,
> che qual l'avesse voluta mirare
> sarebbe innanzi lei piangendo morta.

22:17   Questo sonetto ha quattro parti, secondo che quattro modi di parlare ebbero in loro le donne per cui rispondo; e però che sono di sopra assai manifesti, non m'intrametto di narrare la sentenzia de le parti, e però le distinguo solamente. La seconda comincia quivi: *E perché piangi*; la terza: *Lascia piangere noi*; la quarta: *Ell'ha nel viso*.

23:1   Appresso ciò per pochi dì avvenne che in alcuna parte de la mia persona mi giunse una dolorosa infermitade, onde io continuamente soffersi per nove dì amarissima pena; la quale mi condusse a tanta debolezza, che me

23:2   convenia stare come coloro li quali non si possono muovere. Io dico che ne lo nono giorno, sentendome dolere quasi intollerabilemente, a me giunse uno

23:3   pensero lo quale era de la mia donna. E quando ei pensato alquanto di lei, ed io ritornai pensando a la mia debilitata vita; e veggendo come leggiero era lo suo durare, ancora che sana fosse, sì cominciai a piangere fra me stesso di tanta miseria. Onde, sospirando forte, dicea fra me medesimo: "Di necessitade

23:4   convene che la gentilissima Beatrice alcuna volta si muoia." E però mi giunse uno sì forte smarrimento, che chiusi li occhi e cominciai a travagliare

This sonnet divides into two parts: in the first I call upon and ask these ladies   22:11
if they come from her, telling them that I so believe, because they return
ennobled; in the second I beseech them to tell me of her. The second begins:
And if you return. Here following is the other sonnet, as we have already   22:12
discussed.

> Are you he who has often spoken   22:13
> of our lady, speaking only to us?
> You seem in voice to be truly he,
> but your countenance seems of someone else.   v. 4
> And why do you weep so from the heart,   22:14
> that you cause pity for you in others?
> Did you see her weep, that you cannot
> fully hide your doleful mind?   v. 8
> Leave weeping to us and sad faring   22:15
> (and one sins who ever comforts us),
> for in her cries we heard her speak.
> She bears in her face pity so present   22:16
> that who might have wished to behold her
> would in her presence have died weeping.

This sonnet has four parts, in that four manners of speaking were employed   22:17
by the ladies for whom I respond; and because in the poem above they are
quite clear, I do not interpose myself to recount the meaning of the parts, and
thus I distinguish them only. The second begins: *And why do you weep*; the
third: *Leave weeping to us*; the fourth: *She bears in her face.*

A few days after that, it happened that in a part of my body I was   23:1
seized by a dolorous illness, from which continuously for nine days I
suffered bitterest pain, which reduced me to such weakness that I was obliged
to lie down like those who cannot move. I say that on the ninth day, feeling   23:2
myself in pain almost intolerably, I was taken by a thought that concerned
my lady. And when I had thought somewhat about her, and returned to think-   23:3
ing about my enfeebled life, and to seeing how fleeting was its duration, even
when it was healthy, I began to weep within myself over such misery. Hence,
sighing heavily, I said within myself: "Of necessity it must happen that the
most gentle Beatrice one day will die." And thus came over me so powerful   23:4
a sense of loss that I closed my eyes and began to be agitated like a frantic

sì come farnetica persona ed a imaginare in questo modo: che ne lo incominciamento de lo errare che fece la mia fantasia, apparvero a me certi visi di donne scapigliate, che mi diceano: "Tu pur morrai"; e poi, dopo queste donne, m'apparvero certi visi diversi e orribili a vedere, li quali mi diceano:

23:5   "Tu se' morto." Così cominciando ad errare la mia fantasia, venni a quello ch'io non sapea ove io mi fosse; e vedere mi parea donne andare scapigliate piangendo per via, maravigliosamente triste; e pareami vedere lo sole oscurare, sì che le stelle si mostravano di colore ch'elle mi faceano giudicare che piangessero; e pareami che li uccelli volando per l'aria cadessero morti, e

23:6   che fossero grandissimi tremuoti. E maravigliandomi in cotale fantasia, e paventando assai, imaginai alcuno amico che mi venisse a dire: "Or non sai? la tua mirabile donna è partita di questo secolo." Allora cominciai a piangere molto pietosamente; e non solamente piangea ne la imaginazione, ma piangea

23:7   con li occhi, bagnandoli di vere lagrime. Io imaginava di guardare verso lo cielo, e pareami vedere moltitudine d'angeli li quali tornassero in suso, ed aveano dinanzi da loro una nebuletta bianchissima. A me parea che questi angeli cantassero gloriosamente, e le parole del loro canto mi parea udire

23:8   fossero queste: *Osanna in excelsis*; e altro non mi parea udire. Allora mi parea che lo cuore, ove era tanto amore, mi dicesse: "Vero è che morta giace la nostra donna." E per questo mi parea andare per vedere lo corpo ne lo quale era stata quella nobilissima e beata anima; e fue sì forte la erronea fantasia, che mi mostrò questa donna morta: e pareami che donne la covrissero, cioè la sua testa, con uno bianco velo; e pareami che la sua faccia avesse tanto aspetto d'umilitade, che parea che dicesse: "Io sono a vedere lo principio

23:9   de la pace." In questa imaginazione mi giunse tanta umilitade per vedere lei, che io chiamava la Morte, e dicea: "Dolcissima Morte, vieni a me, e non m'essere villana, però che tu dei essere gentile, in tal parte se' stata! Or vieni

23:10   a me, che molto ti desidero; tu lo vedi, ché io porto già lo tuo colore." E quando io avea veduto compiere tutti li dolorosi mestieri che a le corpora de li morti s'usano di fare, mi parea tornare ne la mia camera, e quivi mi parea guardare verso lo cielo; e sì forte era la mia imaginazione, che piangendo incominciai a dire con verace voce: "Oi anima bellissima, come è beato colui

23:11   che ti vede!" E dicendo io queste parole con doloroso singulto di pianto, e chiamando la Morte che venisse a me, una donna giovane e gentile, la quale era lungo lo mio letto, credendo che lo mio piangere e le mie parole fossero solamente per lo dolore de la mia infermitade, con grande paura cominciò a

23:12   piangere. Onde altre donne che per la camera erano s'accorsero di me, che io piangea, per lo pianto che vedeano fare a questa; onde faccendo lei partire

person and to imagine in this manner: at the outset of the wandering that my fantasy took to, there appeared to me certain faces of disheveled women, who said to me: "You, too, will die"; then, following these ladies, there appeared certain faces strange and horrible to look at, which said to me: "You are dead." Thus, my fantasy beginning to wander, I reached a point at which   23:5
I knew not where I was; and I seemed to see women roaming disheveled, crying along the way, wondrously sad; and I seemed to see the sun darken, so that the stars appeared of a color that made me think that they wept; and it seemed to me that birds flying through the air fell dead, and that there were tremendous earthquakes. And marveling in that fantasy, and terribly afraid,   23:6
I imagined that a friend came to me to say: "Don't you know yet? Your wonderful lady has departed from this world." With that I began to weep most piteously; and I wept not only in my imagination, but I wept with my eyes, bathing them in true tears. I imagined myself looking toward heaven,   23:7
and I seemed to see multitudes of angels who were returning upward, and they had before them a small cloud of purest white. It seemed to me that these angels sang gloriously, and the words I seemed to hear of their song were these: *Osanna in excelsis* [Glory in the highest]; and nothing else I seemed to hear. Then it seemed to me that my heart, where was much love,   23:8
said to me: "It is true that dead lies our lady." And with that I seemed to go and see the body in which had dwelled that most noble and blessed soul; and so strong was the erroneous fantasy that it showed me that lady dead: and it seemed that women covered her — that is, her head — with a white veil; and it appeared that her face had so much the aspect of humility that she seemed to say: "I am beholding the font of peace." In this imagining I felt such hu-   23:9
mility at seeing her that I summoned Death, and said: "Sweet Death, come to me, and be not unkind, for you must be noble: in such a place have you been! Now come to me, I greatly desire you, as you can see, for I already wear your color." And when I had seen completed all the doleful ministrations that on   23:10
the bodies of the dead it is customary to perform, I seemed to return to my room and there to look toward heaven; and so strong was my imagination that, weeping, I began to utter in my real voice: "Oh, most beautiful of souls, how blessed is the one who sees you!" And as I was uttering these words   23:11
with painful convulsions of weeping, and calling on Death to come to me, a lady, young and gentle, who stood alongside my bed, believing that my weeping and my words came solely from the pain of my infirmity, with great fear began to cry. Whereby other ladies who were in the room became aware   23:12
that I was crying, because of the tears they saw this lady shed; hence, making

da me, la quale era meco di propinquissima sanguinitade congiunta, elle si
trassero verso me per isvegliarmi, credendo che io sognasse, e diceanmi:

23:13   "Non dormire più", e "Non ti sconfortare." E parlandomi così, sì mi cessò
la forte fantasia entro in quello punto ch'io volea dicere: "O Beatrice, benedetta
sie tu"; e già detto avea "O Beatrice", quando riscotendomi apersi li occhi, e
vidi che io era ingannato. E con tutto che io chiamasse questo nome, la mia
voce era sì rotta dal singulto del piangere, che queste donne non mi pottero
intendere, secondo il mio parere; e avvegna che io vergognasse molto, tuttavia

23:14   per alcuno ammonimento d'Amore mi rivolsi a loro. E quando mi videro,
cominciaro a dire: "Questi pare morto", e a dire tra loro: "Procuriamo di
confortarlo"; onde molte parole mi diceano da confortarmi, e talora mi

23:15   domandavano di che io avesse avuto paura. Onde io, essendo alquanto
riconfortato, e conosciuto lo fallace imaginare, rispuosi a loro: "Io vi diroe
quello ch'i' hoe avuto." Allora, cominciandomi dal principio infino a la
fine, dissi loro quello che veduto avea, tacendo lo nome di questa gentilissima.

23:16   Onde poi, sanato di questa infermitade, propuosi di dire parole di questo che
m'era addivenuto, però che mi parea che fosse amorosa cosa da udire; e però
ne dissi questa canzone: *Donna pietosa e di novella etade*, ordinata sì come
manifesta la infrascritta divisione.

23:17   **D**onna pietosa e di novella etate,
                                   adorna assai di gentilezze umane,
                                   ch'era là 'v'io chiamava spesso Morte,
v. 4   veggendo li occhi miei pien di pietate,
                                   e ascoltando le parole vane,
                                   si mosse con paura a pianger forte.
23:18   E altre donne, che si fuoro accorte
v. 8   di me per quella che meco piangia,
                                   fecer lei partir via,
                                   e appressarsi per farmi sentire.
                                   Qual dicea: "Non dormire",
v. 12   e qual dicea: "Perché sì ti sconforte?"
                                   Allora lassai la nova fantasia,
                                   chiamando il nome de la donna mia.
23:19   Era la voce mia sì dolorosa
v. 16   e rotta sì da l'angoscia del pianto,
                                   ch'io solo intesi il nome nel mio core:

her leave me, for she was joined to me by extremely close blood relation, they drew near to waken me, believing that I was dreaming, and said to me: "Don't sleep any more," and "Don't be disheartened." And as they were *speaking* to me like this, my powerful fantasy ceased at the point where I wanted to say: "Oh, Beatrice, blessed are you"; and I had already said "Oh, Beatrice" when, returning to myself, I opened my eyes and saw that I was deceived. Although I had called out this name, my voice was so broken by my weeping and sobbing that these ladies could not understand me, as it seemed to me; and although I felt utterly ashamed, nevertheless, through some warning of Love, I turned toward them. And when they saw me, they began to say: "This one looks dead," and to say among themselves, "Let's try to comfort him"; whereupon many things they said to comfort me, and at times they asked me what I had feared. Hence I, being somewhat comforted and aware of my false imagining, to them responded: "I will tell you what has happened to me." Thereafter, from beginning to end, I told them what I had seen, leaving unmentioned the name of this most gentle one. Then later, cured of this infirmity, I resolved to write verses about what had happened to me, for it seemed to me that it would be an amorous thing to hear; and so I wrote this canzone about it: *A Lady compassionate and young*, structured as indicated by the below-inscribed division.

A lady compassionate and young,

richly adorned with human perfections,

who was there, where often I called on Death,

seeing my eyes filled with pain,

and hearing my empty words,

was moved by fear to bitter weeping.

And other ladies, who became aware

of me through her who with me wept,

made her go away,

and approached to bring me to my senses.

One said: "Do not sleep,"

and another: "Why so disheartened?"

Then I quit the strange fantasy,

calling the name of my lady.

My voice was so woeful

and so broken by the anguish of my tears,

that I alone understood the name in my heart;

23:13

23:14

23:15

23:16

23:17

v. 4

23:18

v. 8

v. 12

23:19

v. 16

e con tutta la vista vergognosa

ch'era nel viso mio giunta cotanto,

v. 20   mi fece verso lor volgere Amore.

23:20   Elli era tale a veder mio colore,

che facea ragionar di morte altrui:

"Deh, consoliam costui",

v. 24   pregava l'una l'altra umilemente;

e dicevan sovente:

"Che vedestù, che tu non hai valore?"

E quando un poco confortato fui,

v. 28   io dissi: "Donne, dicerollo a vui.

23:21   Mentr'io pensava la mia frale vita,

e vedea 'l suo durar com'è leggiero,

piansemi Amor nel core, ove dimora;

v. 32   per che l'anima mia fu sì smarrita,

che sospirando dicea nel pensero:

— Ben converrà che la mia donna mora —

23:22   Io presi tanto smarrimento allora,

v. 36   ch'io chiusi li occhi vilmente gravati,

e furon sì smagati

li spirti miei, che ciascun giva errando;

e poscia imaginando,

v. 40   di caunoscenza e di verità fora,

visi di donne m'apparver crucciati,

che mi dicean pur: — Morra'ti, morra'ti. —

23:23   Poi vidi cose dubitose molte,

v. 44   nel vano imaginare ov'io entrai;

ed esser mi parea non so in qual loco,

e veder donne andar per via disciolte,

qual lagrimando, e qual traendo guai,

v. 48   che di tristizia saettavan foco.

23:24   Poi mi parve vedere a poco a poco

turbar lo sole e apparir la stella,

e pianger elli ed ella;

v. 52   cader li augelli volando per l'are,

e la terra tremare;

ed omo apparve scolorito e fioco,

dicendomi: — Che fai? non sai novella?

and despite the look of shame
that in my face so mounted,
Love made me turn toward them.   v. 20
My color was such that seeing it   23:20
made them speak of death:
"Come, let us console him,"
one implored the other humbly;   v. 24
and they asked repeatedly:
"What have you seen, that you have no strength?"
And when I felt a bit comforted,
I replied: "Ladies, I will tell you.   v. 28
As I reflected upon my frail life,   23:21
and saw its duration so unstable,
Love wept in my heart, where it dwells;
for which my soul became so lost   v. 32
that sighing I said in thought:
— The time must come when my lady dies.—
I took on such dismay, then,   23:22
that I closed my vilely burdened eyes,   v. 36
and so confounded were
my spirits that each wandered off;
and afterward, imagining,
to all knowledge and truth lost,   v. 40
I seemed to see faces of women disconsolate,
who told me over and again: —You will die, you will die.—
Then I saw things greatly fearsome   23:23
in the empty imagining into which I entered;   v. 44
I seemed to be in I don't know which place,
and saw ladies go along all disheveled,
some weeping, some crying out their laments,
so that of grief they let fly the fire.   v. 48
Then I seemed to see, little by little,   23:24
the sun grow dim and stars appear
and the one and the others weep;
birds in flight fell from the air,   v. 52
and the earth shook;
and a man appeared, pale and weak,
saying: — What, have you not heard the news?

v. 56   morta è la donna tua, ch'era sì bella.—

23:25   Levava li occhi miei bagnati in pianti,

     e vedea, che parean pioggia di manna,

     li angeli che tornavan suso in cielo,

v. 60   e una nuvoletta avean davanti,

     dopo la qual gridavan tutti: *Osanna*;

     e s'altro avesser detto, a voi dire'lo.

23:26   Allor diceva Amor: — Più nol ti celo;

v. 64   vieni a veder nostra donna che giace.—

     Lo imaginar fallace

     mi condusse a veder madonna morta;

     e quand'io l'avea scorta,

v. 68   vedea che donne la covrian d'un velo;

     ed avea seco umilità verace,

     che parea che dicesse: — Io sono in pace.—

23:27   Io divenia nel dolor sì umile,

v. 72   veggendo in lei tanta umiltà formata,

     ch'io dicea: — Morte, assai dolce ti tegno;

     tu dei omai esser cosa gentile,

     poi che tu se' ne la mia donna stata,

v. 76   e dei aver pietate e non disdegno.

     Vedi che sì desideroso vegno

     d'esser de' tuoi, ch'io ti somiglio in fede.

     Vieni, ché 'l cor te chiede.—

23:28   Poi mi partia, consumato ogne duolo;

     e quand'io era solo,

     dicea, guardando verso l'alto regno:

     — Beato, anima bella, chi te vede! —

v. 84   Voi mi chiamaste allor, vostra merzede."

23:29   Questa canzone ha due parti: ne la prima dico, parlando a indiffinita persona, come io fui levato d'una vana fantasia da certe donne, e come promisi

23:30   loro di dirla; ne la seconda dico come io dissi a loro. La seconda comincia quivi: *Mentr'io pensava.* La prima parte si divide in due: ne la prima dico quello che certe donne, e che una sola, dissero e fecero per la mia fantasia quanto è dinanzi che io fossi tornato in verace condizione; ne la seconda dico quello che queste donne mi dissero poi che io lasciai questo farneticare; e

23:31   comincia questa parte quivi: *Era la voce mia.* Poscia quando dico: *Mentr'io*

Dead is your lady, who was so lovely.—   v. 56

I raised my eyes, wet with tears,   23:25

and saw what looked like a shower of manna,

angels returning to heaven above,

and a small cloud they had before them,   v. 60

after which all were crying out: *Hosanna*;

and had they said something else, I would tell you.

Then spoke Love: — No more will I conceal from you;   23:26

come and see our lady who lies dead.—   v. 64

My false imagining

took me to see my dead lady;

and after I had seen her,

I saw ladies cover her with a veil;   v. 68

and with her she had true humility,

that seemed to say: —I rest in peace.—

I became in my sorrow so humble,   23:27

seeing in her so much humility personified,   v. 72

that I said: —Death, in great sweetness I hold you;

you must hereafter be a noble thing,

because you have been in my lady,

and you must have compassion and not disdain.   v. 76

See how desirous I come

to be one of yours, for I resemble you truly.

Come, for my heart calls you.—

Then I departed, all grief ended;   23:28

and when I was alone,

I said, turning toward the high kingdom:

—Blessed is the one, sweet soul, who sees you!—

You called me then, in your mercy."   v. 84

This canzone has two parts: in the first I say, speaking to an unspecified   23:29
person, how I was recalled from an empty fantasy by certain ladies, and
how I promised to relate it to them; in the second, I recount what I said to
them. The second begins: *As I reflected upon.* The first part divides in   23:30
two: in the first I recount what certain ladies, and one in particular, said
and did about my fantasy before I returned to my true condition; in the
second I recount what these ladies told me after I emerged from this rav-
ing; and this part begins: *My voice.* Then, when I say: *As I reflected*   23:31

pensava, dico come io dissi loro questa mia imaginazione. Ed intorno a ciò foe due parti: ne la prima dico per ordine questa imaginazione; ne la seconda, dicendo a che ora mi chiamaro, le ringrazio chiusamente; e comincia quivi questa parte: *Voi mi chiamaste.*

24:1   **A**ppresso questa vana imaginazione, avvenne uno die che, sedendo io pensoso in alcuna parte, ed io mi sentio cominciare un tremuoto nel

24:2   cuore, così come se io fosse stato presente a questa donna.   Allora dico che mi giunse una imaginazione d'Amore; che mi parve vederlo venire da quella parte ove la mia donna stava, e pareami che lietamente mi dicesse nel cor mio: "Pensa di benedicere lo dì che io ti presi, però che tu lo dei fare."   E certo me parea avere lo cuore sì lieto, che me non parea che fosse lo mio

24:3   cuore, per la sua nuova condizione.   E poco dopo queste parole, che lo cuore mi disse con la lingua d'Amore, io vidi venire verso me una gentile donna, la quale era di famosa bieltade, e fue già molto donna di questo primo mio amico.   E lo nome di questa donna era Giovanna, salvo che per la sua bieltade, secondo che altri crede, imposto l'era nome Primavera; e così era chiamata.

24:4   E appresso lei, guardando, vidi venire la mirabile Beatrice.   Queste donne andaro presso di me così l'una appresso l'altra, e parve che Amore mi parlasse nel cuore, e dicesse: "Quella prima è nominata Primavera solo per questa venuta d'oggi; ché io mossi lo imponitore del nome a chiamarla così Primavera, cioè prima verrà lo die che Beatrice si mosterrà dopo la imaginazione del suo fedele.   E se anche vogli considerare lo primo nome suo, tanto è quanto dire 'prima verrà', però che lo suo nome Giovanna è da quello Giovanni lo quale precedette la verace luce, dicendo: 'Ego vox

24:5   clamantis in deserto: parate viam Domini.'"   Ed anche mi parve che mi dicesse, dopo queste parole: "E chi volesse sottilmente considerare, quella Beatrice

24:6   chiamerebbe Amore per molta simiglianza che ha meco."   Onde io poi, ripensando, propuosi di scrivere per rima a lo mio primo amico (tacendomi certe parole le quali pareano da tacere), credendo io che ancor lo suo cuore mirasse la bieltade di questa Primavera gentile; e dissi questo sonetto, lo quale comincia: *Io mi senti' svegliar.*

24:7   **I**o mi senti' svegliar dentro a lo core
                 un spirito amoroso che dormia:
                 e poi vidi venir da lungi Amore
v. 4   allegro sì, che appena il conoscia,

upon, I tell how I recounted to them my imagining. And concerning this, I make two parts: in the first I relate in order my imagining; in the second, saying at what hour they called me, I thank those ladies implicitly; and this part begins: *You called me*.

A fter this empty imagining, it happened one day that, sitting pensive in a   24:1
place, I felt the beginning of a tremor in my heart, as if I were in the presence of this lady. Then, I say that there came to me an imagining of   24:2
Love, whom I seemed to see coming from the place where my lady dwelt, and he seemed to say joyously in my heart: "Think about blessing the day I took you captive, for you must do so." And certainly I seemed to have a heart so happy that I thought it could not be my heart, because of its new condition. And shortly after these words, which my heart spoke with the tongue of Love,   24:3
I saw coming towards me a gentle lady, who was famously beautiful and was the much beloved lady of this foremost of my friends. The name of this lady was Giovanna, except that because of her beauty — as people believe — she was given the name *Primavera* [Springtime]; and so was she called. And behind her, when I looked, I saw approaching the wondrous Beatrice. These   24:4
ladies passed near me, one after the other, and Love seemed to speak in my heart, and to say: "She who comes first is called *Primavera* uniquely for this, today's coming; for I inspired the bestower of her name to call her *Primavera*, because she will come first [*prima verrà*] on the day that Beatrice will show herself following the imagining of her faithful one. And if you also wish to consider her first name, it is tantamount to saying, 'She will come first,' in that her name Giovanna derives from that John who preceded the true light, saying: 'Ego vox clamantis in deserto: *parate viam Domini*'" ['I am the voice crying in the wilderness: prepare the way of the Lord']. And after   24:5
these words, Love also seemed to say: "And who wishes subtly to consider would call Beatrice Love for the great likeness she bears to me." Thus, upon   24:6
reflection, I resolved to write in rhyme to my best friend (omitting certain words that seemed better left unsaid), believing that his heart still beheld the beauty of this gentle *Primavera*; and I wrote this sonnet, which begins: *I felt awakening*.

I felt awakening in my heart   24:7
an amorous spirit that slept:
and then I saw, approaching from afar, Love,
so joyous that I hardly recognized him,   v. 4

dicendo: "Or pensa pur di farmi onore";
e 'n ciascuna parola sua ridia.

24:8   E poco stando meco il mio segnore,
v. 8   guardando in quella parte onde venia,
io vidi monna Vanna e monna Bice
venire inver lo loco là 'v'io era,
l'una appresso de l'altra maraviglia;
24:9   e sì come la mente mi ridice,
Amor mi disse: "Quell'è Primavera,
e quell'ha nome Amor, sì mi somiglia."

24:10   Questo sonetto ha molte parti: la prima delle quali dice come io mi senti'
svegliare lo tremore usato nel cuore, e come parve che Amore m'apparisse
allegro nel mio cuore da lunga parte; la seconda dice come me parea che
Amore mi dicesse nel mio cuore, e quale mi parea; la terza dice come, poi
che questi fue alquanto stato meco cotale, io vidi e udio certe cose.   La
seconda parte comincia quivi: *dicendo: Or pensa*; la terza quivi: *E poco*
24:11   *stando.* La terza parte si divide in due: ne la prima dico quello che io
vidi; ne la seconda dico quello che io udio. La seconda comincia quivi:
25:1   *Amor mi disse.* Potrebbe qui dubitare persona degna da dichiararle onne
dubitazione, e dubitare potrebbe di ciò, che io dico d'Amore come se
fosse una cosa per sé, e non solamente sustanzia intelligente, ma sì come
fosse sustanzia corporale: la quale cosa, secondo la veritade, è falsa; ché
Amore non è per sé sì come sustanzia, ma è uno accidente in sustanzia.
25:2   E che io dica di lui come se fosse corpo, ancora sì come se fosse uomo,
appare per tre cose che dico di lui. Dico che lo vidi venire; onde, con ciò
sia cosa che venire dica moto locale, e localmente mobile per sé, secondo
lo Filosofo, sia solamente corpo, appare che io ponga Amore essere corpo.
Dico anche di lui che ridea, e anche che parlava; le quali cose paiono
essere proprie de l'uomo, e spezialmente essere risibile; e però appare
25:3   ch'io ponga lui essere uomo. A cotale cosa dichiarare, secondo che è
buono a presente, prima è da intendere che anticamente non erano dicitori
d'amore in lingua volgare, anzi erano dicitori d'amore certi poete in lingua latina; tra noi, dico, avvegna forse che tra altra gente addivenisse, e
addivegna ancora, sì come in Grecia, non volgari ma litterati poete queste
25:4   cose trattavano. E non è molto numero d'anni passati, che appariro prima

saying: "Now think indeed of paying me honor";
and with each word he smiled.
And shortly after my Lord was with me,   24:8
looking in the direction whence he had come,   v. 8
I saw Lady Vanna and Lady Bice
coming toward the place where I was,
one after the other wonder;
and as my memory retells me,   24:9
Love said to me: "This one is Primavera,
and that other is named Love, so like me is she."

This sonnet has many parts, the first of which says how I felt the awakening   24:10
of the wonted tremor in my heart, and how it seemed that Love appeared
happy in my heart coming from a distance; the second says what Love seemed
to say to me in my heart, and how he looked; the third tells how, after he had
lingered with me awhile, I saw and heard certain things. The second part
begins: *saying: "Now think"*; the third: *And shortly after*. The third part   24:11
divides in two: in the first I tell what I saw; in the second I tell what I heard.
The second begins: *Love said to me*. Here might doubt a person worthy of   25:1
having every doubt explained, and one might be doubtful of this, that I speak
of Love as a thing in itself, and not only an intelligent substance but also a
corporeal substance: which, according to truth, is false; for Love is not in
himself a substance, but is an accident inherent in a substance. And that I   25:2
speak of him as if he were a body, indeed as if he were a human being, is
clear from three things that I say about him. I say that I saw him approach;
hence, since coming implies local motion, and local mobility as such, according to the Philosopher, belongs to bodies only, I seem to posit Love as a
body. I also say of him that he smiled, and also that he spoke, which things
seem to be properties of a human being, especially that of being risible; and
so it appears that I posit him human. To explain such a matter, to the extent   25:3
appropriate at present, it must first be understood that in antiquity there were
no versifiers of love in the vernacular language, but rather there were versifiers of love who were poets in the Latin language; I say that among us —
although perhaps among other peoples it might have happened and it might
still happen, just as in Greece — not vernacular but educated poets dealt with
these subjects. And not a great number of years have passed since first ap-   25:4
peared these vernacular poets; for to compose rhymes in the vernacular is
tantamount to composing verses in Latin, according to a certain proportion.

questi poete volgari; ché dire per rima in volgare tanto è quanto dire per versi in latino, secondo alcuna proporzione. E segno che sia picciolo tempo, è che se volemo cercare in lingua d'*oco* e in quella di *sì*, noi non

25:5 troviamo cose dette anzi lo presente tempo per cento e cinquanta anni. E la cagione per che alquanti grossi ebbero fama di sapere dire, è che quasi

25:6 fuoro li primi che dissero in lingua di *sì*. E lo primo che cominciò a dire sì come poeta volgare, si mosse però che volle fare intendere le sue parole a donna, a la quale era malagevole d'intendere li versi latini. E questo è contra coloro che rimano sopra altra matera che amorosa, con ciò sia cosa che cotale modo di parlare fosse dal principio trovato per dire

25:7 d'amore. Onde, con ciò sia cosa che a li poete sia conceduta maggiore licenza di parlare che a li prosaici dittatori, e questi dicitori per rima non siano altro che poete volgari, degno e ragionevole è che a loro sia maggiore licenzia largita di parlare che a li altri parlatori volgari: onde, se alcuna figura o colore rettorico è conceduto a li poete, conceduto è a li rimatori.

25:8 Dunque, se noi vedemo che li poete hanno parlato a le cose inanimate, sì come se avessero senso e ragione, e fattele parlare insieme; e non solamente cose vere, ma cose non vere, cioè che detto hanno, di cose le quali non sono, che parlano, e detto che molti accidenti parlano, sì come se fossero sustanzie e uomini; degno è lo dicitore per rima di fare lo somigliante, ma non sanza ragione alcuna, ma con ragione la quale poi

25:9 sia possibile d'aprire per prosa. Che li poete abbiano così parlato come detto è, appare per Virgilio; lo quale dice che Iuno, cioè una dea nemica de li Troiani, parloe ad Eolo, segnore de li venti, quivi nel primo de lo Eneida: *Eole, nanque tibi*, e che questo segnore le rispuose, quivi: *Tuus, o regina, quid optes explorare labor; michi iussa capessere fas est.* Per questo medesimo poeta parla la cosa che non è animata a le cose animate, nel terzo de lo Eneida: quivi: *Dardanide duri.* Per Lucano parla la cosa animata a la cosa inanimata, quivi: *Multum, Roma, tamen debes civilibus armis.* Per Orazio parla l'uomo a la scienzia medesima sì come ad altra persona; e non solamente sono parole d'Orazio, ma dicele quasi recitando lo modo del buono Omero, quivi ne la sua Poetria: *Dic michi, Musa, virum.* Per Ovidio parla Amore sì come se fosse persona umana, ne lo principio de lo libro c'ha nome Libro di Remedio d'Amore, quivi: *Bella michi video, bella parantur, ait.* E per questo puote essere manifesto a

25:10 chi dubita in alcuna parte di questo mio libello. E acciò che non ne pigli

And a proof that only a short time has passed is that if we research the language of *oco* and that of *sì*, we will not find poetry written before the present time by more than one hundred and fifty years. And the reason some unschooled individuals achieved fame for knowing how to versify is that they were almost the first to versify in the language of *sì*. And the first who began writing as a poet of the vernacular was prompted by the desire to make his words understandable to ladies, to whom it was difficult to understand Latin verses. And this counters those who rhyme on other matters than the amorous, for that mode of versification was developed from the beginning in order to write of love. Consequently, because to poets is granted greater license of expression than to prose writers, and these writers in rhyme are none other than poets of the vernacular, worthy and reasonable it is that to them is granted a greater license to speak than is granted to the other writers in the vernacular; hence, if a certain figure or rhetorical color is granted to poets, it is granted to vernacular versifiers. Therefore, if we see that poets have addressed inanimate things as if they had sense and reason, and have made them speak to each other: and not only of true things but of things not true: that is, they have said of things non-existent that they speak, and said that many accidents speak as if they were substances and human beings; worthy is the vernacular writer in rhyme to do the same, but not without a reason, rather with a reason that is then possible to disclose in prose. That poets have written as I have said above is evident in Vergil, who says that Juno, who is a goddess enemy of the Trojans, spoke to Aeolus, Lord of the winds, in the first book of the *Aeneid*: *Eole, nanque tibi* [Oh Aeolus, to you], and this Lord replied: *Tuus, o regina, quid optes explorare labor; michi iussa capessere fas est* [Yours, o queen, is the task of examining your wishes; mine, the duty to carry out orders]. Through the same poet speaks an inanimate thing to things animate, in the third book of the *Aeneid*, with: *Dardanide duri* [You hard Trojans]. Through Lucan a thing animate speaks to a thing inanimate, with: *Multum, Roma, tamen debes civilibus armis* [Much, oh Rome, do you nevertheless owe to civil wars]. Through Horace one speaks to one's own poetic faculty as to another person — and not only are they Horace's words, but he speaks them while reciting in the manner of the good Homer — here in his *Art of Poetry*: *Dic michi, Musa, virum* [Tell me, oh Muse, about the man]. Through Ovid, Love speaks as if it were a human being, in the beginning of the book entitled *The Book of the Remedies of Love*, with: *Bella michi, video, bella parantur, ait* [Wars against me, I see, wars are being prepared, he says]. And all this should be manifest to whoever

25:5

25:6

25:7

25:8

25:9

alcuna baldanza persona grossa dico che né li poete parlavano così sanza ragione, né quelli che rimano deono parlare così non avendo alcuno ragionamento in loro di quello che dicono, però che grande vergogna sarebbe a colui che rimasse cose sotto vesta di figura o di colore rettorico, e poscia, domandato, non sapesse denudare le sue parole da cotale vesta, in guisa che avessero verace intendimento.   E questo mio primo amico e io ne sapemo bene di quelli che così rimano stoltamente.

26:1   **Q**uesta gentilissima donna, di cui ragionato è ne le precedenti parole, venne in tanta grazia de le genti, che quando passava per via, le persone correano per vedere lei; onde mirabile letizia me ne giungea.   E quando ella fosse presso d'alcuno, tanta onestade giungea nel cuore di quello, che non ardia di levare li occhi, né di rispondere a lo suo saluto; e di questo molti, sì

26:2   come esperti, mi potrebbero testimoniare a chi non lo credesse.   Ella coronata e vestita d'umilitade s'andava, nulla gloria mostrando di ciò ch'ella vedea e udia.   Diceano molti, poi che passata era: "Questa non è femmina, anzi è uno de li bellissimi angeli del cielo."   E altri diceano: "Questa è una maraviglia;

26:3   che benedetto sia lo Segnore, che sì mirabilemente sae adoperare!"   Io dico ch'ella si mostrava sì gentile e sì piena di tutti li piaceri, che quelli che la miravano comprendeano in loro una dolcezza onesta e soave, tanto che ridicere non lo sapeano; né alcuno era lo quale potesse mirare lei, che nel principio

26:4   nol convenisse sospirare.   Queste e più mirabili cose da lei procedeano virtuosamente: onde io pensando a ciò, volendo ripigliare lo stilo de la sua loda, propuosi di dicere parole, ne le quali io dessi ad intendere de le sue mirabili ed eccellenti operazioni; acciò che non pur coloro che la poteano sensibilmente vedere, ma li altri sappiano di lei quello che le parole ne possono fare intendere.   Allora dissi questo sonetto, lo quale comincia: *Tanto gentile*.

26:5   **T**anto gentile e tanto onesta pare
la donna mia quand'ella altrui saluta,
ch'ogne lingua deven tremando muta,
v. 4   e li occhi no l'ardiscon di guardare.
26:6   Ella si va, sentendosi laudare,
benignamente d'umiltà vestuta;
e par che sia una cosa venuta
v. 8   da cielo in terra a miracol mostrare.

objects to any part of my little book. And so that no unschooled person may   25:10
become emboldened from this, I say that neither Latin poets wrote in this
manner without reason, nor vernacular poets should write like this without
having any reasons in mind for what they write; for a great shame would
befall those who put things under the veil of a figure or rhetorical color and
then, when asked, could not unveil their words in a way that would show their
true reasoning. And this best friend of mine and I know well some who rhyme
so senselessly.

This most gentle lady, of whom it has been spoken in the preceding words,   26:1
came into such favor among the people that when she passed along the
way, people ran to see her, for which a great joy came over me. And when
she was near anyone, such honesty came into one's heart that one ventured
neither to raise the eyes nor to respond to her greeting; and to this, many who
experienced it could testify for me to whoever might not believe it. She,   26:2
crowned and clothed with humility, would go her way, showing no glory in
what she saw and heard. Many said, after she had passed: "She is no earthly
woman, but one of those most beautiful angels of heaven." And others said:
"She is a marvel; blessed be the Lord, who so marvelously can work!" I say   26:3
that she appeared so gentle and so full of every beauty that those who beheld
her conceived in themselves such honest and soothing sweetness that they
knew not how to retell it; nor was there anyone who could behold her and
need not immediately sigh. These and more wonderful operations proceeded   26:4
from her virtuousness; hence, reflecting upon this and wanting to resume my
mode of praising her, I resolved to write words in which I would make known
her wondrous and excellent operations, so that not only those who could
physically see her, but also all others, might know of her what words can
make one understand. Then I wrote this sonnet, which begins: *So gentle.*

So gentle and so honest appears   26:5
my lady when she greets others
that every tongue, trembling, becomes mute,
and eyes dare not look at her.   v. 4
She goes hearing herself praised,   26:6
benevolently clothed in humility,
and seems a thing come down
from heaven to earth to reveal miraculousness.   v. 8

26:7

> Mostrasi sì piacente a chi la mira,
> che dà per li occhi una dolcezza al core,
> che 'ntender no la può chi no la prova:

v. 12

> e par che de la sua labbia si mova
> un spirito soave pien d'amore,
> che va dicendo a l'anima: Sospira.

26:8 Questo sonetto è sì piano ad intendere, per quello che narrato è dinanzi, che non abbisogna d'alcuna divisione; e però lassando lui, dico che questa mia donna venne in tanta grazia, che non solamente ella era onorata e laudata, ma

26:9 per lei erano onorate e laudate molte. Ond'io, veggendo ciò e volendo manifestare a chi ciò non vedea, propuosi anche di dire parole, ne le quali ciò fosse significato; e dissi allora questo altro sonetto, che comincia: *Vede perfettamente onne salute*, lo quale narra di lei come la sua vertude adoperava ne l'altre, sì come appare ne la sua divisione.

26:10

> **V**ede perfettamente onne salute
> chi la mia donna tra le donne vede;
> quelle che vanno con lei son tenute

v. 4

> di bella grazia a Dio render merzede.

26:11

> E sua bieltate è di tanta vertute,
> che nulla invidia a l'altre ne procede,
> anzi le face andar seco vestute

v. 8

> di gentilezza, d'amore e di fede.

26:12

> La vista sua fa onne cosa umile;
> e non fa sola sé parer piacente,
> ma ciascuna per lei riceve onore.

26:13

> Ed è ne li atti suoi tanto gentile,
> che nessun la si può recare a mente,
> che non sospiri in dolcezza d'amore.

26:14 Questo sonetto ha tre parti: ne la prima dico tra che gente questa donna più mirabile parea; ne la seconda dico sì come era graziosa la sua compagnia; ne la terza dico di quelle cose che vertuosamente operava in altrui. La seconda

26:15 parte comincia quivi: *quelle che vanno*; la terza quivi: *E sua bieltate*. Questa ultima parte si divide in tre: ne la prima dico quello che operava ne le donne, cioè per loro medesime; ne la seconda dico quello che operava in loro per altrui; ne la terza dico come non solamente ne le donne, ma in tutte le persone,

She appears so pleasing to whoever beholds her   26:7
that she sends through the eyes a sweetness to the heart,
which no one understands who does not feel it:
and it seems that from her lips moves   v. 12
a spirit, soothing and full of love,
that goes saying to the soul: Sigh.

This sonnet is so open to understanding through what has been narrated above   26:8
that it needs no division; and therefore leaving it, I say that my lady came
into such great favor that not only was she honored and praised, but because
of her were honored and praised many other ladies. Hence I, seeing this and   26:9
wanting to manifest it to whoever did not see it, resolved to write additional
words in which it would be expressed: I then wrote this other sonnet, which
begins: *One sees perfectly every salvation*, and which narrates how her virtue served the other ladies in the way evident in its division.

One sees perfectly every salvation   26:10
who sees my lady among the ladies;
they who go with her are bound,
for beauteous grace, to render thanks to God.   v. 4
And her beauty is of such power   26:11
that no envy flows to the others from it;
rather it makes them go with her clothed
in gentleness, love, and devotion.   v. 8
The sight of her makes all creatures humble;   26:12
and makes not only herself appear beautiful,
but each lady, because of her, receives honor.
And she is in her acts so gentle,   26:13
that no one can call her to mind
who does not sigh because of love's sweetness.

This sonnet has three parts: in the first I say among what people my lady   26:14
appeared most admirable; in the second I say how gentle was her company;
in the third I speak of those things that through her power she brought about
in others. The second part begins: *they who go with her*; the third: *And her
beauty*. This last part divides in three: in the first I tell what she brought   26:15
about in the ladies, that is, what they themselves became; in the second I
describe what she worked in them in the eyes of the others; in the third I say

e non solamente ne la sua presenzia, ma ricordandosi di lei, mirabilemente operava. La seconda comincia quivi: *La vista sua*; la terza quivi: *Ed è ne li atti.*

27:1   Appresso ciò, cominciai a pensare uno giorno sopra quello che detto avea de la mia donna, cioè in questi due sonetti precedenti; e veggendo nel mio pensero che io non avea detto di quello che al presente tempo adoperava 27:2 in me, pareami defettivamente avere parlato. E però propuosi di dire parole, ne le quali io dicesse come me parea essere disposto a la sua operazione, e come operava in me la sua vertude; e non credendo potere ciò narrare in brevitade di sonetto, cominciai allora una canzone, la quale comincia: *Sì lungiamente.*

27:3   Sì lungiamente m'ha tenuto Amore
                     e costumato a la sua segnoria,
                     che sì com'elli m'era forte in pria,
v. 4   così mi sta soave ora nel core.
27:4   Però quando mi tolle sì 'l valore,
                     che li spiriti par che fuggan via,
                     allor sente la frale anima mia
v. 8   tanta dolcezza, che 'l viso ne smore,
                     poi prende Amore in me tanta vertute,
                     che fa li miei spiriti gir parlando,
                     ed escon for chiamando
v. 12   la donna mia, per darmi più salute.
27:5   Questo m'avvene ovunque ella mi vede,
                     e sì è cosa umil, che nol si crede.

28:1   *Quomodo sedet sola civitas plena populo! facta est quasi vidua domina gentium.* Io era nel proponimento ancora di questa canzone, e compiuta n'avea questa soprascritta stanzia, quando lo segnore de la giustizia chiamoe questa gentilissima a gloriare sotto la insegna di quella regina benedetta virgo Maria, lo cui nome fue in grandissima reverenzia ne le parole di questa Beatrice 28:2 beata. E avvegna che forse piacerebbe a presente trattare alquanto de la sua partita da noi, non è lo mio intendimento di trattarne qui per tre ragioni: la prima è che ciò non è del presente proposito, se volemo guardare nel proemio che precede questo libello; la seconda si è che, posto che fosse del presente

how, not only in the women but in all people, and not only by her presence but through their remembrance of her, she worked wondrously. The second begins: *The sight of her*; the third: *And she is in her acts.*

A fter that, I began to reflect one day about what I had said about my   27:1
lady: that is, in these two preceding sonnets; and seeing, as I reflected, that I had not spoken of what at that time she worked in me, I seemed to have spoken imperfectly. I therefore resolved to write verses in which I would say   27:2
how I seemed to be disposed to her working, and how her power worked in me; and not believing that I could relate this in the brevity of a sonnet, I therefore began a canzone, which begins: *For so long.*

> F or so long has Love possessed me   27:3
> and accustomed me to his lordship
> that as much as he was harsh to me at first
> is he now gentle in my heart.   v. 4
> Therefore, when he takes away my strength so   27:4
> that my spirits seem to flee,
> then my frail soul feels
> so much sweetness that my face pales from it,   v. 8
> for Love grows in me to such power
> that it makes my spirits go speaking,
> and they issue forth calling
> my lady to give me greater beatitude.   v. 12
> This occurs to me wherever she sees me,   27:5
> and is a thing so humble, it can hardly be believed.

Q uomodo sedet sola civitas plena populo! facta est quasi vidua domina   28:1
gentium [How solitary lies the city, once full of people! Once great among the nations, she has become like a widow]. I was still intent on this canzone, of which I had completed the stanza transcribed above, when the Lord of Justice called this most gentle one to glory under the sign of the blessed queen, the virgin Mary, whose name was in greatest reverence in the words of this blessed Beatrice. And although it might perhaps be pleasing at   28:2
this point to treat somewhat her departure from us, it is not my purpose to deal with it here for three reasons: the first is that it is not part of the present purpose, if we want to consider the proem that precedes this little book; the second is that, supposing it did pertain to the present purpose, my language

proposito, ancora non sarebbe sufficiente la mia lingua a trattare come si converrebbe di ciò; la terza si è che, posto che fosse l'uno e l'altro, non è convenevole a me trattare di ciò, per quello che, trattando, converrebbe essere me laudatore di me medesimo, la quale cosa è al postutto biasimevole a chi lo fae; e però lascio cotale trattato ad altro chiosatore.   Tuttavia, però che molte volte lo numero del nove ha preso luogo tra le parole dinanzi, onde pare che sia non sanza ragione, e ne la sua partita cotale numero pare che avesse molto luogo, convenesi di dire quindi alcuna cosa, acciò che pare al proposito convenirsi.   Onde prima dicerò come ebbe luogo ne la sua partita, e poi n'assegnerò alcuna ragione, per che questo numero fue a lei cotanto amico.   Io dico che, secondo l'usanza d'Arabia, l'anima sua nobilissima si partio ne la prima ora del nono giorno del mese; e secondo l'usanza di Siria, ella si partio nel nono mese de l'anno, però che lo primo mese è ivi Tisirin primo, lo quale a noi è Ottobre; e secondo l'usanza nostra, ella si partio in quello anno de la nostra indizione, cioè de li anni Domini, in cui lo perfetto numero nove volte era compiuto in quello centinaio nel quale in questo mondo ella fue posta, ed ella fue de li cristiani del terzodecimo centinaio.   Perché questo numero fosse in tanto amico di lei, questa potrebbe essere una ragione: con ciò sia cosa che, secondo Tolomeo e secondo la cristiana veritate, nove siano li cieli che si muovono, e, secondo comune oppinione astrologa, li detti cieli adoperino qua giuso secondo la loro abitudine insieme, questo numero fue amico di lei per dare ad intendere che ne la sua generazione tutti e nove li mobili cieli perfettissimamente s'aveano insieme.   Questa è una ragione di ciò; ma più sottilmente pensando, e secondo la infallibile veritate, questo numero fue ella medesima; per similitudine dico, e ciò intendo così.   Lo numero del tre è la radice del nove, però che, sanza numero altro alcuno, per sé medesimo fa nove, sì come vedemo manifestamente che tre via tre fa nove.   Dunque se lo tre è fattore per se medesimo del nove, e lo fattore per se medesimo de li miracoli è tre, cioè Padre e Figlio e Spirito Santo, li quali sono tre e uno, questa donna fue accompagnata da questo numero del nove a dare ad intendere ch'ella era uno nove, cioè uno miracolo, la cui radice, cioè del miracolo, è solamente la mirabile Trinitade.   Forse ancora per più sottile persona si vederebbe in ciò più sottile ragione; ma questa è quella ch'io ne veggio, e che più mi piace.

Poi che fue partita da questo secolo, rimase tutta la sopradetta cittade quasi vedova dispogliata da ogni dignitade; onde io, ancora lagrimando in questa desolata cittade, scrissi a li principi de la terra alquanto de la sua

would still be inadequate to deal with it properly; the third is that, given the first and second conditions, it is not becoming for me to treat of it, for the reason that, by treating it, I would be obliged to be a praiser of myself, which thing is at all times reprehensible to whoever does it; and therefore I leave this matter to some other glossator. Nevertheless, since the number nine has many times occurred among the previous words, which evidently is not without a reason, and because in her departure that number has clearly figured repeatedly, it is fitting, therefore, to say a few things, for it appears to befit my purpose. Hence, first I will say how this number figured in her departure, and then I will give a reason why this number was so much her friend. I say that, according to the custom of Arabia, her most noble soul departed in the first hour of the ninth day of the month; and according to the custom of Syria, she departed in the ninth month of the year, for there the first month is Tixryn the first, which for us is October; and according to our custom, she departed in that year of our indiction, that is, of the years of our Lord, in which the perfect number nine had been completed nine times in that century in which she had come into this world, and she was a Christian of the thirteenth century. As to why this number was so much her friend, this could be one reason: since, according to Ptolemy and according to Christian truth, nine are the heavens that move, and according to common astrological opinion, the said heavens influence the earth below according to their reciprocal relation, this number was a friend to her to make it understood that at her conception all nine moving heavens were in the most perfect relationship to one another. This is one reason for it; but if we consider more subtly and according to infallible truth, this number was she herself; I speak by similitude, and I explicate it thusly. The number three is the radical of nine, since, without any other number, through itself it makes nine, as we see self-evidently that three times three is nine. Therefore, if three multiplied by itself is the factor of nine, and the factor of miracles multiplied by itself is three, that is, Father, Son, and Holy Spirit, who are three and one, this lady was accompanied by this number nine to make it understood that she was a nine, that is, a miracle, whose root — that is, of the miracle — is solely the wondrous Trinity. Perhaps a still more subtle person might see in this matter a more subtle reason; but this is the one I see in it, and which most pleases me.

A fter she had departed from this century, the entire aforementioned city was left like a widow dispossessed of every dignity; hence, still weeping in this desolate city, I wrote to the princes of the earth somewhat about its

condizione, pigliando quello cominciamento di Geremia profeta che dice: *Quomodo sedet sola civitas.* E questo dico acciò che altri non si maravigli perché io l'abbia allegato di sopra, quasi come entrata de la nuova materia che appresso vene. E se alcuno volesse me riprendere di ciò, ch'io non scrivo qui le parole che seguitano a quelle allegate, escusomene, però che lo intendimento mio non fue dal principio di scrivere altro che per volgare; onde, con ciò sia cosa che le parole che seguitano a quelle che sono allegate, siano tutte latine, sarebbe fuori del mio intendimento se le scrivessi. E simile intenzione so ch'ebbe questo mio primo amico a cui io ciò scrivo, cioè ch'io li scrivessi solamente volgare.

31:1 Poi che li miei occhi ebbero per alquanto tempo lagrimato, e tanto affaticati erano che non poteano disfogare la mia tristizia, pensai di volere disfogarla con alquante parole dolorose; e però propuosi di fare una canzone, ne la quale piangendo ragionassi di lei per cui tanto dolore era fatto distruggitore de l'anima mia; e cominciai allora una canzone, la qual comincia: 31:2 *Li occhi dolenti per pietà del core.* E acciò che questa canzone paia rimanere più vedova dopo lo suo fine, la dividerò prima che io la scriva e cotale modo 31:3 terrò da qui innanzi. Io dico che questa cattivella canzone ha tre parti: la prima è proemio; ne la seconda ragiono di lei; ne la terza parlo a la canzone pietosamente. La seconda parte comincia quivi: *Ita n'è Beatrice*; la terza 31:4 quivi: *Pietosa mia canzone.* La prima parte si divide in tre: ne la prima dico perché io mi muovo a dire; ne la seconda dico a cui io voglio dire; ne la terza dico di cui io voglio dire. La seconda comincia quivi: *E perché me ricorda*; 31:5 la terza quivi: *e dicerò.* Poscia quando dico: *Ita n'è Beatrice*, ragiono di lei; e intorno a ciò foe due parti: prima dico la cagione per che tolta ne fue; appresso dico come altri si piange de la sua partita, e comincia questa parte 31:6 quivi: *Partissi de la sua.* Questa parte si divide in tre: ne la prima dico chi non la piange; ne la seconda dico chi la piange; ne la terza dico de la mia condizione. La seconda comincia quivi: *ma ven tristizia e voglia*; la terza 31:7 quivi: *Dannomi angoscia.* Poscia quando dico: *Pietosa mia canzone*, parlo a questa canzone, disignandole a quali donne se ne vada, e steasi con loro.

31:8
Li occhi dolenti per pietà del core
hanno di lagrimar sofferta pena,
sì che per vinti son remasi omai.
v. 4
Ora, s'i' voglio sfogar lo dolore,

condition, taking the beginning from Jeremiah the prophet, who says: *Quomodo sedet sola civitas* [How solitary lies the city]. And I say this so that no one may wonder why I have cited it above as the introduction to the new matter that comes after. And if any one should want to blame me for not 30:2 transcribing here the words that follow those quoted, I justify myself, for my intention from the beginning has been not to write anything but in the vernacular; hence, since the words that follow those that have been quoted are all in Latin, it would be outside my intention if I wrote them. And the same intention I know had my first friend to whom I write this; that is, that I would write to him only in the vernacular.

After my eyes had for some time wept, and were so tired that they could 31:1 not relieve my sorrow, I thought I would relieve it with some sorrowful verses; so I resolved to write a canzone in which, weeping, I would speak about her because of whom so much pain had become the destroyer of my soul; and then I began a canzone, which begins: *The eyes grieving for the heart's pity.* And so that this canzone may seem to remain all the more 31:2 widowed after its end, I will divide it before I transcribe it; and I will hold to such a mode from now on. I say that this somewhat rueful canzone has three 31:3 parts: the first is a proem; in the second I speak of her; in the third I address the canzone sorrowfully. The second part begins: *Gone has Beatrice*; the third: *My rueful canzone.* The first part divides in three: in the first I tell why 31:4 I am prompted to write; in the second I say to whom I want to speak; in the third I speak about whom I want to write. The second begins: *And because I remember*; the third: *and I will write.* Then when I say: *Gone has Beatrice*, I 31:5 speak about her; and of this I make two parts; first I tell the reason she was taken away from us; after it, I tell how the others wept over her parting, and this part begins: *Departed from her.* This part divides in three: in the first I 31:6 say who does not weep for her; in the second I say who does weep for her; in the third I speak of my condition. The second begins: *otherwise comes sadness and a desire*; the third: *My sighs give me great anguish.* Afterward, 31:7 when I say: *My rueful canzone*, I address this canzone, indicating to which ladies it should go, and that it should remain among them.

> The eyes grieving for the heart's pity   31:8
> have from weeping suffered pain,
> so that overwhelmed they desist in the end.
> Now, if I wish to relieve my grief,   v. 4

che a poco a poco a la morte mi mena,
convenemi parlar traendo guai.

31:9
v. 8

E perché me ricorda ch'io parlai
de la mia donna, mentre che vivia,
donne gentili, volentier con vui,
non voi parlare altrui,
se non a cor gentil che in donna sia;

v. 12

e dicerò di lei piangendo, pui
che si n'è gita in ciel subitamente,
e ha lasciato Amor meco dolente.

31:10
v. 16

Ita n'è Beatrice in l'alto cielo,
nel reame ove li angeli hanno pace,
e sta con loro, e voi, donne, ha lassate:
no la ci tolse qualità di gelo
né di calore, come l'altre face,

v. 20

ma solo fue sua gran benignitate;
ché luce de la sua umilitate
passò li cieli con tanta vertute,
che fé maravigliar l'etterno sire,

v. 24

sì che dolce disire
lo giunse di chiamar tanta salute;
e fella di qua giù a sé venire,
perché vedea ch'esta vita noiosa

v. 28

non era degna di sì gentil cosa.

31:11

Partissi de la sua bella persona
piena di grazia l'anima gentile,
ed èssi gloriosa in loco degno.

v. 32

Chi no la piange, quando ne ragiona,
core ha di pietra sì malvagio e vile,
ch'entrar no i puote spirito benegno.
Non è di cor villan sì alto ingegno,

v. 36

che possa imaginar di lei alquanto,
e però no li ven di pianger doglia:

31:12

ma ven tristizia e voglia
di sospirare e di morir di pianto,

v. 40

e d'onne consolar l'anima spoglia
chi vede nel pensero alcuna volta
quale ella fue, e com'ella n'è tolta.

which little by little leads me toward death,

I must speak, dragging up woes.

And because I remember that I spoke   31:9

of my lady, while she lived,   v. 8

gentle ladies, willingly to you,

I wish to speak to no other

than the gentle heart that is in a lady;

and I will write of her as I weep, for   v. 12

she has gone from us to heaven suddenly,

and has left Love with me, sorrowing.

Gone has Beatrice to high heaven,   31:10

to the realm where the angels have peace,   v. 16

and lives with them, and you, ladies, she has left:

what took her from us was not any quality of cold

or heat, as it does with others,

but was only her great goodness;   v. 20

for a ray of her humility

went beyond the heavens with such power

as to make the eternal Lord marvel

so that sweet desire   v. 24

came upon him to summon so much perfection;

and he made her, from here below, come to him,

because he saw that this abject life

was not worthy of so gentle a thing.   v. 28

Departed from her beautiful person is   31:11

this gentle soul full of grace,

and in a worthy place dwells in glory.

Who weeps not for her, when speaking of her,   v. 32

has a heart of stone so wicked and base

that no good spirit can enter it.

No villainous heart's mind is so high

that it can imagine her in some degree,   v. 36

and hence no pain of weeping comes to it:

otherwise comes sadness and a desire   31:12

to sigh and die of weeping,

and of every consolation the soul is stripped   v. 40

when one who sees in thought at times

what she was, and that she has been taken from us.

31:13	Dannomi angoscia li sospiri forte,
v. 44	quando 'l pensero ne la mente grave
	mi reca quella che m'ha 'l cor diviso:
	e spesse fiate pensando a la morte,
	venemene un disio tanto soave,
v. 48	che mi tramuta lo color nel viso.
31:14	E quando 'l maginar mi ven ben fiso,
	giugnemi tanta pena d'ogne parte,
	ch'io mi riscuoto per dolor ch'i' sento;
v. 52	e sì fatto divento,
	che da le genti vergogna mi parte.
	Poscia piangendo, sol nel mio lamento
	chiamo Beatrice, e dico: "Or se' tu morta?";
v. 56	e mentre ch'io la chiamo, me conforta.
31:15	Pianger di doglia e sospirar d'angoscia
	mi strugge 'l core ovunque sol mi trovo,
	sì che ne 'ncrescerebbe a chi m'audesse:
v. 60	e quale è stata la mia vita, poscia
	che la mia donna andò nel secol novo,
	lingua non è che dicer lo sapesse:
31:16	e però, donne mie, pur ch'io volesse,
v. 64	non vi saprei io dir ben quel ch'io sono,
	sì mi fa travagliar l'acerba vita:
	la quale è sì 'nvilita,
	che ogn'om par che mi dica: "Io t'abbandono",
v. 68	veggendo la mia labbia tramortita.
	Ma qual ch'io sia la mia donna il si vede,
	e io ne spero ancor da lei merzede.
31:17	Pietosa mia canzone, or va piangendo;
v. 72	e ritruova le donne e le donzelle
	a cui le tue sorelle
	erano usate di portar letizia;
	e tu, che se' figliuola di tristizia,
v. 76	vatten disconsolata a star con elle.

31:1   **P**oi che detta fue questa canzone, sì venne a me uno, lo quale, secondo li gradi de l'amistade, è amico a me immediatamente dopo lo primo, e questi fue tanto distretto di sanguinitade con questa gloriosa, che nullo più

My sighs give me great anguish, 31:13

when thought in the oppressed mind v. 44

brings before me her who has divided my heart:

and many times, thinking of death,

there comes to me a desire so sweet

that it alters the color of my face. v. 48

And when the imagining is well fixed in me, 31:14

so much pain comes upon me in every part

that I am startled by the suffering that I feel;

and I become so, v. 52

that from others shame drives me away.

Then weeping, alone in my lament,

I call Beatrice, and I say: "Are you now dead?";

and as I call her, I am comforted. v. 56

To weep in pain and sigh in anguish 31:15

destroys my heart wherever I find myself alone,

so that it would pain whoever heard me:

and what my life has been, since v. 60

my lady went to the new world,

there is not a tongue that knows how to tell it:

and therefore, my ladies, even if I wished, 31:16

I would know not how to tell you fully what I am, v. 64

so does bitter life torment me;

life has fallen so low

that every one seems to tell me: "I forsake you,"

seeing my lips lifeless. v. 68

But whatever I am my lady sees it,

and I still hope for mercy from her.

My rueful canzone, now go, weeping; 31:17

and find again the ladies and the maidens v. 72

to whom your sisters

were accustomed to offering delight;

and you, who are a child of sadness,

go disconsolate to stay with them. v. 76

After I wrote this canzone, there came to me one who, according to the 32:1
degrees of friendship, is friend to me immediately after the first; and he
was by blood relation so close to the glorious one that no one was closer to

32:2 presso l'era. E poi che fue meco a ragionare, mi pregoe ch'io li dovessi dire alcuna cosa per una donna che s'era morta; e simulava sue parole, acciò che paresse che dicesse d'un'altra, la quale morta era certamente: onde io, accorgendomi che questi dicea solamente per questa benedetta, sì li dissi di

32:3 fare ciò che mi domandava lo suo prego. Onde poi, pensando a ciò, propuosi di fare uno sonetto, nel quale mi lamentasse alquanto, e di darlo a questo mio amico, acciò che paresse che per lui l'avessi fatto; e dissi allora questo sonetto,

32:4 che comincia: *Venite a intender li sospiri miei.* Lo quale ha due parti: ne la prima chiamo li fedeli d'Amore che m'intendano; ne la seconda narro de la mia misera condizione. La seconda comincia quivi: *li quai disconsolati.*

32:5   **V**enite a intender li sospiri miei,
          oi cor gentili, ché pietà 'l disia:
          li quai disconsolati vanno via,

v. 4   e s'e' non fosser, di dolor morrei;
          però che gli occhi mi sarebber rei,
          molte fiate più ch'io non vorria,
          lasso!, di pianger sì la donna mia,

v. 8   che sfogasser lo cor, piangendo lei.

32:6   **V**oi udirete lor chiamar sovente
          la mia donna gentil, che si n'è gita
          al secol degno de la sua vertute;

v. 12   e dispregiar talora questa vita
          in persona de l'anima dolente
          abbandonata de la sua salute.

33:1 Poi che detto ei questo sonetto, pensandomi chi questi era a cui lo intendea dare quasi come per lui fatto, vidi che povero mi parea lo servigio e nudo a

33:2 così distretta persona di questa gloriosa. E però anzi ch'io li dessi questo soprascritto sonetto, sì dissi due stanzie d'una canzone, l'una per costui veracemente, e l'altra per me, avvegna che paia l'una e l'altra per una persona detta, a chi non guarda sottilmente; ma chi sottilmente le mira vede bene che diverse persone parlano, acciò che l'una non chiama sua donna

33:3 costei, e l'altra sì, come appare manifestamente. Questa canzone e questo

33:4 soprascritto sonetto li diedi, dicendo io lui che per lui solo fatto l'avea. La canzone comincia: *Quantunque volte,* e ha due parti: ne l'una, cioè ne la prima stanzia, si lamenta questo mio caro e distretto a lei; ne la seconda mi lamento io, cioè ne l'altra stanzia, che comincia: *E' si raccoglie ne li miei.* E

her. And after he lingered with me in conversation, he requested that I write   32:2
something for him about a lady who had died; and he dissembled his words
in order to seem to speak of another lady, who had in fact died: therefore I,
aware that he spoke only of this blessed one, said that I would do what he
asked in his request. Later, pondering the matter, I resolved to write a son-   32:3
net, in which I would lament somewhat, and to give it to this my friend, so
that it would appear that I had done it for him; and I then wrote this sonnet,
which begins: *Come and listen to my sighs*. It has two parts: in the first I call   32:4
upon Love's faithful to listen to me; in the second I speak of my sorrowful
condition. The second begins: *for they issue forth disconsolate.*

> Come and listen to my sighs,   32:5
> you gentle hearts, for pity desires it:
> for they issue forth disconsolate,
> and were it not so, of grief I would die;   v. 4
> because my eyes would be my debtors,
> many times more than I would desire,
> alas, of weeping for my lady, so
> as to relieve my heart, weeping for her.   v. 8
> You will hear them call often   32:6
> to my gentle lady, who has gone
> to the world worthy of her virtue,
> and despise now and then this life   v. 12
> in the name of the suffering soul
> abandoned by its salvation.

After I had written this sonnet, thinking who he was to whom I intended to   33:1
give it as a poem written by him, I saw how poor and bare a service it seemed
for so close a relative of the glorious one. And therefore before I gave him   33:2
the sonnet transcribed above, I wrote two stanzas of a canzone, one truly for
him and the other for me, although both appear written by the same person to
whoever does not look carefully; but who examines them closely sees clearly
that different persons speak, because one does not call the lady his own, and
the other does, as manifestly appears. This canzone and the sonnet transcribed   33:3
above I gave to him, telling him that I had written them for him alone. The
canzone begins: *Every time*, and has two parts: in one, that is in the first   33:4
stanza, this dear friend of mine and relative of hers laments; in the second I
lament: that is, in the other stanza, which begins: *There gathers in my sighs.*

così appare che in questa canzone si lamentano due persone, l'una de le quali
si lamenta come frate, l'altra come servo.

33:5   Quantunque volte, lasso!, mi rimembra
                ch'io non debbo già mai
                veder la donna ond'io vo sì dolente,
v. 4   tanto dolore intorno 'l cor m'assembra
                la dolorosa mente,
                ch'io dico: "Anima mia, ché non ten vai?
                ché li tormenti che tu porterai
v. 8   nel secol, che t'è già tanto noioso,
                mi fan pensoso di paura forte."
33:6   Ond'io chiamo la Morte,
                come soave e dolce mio riposo;
v. 12   e dico "Vieni a me" con tanto amore,
                che sono astioso di chiunque more.
33:7   E' si raccoglie ne li miei sospiri
                un sono di pietate,
v. 16   che va chiamando Morte tuttavia:
                a lei si volser tutti i miei disiri,
                quando la donna mia
                fu giunta da la sua crudelitate;
33:8   perché 'l piacere de la sua bieltate,
                partendo sé da la nostra veduta,
                divenne spirital bellezza grande,
                che per lo cielo spande
v. 24   luce d'amor, che li angeli saluta,
                e lo intelletto loro alto, sottile
                face maravigliar, sì v'è gentile.

34:1   In quello giorno nel quale si compiea l'anno che questa donna era fatta
        de li cittadini di vita eterna, io mi sedea in parte ne la quale, ricordandomi
        di lei, disegnava uno angelo sopra certe tavolette; e mentre io lo disegnava,
34:2   volsi li occhi, e vidi lungo me uomini a li quali si convenia di fare onore. E'
        riguardavano quello che io facea; e secondo che me fu detto poi, elli erano
        stati già alquanto anzi che io me ne accorgesse. Quando li vidi, mi levai, e
34:3   salutando loro dissi: "Altri era testé meco, però pensava." Onde partiti
        costoro, ritornaimi a la mia opera, cioè del disegnare figure d'angeli: e

And thus it is clear that in this canzone two persons lament, one as a brother,
the other as a servant.

Every time, alas, I remember   33:5
that I shall never again
see the lady for whom I go so painfully,
such grief around my heart is gathered   v. 4
by my grieving mind
that I say, "My soul, why don't you go?
for the torments you will suffer
in this world, which already burdens you so,   v. 8
make me most pensive with fear."
Whence I call upon Death   33:6
as my soothing and sweet repose,
and say, "Come to me" with such love   v. 12
that I envy anyone who dies.
There gathers in my sighs   33:7
a voice of pity
that goes calling upon Death endlessly;   v. 16
toward it turned all my desires
when my lady
was overtaken by its cruelties,
because the pleasure of her beauty,   33:8
taking itself from our sight,
became great spiritual beauty
that throughout heaven spreads
light of love, which beatifies the angels,   v. 24
and makes their intellect, lofty and fine,
marvel, so gentle is she there.

On that day when a year was completed since this lady had become a   34:1
citizen of life eternal, I was sitting in a place where, thinking of her, I
was designing an angel on certain panels; and while I was drawing it, I turned
my eyes and saw beside me men to whom it was proper to pay respects.   34:2
They were watching what I was doing; and according to what I was later
told, they had been there some time before I noticed them. When I saw them,
I arose, and greeting them, said: "Someone was just now with me, therefore   34:3
I was in thought." After they had left, I returned to my work, that is, to de-

faccendo ciò, mi venne uno pensero di dire parole, quasi per annovale, e scrivere a costoro li quali erano venuti a me; e dissi allora questo sonetto, lo quale comincia: *Era venuta*; lo quale ha due cominciamenti, e però lo dividerò

34:4   secondo l'uno e secondo l'altro.   Dico che secondo lo primo questo sonetto ha tre parti: ne la prima dico che questa donna era già ne la mia memoria; ne la seconda dico quello che Amore però mi facea; ne la terza dico de gli effetti d'Amore. La seconda comincia quivi: *Amor, che*; la terza quivi: *Piangendo*

34:5   *uscivan for.*   Questa parte si divide in due: ne l'una dico che tutti li miei sospiri uscivano parlando; ne la seconda dico che alquanti diceano certe pa-

34:6   role diverse da gli altri. La seconda comincia quivi: *Ma quei.* Per questo medesimo modo si divide secondo l'altro cominciamento, salvo che ne la prima parte dico quando questa donna era così venuta ne la mia memoria, e ciò non dico ne l'altro.

Primo cominciamento

34:7   Era venuta ne la mente mia

la gentil donna che per suo valore

fu posta da l'altissimo signore

v. 4   nel ciel de l'umiltate, ov'è Maria.

Secondo cominciamento

34:8   Era venuta ne la mente mia

quella donna gentil cui piange Amore,

entro 'n quel punto che lo suo valore

v. 4   vi trasse a riguardar quel ch'eo facia.

34:9   Amor, che ne la mente la sentia,

s'era svegliato nel destrutto core,

e diceva a' sospiri: "Andate fore";

v. 8   per che ciascun dolente si partia.

34:10   Piangendo uscivan for de lo mio petto

con una voce che sovente mena

le lagrime dogliose a li occhi tristi.

34:11   Ma quei che n'uscian for con maggior pena,

venian dicendo: "Oi nobile intelletto,

oggi fa l'anno che nel ciel salisti."

35:1   Poi per alquanto tempo, con ciò fosse cosa che io fosse in parte ne la quale mi ricordava del passato tempo, molto stava pensoso, e con dolorosi

signing figures of angels: and while doing that, there came to me the thought of writing words in rhyme as for her anniversary, and to address those who had come to me; and I then wrote this sonnet, which begins: *Into my mind had come*, which has two beginnings, and so I will make divisions according to the one and the other. I say, with regard to the first, that this sonnet has three parts: in the first I say that this lady was already in my memory; in the second I say what Love therefore worked within me; in the third I speak about the effects of Love. The second begins: *Love, who*; the third: *Weeping they issued forth.* This part is divided in two: in the first I say that all my sighs issued speaking; in the second I say that some were saying certain words different from the others. The second begins: *But those.* In this same way does the sonnet divide according to the other beginning, except that in the first part I say when this lady had thus come into my memory, and I do not say that in the other.

34:4

34:5

34:6

> *First beginning*
> Into my mind had come
> the gentle lady who for her worth
> was placed by the most high Lord
> in the heaven of the humble, where Mary dwells.

34:7

v. 4

> *Second beginning*
> Into my mind had come
> that gentle lady for whom weeps Love,
> at the moment when her worth
> led you to watch what I was doing.
> Love, who in my mind perceived her,
> was awakened in the ravaged heart,
> and said to the sighs: "Go forth";
> at which each one sadly departed.
> Weeping they issued forth from my breast
> with a voice that often calls up
> tears of grief to my sad eyes.
> But those that went forth from there with greatest pain
> issued saying: "Oh, noble intellect,
> today makes a year since to heaven you ascended."

34:8

v. 4

34:9

v. 8

34:10

34:11

Some time afterwards, because I happened to be in a place in which I remembered times past, I became pensive and with painful thoughts

35:1

pensamenti, tanto che mi faceano parere de fore una vista di terribile

35:2   sbigottimento. Onde io, accorgendomi del mio travagliare, levai li occhi per
vedere se altri mi vedesse. Allora vidi una gentile donna giovane e bella
molto, la quale da una finestra mi riguardava sì pietosamente, quanto a la

35:3   vista, che tutta la pietà parea in lei accolta. Onde, con ciò sia cosa che
quando li miseri veggiono di loro compassione altrui, più tosto si muovono a
lagrimare, quasi come di se stessi avendo pietade, io senti' allora cominciare
li miei occhi a volere piangere; e però, temendo di non mostrare la mia vile
vita, mi partio dinanzi da li occhi di questa gentile; e dicea poi fra me
medesimo: "E' non puote essere che con quella pietosa donna non sia

35:4   nobilissimo amore." E però propuosi di dire uno sonetto, ne lo quale io
parlasse a lei, e conchiudesse in esso tutto ciò che narrato è in questa ragione.
E però che per questa ragione è assai manifesto, sì nollo dividerò. Lo sonetto
comincia: *Videro li occhi miei.*

35:5   **V**idero li occhi miei quanta pietate
                            era apparita in la vostra figura,
                            quando guardaste li atti e la statura
v. 4   ch'io faccio per dolor molte fiate.
35:6   Allora m'accorsi che voi pensavate
                            la qualità de la mia vita oscura,
                            sì che mi giunse ne lo cor paura
v. 8   di dimostrar con li occhi mia viltate.
35:7   E tolsimi dinanzi a voi, sentendo
                            che si movean le lagrime dal core,
                            ch'era sommosso da la vostra vista.
35:8   Io dicea poscia ne l'anima trista:
                            "Ben è con quella donna quello Amore
                            lo qual mi face andar così piangendo."

36:1   Avvenne poi che là ovunque questa donna mi vedea, sì si facea d'una vista
pietosa e d'un colore palido quasi come d'amore; onde molte fiate mi ricordava

36:2   de la mia nobilissima donna, che di simile colore si mostrava tuttavia. E
certo molte volte non potendo lagrimare né disfogare la mia tristizia, io andava
per vedere questa pietosa donna, la quale parea che tirasse le lagrime fuori de

36:3   li miei occhi per la sua vista. E però mi venne volontade di dire anche
parole, parlando a lei, e dissi questo sonetto, lo quale comincia: *Color
d'amore*; ed è piano sanza dividerlo, per la sua precedente ragione.

to such an extent that they gave my outward appearance a look of dreadful dismay. Hence, becoming aware of my travail, I raised my eyes to see   35:2
if others saw me. I then saw a gentle lady, young and very beautiful, who
from a window watched me so compassionately, to judge by her look,
that all pity seemed to be gathered in her. With that, because when the   35:3
unhappy see that others have compassion for them, they are more quickly
moved to tears, as if they had pity for themselves, I then felt my own eyes
begin wanting to weep; hence, fearing lest I display my wretched life, I
left the view of this gentle one; and later I said within myself: "It cannot
be but in that compassionate lady there is a most noble love." Therefore I
resolved to write a sonnet, in which I would speak to her, and would include   35:4
in it all that is narrated in this account. And because through this account it
is quite clear, I will not analyze it. The sonnet begins: *My eyes saw.*

> **M**y eyes saw how much pity   35:5
> had appeared on your face
> when you watched the acts and state
> that I bear through sorrow many times.   v. 4
> Then I realized that you were thinking   35:6
> about the quality of my dark life,
> so that over my heart came a fear
> of revealing with my eyes my wretchedness.   v. 8
> And I took myself away from you, feeling   35:7
> that tears were welling in my heart,
> which was moved by your sight.
> I said then in my sad soul: 35:8
> "Surely, with that lady is that Love
> who makes me go thus weeping."

It then happened that wherever this lady saw me, she indeed took on a com-   36:1
passionate look and a pale color like that of love; so I often remembered my
most noble lady, for a similar color she showed continuously. And certainly   36:2
often, unable to weep or relieve my sadness, I went to see this compassionate
lady, who seemed to draw tears from my eyes by her sight. And so I felt the
desire to write some words, addressing her, and I wrote this sonnet, which   36:3
begins: *Color of love*; and it is clear without dividing it, because of the
previous account.

36:4   Color d'amore e di pietà sembianti
non preser mai così mirabilmente
viso di donna, per veder sovente
v. 4   occhi gentili o dolorosi pianti,
come lo vostro, qualora davanti
vedetevi la mia labbia dolente;
sì che per voi mi ven cosa a la mente,
v. 8   ch'io temo forte non lo cor si schianti.
36:5   Eo non posso tener li occhi distrutti
che non reguardin voi spesse fiate,
per desiderio di pianger ch'elli hanno:
v. 12   e voi crescete sì lor volontate,
che de la voglia si consuman tutti;
ma lagrimar dinanzi a voi non sanno.

37:1   Io venni a tanto per la vista di questa donna, che li miei occhi si cominciaro a dilettare troppo di vederla; onde molte volte me ne crucciava nel mio cuore
37:2   ed aveamene per vile assai.   Onde più volte bestemmiava la vanitade de li occhi miei, e dicea loro nel mio pensero: "Or voi solavate fare piangere chi vedea la vostra dolorosa condizione, e ora pare che vogliate dimenticarlo per questa donna che vi mira; che non mira voi, se non in quanto le pesa de la gloriosa donna di cui piangere solete; ma quanto potete fate, ché io la vi pur rimembrerò molto spesso, maladetti occhi, ché mai, se non dopo la morte,
37:3   non dovrebbero le vostre lagrime avere restate."   E quando così avea detto fra me medesimo a li miei occhi, e li sospiri m'assalivano grandissimi e angosciosi.   E acciò che questa battaglia che io avea meco non rimanesse saputa pur dal misero che la sentia, propuosi di fare un sonetto, e di comprendere in ello questa orribile condizione.   E dissi questo sonetto, lo
37:4   quale comincia: _L'amaro lagrimar._ Ed hae due parti: ne la prima parlo a li occhi miei sì come parlava lo mio cuore in me medesimo; ne la seconda rimuovo alcuna dubitazione manifestando chi è che così parla; e comincia
37:5   questa parte quivi: _Così dice._ Potrebbe bene ancora ricevere più divisioni, ma sariano indarno, però che è manifesto per la precedente ragione.

37:6   "L'amaro lagrimar che voi faceste,
oi occhi miei, così lunga stagione,

Color of love and pity's semblance   36:4
never possessed so wondrously
the face of a lady, from seeing often
gentle eyes or sorrowful tears,   v. 4
as do yours, whenever before you
you see my suffering countenance;
so that through you comes such a thing to mind
that I strongly fear lest my heart should break.   v. 8
I cannot restrain these ravaged eyes   36:5
from looking at you often,
so much desire to weep do they feel:
and you so increase their longing   v. 12
that by this desire they are wholly consumed;
but weep in your presence they cannot.

I came to such a point through the sight of this lady that my eyes began to   37:1
delight excessively in seeing her; so that I often became angry about it in
my heart and considered myself base. Consequently, time and again I   37:2
cursed the vanity of my eyes and spoke to them in my mind: "Until now
you used to make weep whoever saw your mournful condition, and now
you seem willing to forget it because of this lady who gazes at you; but
she does not gaze at you except insofar as she grieves for the glorious
lady for whom you used to weep; but do what you will, for I will nevertheless remind you of her again and again, cursed eyes, for never, except
after your death, should your tears have ceased." And when I had thus   37:3
spoken within myself to my eyes, the most profound and anguished sighs
assailed me. And so that this battle that I had with myself would not
remain known only to the wretch who experienced it, I resolved to write
a sonnet, and to express in it this horrible condition. And I wrote this
sonnet, which begins: *The bitter weeping*. It has two parts: in the first I   37:4
address my eyes just as my heart spoke within me; in the second I remove
some doubt, indicating who it is that speaks this way; and this part begins: *So says*. It could well receive further divisions, but they would be   37:5
unnecessary, because all is made clear by the previous account.

"The bitter weeping that you did,   37:6
oh eyes of mine, for so long a season,

facea lagrimar l'altre persone
v. 4   de la pietate, come voi vedeste.
37:7   Ora mi par che voi l'obliereste,
s'io fosse dal mio lato sì fellone
ch'i' non ven disturbasse ogne cagione,
v. 8   membrandovi colei cui voi piangeste.
37:8   La vostra vanità mi fa pensare,
e spaventami sì, ch'io temo forte
del viso d'una donna che vi mira.
v. 12   Voi non dovreste mai, se non per morte,
la vostra donna, ch'è morta, obliare."
Così dice 'l meo core, e poi sospira.

38:1   Ricovrai la vista di quella donna in sì nuova condizione, che molte volte ne
pensava sì come di persona che troppo mi piacesse; e pensava di lei così:
"Questa è una donna gentile, bella, giovane e savia, e apparita forse per
volontade d'Amore, acciò che la mia vita si riposi." E molte volte pensava
più amorosamente, tanto che lo cuore consentiva in lui, cioè nel suo ragionare.
38:2   E quando io avea consentito ciò, e io mi ripensava sì come da la ragione
mosso, e dicea fra me medesimo: "Deo, che pensero è questo, che in così vile
38:3   modo vuole consolare me e non mi lascia quasi altro pensare?" Poi si rilevava
un altro pensero, e diceame: "Or tu se' stato in tanta tribulazione, perché non
vuoli tu ritrarre te da tanta amaritudine? Tu vedi che questo è uno spiramento
d'Amore, che ne reca li disiri d'amore dinanzi, ed è mosso da così gentil
parte com'è quella de li occhi de la donna che tanto pietosa ci s'hae mostrata."
38:4   Onde io, avendo così più volte combattuto in me medesimo, ancora ne volli
dire alquante parole; e però che la battaglia de' pensieri vinceano coloro che
per lei parlavano, mi parve che si convenisse di parlare a lei; e dissi questo
sonetto, lo quale comincia: *Gentil pensero*; e dico "gentile" in quanto
38:5   ragionava di gentile donna, ché per altro era vilissimo. In questo sonetto fo
due parti di me, secondo che li miei pensieri erano divisi. L'una parte chiamo
cuore, cioè l'appetito; l'altra chiamo anima, cioè la ragione; e dico come
l'uno dice con l'altro. E che degno sia di chiamare l'appetito cuore, e la
ragione anima, assai è manifesto a coloro cui mi piace che ciò sia aperto.
38:6   Vero è che nel precedente sonetto io fo la parte del cuore contra quella de li
occhi, e ciò pare contrario di quello che io dico nel presente; e però dico che

made other persons weep

out of pity, as you saw.   v. 4

Now it seems to me you would forget,   37:7

were I on my part so disloyal

as not to remove from you its every reason,

reminding you of her for whom you wept.   v. 8

Your inconstancy afflicts me,   37:8

and frightens me so, that I greatly fear

the face of a lady who gazes at you.

You should never, except through death,   v. 12

put your lady, who is dead, out of memory."

So says my heart, and then it sighs.

I recovered the sight of this lady in so new a condition that I often thought of   38:1
her as a person who greatly appealed to me; and I thought of her in this way:
"This lady is gentle, beautiful, young, and wise, and she has appeared perhaps through the will of Love, so that my life might find some rest." And I
often thought more amorously, so much so that my heart consented to it, that
is, to that reasoning. And after I had consented to it, moved by reason, I   38:2
reflected about it, and I said within myself: "God, what thought is this, that in
such a base manner wants to console me and lets me think of almost nothing
else?" Then arose another thought, and it said to me: "Now that you have   38:3
endured so much tribulation, why don't you want to pull yourself out of such
bitterness? You see that this is an inspiration of Love, who brings the desires
of love into our presence and is derived from so gentle a place as the eyes of
the lady who has shown herself so compassionate to us." Hence, having in   38:4
this way been often embattled within myself, I wanted to write more words
about it; and because the battle of thoughts was being won by those who
spoke for her, it seemed necessary to speak to her, and I wrote this sonnet,
which begins: *A gentle thought*; and I say "gentle" insofar as it spoke of a
gentle lady, for in other respects the thought was extremely base. In this   38:5
sonnet I make two parts of myself, according as my thoughts were divided.
One part, that is, appetite, I call heart; the other, that is, reason, I call soul;
and I tell how one speaks against the other. And that it is proper to call the
heart "appetite" and the reason "soul" is sufficiently manifest to those to
whom I am pleased to make these things open. It is true that in the preceding   38:6
sonnet I take the part of the heart against that of the eyes, and that seems
contrary to what I say in the present one; therefore, I say that also there by the

ivi lo cuore anche intendo per lo appetito, però che maggiore desiderio era lo mio ancora di ricordarmi de la gentilissima donna mia, che di vedere costei, avvegna che alcuno appetito n'avessi già, ma leggiero parea: onde appare

38:7   che l'uno detto non è contrario a l'altro.   Questo sonetto ha tre parti: ne la prima comincio a dire a questa donna come lo mio desiderio si volge tutto verso lei; ne la seconda dico come l'anima, cioè la ragione, dice al cuore, cioè a lo appetito; ne la terza dico com'e' le risponde.   La seconda parte comincia quivi: *L'anima dice*; la terza quivi: *Ei le risponde.*

38:8   Gentil pensero che parla di vui
                sen vene a dimorar meco sovente,
                e ragiona d'amor sì dolcemente,
v. 4   che face consentir lo core in lui.
38:9   L'anima dice al cor: "Chi è costui,
                che vene a consolar la nostra mente,
                ed è la sua vertù tanto possente,
v. 8   ch'altro penser non lascia star con nui?"
38:10   Ei le risponde: "Oi anima pensosa,
                questi è uno spiritel novo d'amore,
                che reca innanzi me li suoi desiri;
v. 12   e la sua vita, e tutto 'l suo valore,
                mosse de li occhi di quella pietosa
                che si turbava de' nostri martiri."

39:1   Contra questo avversario de la ragione si levoe un die, quasi ne l'ora de la nona, una forte imaginazione in me, che mi parve vedere questa gloriosa Beatrice con quelle vestimenta sanguigne co le quali apparve prima a li occhi miei; e pareami giovane in simile etade in quale io prima la vidi.

39:2   Allora cominciai a pensare di lei: e ricordandomi di lei secondo l'ordine del tempo passato, lo mio cuore cominciò dolorosamente a pentere de lo desiderio a cui sì vilmente s'avea lasciato possedere alquanti die contra la costanzia de la ragione: e discacciato questo cotale malvagio desiderio, sì si rivolsero tutti

39:3   li miei pensamenti a la loro gentilissima Beatrice. E dico che d'allora innanzi cominciai a pensare di lei sì con tutto lo vergognoso cuore, che li sospiri manifestavano ciò molte volte; però che tutti quasi diceano nel loro uscire quello che nel cuore si ragionava, cioè lo nome di quella gentilissima, e come si partio da noi. E molte volte avvenia che tanto dolore avea in sé alcuno

heart I mean appetite, because my greater desire was still to remember my most gentle lady than to see this other one, for even though I had some appetite for it already, it seemed slight: thus it is clear that the one way of speaking is not contrary to the other. This sonnet has three parts: in the first I begin by telling this lady how my desire is wholly turned toward her; in the second I tell how my soul, that is, my reason, speaks to my heart, that is, my appetite; in the third I tell how my heart responds. The second part begins: *The soul says*; the third: *The heart replies*. 38:7

> **A** gentle thought that speaks of you   38:8
> comes to linger with me often,
> and speaks of love so sweetly
> that it makes the heart consent to it.   v. 4
> The soul says to the heart: "Who is this one,   38:9
> who comes to console our mind,
> and whose power is so mighty
> that it lets no other thought stay with us?"   v. 8
> The heart replies: "Oh, pensive soul,   38:10
> this is a new little spirit of love,
> who brings before me its desires;
> and its life, and all its power,   v. 12
> come from the eyes of that compassionate one
> who became perturbed at our sufferings."

Against this adversary of reason arose in me one day, at about the ninth hour, a powerful imagining: that is, I seemed to see this glorious Beatrice with those crimson vestments in which she first appeared before my eyes; and to me she seemed young and of the same age as when I first saw her. I then began to think about her; and remembering her according to the order of time past, my heart began painfully to repent the desire by which it had so basely allowed itself to be possessed for several days against the constancy of reason: and after casting out this malicious desire, all my thoughts began to revert to their most gentle Beatrice. And I say that from then on I began to think of her so much with all my shameful heart that my sighs manifested this many times; in fact, almost all of them said, in their issuing forth, what was said within my heart: that is, the name of that most gentle one, and that she had departed from us. And it often happened that one of my thoughts had within itself so much suffering that I would forget it and the place where I 39:1

39:2

39:3

39:4 pensero, ch'io dimenticava lui e là dov'io era. Per questo raccendimento de'
sospiri si raccese lo sollenato lagrimare in guisa che li miei occhi pareano
due cose che disiderassero pur di piangere; e spesso avvenia che per lo lungo
continuare del pianto, dintorno loro si facea uno colore purpureo, lo quale
39:5 suole apparire per alcuno martirio che altri riceva.   Onde appare che de la
loro vanitade fuoro degnamente guiderdonati; sì che d'allora innanzi non
potero mirare persona che li guardasse sì che loro potesse trarre a simile
39:6 intendimento.   Onde io, volendo che cotale desiderio malvagio e vana
tentazione paresse distrutto, sì che alcuno dubbio non potessero indurre le
rimate parole ch'io avea dette innanzi, propuosi di fare uno sonetto ne lo
quale io comprendesse la sentenzia di questa ragione.   E dissi allora: *Lasso!*
per forza di molti sospiri; e dissi "lasso" in quanto mi vergognava di ciò, che
39:7 li miei occhi aveano così vaneggiato.   Questo sonetto non divido, però che
assai lo manifesta la sua ragione.

39:8   Lasso! per forza di molti sospiri,
                             che nascon de' penser che son nel core,
                             li occhi son vinti, e non hanno valore
v. 4   di riguardar persona che li miri.
39:9   E fatti son che paion due disiri
                             di lagrimare e di mostrar dolore,
                             e spesse volte piangon sì, ch'Amore
v. 8   li 'ncerchia di corona di martìri.
39:10   Questi penseri, e li sospir ch'eo gitto,
                             diventan ne lo cor sì angosciosi,
                             ch'Amor vi tramortisce, sì lien dole;
v. 12   però ch'elli hanno in lor li dolorosi
                             quel dolce nome di madonna scritto,
                             e de la morte sua molte parole.

40:1   Dopo questa tribulazione avvenne, in quello tempo che molta gente va
             per vedere quella imagine benedetta la quale Iesu Cristo lasciò a noi
per essemplo de la sua bellissima figura, la quale vede la mia donna
gloriosamente, che alquanti peregrini passavano per una via la quale è quasi
40:2 mezzo de la cittade ove nacque e vivette e morio la gentilissima donna.   Li
quali peregrini andavano, secondo che mi parve, molto pensosi; ond'io,

was. Through this rekindling of my sighs was rekindled my alleviated weep-   39:4
ing in such a way that my eyes appeared to be two things that desired only to
weep; and it often happened that through long, incessant weeping, around
them would form a purplish color, such as usually appears for some torment
that one may suffer. Thus it is clear that for their inconstancy they were   39:5
worthily rewarded; so that from then on they could not gaze upon any person
who might look at them in such a way as to induce them into a similar intent.
Hence, wanting that such a wicked desire and vain temptation should clearly   39:6
appear destroyed, so that no doubt could arise from the words in rhyme that
I had written previously, I resolved to compose a sonnet in which I would
express the substance of this account. And I then wrote: *Alas! through the
might of many sighs*; and I wrote "alas" because I was ashamed that my eyes
had so strayed. This sonnet I do not divide, because its account makes it   39:7
sufficiently clear.

> Alas! through the might of many sighs   39:8
> that issue from the thoughts that dwell in the heart,
> the eyes are vanquished and have not the strength
> to look on anyone who gazes upon them.   v. 4
> And they have become such that they seem two desires   39:9
> to weep and display suffering,
> and oftentimes they cry so, that Love
> encircles them with the crown of martyrs.   v. 8
> These thoughts, and the sighs I send forth,   39:10
> become in the heart so anguished
> that Love there faints, so much does he suffer from them;
> for they have in themselves, the sorrowful ones,   v. 12
> that sweet name of the lady inscribed,
> and of her death many words.

After this tribulation, at the time when many folk go to see   40:1
that blessed image that Jesus Christ left to us as a likeness of his most
beautiful countenance, which my lady sees in glory, it happened that some
pilgrims passed through a street that is like the middle of the city where was
born, lived, and died the most gentle lady. These pilgrims were going, as it   40:2
seemed to me, most pensively; therefore, thinking of them, I said within myself: "These pilgrims seem to me from a faraway place, and I do not believe
that they have ever heard speak of this lady, and know nothing of her; rather,

pensando a loro, dissi fra me medesimo: "Questi peregrini mi paiono di lontana parte, e non credo che anche udissero parlare di questa donna, e non ne sanno neente; anzi li loro penseri sono d'altre cose che di queste qui, ché forse

40:3   pensano de li loro amici lontani, li quali noi non conoscemo." Poi dicea fra me medesimo: "Io so che s'elli fossero di propinquo paese, in alcuna vista

40:4   parrebbero turbati passando per lo mezzo de la dolorosa cittade." Poi dicea fra me medesimo: "Se io li potesse tenere alquanto, io li pur farei piangere anzi ch'elli uscissero di questa cittade, però che io direi parole le quali

40:5   farebbero piangere chiunque le intendesse." Onde, passati costoro da la mia veduta, propuosi di fare uno sonetto, ne lo quale io manifestasse ciò che io avea detto fra me medesimo; e acciò che più paresse pietoso, propuosi di dire come se io avesse parlato a loro; e dissi questo sonetto, lo quale comincia:

40:6   *Deh peregrini che pensosi andate.* E dissi "peregrini" secondo la larga significazione del vocabulo; ché peregrini si possono intendere in due modi, in uno largo e in uno stretto: in largo, in quanto è peregrino chiunque è fuori de la sua patria; in modo stretto non s'intende peregrino se non chi va verso

40:7   la casa di sa' Iacopo o riede. E però è da sapere che in tre modi si chiamano propriamente le genti che vanno al servigio de l'Altissimo: chiamansi palmieri in quanto vanno oltremare, là onde molte volte recano la palma; chiamansi peregrini in quanto vanno a la casa di Galizia, però che la sepultura di sa' Iacopo fue più lontana de la sua patria che d'alcuno altro apostolo; chiamansi romei in quanto vanno a Roma, là ove questi cu' io chiamo peregrini andavano.

40:8   Questo sonetto non divido, però che assai lo manifesta la sua ragione.

40:9   **D**eh peregrini che pensosi andate,
                  forse di cosa che non v'è presente,
                  venite voi da sì lontana gente,
v. 4   com'a la vista voi ne dimostrate,
                  che non piangete quando voi passate
                  per lo suo mezzo la città dolente,
                  come quelle persone che neente
v. 8   par che 'ntendesser la sua gravitate?
40:10   **S**e voi restaste per volerlo audire,
                  certo lo cor de' sospiri mi dice
                  che lagrimando n'uscireste pui.
v. 12   Ell'ha perduta la sua beatrice;
                  e le parole ch'om di lei pò dire
                  hanno vertù di far piangere altrui.

their thoughts are on other things than these here, because they perhaps think
about their distant friends, whom we do not know." Then I said within my-   40:3
self, "I know that if they were from a nearby place, in some aspect they
would appear disturbed, passing through the center of the sorrowful city."
After that I said within myself: "If I could detain them awhile, I would nev-   40:4
ertheless make them weep before they left this city, because I would speak
words that would make anyone weep who heard them." Therefore, after they   40:5
had passed from sight, I resolved to write a sonnet in which I would manifest
what I had said within myself; and so that it would appear all the more moving, I resolved to write as if I had spoken to them; and I wrote this sonnet,
which begins: *Oh pilgrims, who go along in thought.* And I wrote "pilgrims"   40:6
according to the broad signification of the word; for pilgrims may be understood in two ways, one broad and the other strict: in the broad sense, in that a
pilgrim is anyone outside one's country; in the strict sense no one is considered a pilgrim but who goes to the house of Saint James or returns from
there. Therefore, it must be known that in three ways are properly called   40:7
those who journey in the service of the Most High: they are called palmers
inasmuch as they go overseas, from where they often bring back palms; they
are called pilgrims inasmuch as they go to the house in Galicia, because the
sepulcher of Saint James was farther from his homeland than that of any
other apostle; they are called Romers inasmuch as they go to Rome, where
these I call pilgrims were going. This sonnet I do not divide, because its   40:8
account makes it sufficiently clear.

> Oh pilgrims who go along in thought,   40:9
> perhaps of something not present to you,
> do you come from such distant folk,
> as by your appearance you show us,   v. 4
> that you weep not when you pass
> through the center of the sorrowing city,
> like those people who nothing,
> it seems, could comprehend of its pain?   v. 8
> If you would linger to hear of it,   40:10
> surely the heart of many sighs tells me
> that in tears would you then depart from here.
> The city has lost its *beatrice*;   v. 12
> and the words that one may say of her
> have the power to make one cry.

41:1 **P**oi mandaro due donne gentili a me pregando che io mandasse loro di queste mie parole rimate; onde io, pensando la loro nobilitade, propuosi di mandare loro e di fare una cosa nuova, la quale io mandasse a loro con esse, acciò che più onorevolemente adempiesse li loro prieghi. E dissi allora uno sonetto, lo quale narra del mio stato, e manda'lo a loro co lo precedente

41:2 sonetto accompagnato, e con un altro che comincia: *Venite a intender*. Lo sonetto lo quale io feci allora, comincia: *Oltre la spera*; lo quale ha in sé

41:3 cinque parti. Ne la prima dico ove va lo mio pensero, nominandolo per lo

41:4 nome d'alcuno suo effetto. Ne la seconda dico perché va là suso, cioè chi lo

41:5 fa così andare. Ne la terza dico quello che vide, cioè una donna onorata là suso; e chiamolo allora "spirito peregrino", acciò che spiritualmente va là

41:6 suso, e sì come peregrino lo quale è fuori de la sua patria, vi stae. Ne la quarta dico come elli la vede tale, cioè in tale qualitade, che io non lo posso intendere, cioè a dire che lo mio pensero sale ne la qualitade di costei in grado che lo mio intelletto no lo puote comprendere; con ciò sia cosa che lo nostro intelletto s'abbia a quelle benedette anime sì come l'occhio debole a

41:7 lo sole: e ciò dice lo Filosofo nel secondo de la Metafisica. Ne la quinta dico che, avvegna che io non possa intendere là ove lo pensero mi trae, cioè a la sua mirabile qualitade, almeno intendo questo, cioè che tutto è lo cotale pensare de la mia donna, però ch'io sento lo suo nome spesso nel mio pensero: e nel fine di questa parte dico "donne mie care", a dare ad intendere che sono

41:8 donne coloro a cui io parlo. La seconda parte comincia quivi: *intelligenza nova*; la terza quivi: *Quand'elli è giunto*; la quarta quivi: *Vedela tal*; la quinta

41:9 quivi: *So io che parla*. Potrebbesi più sottilmente ancora dividere, e più sottilmente fare intendere; ma puotesi passare con questa divisa, e però non m'intrametto di più dividerlo.

41:10   **O**ltre la spera che più larga gira
     passa 'l sospiro ch'esce del mio core:
     intelligenza nova, che l'Amore

v. 4   piangendo mette in lui, pur su lo tira.

41:11   Quand'elli è giunto là dove disira,
     vede una donna, che riceve onore,
     e luce sì, che per lo suo splendore

v. 8   lo peregrino spirito la mira.

41:12   Vedela tal, che quando 'l mi ridice,
     io no lo intendo, sì parla sottile
     al cor dolente, che lo fa parlare.

Then two gentle ladies sent word to me requesting that I send them 41:1
some of these verses of mine; hence, considering their nobility, I
resolved to send them some and to write something new, which I might
send them along with the others, in order more honorably to fulfill their
petitions. I then wrote a sonnet, which tells of my condition, and I sent it
to them accompanied by the previous sonnet, and another that begins:
Come and hear. The sonnet that I then wrote begins: *Beyond the sphere*; 41:2
it has in it five parts. In the first I tell where my thought goes, naming it 41:3
by the name of one of its effects. In the second I say why it ascends on 41:4
high: that is, who makes it go thus. In the third I tell what it saw: namely, 41:5
a lady honored up above; and I call it then "pilgrim spirit," since it ascends on high spiritually, and like a pilgrim who is outside his fatherland,
there abides. In the fourth I say that it sees her such, that is, in such a 41:6
quality that I cannot understand it: that is to say that my thought ascends,
in contemplating the quality of her, to a degree that my intellect cannot
comprehend; for our intellect is to those blessed souls just as a weak eye
is to the sun; and this the Philosopher says in the second book of the
Metaphysics. In the fifth I say that, although I cannot understand that to 41:7
which my thought takes me, namely, to her wonderful quality, this at
least I understand, that all such thinking is about my lady, because I often
hear her name in my thought; and at the end of this fifth part I say "dear
my ladies," to make it clear that they are ladies to whom I speak. The 41:8
second part begins: *a new intelligence*; the third: *When he arrives*; the fourth:
He sees her such; the fifth: *I know that he speaks.* The sonnet could be 41:9
divided more subtly, and more subtly clarified; but it may pass with this
division, and therefore I do not concern myself to divide it any further.

Beyond the sphere that circles widest 41:10
penetrates the sigh that issues from my heart:
a new intelligence, which Love,
weeping, places in him, draws him ever upward. v. 4
When he arrives where he desires, 41:11
he sees a lady, who receives honor,
and so shines that, because of her splendor,
the pilgrim spirit gazes upon her. v. 8
He sees her such that when he tells me of it, 41:12
I do not understand him, so subtly does he speak
to the sorrowing heart, which makes him speak.

41:13
> So io che parla di quella gentile,
> però che spesso ricorda Beatrice,
> sì ch'io lo 'ntendo ben, donne mie care.

42:1   **A**ppresso questo sonetto apparve a me una mirabile visione, ne la quale io vidi cose che mi fecero proporre di non dire più di questa benedetta 42:2 infino a tanto che io potessi più degnamente trattare di lei. E di venire a ciò io studio quanto posso, sì com'ella sae veracemente. Sì che, se piacere sarà di colui a cui tutte le cose vivono, che la mia vita duri per alquanti anni, io 42:3 spero di dicer di lei quello che mai non fue detto d'alcuna. E poi piaccia a colui che è sire de la cortesia, che la mia anima se ne possa gire a vedere la gloria de la sua donna, cioè di quella benedetta Beatrice, la quale gloriosamente mira ne la faccia di colui *qui est per omnia saecula benedictus.*

Qui finisce

la

Vita Nuova

di

Dante Alighieri

I know that he speaks of that gentle one,   41:13
for he often remembers Beatrice,
so that I understand him well, dear my ladies.

After this sonnet there appeared to me a wonderful vision, in which I saw   42:1
things that made me resolve to write no more of this blessed one until I
could more worthily treat of her. And to arrive at that, I apply myself as   42:2
much as I can, as she truly knows. So that, if it be pleasing to Him for whom
all things live that my life may last for some years, I hope to say of her what
was never said of any other woman. And then may it please Him who is the   42:3
Lord of courtesy that my soul may go to see the glory of his lady: namely,
that blessed Beatrice, who in glory gazes upon the face of Him *qui est per
omnia secula benedictus* [who is for all ages blessed].

Here ends
the
New Life
of
Dante Alighieri

TOPICAL INDEX

The names, titles, terms, quotations, and topics indexed here address the range of interests raised in this volume's introduction and in volume two's commentary, as well as topics raised by the *Vita nuova* itself. The English citations for each topic comprise all instances of usage, and complex topics are subdivided according to their varied aspects. Although this index facilitates reference to the English translation, the international standard numbering and the bracketed Italian terms locate the citations in the Italian original. The concordance that follows this index provides exhaustive access to the *Vita nuova*'s Italian text.

accident [accidente] **25:1** (Love . . . is an accident inherent in a substance), **8** (many accidents speak as if they were substances).

account [narrazione, parlare, ragione] **10:1** (to abbreviate this account), **15:8** (according to five different accounts), **35:4** (all that is narrated in this account), **4** (through this account it is quite clear), **36:3** (because of the previous account), **37:5** (all is made clear by the previous account), **39:6** (the substance of this account), **7** (its account makes it sufficiently clear), **40:8** (its account makes it sufficiently clear).

act [atto, operazione] **2:10** (dwelling on the passions and acts of such a youthful age), **19:7** (a marvel in the act that comes forth / from a soul), **20** (this lady's salutation, which belongs to the acts of her mouth), **20:6** (Love . . . insofar as from potentiality he is reduced to act), **8** (this potentiality is reduced to act), **21:5** (this lady reduces this potentiality to act), **6** (she brings Love forth into actuality), **8** (according to the two acts of her mouth), **35:5** (the acts and state / that I create through sorrow). See **bearing, operation**.

Aeneid [*Eneide*] **25:9** [*Aeneid: Eole, nanque tibi*] (Oh Aeolus, to you), **9** (in the third book of the *Aeneid*).

Aeolus [Eolo)] **25:9** (Juno . . . spoke to Aeolus), **9** (Oh Aeolus, to you).

Alas! through the might of many sighs [*Lasso! per forza di molti sospiri*] **39:8**.

All my thoughts speak of Love [*Tutti li miei penser parlan d'Amore*] **13:8**.

angel [angelo]:

— Celestial: **8:1** (the will of the Lord of the angels). **19:7** (An angel entreats within the divine mind), **15** (*And angel entreats*), **17** (*An angel entreats*), **23:7** (I seemed to see multitudes of angels), **7** (these angels sang gloriously), **25** (angels returning to heaven above), **26:2** ("She is no earthly woman, but one of those most beautiful angels of heaven"), **31:10** (to the realm where the angels have peace), **33:8** (light of love, which beatifies the angels).

— Human: **2:8.** (I seek to behold this youthful angel).

— Pictured: **34:1** (I was designing an angel on certain panels), **3** (I returned . . . to designing figures of angels).

"Apparuit iam beatitudo vestra" ("Now has appeared your beatitude") **2:5**.

appear [apparire, apparimento, parere, vista]:

— Of Beatrice: **2:1** (to my eyes first appeared the glorious lady of my mind), **2** (at about the beginning of her ninth year did she appear to me), **3** (She appeared humbly and properly dressed in a most noble color), **4** (the spirit of life . . . appeared in its smallest veins terrifying), **2** ("Now has appeared your beatitude"), **3:1** (the appearance described above of this most gentle lady), **1** (this marvelous lady appeared to me dressed in purest white), **3** (there appeared to me a marvelous vision), **8** (the hour in which this vision had appeared to me had been the fourth hour of the night), **11:1** (when she appeared from any direction), **23:4** (it appeared that her face had so much the aspect of humility), **26:3** (she appeared so gentle and so full of every beauty), **5** (So gentle and so honest appears / my lady), **7** (She appears so pleasing to whoever beholds her), **12** (makes not only herself appear beautiful, / but each lady), **14** (my lady appeared most admirable), **39:1** (Beatrice with those crimson vestments in which she first appeared), **42:1** (After this sonnet there appeared to me a wonderful vision).

— Of Love: **3:3** (he appeared so happy in himself), **5** (he appeared to hold something all aflame), **6** (he appeared to waken her who slept), **7** (with her he appeared to ascend toward heaven), **11** (to me appeared Love suddenly), **9:3** (the sweetest Lord . . . appeared in my imagination as a pilgrim), **7** (this image of mine disappeared all suddenly), **12** (he disappeared, and I knew not how), **13** (I tell how he disappeared), **12:9** (having said these words, he disappeared).

— Of narrator-protagonist: **4:1** (friends worried about my appearance), **9:9** (to all appearances I kept company with many), **12** (Love . . . / changes, at will, that one's appearance), **15:1** ("you take on so ridiculous an appearance"), **8** (the piteous sight that appears in my eyes), **24:10** (Love appeared happy in my heart coming from a distance), **35:1** (painful thoughts . . . gave my outward appearance a look of dreadful dismay), **39:4** (my eyes appeared to be two things that desired only to weep).

— Of other: **19:9** (let who wishes to appear a gentle lady / go with her), **20:5** (Beauty appears in a wise lady, then), **6** (*Beauty appears*), **8** (*Beauty appears*), **22:9** (whence do you come that your color / appears changed into pity's own?), **23:4** (there appeared to me certain faces of disheveled women), **4** (there appeared certain faces strange and horrible to look at), **5** (the stars appeared of a color that made me think that they wept), **22** (faces of women appeared to me disconsolate), **24** (Then I seemed to see, little by little, / the sun grow dim and the star appear), **24** (a man appeared, pale and weak), **25:4** (years have passed since first appeared these vernacular poets), **35:5** (much pity / had appeared on your face), **38:1** (she has appeared perhaps through the will of Love), **40:3** (if they were from a nearby town, in some aspect they would appear disturbed).

— Reflections: **3:8** (it appears manifestly to have been the first of the nine last hours of the night), **9** (Thinking upon that which had appeared to me), **10:2** (these excessive voices that appeared to defame me), **11:4** (it plainly appears that in her greetings lay my beatitude), **25:2** (it appears that I posit him [Love] human), **29:3** (it appears to befit my purpose), **32:3** (it would appear that I had done it [sonnet] for him [friend]), **33:2** (both [sonnets] appear written by the same person), **2** (as manifestly appears), **5** (it appears that in this canzone two persons lament), **39** (as usually appears for some torment that one may suffer), **5** (such a wicked desire and vain temptation should clearly appear destroyed), **40:5** (it [sonnet] would appear all the more sorrowful).

appetite [appetito] **38:5** (One part, that is, appetite, I call heart), **5** (it is proper to call the heart "appetite"), **6** (by heart I mean appetite), **6** (even though I had some appetite), **7** (my soul . . . speaks to my heart, that is, my appetite).

Are you he who has often spoken [*Se' tu colui c'hai trattato sovente*] **22:13**.

Aristotle [Il Filosofo] **25:2** (local mobility as such, according to the Philosopher, belongs to bodies only), **41:6** (and this the Philosopher says).

Arabia [Arabia] **29:1** (according to the custom of Arabia).

ascend [various expressions] **3:7** (with her he appeared to ascend toward heaven [si ne gisse verso lo cielo), **34:11** ("today makes a year since to heaven you ascended [nel ciel salisti]"), **41:4** (In the second I say why it ascends on high [va là suso]), **5** (I call it then "pilgrim spirit," since it ascends [va là suso] on high spiritually), **6** my thought ascends [va là suso], in contemplating the quality of her, to a degree that my intellect cannot comprehend).

awake [svegliare] **3:7** (I could not sustain my fragile sleep, which indeed broke and I awakened), **21.1** (through her this Love awakens), **1** (how he [Love] awakens where he sleeps), **24:6** (*I felt awakening*), **7** (I felt awakening in my heart), **24:10** (the awakening of the wonted tremor in my heart), **34:9** (Love . . . / was awakened in the ravaged heart).

ballade [ballata] **12:9** (I resolved to compose a ballade), **9** (I then composed this ballade), **9** (*Ballade, I want*), **10** (Ballade, I want you to seek out Love), **11** (You must go, ballade, courteously), **15** (My gentle ballade, when it pleases you), **16** (This ballade divides into three parts), **16** (*My gentle ballade*), **17** (the ballade is none other than these words that I speak).

Ballade, I want you to seek out Love [*Ballata, i' voi che tu ritrovi Amore*] **12:10**.

battle [battaglia]:

— Of Love: **16:4** (this battle with Love battered me so), **4** (the sight of her would shield me from this battle).

— Of thoughts: **14:1** (the battle of the diverse thoughts), **37:3** (this battle that I had with myself), **38:4** (often embattled with myself), **4** (the battle of thoughts was being won).

bearing [atto, portamento] **2:8** (I saw in her such noble and laudable bearing), **22:9** (I see you go with no mean bearing), **26:13** (she is in her bearing so gentle), **15** (*she is in her bearing*). See **act, operation**.

beatitude [beatitudine, salute]:

— Related to Beatrice's greeting: **3:1** (I then seemed to see all the terms of beatitude), **10:2** (her so dear greeting, in which was all my beatitude), **11:3** (it was not that Love . . . might shade me from the unbearable beatitude), **4** (in her greetings lay my beatitude), **12:1** (after my beatitude was denied me), **18:4** ("and in that greeting lay my beatitude"), **27:4** (calling / my lady, to give me greater beatitude).

— Related to the "praising style": **18:4** ("my Lord Love . . . has placed all my beatitude in that which cannot fail me"), **6** ("tell us where this your beatitude lies"), **8** ("so much beatitude lies in those words that praise my lady").

— Synonym for Beatrice: **2:5** [*"Apparuit iam beatitudo vestra"*] ("Now has appeared your beatitude"), **5:1** (in a location from which I beheld my beatitude), **9:2** (I was distancing myself from my beatitude).

Beatrice [Beatrice, Bice] **2:1** (the glorious lady of my mind, who was called Beatrice), **5:2** (the direct line that proceeded from the most gentle Beatrice), **4** (it might serve to speak of that most gentle Beatrice), **12:6** ("Our Beatrice heard from certain people"), **14:4** (I saw among them the most gentle Beatrice), **22:1** (so great a marvel as evidently was this most noble Beatrice), **3** (ladies gathered where this Beatrice piteously wept), **23:3** ("the most gentle Beatrice one day will die"), **13** ("Oh, Beatrice, blessed are you"), **13** ("Oh, Beatrice"), **24:3** (I saw approaching the wondrous Beatrice), **4** ("she will come first [*prima verrá*] on the day that Beatrice will show herself"), **5** ("who wishes subtly to consider would call Beatrice Love"), **8** (I saw Lady Vanna and Lady Bice), **28:1** (the virgin Mary, whose name was in greatest reverence in the words of this blessed Beatrice), **31:3** (*Gone has Beatrice*), **5** (*Gone has Beatrice*), **10** (Gone has Beatrice to high heaven), **14** (I call Beatrice, and I say: "Are you now dead?"), **39:1** (I seemed to see this glorious Beatrice), **2** (all my thoughts began to revert to their most gentle Beatrice), **40:10** (This place has lost its *beatrice*), **41:13** (he often remembers Beatrice), **42:3** (my soul may go to see the glory of his lady: namely, that blessed Beatrice). See **gentle**, **glorious one**.

Bella michi, video, bella parantur, ait (Wars against me, I see, wars are being prepared, he says) **25:9**.

Beyond the sphere that circles widest [*Oltre la spera che più larga gira*] **41:10**.

birds [uccelli] **23:5** (birds flying through the air fell dead), **24** (birds in flight fell from the air).

"The bitter weeping that you did" [*"L'amaro lagrimar che voi faceste"*] **37:6**.

blessed [beato] **19:8** ("I beheld the hope of the blessed"), **23:8** (the body in which had dwelled that most noble and blessed soul), **10** ("Oh, most beautiful of souls, how blessed is the one who sees you!"), **13** ("Oh, Beatrice, blessed are you"), **28** (Blessed is the one, sweet soul, who sees you), **24:2** ("Think about blessing the day I took you captive"), **26:2** ("She is a marvel; blessed be the Lord, who so marvelously can work!"), **28:1** (under the sign of the blessed queen, the virgin Mary), **1** (in the words of this blessed Beatrice), **32:2** (I, aware that he spoke only of this blessed one), **40:1** (the time when many folk go to see that blessed image that Jesus Christ left to us), **41:6** (our intellect is to those blessed souls just as a weak eye is to the sun), **42:1** (I saw things that made me resolve to write no more of this blessed one), **3** (that blessed Beatrice), **3** (the face of Him *qui est per omnia secula benedictus* [who is for all ages blessed]).

body [corpo] **8:1** (her body I saw lying soulless), **11:3** (my body . . . often moved like a heavy, inanimate thing), **14:4** (a wondrous tremor . . . quickly spread throughout my body), **4** (I rested my body), **19:18** (the nobility of her body), **23:1** (in a part of my body), **8** (I seemed to go and see the body), **10** (doleful ministrations that on the bodies of the dead it is customary to perform), **25:2** (I speak of him as if he were a body), **2** (Local mobility as such . . . belongs to bodies only), **2** (I seem to posit Love as a body). See **corporeal**.

book. See **little book**.

book of memory. See **memory**.

The Book of the Remedies of Love [*Libro di Remedio d'Amore*] **25:9** (the book entitled *The Book of the Remedies of Love*).

Brother of Beatrice. See **friend**.

canzone [canzone] **19:3** (I began a canzone), **3** (The canzone begins: *Ladies who have*), **13** (Canzone, I know that you will go forth speaking), **15** (This canzone . . . I will divide more subtly),**15** (*Canzone, I know that*), **21** (*Canzone, I know that you*), **21** (what I hope for from this canzone), **22** (to open further the meaning of this canzone), **20:1** (this canzone was somewhat divulged), **23:16** (I wrote this canzone), **29** (This canzone has two parts), **27:2** (I therefore began a canzone), **28:1** (I was still intent on this canzone), **31:1** (I resolved to write a canzone), **1** (then I began a canzone), **2** (this canzone may seem to remain all the more widowed), **3** (this somewhat sorrowful canzone), **3** (I address the canzone sorrowfully), **3** (*My rueful canzone*), **7** (*My rueful canzone*), **7** (I address this canzone), **17** (My rueful canzone, now go, weeping) **32:1** (I wrote this canzone), **33:2** (I wrote two stanzas of a canzone), **3** (This canzone and the sonnet), **4** (The canzone begins: *Every time)* **4** (it appears that in this canzone two persons lament).

cause [cagione, ragione] **7:2** (my lady was the immediate cause of certain words), **8:4** (you hear what cause makes him weep), **7** ("what cause makes him weep"), **7** (I relate the cause), **8:12** (I tell the cause that moves me), **10.2** (for this cause), **12:6** (asked him the cause), **14** (plead my good cause to her), **14:10** (the cause of my transfiguration), **10** (this cause is unknown), **13** (it is quite evident through its narrated cause).

cause [varied expressions] **12:14** (forgiving might cause [se le fosse] her displeasure), **15:5** (intoxication caused by [per la ebrietà del] great trembling), **16:10** a tremor that from my pulses causes [fa] the soul to part), **19:8** (Pity alone our cause [parte] defends), **22:14** (you cause [fai] pity for you in others).

Cavalcanti Guido. See **Guido Cavalcanti.**

Cavalcanti's Lady. See **Primavera.**

century. See **time.**

chamber [camera] **2:4** (the spirit of life, which dwells in the most secret chamber of the heart), **5** (the animal spirit, which dwells in the upper chamber). See **room.**

chance [avventura] **14:10** (I resolved to write these words in the hope that they would by chance come to her hearing). See **happen.**

Christ [Iesu Cristo] **22:1** (the Lord of Glory who did not negate death for himself), **24:4** (that John who preceded the true light), **40:1** (the blessed image that Jesus Christ left to us).

Christian [Cristiano] **29:1** (she was a Christian of the thirteenth century), **2** (according to Christian truth).

Color of love and pity's semblance [*Color d'amore e di pietà sembianti*] **36:4.**

color [colore]:

— Of aspect: **15:5** (My face shows the color of my heart), **16:4** (I went, almost wholly drained of color), **19:11** (Color like that of pearls she has), **22:9** (your color / appears changed into pity's own), **31:13** (it alters the color of my face) **39:4** (around them would form a purplish color).

— Of love: **3:3** (a cloud the color of fire), **36:1** (a pale color like that of love), **1** (a similar color she showed continuously), **3** (*Color of love*), **4** (Color of love and pity's semblance).

— Of dress: **2:3** (She appeared humbly and properly dressed in a most noble color).

— Of stars: **23:5** (the stars appeared of a color that made me think they wept).

— Of death: **15:5** (My face shows the color of my heart), **23:9** ("I already wear your color"), **20** (my color / . . . made them speak of death).

— Of rhetoric: **25:7** (rhetorical color is granted to poets), **10** (under the veil of a figure, or rhetorical color).

Come and listen [*Venite a intender*] **41:1**.

Come and listen to my sighs [*Venite a intender li sospiri miei*] **32:5**.

compassion [pietà]:

— Of Love: **12:14** (tell him who is every compassion's key).

— Of Death: **23: 27** (you [Death] must have compassion and not disdain).

— Of others: **14:10** (I believe that compassion would grow in others), **15:8** (they sin who do not show compassion for me), **8** (I say why one should have compassion), **22:3** ("Surely she weeps so, that whoever sees her must die of compassion"), **23:16** (*A Lady compassionate and young*), **17** (A lady compassionate and young), **35:2** (a gentle lady . . . watched me so compassionately), **3** (when the unhappy see that others have compassion), **3** ("in that compassionate lady there is a most noble love"), **36:1** (she indeed took on a compassionate look), **2** (I went to see this compassionate lady), **38:3** ("the lady who has shown herself so compassionate to us"), **10** (the eyes of that compassionate one). See **mercy, pity**.

conceive [pensare, comprendere] **19:1** (I began to conceive the mode I might follow), **22:7** (I conceived of this matter), **26:3** (those who beheld her conceived in themselves . . . honest and soothing sweetness). See **consider, pensive, ponder, reflect, think**.

consider [pensare] **24:4** (to consider her first name), **5** (who wishes subtly to consider would call Beatrice Love), **28:2** (consider the proem), **29:3** (considering more subtly), **37:1** (I . . . considered myself base), **41:1** (considering their nobility). See **conceive, pensive, ponder, reflect, think**.

converse [parlare, ragionare] **12:6** (I then began to converse with [Love]), **15:1** ([a thought's] conversation with me), **18:5** (these ladies began conversing among themselves), **19:4** (to converse to ease my mind), **32:2** (he [Beatrice's brother] lingered with me in conversation).

corporeal [corporale] **25:1** (I speak of Love as . . . a corporeal substance). See **body**.

courtesy [cortesia] **3:1** (her ineffable courtesy), **2** (this most courteous one), **8:10** (From this world you have separated courtesy), **10:1** (too many spoke about it beyond the bounds of courtesy), **12:2** (asking pity of the lady of courtesy), **12:11** (You must go, ballade, courteously), **42:3** (may it please Him who is the Lord of courtesy).

cry. See **tears, weep**.

Dic michi, Musa, virum (Tell me, oh Muse, about the man) **25:9**.

Death [morte, partita] **7:2** (if of her departure I did not write somewhat sorrowfully), **8:2** (I resolved to write some words about her [a lady's] death), **3** (*Death villainous*), **5** (villainous Death in a gentle heart / has set its cruel working), **6** (I saw him lament in his true form / over the lovely dead image) **8** (Death villainous, pity's foe), **12** (in the first part I summon Death), **9:1** (after the death of this lady), **14:8** (my dead spirits having resurrected), **15:4** ("Flee, if death disquiets you"), **6** (my eyes, who desire their own death), **22:1** (the Lord of Glory who did not negate death for himself), **1** (the parent of . . . Beatrice . . . to eternal glory passed truly), **2** (parting is painful to those who remain and who have been friends of the departed), **23:4** (faces . . . said to me: "You are dead."), **5** (birds flying through the air fell dead), **6** ("Your wonderful lady has departed from this world"), **8** ("It is true that dead lies our lady"), **8** (the erroneous fantasy that it showed me that lady dead), **9** (I felt such humility at seeing her that I summoned Death), **9** ("Sweet Death, come to me"), **10** (the doleful ministrations that on the bodies of the dead it is customary to perform), **11** (I . . . , calling on Death to come to me), **14** ("This one looks dead"), **17** (there, where often I called on Death), **20** (my color / . . . made them speak of death), **24** (Dead is your lady), **26** (come and see our lady who lies dead), **27** (My false imagining / took me to see my dead lady), **27** (Death, in great sweetness I hold you), **28:2** (although it might perhaps be pleasing at this point to treat somewhat her departure from us, it is not my purpose), **3** (in her departure that number has clearly figured repeatedly), **3** (I will say how this number figured in her departure), **29:1** (her most noble soul departed in the first hour of the ninth day of the month), **1** (according to the custom of Syria, she departed in the ninth month of the year), **1** (she departed in that year of our indiction), **30:1** (After she had departed from this century), **31:5** (After she had departed from this century), **8** (my grief, / which little by little leads me toward death), **11** (Departed from her beautiful person is / this gentle soul full of grace), **13** (thinking of death, / there comes to me a desire so sweet), **14** (I call Beatrice, and I say: "Are you now dead?"), **33:6** (Whence I call upon Death), **7** (a song of pity / that goes calling upon Death endlessly), **37:3** ("cursed eyes, for never, except after your death, should your tears have ceased"), **8** ("You should never, except through death, / put your lady, who is dead, out of memory"), **39:3** (the name of that most gentle one, and how she departed from us), **10** (These thoughts, and the sighs I send forth, / . . . have in themselves . . . / that sweet name of the lady inscribed, / and of her death many words). See **die**.

Death villainous, pity's foe [*Morte villana, di pietà nemica*] **8:8**.

desire [volere, volontade]:

— Amorous: **6:1** (the desire arose in me to recollect the name of this most gentle one), **12:12** (he who sends me to you, / . . . desires / that if he has an excuse, you may hear it from me), **13:8** (one [thought] makes me desire its [Love's] power), **15:2** (I am immediately overcome by a desire to see her), **2** (a desire to see her . . . slays and destroys . . . what might arise against that desire), **18:4** (the greeting of this lady . . . was the end of all my desires), **19:20** (this lady's salutation . . . was the end of my desire), **20:5** (in the heart / is born a desire for that which pleases), **38:3** (Love, who brings the desires of love into our presence), **6** (my greater desire was still to remember my most gentle lady), **7** (my desire is wholly turned toward her), **10** (a new little spirit of love, / who brings before me its desires), **39:2** (my heart began painfully to repent the desire), **2** (after casting out this malicious desire), **6** (wanting that such a wicked desire and vain temptation should clearly appear destroyed).

— Figurative: **15:6** (my eyes . . . desire their own death), **19:9** (The lady is desired in highest heaven), **17** (*The lady is desired*), **23:9** (Sweet Death . . . I greatly desire you), **27** (See how desirous I come / to be one of yours [death]), **31:6** (*otherwise comes sadness and a desire*), **10** (that

doubt [dubbio] **12:17** (this doubt I intend to solve and explain in this little book), **14:14** (This doubt is impossible to solve), **25:1** (Here might doubt a person worthy of having every doubt explained and one might be doubtful of this, that I speak of Love as a thing in itself), **37:4** (in the second I remove some doubt, indicating who it is that speaks this way), **39:6** (no doubt about this could be inferred).

"Ecce deus fortior me, qui veniens dominabitur michi" ("Behold a god more powerful than I, who comes to rule over me") **2:4**.
"Ego dominus tuus" ("I am your Lord") **3:3**.
"Ego tanquam centrum circuli, cui simili modo se habent circumferentie partes; tu autem non sic" ("I am like the center of a circle, to which all the points of the circumference bear the same relation; you, however, are not") **12:4**.
"Ego vox clamantis in deserto: parate viam Domini" ("I am the voice crying in the wilderness: prepare the way of the Lord"] **24:4**.
end [fine]:
— Purpose: **18:3** ("To what end do you love this lady of yours . . . "), **3** ("the end of such a love"), **4** ("the end of my love was indeed the greeting of this lady"), **4** ("it was the end of all my desires"), **19:20** (which is the end of love), **20** (this lady's salutation . . . was the end of my desire).
— Terminus: **2:1** (at about the end of my ninth [year]), **5:2** (the direct line that proceeded from the most gentle Beatrice and ended in my eyes), **12:3** ("My son, it is time to end our fabrications"), **12:13** (at the end offer her a humble prayer), **13:3** ("To what end do you love this lady of yours"), **3** ("the end of such a love must be extraordinary"), **4** ("the end of my love was indeed the greeting of this lady"), **4** ("that greeting . . . was the end of all my desires"), **19:10** (one cannot end in evil who has spoken to her), **20** (her mouth, which is the end of love), **20** (the acts of her mouth, was the end of my desire), **23:15** (from beginning to end), **28** (Then I departed, all grief ended), **31:2** (all the more widowed after its end), **8** (overwhelmed they desist in the end), **33:7** (a song of pity / that goes calling upon Death endlessly), **41:7** (at the end of this fifth part I say "dear my ladies").
envy [invidia] **4:1** (many who were filled with envy sought at once to know what I wanted wholly to conceal), **26:11** (her beauty is of such power / that no envy flows to the others from it), **33:6** (I envy anyone who

dies).

Eole, nanque tibi (Oh Aeolus, to you) **25:9**.

eternity [eternità] **22:1** (Beatrice, from this life issuing, to eternal glory passed truly), **31:10** (to make the eternal Lord marvel), **34:1** (a year was completed since this lady had become a citizen of life eternal), **42:3** [*qui est per omnia secula benedictus*] (who is for all ages blessed).

Every time, alas, I remember [Quantunque volte, lasso!, mi rimembra] **33:5**.

eyes [occhi]:

— Beatrice's: **3:1** (she turned her eyes to that place where I stood), **19:12** (From her eyes . . . / issue spirits of love inflamed), **19** (*From her eyes*), **20** (in one I speak of her eyes), **21:1** (*In her eyes my lady brings*), **2** (In her eyes my lady brings Love), **5** (the very noble part which are her eyes), **22:9** (Have you seen our gentle lady / bathe Love with her eyes' tears).

— Love's: **9:4** (at times his eyes seemed to turn toward a river).

— Narrator's: **2:1** (to my eyes first appeared the glorious lady of my mind), **5:2** (the direct line that proceeded from the most gentle Beatrice and ended in my eyes), **11:2** (whoever wanted to know Love could do so by looking at the tremor of my eyes), **14:4** (fearing lest one might notice my trembling, I raised my eyes), **15:6** (pity . . . / is reborn in the dying sight / of my eyes), **8** (for the piteous sight that appears in my eyes), **16:10** (if I raise my eyes to look), **21:2** (lowering the eyes, one grows all pale), **22:4** (I covered myself by placing my hands frequently over my eyes), **23:4** so powerful a sense of loss that I closed my eyes), **6** (I wept with my eyes), **13** (I opened my eyes and saw that I was deceived), **17** (seeing my eyes fill with pain), **22** (I closed my vilely burdened eyes), **25** (I raised my eyes, wet with tears), **31:1** (After my eyes had for some time wept), **1** (*The eyes grieving for the heart's pity*), **8** (The eyes grieving for the heart's pity), **32:5** (my eyes would be my debtors), **34:1** (I turned my eyes and saw beside me men), **10** (a voice that often calls up / tears of grief to my sad eyes), **35:2** (I raised my eyes to see if others saw me), **3** (I then felt my own eyes begin wanting to weep), **4** (*My eyes saw*), **5** (My eyes saw how much pity / had appeared on your face), **6** (revealing with my eyes my wretchedness), **36:2** (this compassionate lady, who seemed to draw tears from my eyes), **4** (from seeing often / gentle eyes or sorrowful tears), **5** (I cannot restrain these

ravaged eyes), **37:1** (my eyes began to delight excessively), **2** (I cursed
the vanity of my eyes), **2** ("I will nevertheless remind you of her again
and again, cursed eyes"), **3** (when I had thus spoken within myself to my
eyes), **4** (I address my eyes), **6** (The bitter weeping that you did, / oh
eyes of mine), **6** (the part of the heart against that of the eyes), **39:1**
(those crimson vestments in which she first appeared before my eyes), **4**
(my eyes appeared to be two things that desire only to weep), **6** (I was
ashamed that my eyes had so strayed), **8** (the eyes are vanquished and
have not the strength), **41:6** (our intellect is to those blessed souls just
as a weak eye is to the sun).

— Others': **8:5** (ladies invoke Pity, / showing bitter sorrow through their
eyes), **18:3** (One of them, turning her eyes toward me), **19:12** (spirits
of love . . . / wound the eyes of whoever then beholds her), **20:5**
(Beauty appears in a wise lady, then, / which so pleases the eyes), **22:9**
(with eyes lowered, showing sorrow), **10** (I see your eyes, which have
wept), **26:1** (one ventured neither to raise the eyes nor to respond to her
greeting), **5** (eyes dare not look at her), **7** (she sends through the eyes a
sweetness to the heart), **38:3** (so gentle a place as the eyes of the lady),
10 (the eyes of that compassionate one).

The eyes grieving for the heart's pity [*Li occhi dolenti per pietà del
core*] **31:8**.

faculty [virtù, vertude] **15:1** (assuming your were free to apply all your
faculties), **2** ("If I did not lose my faculties and were free enough to
answer her"), **25:9** (through Horace one speaks to one's own poetic
faculty).

faithful of love. See **love.**

fantasy [fantasia]:

— Faculty: **16:2** (when memory moved my fantasy to imagine what Love
was doing to me), **23:4** (at the outset of the wandering that my fantasy
took to), **5** (my fantasy beginning to wander).

— Imagined object: **23:6** (And marveling in that fantasy), **8** (so strong was
the erroneous fantasy), **13** (my powerful fantasy ceased), **18** (Then I quit
the strange fantasy), **29** (I was recalled from an empty fantasy), **30** (what
certain ladies . . . said and did about my fantasy).

fear [paura] **3:1** (that place where I stood in great fear), **7:1** (fearful that my
fair defense was being lost), **5** (in a way I fear to speak of), **9:13** (the

fear I had of revealing my secret), **12:6** (fearing you might be shameful), **13:8** (trembling with the fear that is in my heart), **14:4** (fearing lest one might notice my trembling), **18:9** (I tarried for some days with the desire to speak and the fear of beginning), **19:21** (I fear having communicated its meaning to too many people), **23:11** (with great fear began to cry), **14** (they asked me what I had feared), **17** ([a lady] was moved by fear to bitter weeping), **23** (I saw things greatly fearsome), **33:5** ("the torments you will suffer / . . . / make me most pensive with fear."), **35:5** (fearing lest I display my wretched life), **6** (fear / of revealing with my eyes my wretchedness), **36:4** (I strongly fear lest my heart should break), **37:8** (I greatly fear / the face of a lady who gazes at you).

"Fili mi, tempus est ut pretermictantur simulacra nostra" ("My son, it is time to end our fabrications") **12:3**.

Florence [cittade] **6:2** (the most beautiful ladies of the city), **7:1** (The lady . . . was obliged to leave the aforementioned city), **8:1** (a lady . . . greatly favored in the city), **9:1** (necessary for me to leave the aforementioned city), **14:3** (according to the custom of the city mentioned above), **19:3** (returning to the city mentioned above), **22:3** (the custom of the aforementioned city), **28:1** (How solitary lies the city, once full of people), **30:1** (the entire aforementioned city was left like a widow), **1** (still weeping in this desolate city), **1** (How solitary lies the city), **40:1** (a street that goes through almost the middle of the city), **1** (the city where was born, lived, and died the most gentle lady), **3** (passing through the center of this sorrowful city), **4** (make them weep before they left this city), **9** (through the center of the sorrowing city), **10** (The city has lost its *beatrice*).

For so long has love possessed me [*Sì lungiamente m'ha tenuto Amore*] **27:3**.

form [forma] **6:2** (in the form of a *serventese*), **8:6** (I saw [Love] lament in his true form), **19:11** (in just the form as becomes a lady), **20:7** (one relates to the other as form to matter), **39:4** (around [the eyes] would form a purplish color).

four [quattro] **3:8** (this vision had appeared to me had been the fourth hour of the night), **8:12** (This sonnet divides into four parts), **12** (in the fourth, I turn to speak to a person undefined), **12** (the fourth begins: *Let him who does not merit salvation*), **13:1** (among which thoughts four seemed most to disrupt my life's peace), **5** (The fourth was: the lady through whom Love binds you), **10** (This sonnet can be divided into four parts), **10** (in the fourth I say that desiring to speak of Love), **10** (the fourth: *Then I know not*), **15:8** (in the fourth, I say that they sin who do not show compassion for me), **15:9** (the fourth: *One sins*), **16:1** (four more thoughts about my condition), **5** (The fourth is how that sight not only failed to shield me), **11** (This sonnet divides into four parts), **11** (four things are recounted in it), **11** (the fourth: *and if I raise*), **19:16** (The first part divides into four), **16** (in the fourth, again saying to whom I wish to speak), **16** (the fourth: *ladies and amorous maidens*), **22:17** (This sonnet has four parts), **17** (four manners of speaking were employed by the ladies), **17** (*She bears in her face*), **41:6** (In the fourth I say that it sees her such), **9** (the fourth: *It so beholds her*).

friend [amico] **3:14** (one [Cavalcanti] whom I call first among my friends), **14** (the beginning of friendship between him [Cavalcanti] and me), **4:1** (many friends worried about my appearance), **14:1** (to which place I was taken by a friend), **2** (trusting in a person who had accompanied a friend of his to the extremity of life), **3** (thinking to please this friend), **7** (my deceived friend of good faith), **8** (I said to my friend these words), **20:1** (a certain friend happened to hear it [a canzone]), **2** (thinking that the friend should be served), **22:2** (those who remain and who have been friends of the departed), **2** (no friendship is as intimate as that of a good father to a good child), **23:6** (I imagined that a friend came to me to say), **24:3** (the much beloved lady of this foremost of my friends), **6** (I resolved to write in rhyme to my best friend [Cavalcanti]), **25:10** (this best friend of mine [Cavalcanti]), **28:3** (I will give a reason why this number [nine] was so much her friend), **29:2** (As to why this number was so much her friend), **2** (this number was her friend), **30:3** (my first friend [Cavalcanti] to whom I write this), **32:1** (one [Beatrice's brother] who . . . is friend to me immediately after the first [Cavalcanti]), **3** (give it [a sonnet] to this my friend), **33:4** (this dear friend of mine and relative of hers), **40:2** (These pilgrims . . . perhaps think about their distant friends).

Galicia [Galizia] **40:7** (pilgrims . . . go to the house in Galicia).
gentle [gentile]:
— Of Beatrice: **3:1** (the appearance described above of this most gentle lady),

(After the departure of this gentle lady), **1** (a lady, young and of quite gentle aspect), **5** (villainous Death in a gentle heart / has imposed its cruel working), **5** (what in this world must be praised / in a gentle lady besides honor), **6** (where the gentle soul already dwelled), **9:1** the gentle lady who had been my defense), **14:3** (there in the company of a gentle lady who had married), **18:1** (I was addressed by one of these gentle ladies), **19:1** (those who are gentle and not just women), **9** (let who wishes to appear a gentle lady / go with her), **23:11** (a lady, young and gentle, who stood alongside my bed), **24:3** (I saw coming towards me a gentle lady), **6** (the beauty of this gentle *Primavera:*), **26:11** (it makes them go with her clothed / in gentleness, love, and devotion), **31:9** (I spoke / of my lady, while she lived, / gentle ladies, willingly to you), **9** (the gentle heart that is in a lady), **32:5** (Come and listen to my sighs, / you gentle hearts), **35:2** (I then saw a gentle lady, . . . who from a window watched me), **3** (I left the view of this gentle one), **38:1** ("This lady is gentle"), **3** (such a gentle place as the eyes of the lady), **4** (I say "gentle" insofar as it spoke of a gentle lady), **8** (A gentle thought that speaks of you), **41:1** (Then two gentle ladies sent word to me).

— Figurative: **11:3** (when this most gentle salutation greeted me), **12:15** (My gentle ballade), **16** (*My gentle ballade*), **16:4** (what approaching so much gentleness brought on), **19:6** (I will speak of her gentle estate), **20:2** (*Love and the gentle heart*), **3** (Love and the gentle heart are one thing), **27:3** (as much as he was harsh to me at first / is he now gentle in my heart), **36:4** (from seeing often / gentle eyes or sorrowful tears), **38:4** (*A gentle thought*), **8** (A gentle thought that speaks of you).

— See **noble.**

A gentle thought that speaks of you [*Gentil pensero che parla di vui*] **38:4**.

Giovanna [Giovanna, Vanna] **24:3** (The name of this lady was Giovanna), **4** (her name Giovanna derives from that John who preceded the true light), **8** (I saw Lady Vanna and Lady Bice).

God [Dio] **19:8** (God speaks, having my lady in mind), **10** (God has given her an even greater grace), **11** (God intends to make of her something new), **26:10** (they who go with her are bound, / for beauteous grace, to render thanks to God), **38:2** ("God, what thought is this, that in such a base manner wants to console me").

— **Him** [colui] **42:2** (if it be pleasing to Him for whom all things live), **3** (may it please Him who is the Lord of courtesy), **3** (blessed Beatrice, who in glory gazes upon the face of Him).

— **Lord** [Deo, Segnore, Sire]: **6:2** (the city where my lady was placed by the most high Lord), **7:4** ("Lord, for what merit / has he so lively a heart"), **8:1** (the will of the Lord of the angels), **19:7** ("Lord, in the world is seen / a marvel"), **7** ([Heaven] asks her of its Lord), **22:1** (as it pleased the Lord of Glory), **24:4** ('I am the voice crying in the wilderness: prepare the way of the Lord'), **26:2** ("blessed be the Lord, who so marvelously can work"), **28:1** (the Lord of justice called this most gentle one to glory), **29:1** (that year of our indiction, that is, of the years of our Lord), **31:10** (to make the eternal Lord marvel), **34:7** (placed by the most high Lord), **42:3** (may it please Him who is the Lord of courtesy).

— **Most High** [L'Altissimo] **40:7** (those who journey in the service of the Most High).

— See **spirit**.

God of Love [Dio d'Amore]. See **Love**.

glorious one [gloriosa] **2:1** (the glorious lady of my mind), **32:1** (he was by blood relation so close to the glorious one), **33:1** (so close a relative to the glorious one), **37:2** (she grieves for the glorious lady for whom you used to weep), **39:1** (I seemed to see this glorious Beatrice with those crimson vestments in which she first appeared before my eyes). See **Beatrice, gentle**.

Greece [Grecia] **25:3** (it might still happen, just as in Greece).

greeting [saluto] **3:1** (she greeted me with exceeding virtue), **2** (the hour in which her most sweet greeting reached me), **4** (the lady of the salutation, who the day before had deigned to greet me), **9** (a sonnet, in which I would greet all the faithful of Love), **10** (greeting in their Lord, who is Love), **13** (in the first part I greet and ask a response), **10:2** (that most gentle lady . . . denied me her so dear greeting), **3** (what her greeting worked in me), **11:1** (in the hope of her miraculous greeting), **2** (on the verge of the greeting), **3** (when this most gentle salutation greeted me), **4** (in her greetings lay my beatitude), **12:6** (the greeting that was denied me), **6** (this gentlest one, who is the adversary of all harms, did not deign to greet your person), **18:2** (with assurance I greeted them), **4** (the end of my love was indeed the greeting of this lady), **4** (in that greeting lay my beatitude), **21:2** (whomever she greets trembles at heart), **6** (*and* *whomever she greets*), **26:1** (neither to raise the eyes nor to respond to her greeting), **5** (when she greets others / . . . every tongue, trembling, becomes mute), **34:2** (greeting them, said: "Someone was just now with me").

grief [dolore] **7:3** (attend and see / if there be any grief as heavy as mine), **8:8** (you have given reasons to the grieving heart), **12:1** (much grief seized me), **13:3** (the more heavy and grievous trials), **14:6** (I grieved much for these little spirits), **16:2** (I often grieved when memory moved my fantasy), **22:3** (women with women and men with men assemble for such grief), **3** (they spoke regarding this most gentle one, how she grieved), **23:23** (of grief they [ladies] let fly the fire), **23** (all grief ended), **31:1** (*The eyes grieving for the heart's pity*), **31:8** (The eyes grieving for the heart's pity), **8** (I wish to relieve my grief), **32:6** (were it not so, of grief I would die), **33:5** (such grief around my heart is gathered), (my grieving mind), **34:10** (a voice that often calls up / tears of grief), **37:2** (she grieves for the glorious lady for whom you used to weep). See **mourn, sadness**.

Guido Cavalcanti. See **friend**.

Guido Guinizzelli 20:3 (even as the sage affirms in his poem).

happen [addivenire, avere, avvenire] **3:1** (it happened that on the last of these days), **5:1** (One day it happened that this most gentle one was seated), **9:1** (after the death of this lady something happened), **12:3** (It happened that almost in the middle of my sleep), **14:1** (it happened that this most gentle one came), **16:8** ("Ah! can this happen to someone"), **19:1** (It then happened that walking along a path), **20:1** (a certain friend happened to hear it), **23:1** (it happened that in a part of my body I was seized by a dolorous illness), **3** ("Of necessity it must happen that the most gentle Beatrice one day will die"), **15** ("I will tell you what has happened to me"), **16** (I resolved to write verses about what had happened to me), **24:1** (it happened one day), **3** (it might have happened and it might still happen), **35:1** (I happened to be in a place in which I remembered times past), **36:1** (It then happened that wherever this lady saw me), **39:3** (it often happened that one of my thoughts), **4** (it often happened that through long, incessant weeping), **40:1** (it happened, at the time when many folk go to see that blessed image). See **chance**.

harmony [armonia] **12:8** (Let these words . . . be adorned with sweet harmony). See **melody, song**.

hear [sentire] **5:1** (where one heard words about the queen of glory), **2** (I heard it said behind me), **7:3** (I pray only that you bear to hear me), **4** (I heard it said behind me), **7** (to pray that they [the faithful of Love] suffer to hear me), **8:4** (you [lovers] hear what cause makes him weep), **5** (Love hears ladies invoke Pity), **6** (Hear how much Love paid her honor), **7** ("as you hear what cause makes him weep"), **7** (*Love hears*), **7** (*Hear*), **12:2** (where I could lament without being heard), **6** ("Our Beatrice heard from certain people"), **8** (where she might hear them), **11** (she who must hear you [ballade]), **13**: (if he has an excuse, you may hear it from me [ballade]), **13:4** (Love is so sweet to hear), **14:10** (I resolved to write these words in the hope that they would by chance come to her hearing), **12** ([I] do not hear well / the wailings of those tormented [spirits]), **15:4** (when I am near you, I hear Love / say: "Flee, if death disquiets you."), **17:1** (the reason for taking up the new matter is delightful to hear), **18:5** (I seemed to hear their words come forth mixed with sighs), **19:21** (should it come to pass that many were to hear them [a canzone's divisions]), **20:1** (a certain friend happened to hear it [a canzone]), **1** (having perhaps, through the words he heard, more hope in me than I deserved), **21:3** (Every sweetness, every humble thought / is born in the heart of whoever hears her speak), **22:3** (heard the words they spoke regarding this most gentle one), **3** (among which words I heard them say), **4** (I expected to hear more about her), **5** ("Who can ever be happy among us, having heard this lady speak so piteously?"), **7** (I heard words about her and about me), **7** (all I had from these ladies), **8** (taking what I heard from them), **22:15** (in her [Beatrice's] cries we heard her speak), **23:7** (the words I seemed to hear of their song), **7** (nothing else I seemed to hear), **16** (it [an imagining] would be an amorous thing to hear), **17** (hearing my empty words), **24** (have you not heard the news), **24:10** (I saw and heard certain things), **11** (I tell what I heard), **26:2** (showing no glory in what she [Beatrice] saw and heard), **6** (She [Beatrice] goes hearing herself praised), **31:5** (it would pain whoever heard me), **32:6** (You will hear them [my eyes] call often), **40:2** (I do not believe that they have yet heard speak of this lady), **4** ("I would speak words that would make anyone weep who heard them"), **10** (If you would linger to hear of it [the city's loss]), **41:7** (I often hear her name in my thought). See **listen**.

heart [cuore] **2:4** (the spirit of life, which dwells in the most secret chamber of the heart), **3:5** ("Behold your heart"), **10** (To every captive soul and gentle heart), **12** (Love, holding / my heart in hand), **12** (this burning heart / to the frightened one he humbly fed), **7:4** ("Lord, for what merit / has he so lively a heart?"), **6** (inwardly at the heart I waste away and weep), **8:5** (villainous Death in a gentle heart / has imposed its cruel working), **8:8** (you have given reasons to the grieving heart), **9:2** (my sighs could hardly relieve the anguish that my heart felt), **5** ("the heart that I had you owe to her"), **11** ("I come from distant parts, / where your heart was"), **12:12** ("he has not changed his heart"), **13** ("My lady, his heart has attended"), **13:5** (she may lightly move from her heart's resolve), **8** (the fear that is in my heart), **15:5** (My face shows the color of my heart), **8** (I express the state of my heart), **16:10** (in my heart arises a tremor), **18:1** (the secret of my heart), **1** (certain ladies . . . knew my heart well), **19:5** (if I then were not to lose heart), **9** (into villainous hearts Love casts a chill), **12** (each [spirit of love] finds the heart), **16** (what I would say if I did not lose heart), **20:2** (*Love and the gentle heart*), **3** (Love and the gentle heart are one thing), **4** (Love as Lord and the heart as his mansion), **5** (in the heart / is born a desire), **21:2** (whoever she greets trembles at heart), **3** (every humble thought / is born in the heart of whoever hears her speak), **6** (she brings Love forth into actuality in the hearts of all those whom she beholds), **6** (what, by her virtue, she then effects in their hearts), **8** (in the hearts of others), **22:9** (so tells me my heart), **10** (my heart trembles to see so much), **14** (why do you weep so from the heart), **23:8** (my heart, where was much love), **19** (I alone understood the name in my heart), **21** (Love wept in my heart, where it dwells), **27** (Come, for my heart calls you), **24:1** (I felt the beginning of a tremor in my heart), **2** (Love . . . seemed to say joyously in my heart), **2** (I seemed to have a heart so happy that I thought it could not be my heart), **3** (these words, which my heart spoke with the tongue of Love), **4** (Love seemed to speak in my heart), **6** (his heart still beheld the beauty of this gentle *Primavera*), **7** (I felt awakening in my heart / an amorous spirit), **10** (the wonted tremor in my heart), **10** (Love appeared happy in my heart), **10** (Love seemed to say to me in my heart), **26:1** (honesty came into one's heart), **7** (she sends through the eyes a sweetness to the / heart), **27:3** ([Love] now gentle in my heart), **31:1** (*The eyes grieving for the heart's pity*), **8** (The eyes grieving for the heart's pity), **9** (the gentle heart that is in a lady), **11** (a heart of stone so wicked and base), **11** (No villainous heart's mind is so high), **13** (thought in the oppressed mind / brings before me her who has divided my heart), **15** (To weep in pain and sigh in anguish / destroys my heart), **32:5** (you gentle hearts), **5** (to relieve my heart, weeping for her), **33:5** (grief around my heart is gathered), **34:9** ([Love] was awakened in the ravaged heart), **35:6** (over my heart came a fear), **7** (tears were welling in my heart), **36:4** (I strongly fear lest my heart should break), **37:1** (I often became angry about it in my heart), **4** (as my heart spoke within me), **5** (my heart spoke within me), **8** (So says my heart, and then it sighs), **38:1** (my heart consented to it), **5** (One part, that is, appetite, I call heart), **5** (it is proper to call the heart "appetite"), **6** (I take the part of the heart), **6** (there by the heart I mean appetite), **7** (my reason, speaks to my heart, that is, my appetite), **7** (I tell how my heart responds), **7** (*The heart replies*), **8** (it makes the heart consent to it), **9** (The soul says to the heart), **10** (The heart replies), **39:2** (my heart began painfully to repent), **3** (with all my shameful heart), **3** (what was said within my heart), **9** (thoughts that dwell in the heart), **10** (the heart so anguished / that Love there faints), **40:10** (the heart of many sighs), **41:12** (the sorrowing heart).

heaven [cielo]:

— Astronomical: **2:1** (the heaven of light), **2** (the heaven of fixed stars), **29:2** (nine are the heavens that move), **2** (at her conception, all nine moving heavens were in the most perfect relationship to one another) **31:10** (a ray of her humility / went beyond the heavens).

— Astrological: **29:2** (the said heavens influence the earth).

— Theological: **3:7** (with her he appeared to ascend toward heaven), **8:6** (he looked toward heaven again and again), **19:7** (Heaven, which has no other defect / but to have her), **9** (The lady is desired in highest heaven), **17** (I say what is understood of her in heaven), **23:7** (I imagined myself looking toward heaven), **10** (I seemed to return to my room and there to look toward heaven), **25** (angels returning to heaven above), **26:2** ("one of the most beautiful angels of heaven"), **6** (seems a thing come down / from heaven to earth), **31:9** (she has gone from us to heaven suddenly), **10** (Gone has Beatrice to high heaven), **33:8** (spiritual beauty / that throughout heaven spreads), **34:7** (in the heaven of the humble, where Mary dwells), **11** (today makes a year since to heaven you ascended).

Here begins the new life [*Incipit vita nova*] **1:1.**

"Heu miser, quia frequenter impeditus ero deinceps!" ("Wretched me, for often hereafter shall I be impeded!") **2:7.**

Homer [Omero] **2:8** (of her could be said those words of the poet Homer), **25:9** (reciting in the manner of the good Homer).

honor [onore] **8:5** (what in this world must be praised / in a gentle lady besides honor), **6** (Hear how much Love paid her honor), **7** (honor that Love paid this lady), **11:2** ("Go and honor your lady"), **12:11** (she may not do you honor), **15** (you may receive honor), **21:3** (Help me, ladies, to do her honor), **7** (calling upon the ladies to help me honor her), **24:7** ("Now think indeed of paying me honor"), **26:8** (she was honored and praised), **8** (because of her were honored and praised many other ladies), **12** (each lady, because of her, receives honor), **41:1** (in order more honorably to fulfill their petitions), **5** (a lady honored up above), **12** (a lady, who receives honor).

hope [sperare] **8:11** (Let him who does not merit salvation / never hope to have her company), **11:1** (in the hope of her miraculous greeting I was left with no enemy), **13:8** (another [thought], hopeful, brings me sweetness), **14:11** (I resolved to write these words in the hope that they would by chance come to her hearing), **19:8** (your hope may be as long as I please / there where one is who expects to lose her), **8** ("I beheld the hope of the blessed"), **16** (I say how I hope to speak about her), **21** (I say what I hope for from this canzone of mine), **20:2** (having perhaps, through the words he heard, more hope in me than I deserved), **31:16** (I still hope for mercy from her), **42:2** (I hope to say of her what was never said of any other woman).

Horace [Orazio] **25:9** (Through Horace one speaks to one's own poetic faculty), **9** (not only are they Horace's words).

human [umano] **23:17** (A lady compassionate and young, / richly adorned with human perfections), **25:2** (as if he [Love] were a human being), **2** (things seem to be properties of a human being), **2** (it appears that I posit him [Love] human), **8** (accidents speak as if they were substances and human beings), **9** (Love speaks as if it were a human being).

humility [umilitade, umiltà] **2:3** (she appeared humbly and properly dressed in a most noble color), **3:12** (this burning heart / to the frightened one he humbly fed), **11:1** (with a countenance clothed in humility), **12:13** (offer her a humble prayer), **15:2** (a humble thought), **19:10** (so humbles him that he forgets every offense), **21:3** (every humble thought / is born in the heart of whoever hears her speak), **23:8** (her face had so much the aspect of humility), **9** (I felt such humility at seeing her), **26** (with her she had true humility), **27** (I became in my sorrow so humble), **27** (seeing in her so much humility personified), **26:2** (She, crowned and clothed with humility), **6** (benevolently clothed in humility),**12** (The sight of her makes all creatures humble), **27:5** (so humble is this thing that it can hardly be believed), **31:10** (a ray of her humility), **34:7** (in the heaven of the humble, where Mary dwells).

I felt awakening in my heart [*Io mi senti' svegliar dentro a lo core*] **24:7.**

image [imaginazione] **2:9** (her image, which continually stayed with me, gave Love its strength to rule over me), **8:6** (the lovely dead image), **40:1** (that blessed image that Jesus Christ left to us as a likeness of his most beautiful countenance).

imagination [imaginazione] **2:7** (through the power that my imagination gave him [Love]), **7:3** (then imagine / if I am every torment's hostel and key), **9:3** ([Love] appeared in my imagination as a pilgrim dressed meagerly and in simple vestments), **7** (this imagining of mine disappeared), **15:2** (I imagine her wondrous beauty), **16:2** (memory moved my fantasy to imagine what Love was doing to me), **23:4** (I closed my eyes and began . . . to imagine in this manner), **6** (I imagined that a friend came to me), **6** (I wept not only in my imagination), **7** (I imagined myself looking toward heaven), **9** (In this imagining), **10** (so strong was my imagination), **15** (aware of my false imagining), **22** (afterward, imagining), **23** (in the empty imagining), **26** (My false imagining), **31** (I recounted to them my imagining), **31** (I relate in order my imagining), **24:1** (After this empty imagining), **2** (there came to me an imagining of Love), **5** (following the imagining of her faithful one), **31:11** (No villainous heart's mind is so high / that it can imagine her in some degree), **14** (when the imagining is well fixed in me), **39:1** (a powerful imagining).

In her eyes my lady brings Love [*Ne li occhi porta la mia donna Amore*] **21:2.**

Incipit vita nova (Here begins the new life) **1:1.**

ineffable [ineffabile] **3:1** (in her ineffable courtesy).

intellect [intelletto]:

— Divine: **19:7** (An angel entreats within the divine mind [intelletto]).

— Angelic: **33:8** [beatifies the angels, / and makes their intellect . . . / marvel), **34:11** (Oh, noble intellect).

— Human: **19:2** (*Ladies who have understanding* [intelletto] *of love*), **4** (Ladies who have understanding of love), **41:6** (to a degree that my intellect cannot comprehend), **6** (our intellect is . . . as a weak eye).

intelligence [intelligenza] **25:1** (not only an intelligent being but also a corporeal substance), **41:8** (*a new intelligence*), **10** (a new intelligence, which Love, / weeping, places in him].

Into my mind had come [*Era venuta ne la mente mia*] **34:3**.

James. See **Saint James**.

Jeremiah [Geremia] **7:7** (the words of Jeremiah the prophet).

Jesus. See **Christ**.

John The Baptist [Giovanni Battista] **34:4** (that John who preceded the true light).

joy [allegria] **3:12** (Joyous to me seemed Love), **7:6** (outwardly I show joy), **15:4** (when I come to see you, beauteous joy), **24:2** ([Love] seemed to say joyously in my heart), **7** (then I saw, approaching from afar, Love, / so joyous that I hardly recognized him), **26:1** (a great joy came over me).

Juno [Iuno] **25:9** (Juno, who is a goddess enemy of the Trojans).

know [canoscere, conoscere, comunicare, sapere] **2:1** (many who did not know her given name), **3:9** (I resolved to make it known), **4:1** (many who were filled with envy sought at once to know what I wanted wholly to conceal), **5:3** (my secret was believed known), **8:10** (through her known qualities), **9:5** (I know that her return will not take place for a long time), **11:2** (who wanted to know Love could do so by looking at the tremor of my eyes), **12** (he disappeared, and I knew not how), **12:7** ("your secret is in truth somewhat known"), **7** ("call as witness him who knows"), **7** ("she will know your will"), **7** ("knowing it, she will recognize the words of those who were deceived"), **13** (ask Love, who knows the truth), **14** (who will know how to plead my good cause), **16** (I say what befits it to make known), **13:6** (each thought assailed me so that it made me stand almost like one who knows not which way to choose for his journey), **6** ([like one] who wants to go but knows not where), **9** (I know not from which [thought] to take my theme), **9** ([I] wish to speak but know not what to say), **10** (I know not from which part to take my subject matter), **10** (*Then I know not*), **14:2** (not knowing to what I was being led), **9** ("If this lady knew my condition"), **10** (I . . . would tell her that I know well that this cause is unknown, for were it known, I believe that compassion would grow in others), **12** (If you knew it, Pity could no / longer hold against me), **18:1** (through my countenance many had known the secret of my heart), **1** (Certain ladies . . . knew my heart well), **7** (those words that you have said to us in making known your condition), **19:9** (I wish to have you know of her virtue), **11** (by her likeness is beauty known), **13** (Canzone, I know that you will go forth speaking), **15** (*Canzone, I know that*), **21** (*Canzone, I know that you*), **21:7** (I make it known to whom I intend to speak), **23:5** (I reached a point at which I knew not where I was), **7** ("Don't you know yet? Your wonderful lady has departed from this world."), **22** (to all knowledge and truth lost), **23** (I seemed to be in I don't know which place), **25:5** (knowing how to versify), **10** (I know well some who rhyme so senselessly), **26:3** (those who beheld her . . . knew not how to tell it), **4** (make known her wondrous and excellent effects), **4** (might know of her what words can make one understand), **30:3** (the same intention I know had this my first friend), **31:15** (there is not a tongue that knows how to tell it), **16** (I would know not how to tell you), **37:3** (so that this battle that I had with myself would not remain known only to the wretch who experienced it, I resolved to write a sonnet), **40:2** (I do not believe that they have yet heard speak of this lady, and know nothing of her), **2** ("their distant friends, whom we do not know"), **3** ("I know that if they were from a nearby town"), **7** (it must be known that in three ways are properly called those who journey), **8** (*I know that it speaks*), **41:13** (I know that he speaks of that gentle one), **42:2** (I apply myself as much as I can, as she truly knows).

lady [donna]:

— Beatrice: **2:1** (The glorious lady of my mind), **3:1** (this most gentle lady), **1** (this marvelous lady), **4** (the lady of the salutation), **7** (he gathered this lady into his arms), **3:12** (my lady wrapped in a cloth asleep), **4:1** (my soul was wholly given to thoughts of this most gentle lady), **6:2** (where my lady was placed by the most high Lord), **2** (in no other number would my lady's name stand), **7:2** (my lady was the immediate cause of certain words), **8:2** (I had seen her with my lady), **9:3** (the power of the most gentle lady), **10:2** (that most gentle lady . . . denied me her so dear greeting), **11:2** ("Go and honor your lady"), **12:2** (the lady of courtesy), **12:10** (go before my lady), **13** ("My lady, he who sends me to you"), **12** ("My lady, his heart has attended), **13:5** (The lady through whom Love binds you), **14:5** (close proximity to this most gentle lady), **5** (in order to behold the admirable lady), **6** ("the wonder of this lady"), **9** ("If this lady knew my condition"), **11** (you do not think, lady, whence it comes / that I resemble a figure so strange), **15:1** ("when you are near this lady"), **7** (I do not refrain from going near this lady), **8** (through the mockery of this lady), **16:3** (a single thought that spoke to me of this lady), **4** (I went, almost wholly drained of color, to see this lady), **17:1** (three sonnets in which I spoke to this lady), **18:2** (my most gentle lady was not with them), **3** ("To what end do you love this lady of yours"), **4** (the greeting of this lady), **6** ("In those words that praise my lady"), **8** ("in those words that praise my lady"), **8** ("Since so much beatitude lies in those words that praise my lady, why have other words been mine?"), **19:4** (I wish to speak with you of my lady), **8** (God speaks, having my lady in mind), **9** (The lady is desired in highest heaven), **16** (I say to whom I wish to speak of my lady), **17** (I begin to speak about this lady), **17** (*The lady is desired*), **20** (this lady's salutation, which belongs to the acts of her mouth, was the end of my desire), **21:1** (*In her eyes my lady brings*), **2** (In her eyes my lady brings Love), **5** (this lady reduces this potentiality to act), **22:2** (this lady was in the highest level of goodness), **5** (having heard this lady speak so piteously?"), **9** (Have you seen our gentle lady / bathe Love with her eyes' tears?), **13** (Are you he who has often spoken / of our lady), **23:2** (a thought that concerned my lady), **6** ("Your wonderful lady has departed from this world"), **8** ("It is true that dead lies our lady"), **8** (the erroneous fantasy . . . showed me that lady dead), **18** (calling the name of my lady), **21** (The time must come when my lady dies), **24** (Dead is your lady), **26** (our lady who lies dead), **26** (took me to see my dead lady), **27** (because you [Death] have been in my lady), **24:1** (in the presence of this lady), **2** (the place where my lady dwelt), **8** (I saw Lady Vanna and Lady Bice), **26:1** (This most gentle lady), **5** (So gentle and so honest

compassionate lady there is . . . a most noble love"), **8** ("Surely, with that lady is that Love"), **36:1** (wherever this lady saw me), **2** (I went to see this compassionate lady), **4** (the face of a lady), **37:1** (the sight of this lady), **2** (this lady who gazes at you), **8** (the face of a lady who gazes at you), **38:1** (I recovered the sight of this lady), **1** ("This lady is gentle, beautiful, young, and wise"), **3** ("so gentle a place as the eyes of the lady"), **3** (the eyes of the lady), **4** (it spoke of a gentle lady), **7** (I begin by telling this lady).

— Acquaintances: **3:1** (between two gentle ladies), **6:1** (names of many ladies), **2** (sixty of the most beautiful ladies), **2** (the ninth position among the names of these ladies), **8:1** (it was the will of the Lord of the angels to call to his glory a lady), **2** (her body I saw lying soulless amid many ladies), **6** (a lady she was of so lively aspect), **10** (all that in a lady is praiseworthy virtue), **10** (No further will I disclose which lady she may be), **8:5** (Love hears ladies invoke Pity), **7** (a certain honor that Love paid this lady), **9:1** (after the death of this lady), **14:1** (where many gentle ladies gathered), **1** (where many ladies presented their beauties), **2** ("Why have we come to these ladies?"), **3** (a gentle lady who had married that day), **3** (I, thinking to please this friend, resolved to serve these ladies), **4** (beholding the ladies), **7** (these ladies, noting my transfiguration, began to wonder), **7** (drawing me from the view of these ladies), **10** (*With the other ladies*), **11** (With the other ladies you mock my aspect), **22:3** (many ladies gathered where this Beatrice piteously wept), **3** (a number of ladies returning from her house), **4** (Then these ladies passed by), **4** (most of the ladies who were leaving her), **5** (ladies also passed near me), **6** (After these came along other ladies), **7** (these ladies thus passing), **7** (all I had heard from these ladies), **23:11** (a lady, young and gentle, who stood alongside my bed), **12** (other ladies who were in the room), **12** (the tears they saw this lady shed), **13** (these ladies could not understand me), **16** (*A Lady compassionate and young*), **17** (A lady compassionate and young), **18** (other ladies, who became aware), **29** (I was recalled from an empty fantasy by certain ladies), **30** (what certain ladies, and one in particular, said), **30** (what these ladies told me), **31** (I thank those ladies implicitly), **24:3** (I saw coming towards me a gentle lady), **3** (the much beloved lady of this foremost of my friends), **3** (The name of this lady was Giovanna), **4** These ladies passed near me), **8** (I saw Lady Vanna), **26:8** (because of her were honored and praised many other ladies), **9** (her virtue served the other ladies), **10** (my lady among the ladies), **12** (each lady, because of her, receives honor), **15** (what she brought about in the ladies), **41:1** (two gentle ladies sent word to me).

— Audience: **14:11** (you do not think, lady, whence it comes), **18:1** (certain ladies . . . knew my heart well), **1** (I was addressed by one of these gentle ladies), **2** (The lady who had called me), **3** (The ladies were many), **4** ("Ladies, the end of my love was indeed the greeting of this lady"), **5** (these ladies began conversing among themselves), **6** (the lady who had first spoken to me), **8** (I . . . in shame departed from those ladies), **19:1** (I addressed ladies in the second person), **1** (not every lady, but only those who are gentle), **2** (*Ladies who have understanding of love*), **3** (*Ladies who have*), **4** (Ladies who have understanding of love), **6** (ladies and amorous maidens), **13** (speaking / to many ladies), **14** (only to ladies or to men of courtly ways), **16** (*ladies and amorous maidens*), **21:2** (Help me, ladies, to do her honor), **5** (*Help me, ladies*), **7** (when I say: *Help me, ladies*), **7** (calling upon the ladies to help me honor her), **22:9** (Tell me, ladies, for so tells me my heart), **11** (I call upon and ask these ladies), **17** (the ladies for whom I respond), **23:4** (following these ladies), **20** (I replied: "Ladies, I will tell you"), **31:7** (indicating to which ladies it [a canzone] should go), **9** (I spoke / of my lady, while she lived, / gentle ladies), **10** (you, ladies, she has left), **16** (therefore, my ladies, even if I wished), **17** (the ladies and the maidens), **41: 7** (I say "dear my ladies," to make it clear that they are ladies to whom I speak), **13** (I understand him well, dear my ladies).

— Other usage: **8:5** (what in this world must be praised / in a gentle lady besides honor), **13:5** (not like the other ladies), **9** (the lady Pity, that she may defend me), **10** (I call on my enemy, the lady Pity), **10** (I say "lady" as a scornful way of speaking), **14:3** (the company of a gentle lady), **19:9** (let who wishes to appear a gentle lady / go with her), **11** (in just the form / as becomes a lady), **20:5** (Beauty appears in a wise lady), **5** (the same to a lady does a worthy man), **23:12** (each lady, because of her, receives honor), **23** (saw ladies go along all disheveled), **26** (I saw ladies cover her with a veil), **25:6** (to make his words understandable to ladies), **31:9** the gentle heart that is in a lady).

A lady compassionate and young [*Donna pietosa e di novella etate*] **23:17**.

Lady Bice [Monna Bice] **24:8** (I saw Lady Vanna and Lady Bice).

Lady Vanna [Monna Vanna] **24:8** (I saw Lady Vanna and Lady Bice).

Ladies who have understanding of Love [*Donne ch'avete intelletto d'amore*] **19:4**.

lament [lamentare] **7:2** [I resolved to express a lamentation in a sonnet], **8:6** (I saw him [Love] lament in his true form / over the lovely dead image), **12:2** (my room, where I could lament without being heard), **14:6** (these little spirits, who lamented strongly), **23:23** (some weeping, some crying out their laments), **31:14** (alone in my lament), **32:3** (a sonnet, in which I would lament somewhat), **33:4** (this dear friend of mine and relative of hers laments), **4** (in the second I lament), **4** (in this canzone two persons lament, one as a brother, the other as a servant).

language [lingua] **25:3** (there were no versifiers of love in the vernacular language), **3** (versifiers of love who were poets in the Latin language), **28:2** (my language would still be inadequate to deal with it properly).

language of *oco* [lingua d'oco] **25:4** (if we research the language of *oco*).

language of *sí* [lingua di sí] **25:4** (if we research the language . . . of *sí*).

Latin [Latino] **25:3** (versifiers of love who were poets in the Latin language), **4** (to compose rhymes in the vernacular is tantamount to composing verses in Latin), **6** (ladies, to whom it was difficult to understand Latin verses), **10** (neither Latin poets wrote in this manner without reason, nor vernacular poets should), **30:2** (the words that follow those that have been quoted are all in Latin).

life [vita] **1:1** (*Incipit vita nova* [Here begins the new life], **2:2** (She had already been in this life), **4** (the spirit of life, which dwells in the most secret chamber of the heart), **3:1** (her ineffable courtesy . . . is rewarded in life everlasting), **7:4** (a life so sweet and serene), **13:1** (among which thoughts four seemed most to disrupt my life's peace), **14:2** (a person who had conducted a friend of his to the extremity of life), **5** (no spirits remained alive [in vita] but those of sight), **8** (I have set my feet in that part of life), **14** (the visual ones remain alive), **16:3** (in me remained no more life), **5** (that sight . . . ultimately discomfited my little life), **8** (life almost abandons me), **22:1** (from this life issuing, to eternal glory passed truly), **23:3** (returned to thinking about my enfeebled life), **21** (I reflected upon my frail life), **31:10** (this abject life / was not worthy of so gentle a thing), **15** (what my life has been), **16** (life has fallen so

Love, so like me is she").

— Personified: **2:7** (Love ruled over my soul), **9** (her image, which continually stayed with me, gave Love its strength), **9** (at no time did it allow Love to rule me without the faithful counsel of reason), **3:3** (a master, of an aspect frightening to . . . behold), **10** (greeting in their Lord, who is Love), **11** (when to me appeared Love), **12** (Joyous to me seemed Love), **4:2** (And I . . . through the will of Love . . . replied that Love it was who had so guided me), **7:7** (I tell where Love has placed me), **8:5** (Love hears ladies invoke Pity), **6** (Hear how much Love paid her honor), **7** (a certain honor that Love paid this lady), **7** (*Love hears*), **9:5** (It seemed that Love called to me), **7** (the great portion that Love seemed to give me of himself), **9** (I met Love in the middle of the way), **13** (I tell how I met Love), **11:3** (it was not that Love interposed), **12:10** (Ballade, I want you to seek out Love), **11** (find Love first), **12** (Love is here, who through your beauty changes), **12** (why Love made him look at another lady), **13** (tell her to ask Love, who knows the truth), **14** (And tell him who is every compassion's key), **13:1** (the words that Love had commanded me to say), **14:5** (the power that Love derived from seeing himself), **5**, (Love wanted to stand in their most noble place), **12** (Love, when he finds me so near you), **15:4** (when I am near you, I hear Love), **8** (I say what Love . . . tells me), **16:2** (what Love was doing to me), **3** (Love often and suddenly assailed me), **7** (the dark quality that Love bestows upon me), **8** (Love assails me suddenly), **11** (*for Love*), **19:11** (Of her says Love, "A mortal thing"), **12** (From her eyes, however she moves them, / issue spirits of love inflamed), **12** (you see Love depicted in her face), **14** (You will find Love abiding with her), **18** (*Of her says Love*), **20:4** (Love as Lord and the heart as his mansion), **23:21** (Love wept in my heart, where it dwells), **26** (Then spoke Love), **24:2** (there came to me an imagining of Love), **3** (my heart spoke with the tongue of Love), **4** (Love seemed to speak in my heart), **5** (after these words, Love also seemed to say), **7** (then I saw, approaching from afar, Love), **9** (Love said to me: "This one is Primavera"), **10** (it appeared that Love seemed happy), **10** (Love seemed to say to me), **11** (*Love said to me*), **25:9** (Through Ovid, Love speaks as if it were a human being), **31:9** ([she] has left Love with me, sorrowing), **34:9** (gentle lady for whom weeps Love), **9** (Love, who in my mind perceived her), **35:8** ("Surely, with that lady is that Love"),

38:1 (she has appeared perhaps through the will of Love), **39:10** (Love there faints, so much does he suffer), **41:10** (a new intelligence, which Love / weeping, places in him). See **Lord**.

— Discourse: **8:10** (you [Death] have destroyed Love's charm), **13:2** (One of them was this: good is the Lordship of Love), **3** (The next thought was this: the Lordship of Love is not good), **4** (the name of Love is so sweet to hear that it seems impossible that in most instances its very operations can be other than sweet), **5** (The fourth was this: The lady through whom Love binds you so is not like the other ladies), **8** (All my thoughts speak of Love), **10** (all my thoughts are of Love), **10** (to speak of Love, I know not from which part to take my subject matter), **16:2** (The first [thought] . . . is . . . what Love was doing to me), **3** (second . . . Love often and suddenly assailed me), **4** (third . . . this battle with Love battered me so), **18:3** ("To what end do you love this lady of yours, since you cannot bear her presence"), **3** (Tell us, for the end of such a love must be extraordinary"), **4** ("Ladies, the end of my love was indeed the greeting of this lady"), **4** ("my Lord Love, in his mercy, has placed all my beatitude in that which cannot fail me."), **19:2** (*ladies who have understanding of love*), **4** (Ladies who have understanding of love), **13** (a daughter of Love), **20:1** (desire moved him to entreat me that I should tell him what Love is), **2** (after that discourse it would be beautiful to treat Love further), **2** (I proposed to write words in which I would speak of Love), **2** (*Love and the gentle heart*), **3** (Love and the gentle heart are one thing), **5** (I speak of Love insofar as he is in potentiality), **21:1** (After I treated of Love in the rhyme inscribed above), **1** (how through her this Love awakens), **2** (In her eyes my lady brings Love), **5** (I tell how this lady reduces [Love's] potentiality to act), **6** (she brings Love forth into potentiality where he is not), **6** (she brings Love forth into actuality in the hearts of those whom she beholds), **25:1** (I speak of Love as a thing in itself), **1** (Love is not in himself a substance), **2** (I seem to posit Love as a body), **3** (versifiers of love in the vernacular language), **3** (versifiers of love who were poets in the Latin language), **6** (versification was developed from the beginning in order to write of love), **9** (*The Book of the Remedies of Love*), **33:8** (throughout heaven spreads / light of love).

— Experience: **6:1** (this lady was a screen to so much love as came from my part), **7:3** (O you who along the way of Love pass by), **4** (Love . . . / . .

. / placed me in a life so sweet and serene), **5** (I have lost all my boldness, / which quickened from Love's treasure), **7** (*Love, certainly not*), **14:14** (Love slays all my spirits), **19:6** (Love so sweet in me makes himself felt), **9** (into villainous hearts Love casts a chill), **20:5** ([desire] wakens the spirit of Love), **22:9** (Have you seen our gentle lady / bathe Love with her eyes' tears?), **23:8** (my heart, where was much love), **13** (through some warning of Love, I turned toward them), **19** (Love made me turn toward them), **26:8** (a spirit, soothing and full of love, / that goes saying to the soul: Sigh), **12** (go with her clothed / in gentleness, love, and devotion) **13** (sigh because of love's sweetness), **27:3** (For so long has Love possessed me), **4** (Love grows in me to such power), **33:6** (I call upon Death / / . . . with such love / that I envy anyone who dies), **34:4** (I say what Love therefore worked within me), **4** (I speak about the effects of Love), **4** (*Love, who*), **38:3** (this is an inspiration of Love), **3** (brings the desires of love into our presence), **8** (speaks of love so sweetly / that it makes the heart consent to it), **10** (this is a new little spirit of love), **39:9** (Love / encircles them with the crown of martyrs), **10** (Love there faints, so much does he suffer).

— Lovers: **3:9** (I resolved to compose a sonnet, in which I would greet all the faithful of Love), **7:7** (I intend to call upon the faithful of Love), **8:3** (*Weep, lovers*), **4** (Weep, lovers, since Love weeps), **7** (I call and urge Love's faithful), **10** (whoever shall henceforth be nurtured of love), **9:6** (the simulated love that you have shown), **11:1** (if anyone had then asked me anything, my answer would have been only, "Love"), **2** (a spirit of love, destroying all other spirits of the senses, drove out the feeble spirits of sight), **2** (who wanted to know Love), **12:2** (saying, "Love, help your faithful one," I fell asleep like a beaten child in tears), **14:14** (one who . . . is not the faithful of Love), **19:13** (as a daughter of Love young and forthright), **14** (You will find Love abiding with her), **20** (her eyes, which are the source of love), **20** (her mouth, which is the end of love), **24:5** (call Beatrice Love for the great likeness she bears to me), **9** ("that other is named Love, so like me is she"), **32:4** (In the first I call upon Love's faithful), **34:3** (in that compassionate lady there is a most noble love), **35:8** ("Surely, with that lady is that Love").

— Signs of Love: **4:2** (I spoke of Love because I bore on my face so many of his signs that it could not be concealed), **3** ("For whom has this Love so ravaged you"), **11:2** (who wanted to know Love could do so by looking at the tremor of my eyes), **36:1** (a pale color like that of love), **3** (*Color of love*), **4** (Color of love and pity's semblance).

— Spirit of Love. See **spirit**.

Love and the gentle heart are one thing [*Amore e 'l cor gentil sono una cosa*] **20:3**.

loss [perdere, venire meno] **7:1** (fearful that my fair defense was being lost), **5** (Now I have lost all my boldness), **7** (I say what I have lost), **9:10** (he had lost his Lordship), **15:2** ("If I did not lose my faculties"), **19:5** (if I then were not to lose heart), **8** (where one is who expects to lose her), **16** (what I would say if I did not lose heart), **23:4** (thus came over me so powerful a sense of loss), **21** (my soul became so lost), **22** (to all knowledge and truth lost), **40:10** (The city has lost its beatrice).

Lucan [Lucano] **25:9** (Through Lucan a thing animate speaks to a thing inanimate).

maiden [donzella] **19:6** (ladies and amorous maidens), **16** (*ladies and amorous maidens*), **31:17** (find again the ladies and the maidens).

manna [manna] **23:25** (what looked like a shower of manna, / angels returning to heaven above).

Mary [Maria] **28:1** (the banner of the blessed queen, the virgin Mary), **34:7** (the heaven of the humble, where Mary dwells). See **queen**.

matter [matera, materia] **13:10** (I know not from which part to take my subject matter), **17:1** (I felt it necessary to take up new matter), **2** (the reason for taking up the new matter), **20:7** (one relates to the other as form to matter), **22:7** (I conceived of this matter), **25:3** (To explain such a matter), **6** (other matters than the amorous), **28:2** (I leave this matter), **29:4** (might see in this matter a more subtle reason), **30:1** (the new matter that comes after), **32:3** (pondering the matter).

meaning [sentenza, sentenzia] **1:1** (if not all of them, at least their substance [sentenza]), **3:15** (The true meaning of the said dream was not seen by anyone then), **7:7** (another meaning that the last parts of the sonnet do not manifest), **14:13** (division is made only to open up the meaning), **19:22** (to open further the meaning of this canzone), **22** (I fear having communicated its meaning to too many people), **22:17** (I do not . . . recount the meaning of the parts), **38:6** (by the heart I mean appetite), **39:6** (a sonnet in which I would express the substance [sentenzia] of this account). See **substance**.

melody [sono] **12:12** (With sweet melody, when you are with him), **12:14** ("Through the grace of my sweet melody"), **16** (*With sweet melody*). See **harmony, song**.

memory [memoria, mente] **1:1** (In that part of the book of my memory), **2:10** (words that are written in my memory), **3:11** (memory of whose being gives me terror), **15:2** (it slays and destroys in my memory), **4** (That which befalls me in my memory dies), **16:2** (I often grieved when memory moved my fantasy), **19:3** (These words I stored in my memory), **21:8** (memory cannot retain her smile), **24:9** (as my memory retells me), **34:4** (this lady was already in my memory), **6** (when this lady had thus come into my memory), **37:8** ("your lady, who is dead, out of memory"). See **mind, remind**.

mercy [grazia, merzede, pietà, pietade, pietate] **8:9** (I want you to beg for mercy), **12:12** (after you have asked for mercy), **18:4** (my Lord Love, in his mercy), **23:28** ("You called me then, in your mercy"), **31:16** (I still hope for mercy from her). See **compassion, pity**.

mind [mente, pensiero]:

— Of God: **19:7** (An angel entreats within the divine mind), **8** (God speaks, having my lady in mind),

— Of the narrator **2:1** (the glorious lady of my mind), **16:7** (Oftentimes there come to mind / the dark qualities that Love bestows upon me), **19:4** (to converse to ease my mind), **31:13** (thought in the oppressed mind / brings before me her), **33:5** (grief around my heart is gathered / by my grieving mind), **34:3** (*Into my mind had come*), **7** (Into my mind had come / the gentle lady), **8** (Into my mind had come / that gentle lady), **9** (Love, who in my mind perceived her), **36:4** (through you comes such a thing to mind), **37:2** (I cursed the vanity of my eyes, and spoke to them in my mind) **38:9** (The soul says to the heart: "Who is this one, / who comes to console our mind").

— Of others: **5:2** (so much mind was paid to it), **21:4** (What she seems when she but smiles / cannot be described nor held in mind), **22:14** (Did you see her weep, that you cannot / fully hide your doleful mind), **25:10** (nor vernacular poets should write like this without having any reasons in mind), **26:13** (no one can call her to mind / who does not sigh) **31:12** (No villainous heart's mind).

— In general: **13:2** (Love . . . removes the mind of his faithful one from all vile things).

— See **memory, remind**.

miracle [miracolo] **11:1** (in the hope of her miraculous greeting I was left with no enemy), **21:1** (she [Beatrice] . . . works miraculously), **4** (so much is she a new miracle), **26:7** (come down / from heaven to earth to reveal miraculousness), **29:3** (the factor of miracles multiplied by itself is three), **3** (she was a nine, that is, a miracle), **3** (whose root — that is, of the miracle — is solely the wondrous Trinity).

mock [gabbare] **14:7** (these ladies . . .mocked me to this most gentle one), **9** ("I do not believe that she would thus mock me"), **11** (With the other ladies you mock my aspect), **15:6** (for the pity that your mockery slays), **8** (through the mockery of this lady).

mourn [dolore] **37:2** (you used to make weep whoever saw your mournful condition). See **grief**.

Multum, Roma, tamen debes civilibus armis (Much, oh Rome, do you nevertheless owe to civil wars) **25:9**.

My eyes saw how much pity [*Videro li occhi miei quanta pietate*] **35:4**.

name [chiamare, nome] **2:1** (the glorious lady of my mind, who was called Beatrice by many who did not know her given name), **5:2** (naming her, it spoke, I understood, of the lady), **6:1** (the name of this most gentle one), **1** (names of many ladies), **1** (the name of this gentle lady), **2** (the names of sixty of the most beautiful ladies), **2** (in no other number would my lady's name stand), **2** (among the names of these ladies), **8:12** (I summon Death through names appropriate to her), **9:6** (he called her for me by name), **11** (When he saw me, he called me by name), **10:1** (that lady whom my Lord had named), **12:6** (the lady whom I named for you on the road of sighs), **13:4** (the name of Love is so sweet to hear), **4** (names are consequent upon the things named), **4** (*Nomina sunt consequentia rerum* [Names are consequent upon things], **18:3** (calling me by name), **23:13** (I had called out this name), **15** (leaving unmentioned the name of this most gentle one), **18** (calling the name of my lady), **19** (I alone understood the name in my heart), **24:3** (The name of this lady was Giovanna), **3** (she was given the name *Primavera* [Springtime]), **4** (I inspired the bestower of her name), **4** (consider her first name), **4** (her name Giovanna derives from that John), **9** (that other is named Love), **28:1** (the virgin Mary, whose name was in greatest reverence), **32:6** (the name of the suffering soul), **39:3** (the name of that most gentle one), **10** (that sweet name of the lady inscribed), **41:3** (naming him by the name of one of his effects), **7** (I often hear her name in my thought).

nature [natura] **2:6** (the natural spirit, which dwells in that part that ministers to our nourishment), **4:1** (my natural spirit began to be hindered), **19:11** (she is as much good as nature can make), **20:4** (Nature creates them when she is amorous), **7** (*Nature creates them*).

nine [nove] **2:1** (Nine times since my birth), **3:1** (precisely nine years were completed), **8** (the first of the nine last hours of the night), **23:1** (for nine days I suffered bitterest pain), **28:3** (the number nine has many times occurred), **29:1** (the years of our Lord, in which the perfect number nine had been completed), **1** (nine times in that century), **2** (nine are the heavens that move), **2** (all nine moving heavens were in the most perfect relationship to one another), **3** (The number three is the radical of nine), **3** (through itself it makes nine), **3** (three time three is nine), **3** (three multiplied by itself is the factor of nine), **3** (this lady was accompanied by this number nine), **3** (she was a nine, that is, a miracle). See **ninth**.

ninth [nono] **2:2** (the beginning of her ninth year), **2** (I saw her at about the end of my ninth), **3:2** (The hour . . . was firmly the ninth), **6:2** (in the ninth position among the names of these ladies), **12:9** (this vision had appeared to me at the ninth hour), **23:2** (I say that on the ninth day), **29:1** (the first hour of the ninth day of the month), **1** (she departed in the ninth month of the year), **39:1** (at about the ninth hour). See **nine**.

noble [nobile]:

— Beatrice: **2:3** (She appeared humbly and properly dressed in a most noble color, crimson), **8** (I saw in her such noble and laudable bearing), **9** (her image . . . was nevertheless of such noble power), **18** (I speak of the nobility of her soul), **18** (I speak of the nobility of her body), **21:5** (in consequence of the very noble part which are her eyes), **5** (in consequence of the very noble part which is her mouth), **22:1** (so great a marvel as evidently was this most noble Beatrice), **23:8** (the body in which had dwelled that most noble and blessed soul), **29:1** (her most noble soul departed in the first hour of the ninth day of the month), **34:11** ("Oh, noble intellect, / today makes a year since to heaven you ascended."), **36:1** (I often remembered my most noble lady),

— Love: **7:4** (Love, certainly not for my little worth / but for his nobility), **12:4** ("Lord of all nobleness, why do you weep?").

— Other: **14:5** (Love wanted to stand in their most noble place), **17:1** (new matter, more noble than the previous), **19:9** (who might suffer to stay and behold her / would change into a noble thing), **21:2** (whereby is ennobled whatever she looks upon), **6** (through her power she makes noble all that she beholds), **22:11** (they return ennobled), **23:9** ("Sweet Death, come to me, and be not unkind, for you must be noble"), **27** ("Death, in great sweetness I hold you; / you must hereafter be a noble thing"), **35:3** ("in that compassionate lady there is a most noble love"), **41:1** (considering their [two ladies] nobility. See **gentle**.

Nomina sunt consequentia rerum (Names are consequent upon things).**13:4**.

"Now has appeared your beatitude" ["*Apparuit iam beatitudo vestra*"] **2:5**.

O vos omnes qui transitis per viam (O all you who pass by) **7:7**.

O you who along the way of Love pass by [O voi che per la via d'Amore passate] **7:3**.

October [Ottobre] **29:1** (Tixryn the first, which for us is October).

Oftentimes there come to mind [*Spesse fiate vegnonmi a la mente*] **16:7**.

O pilgrims who go along in thought [*Deh peregrini che pensosi andate*] **40:9**.

One sees perfectly every salvation [*Vede perfettamente onne salute*] **26:10**.

operation [operazione] **4:1** (my natural spirit began to be hindered in its operations), **13:4** (its own operations can be other than sweet), **15:8** (draws into similar operation), **19:20** (the acts [operazioni] of her mouth), **21:8** (memory cannot retain her smile nor its operation), **26:4** (These and more wonderful operations proceeded from her virtuousness), **4** (make known her wondrous and excellent operations), **27:2** (I would say how I seemed to be disposed to her working [operazioni]). See **act, bearing**.

Osanna in excelsis (Glory in the highest) **23:7** (the words I seemed to hear of their song were these: *Osanna in excelsis*).

Ovid [Ovidio] **25:9** (Through Ovid, Love speaks).

the people that when she passed), **1** (people ran to see her), **14** (I say among what people my lady appeared), **26:15** (not only in the women but in all people), **28:1** (How solitary lies the city, once full of people), **40:9** (those people who nothing, / it seems, could comprehend of its pain).

perfection [gentilezza, perfezione] **3:15** (now it [dream] is perfectly clear to the simplest), **23:17** (richly adorned with human perfections), **26:9** (*One sees perfectly every salvation*), **10** (One sees perfectly every salvation), **27:1** (I seemed to have spoken imperfectly), **29:1** (the perfect number nine), **2** (all nine moving heavens were in the most perfect relationship to one another), **31:10** (to summon so much perfection).

Philosopher. See **Aristotle**.

pilgrim [peregrino]:

— Love's appearance: **9:3** (the sweetest Lord . . . appeared in my imagination as a pilgrim), **9** (Love . . . / in the meager dress of a pilgrim).

— Broad sense: **40:1** (some pilgrims passed through a street), **2** (These pilgrims were going . . . most pensively), **2** ("These pilgrims seem to me from a faraway place"), **5** (*Oh pilgrims, who go along in thought*), **6** (I wrote "pilgrims" according to the broad signification), **6** (pilgrims may be understood in two ways), **6** (a pilgrim is anyone outside one's country), **7** (Rome, where these I call pilgrims were going), **9** (Oh pilgrims who go along in thought), **41:5** (like a pilgrim who is outside his fatherland).

— Strict sense: **40:6** (no one is considered a pilgrim but who goes to the house of Saint James), **7** (they are called pilgrims inasmuch as they go to the house in Galicia).

— In spirit: **41:5** (I call him then "pilgrim spirit"), **11** (the pilgrim spirit gazes upon her).

pity [pietà, pietade, pietate]:

— Personified: **8:5** (Love hears ladies invoke Pity), **13:6** (to throw myself into the arms of Pity), **9** (the lady Pity, that she may defend me), **10** (I call on my enemy, the lady Pity), **14:12** (If you knew it, Pity could no / longer hold against me), **19:8** (Pity alone our cause defends).

— Literal: **8:1** (many ladies, who wept piteously), **8** (Death villainous, pity's foe), **12:2** (asking pity of the lady of courtesy), **4** (he seemed to me to be weeping piteously), **13:8** (they accord only in craving pity), **13:10**, (*and they accord only in craving pity*), **14:9** ("I believe that she would have great pity"), **15:6** (the pity that your mockery slays), **8** (the piteous sight that appears in my eyes), **8** (my eyes, whose pitiful look is destroyed), **8** (those who could perhaps notice this pity), **9** (*for the pity*), **16:7** (there comes to me pity), **22:3** (Beatrice piteously wept), **5** ("having heard this lady speak so piteously"), **9** (your color / appears changed into pity's own), **10** (if you return from so much pity), **14** (you cause pity for you in others), **16** (She bears in her face pity), **23:6** (With that I began to weep most piteously), **31:1** (*The eyes grieving for the heart's pity*), **8** (The eyes grieving for the heart's pity), **32:5** (Come and listen to my sighs, / you gentle hearts, for pity desires it), **33:7** (a song of pity / that goes calling upon Death), **35:2** (all pity seemed to be gathered in her), **3** (as if they had pity for themselves), **5** (My eyes saw how much pity / had appeared on your face), **36:4** (Color of love and pity's semblance), **37:6** (other persons weep / out of pity).

— See **compassion**, **mercy**.

poet [poeta] **2:8** (those words of the poet Homer: "She seemed no child of mortal man, but of god"), **25:3** (there were versifiers of love who were poets in the Latin language), **3** (not vernacular but educated poets), **4** (first appeared these vernacular poets), **6** (the first who began writing as a poet of the vernacular), **7** (to poets is conceded greater license of expression than to prose writers), **7** (these writers in rhyme are none other than poets of the vernacular), **7** (a certain figure or rhetorical color is granted to poets), **8** (we see that poets have addressed inanimate things), **9** (poets have written as I have said), **9** (Through the same poet speaks an inanimate thing), **9** (Through Horace one speaks to one's own poetic faculty), **10** (Latin poets wrote in this manner) **10** (nor vernacular poets should write like this without having any reasons). See **faithful of love**, **Love**, **rhyme**, **vernacular**, **writer**.

Poetry **25:9** (the good Homer— here in his *Art of Poetry*).

poetry [cose dette] **25:4** (we will not find poetry written before the present time by more than one hundred and fifty years).

ponder [pensare] **32:3** (Later, pondering the matter, I resolved to write a sonnet). See **conceive**, **consider**, **pensive**, **reflect**, and **think**.

potentiality [potenzia] **20:6** (I speak of Love insofar as he is in potentiality), **6** (from potentiality he is reduced to act), **7** (in what subject lies this potentiality), **7** (this subject and this potentiality are brought into being), **8** (I say how this potentiality is reduced to act), **21:1** (where he is not in potentiality), **5** (this lady reduces this potentiality to act), **6** (she brings Love forth into potentiality).

power [forza]:

— Of Beatrice: **9** (her image . . . was nevertheless of such noble power), **9:3** (the sweetest Lord, who ruled me through the power of the most gentle lady), **10:3** (what her greeting worked in me because of her power), **19:10** (to behold her, he experiences her power), **18** (the effective powers that emanate from her soul), **21:6** (through her power she makes noble all that she beholds), **26:11** (her beauty is of such power / that no envy flows to the others from it), **14** (things that through her power she brought about in others), **27:2** (how her power worked in me), **31:10** (her humility / went beyond the heavens with such power), **38:9** ("whose power is so mighty / that it lets no other thought stay with us"), **10** (its life, and all its power, / come from the eyes of that compassionate one).

— Of Love: **2:5** ("Behold a god more powerful than I"), **12:8** (make clear the power that I hold over you), **13:8** (one makes me desire its power), **14:5** (the power that Love derived from seeing himself in such close proximity to this most gentle lady), **16:3** (Love often and suddenly assailed me so powerfully), **4** (Love grows in me to such power).

— Of narrator-protagonist: **7** (through the power that my imagination gave him), **15:2** (a desire to see her, which is so powerful), **23:4** (thus came over me so powerful a sense of loss), **13** (my powerful fantasy ceased), **39:1** (arose in me one day, at about the ninth hour, a powerful imagining), **40:10** (the words that one may say of her / have power to make one cry).

— See **rule**.

praise [loda, lodare] **5:4** (I shall write something that will clearly be in praise of her), **8:5** (wasting what in this world must be praised), **10** (and all that in a lady is praiseworthy virtue), **18:6** ("In those words that praise my lady"), **8** ("so much beatitude lies in those words that praise my lady"), **9** (speaking always and ever what would be in praise of this most gentle one), **19:4** (I believe I may exhaust her praise), **13** ("I am sent / to her with whose praise I am adorned"), **21:1** (some words also in praise of this most gentle one), **3** (he is praised who sees her first), **26:4**

(wanting to resume my mode of praising her), **6** (She goes hearing herself praised), **8** (my lady . . . was honored and praised) **8** (because of her were honored and praised many other ladies), **28:2** (I would be obliged to be a praiser of myself).

Primavera [Cavalcanti's Lady] **24:3** (she was given the name *Primavera* [Springtime]), **4** (She who comes first is called *Primavera*), **4** (I inspired the bestower of her name to call her *Primavera*), **6** (his heart still beheld the beauty of this gentle *Primavera*), **9** (Love said to me: "This one is Primavera"). See **Giovanna**, **Vanna**.

prince [principe] **30:1** (I wrote to the princes of the earth).

proem [proemio] **19:15** (the first part is proem to my subsequent words), **28:2** (consider the proem that precedes this little book), **31:3** (this . . . canzone has three parts: the first is a proem).

Ptolemy [Tolomeo] **29:2** (according to Ptolemy . . . nine are the heavens that move).

purpose [intendimento, proposito] **5:4** (it is not my purpose to transcribe here), **10:3** (digressing somewhat from my present purpose), **12:1** (returning to my purpose), **18:7** ("those words that you have said to us in making known your condition you would have used with another purpose"), **28:2** (it is not my purpose to deal with it here), **2** (it is not part of the present purpose), **2** (supposing it did pertain to the present purpose), **3** (this fact appears to befit my purpose).

quality [qualità] **8:10** (No further will I disclose which lady she may be / than through her known qualities), **16:7** (the dark qualities that Love bestows upon me), **31:10** (what took her from us was not any quality of cold), **35:6** (the quality of my dark life), **41:6** (in such a quality that I cannot understand), **6** (contemplating the quality of her), **7** (her wonderful quality).

queen [regina] **5:1** (where one heard words about the queen of glory), **10:2** (destroyer of all vices and queen of virtues), **25:9** (Yours, o queen, is the task of examining your wishes; mine, the duty to carry out orders), **28:1** (the Lord of Justice called this most gentle one to glory under the sign of the blessed queen).

qui est per omnia secula benedictus (who is for all ages blessed) **42:3**.

Quomodo sedet sola civitas (How solitary lies the city) **30:1**.

Quomodo sedet sola civitas plena populo! facta est quasi vidua domina gentium (How solitary lies the city, once full of people! Once great among the nations, she has become like a widow) **28:1**.

read [leggere] **1:1** (In that part of the book of my memory before which little could be read), **19:21** (let whoever reads here remember that above it is written). See **lady: audience**.

reason [cagione, ragione]:
— Causal: **17:2** (the reason for taking up the new matter is delightful to hear), **19:16** (I tell the reason for speaking to them), **22:7** (I had a worthy reason to speak), **25:5** (the reason some unschooled individuals achieved fame), **31:5** (first I tell the reason she was taken away from us), **37:7** (to remove from you its every reason).
— Logical: **8:8** (you have given reasons to the grieving heart), **25:7** (reasonable it is that to them is granted a greater license to speak), **8** (worthy is the vernacular writer in rhyme to do the same, but not without a reason, rather with a reason that is then possible to disclose in prose), **10** (neither Latin poets wrote in this manner without reason, nor vernacular poets should), **10** (without having any reasons in mind), **10** (in a way that would show their true reasoning), **28:2** (it is not my purpose to deal with it here, for three reasons), **2** (for the reason that, by treating it, I would be obliged to be a praiser of myself), **3** (the number nine has many times occurred . . . not without a reason), **3** (I will give a reason why this number was so much her friend), **29:2** (this could be one reason), **3** (This is one reason for it), **4** (a more subtle reason), **31:5** (first I tell the reason she was taken away from us), **38:1** (my heart consented to it, that is, to that reasoning),
— Faculty: **2:9** (at no time did it allow Love to rule me without the faithful counsel of reason), **4:2** (Love, who commanded me according to the counsel of reason), **15:8** (Love, counseled by reason), **20:3** (as much as rational soul without reason), **25:8** (poets have addressed inanimate things as if they had sense and reason), **38:2** (moved by reason I reflected about it), **5** (the other, that is, reason, I call soul), **5** (it is proper to call the heart "appetite" and the reason "soul"), **7** (I tell how my soul, that is, my reason), **39:1** (Against this adversary of reason), **2** (against the constancy of reason).

reflect [pensare] **23:21** (As I reflected upon my frail life), **30** (*As I reflected*

power.

sadness [tristizia] **22:4** (such sadness that some tears at times bathed my
face), **15** (Leave weeping to us and sad faring), **23:5** (women roaming
disheveled, crying along the way, wondrously sad), **31:6** (*otherwise
comes sadness and a desire*), **12** (otherwise comes sadness and a desire),
17 (you, who are a child of sadness), **34:9** (each one sadly departed), **10**
(a voice that often calls up / tears of grief to my sad eyes), **35:8** (I said
then in my sad soul), **36:2** (unable to weep or relieve my sadness). See
grief, mourn.

Saint James [Sa' Iacopo] **40:6** (a pilgrim . . . goes to the house of Saint
James), **7** (the sepulcher of Saint James).

salutation [salute] **3:4** (the lady of the salutation), **11:3** (when this most
gentle salutation greeted me), **19:20** (this lady's salutation). See
greeting.

salvation [salute] **8:11** (Let him who does not merit salvation / never hope
to have her company), **12** (*Let him who does not merit salvation*),
19:10 (what she gives him turns into salvation), **26:9** (*One sees
perfectly every salvation*), **10** (One sees perfectly every salvation), **32:6**
(abandoned by its salvation). See **beatitude, perfection**.

say [dire]:

— Compositional: **2:4** (At that moment I say truly), **7** (I say that from that
time forward, Love ruled over my soul), **9** (the art of saying words in
rhyme), **3:15** (The true meaning of the said dream), **6:1** (I say that
during that time when this lady was a screen), **2** (to say that which, as I
composed it, wonderfully came to pass), **7:7** (the words of Jeremiah the
prophet that say), **7** (I say what I have lost), **8:7** (I say "as you hear
what cause makes him weep"), **10:1** (I say that in a short time I made
her my defense), **11:1** (I say that when she appeared from any direction),
12:1 (I say that after my beatitude was denied), **7** (say that you pray him
to tell it to her), **16** (I say what befits it to make known), **17** (One could
indeed oppose me and say that it is not understood), **17** (I say that this
doubt I intend to solve), **13:1** (having already said the words that Love
had commanded me to say), **9** (wish to speak but know not what to say),
10 (I say and submit that all my thoughts are of Love), **10** (I say that
they are diverse, and I expound their diversity), **10** (I say in what respect
they all seem to accord), **10** (I say that desiring to speak of Love, I know

not from which part to take my subject matter), **10** (I say "lady" as a
scornful way of speaking), **14:4** (I say that I rested my body, to disguise
my tremor, on a painting that went round the walls of the house), **7** (I
say that many of these ladies, noting my transfiguration, began to
wonder), **14** (I say that Love slays all my spirits), **15:7** (I say what
comes over me when I approach her), **8** (I say what Love, counseled by
reason, tells me), **8** (I say how all confidence leaves me), **8** (I say that
they sin who do not show compassion for me), **8** (I say why one should
have compassion), **16:11** (I say that the second part begins with), **19:2**
(I say that my tongue spoke as if it moved by itself), **2** (my tongue
spoke as if it moved by itself, and said), **5** (I say that as I think of her
worth), **9** (I say, let who wishes to appear a gentle lady / go with her),
16 (I say to whom I wish to speak), **16** (I say what I myself seem to
feel), **16** (I say how I hope to speak about her), **16** (saying to whom I
wish to speak), **16** (*I say*), **17** (say: *An angel entreats*), **17** (I say what is
understood of her in heaven), **18** (*Of her says Love*), **21** (I say: *Canzone,
I know that you*), **21** (I say what I hope for from this canzone of mine),
22 (I do say that to open further the meaning of this canzone), **20:7** (I
say in what subject lies this potentiality), **7** (I say how this subject and
this potentiality are brought into being), **8** (say: *Beauty appears*), **8** (I
say how this potentiality is reduced to act), **21:1** (I felt a desire to say
some words also in praise of this most gentle one), **5** (I say the same), **6**
(I say how through her power she makes noble all that she beholds), **6**
(this is tantamount to saying that she brings Love forth into
potentiality), **6** (in the second I say how she brings Love forth into
actuality), **6** (I say what, by her virtue, she then effects in their hearts), **7**
(I say: *Help me, ladies*), **8** (I say: *Every sweetness*), **8** (I say the same as
already said in the first part), **8** (I do not say of the latter how it works),
23:2 (I say that on the ninth day), **29** (I say, speaking to an unspecified
person), **29** (I recount what I said to them), **31** (I say: *As I reflected
upon*), **31** (saying at what hour they called me), **24: 2** (I say that there
came to me an imagining of Love), **6** (omitting certain words that
seemed better left unsaid), **10** (which says how I felt), **10** (second says
what Love seemed to say to me in my heart), **10** (*saying: "Now think"*),
25:2 (three things that I say about him), **2** (I say that I saw him
approach), **2** (I also say of him that he smiled), **3** (I say that among us),
8 ([poets] have said of things non-existent that they speak), **8** ([poets]

words that you have said to us), **8** ([I] departed from those ladies, saying), **19:16** (what I would say if I did not lose heart), **22:3** (I heard them say: "Surely she weeps so, that whoever sees her must die of compassion"), **22** (ladies also passed near me who went along saying among themselves), **6** (other ladies, who approached saying), **6** (Others then said about me), **23:3** (sighing heavily, I said within myself), **4** (disheveled women, who said to me: "You, too, will die"), **4** (faces strange and horrible to look at, which said to me: "You are dead"), **6** (a friend came to me to say), **8** (she seemed to say: "I am beholding the font of peace"), **9** (I summoned Death, and said), **12** ([ladies] believing that I was dreaming, and said), **13** (at the point where I wanted to say), **13** (I had already said "Oh, Beatrice"), **14** (when they saw me, they began to say), **14** (to say among themselves), **14** (many things they said to comfort me), **18** (One said: "Do not sleep," / and another: "Why so disheartened"), **21** (sighing I said in thought), **22** (they said to me time and again: —You will die), **25** (had they said anything else, I would tell you), **27** (I said: —Death, in great sweetness I hold you), **28** (I said, turning toward the high kingdom), **24** (a man appeared, pale and weak, / saying), **30** (what certain ladies, and one in particular, said), **24:4** (John who preceded the true light, saying), **26:2** (Many said, after she had passed), **2** (And others said: "She is a marvel"), **31:14** (I call Beatrice, and I say: "Are you now dead"), **32:2** (I, aware that he spoke only of this blessed one, said that I would do what he asked), **33:6** (I say, "My soul, why don't you go"), **6** (say, "Come to me"), **34:2** (I arose, and greeting them, said), **35:3** (I said within myself), **8** (I said then in my sad soul), **38:2** (I said within myself), **40:2** (I said within myself), **3** (Then I said within myself), **4** (After that I said within myself), **5** (what I had said within myself), **10** (the words that one may say of her).

— Figurative: **1:1** (a rubric is found, which says: *Incipit vita nova* [Here begins the new life]), **2:4** (trembling it said these words), **5** (to the spirits of sight, it said these words), **6** (the natural spirit . . . said these words), **3:5** (he [Love] seemed to say to me these words), **9:5** (Love called to me and said), **7** (these words said, this image of mine disappeared), **11** ([Love] said: "I come from distant parts"), **13** (I tell what he said to me), **11:2** (a spirit of love . . . drove out the feeble spirits of sight, saying to them), **12:4** ([Love] said these words to me), **5** (I said to him [Love] these words), **9** (having said these words, he disappeared), **14:6** (these little spirits, who lamented strongly and said), **15:2** (another, a humble thought, and it said), **4** (I hear Love / say: "Flee, if death disquiets you"), **19:7** (An angel entreats within the divine mind, / and says), **8** (one is who expects to lose her, / and will say in hell: O evil born), **11** (Of her says Love: "A mortal thing"), **13** (where you [canzone] arrive you say), **23:8** (my heart, where was much love, said to me), **26** (true humility, / that seemed to say: —I rest in peace), **24:2** (he [Love] seemed to say joyously in my heart), **4** (Love seemed to speak in my heart, and to say), **4** (it is tantamount to saying, "she will come first"), **5** (Love also seemed to say), **7** (saying: "Now think indeed of paying me [Love] honor"), **9** (Love said to me: "This one is Primavera"), **10** (what Love seemed to say to me in my heart), **11** (*Love said to me*), **25:9** (Wars against me, I see, wars are being prepared, he says]), **26:7** (a spirit, soothing and full of love, / that goes saying to the soul: Sigh), **34:5** (some [sighs] were saying certain words), **9** ([Love] said to the sighs: "Go forth"), **11** ([sighs] issued saying: Oh, noble intellect), **37:8** (So says my heart, and then it sighs), **38:3** (Then arose another thought, and it said to me), **7** (*The soul says*), **9** (The soul says to the heart), **39:3** (almost all of them [sighs] said, in their issuing forth), **3** (what was said within my heart).

— See **speak**.

screen lady. See **lady**.

secret [secreto] **2:4** (the most secret chamber of the heart), **5:3** (my secret had not been revealed), **3** (my secret was believed), **9:13** (the fear I had of revealing my secret), **12:7** (your secret is in truth somewhat known to her), **18:1** (the secret of my heart).

serve [servire] **5:4** (it might serve to speak of that most gentle Beatrice), **9:11** ("I bring it to serve a new delight"), **12:13** ("in your service has he [faith] been molded"), **13** (one shall see a good servant obey) **14** (of your servant speak what you will), **14:2** ("To insure that they are worthily served"), **3** (I, thinking to please this friend, resolved to serve these ladies), **19:15** (the third is almost a servant to the preceding words), **21** (I add a stanza almost as a servant to the others), **20:2** (thinking that the friend should be served), **26:9** (her virtue served the other ladies), **33:1** (I saw how poor and bare a service it seemed for so close a relative of the glorious one), **4** (one as a brother, the other as a servant), **40:7** (journey in the service of the Most High).

serventese **6:2** (I composed an epistle in the form of a *serventese*).

sigh [sospiro] **9:2** (my sighs could hardly relieve the anguish), **7** (accompanied by many sighs), **10** (sighing he came pensively), **10:1** (the lady . . . named on the road of sighs), **12:3** (he seemed to call me, sighing), **6** (the lady whom I named for you on the road of sighs), **18:5** (I seemed to hear their words come forth mixed with sighs), **21:2** (for each fault one then sighs), **23:3** (sighing heavily, I said), **21** (sighing I said), **26:3** (nor was there anyone who . . . need not immediately sigh), **7** (as spirit . . . / goes saying to the soul: Sigh), **13** (who does not sigh because of love's sweetness), **31:6** (*My sighs give me great anguish*), **12** (to sigh and to die of weeping), **13** (My sighs give me great anguish), **15** (To weep in pain and sigh in anguish), **32:3** (*Come and listen to my sighs*), **5** (Come and listen to my sighs), **33:4** (*There gathers in my sighs*), **7** (There gathers in my sighs / a voice of pity), **34:5** (all my signs issued speaking), **9** (said to the sighs: "Go forth"), **37:3** (anguished sighs assailed me), **8** (So says my heart, and then it sighs), **39:3** (my sighs manifested this many times), **4** (this rekindling of my sighs), **39:6** (*Alas! through the might of many sighs*), **8** (Alas! through the might of many sighs), **10** (the sighs I send forth), **40:10** (the heart of many sighs tells me), **41:10** (the sigh that issues from my heart).

sight [viso] **2:5** (the spirits of sight), **11:2** (a spirit of love . . . drove out the feeble spirits of sight), **14:5** (no spirits remained alive but those of sight), **15:6** (the dying sight / of my eyes), **8** (the piteous sight that appears in my eyes), **16:4** (the sight of her would shield me from this battle), **5** (how that sight not only failed), **26:12** (The sight of her makes all creatures humble), **15** (*The sight of her*), **33:7** (her beauty, / taking itself from our sight), **7** (my heart, / which was moved by your sight), **36:2** (this compassionate lady, who seemed to draw tears from my eyes by her sight), **37:1** (the sight of this lady), **38:1** (I recovered the sight of this lady), **40:5** (after they [pilgrims] had passed from sight).

sign [insegna] **4:2** (I spoke of Love because I bore on my face so many of his signs), **28:1** (under the sign of the blessed queen), **40:6** (I wrote "pilgrims" according to the broad signification of the word).

similitude [similitudine] **12:4** (*"Ego tanquam centrum circuli, cui simili modo se habent circumferentie partes; tu autem non sic"* ["I am like the center of a circle, to which all the points of the circumference bear the same relation; you, however, are not"), **15:8** (the mockery of this lady, which draws into similar operation those who could perhaps notice this pity), **29:3** (this number was she herself; I speak by similitude), **36:1** (for a similar color she showed continuously), **39:5** (who might look at them [weeping eyes] in such a way as to induce them into a similar intent).

sin [peccato] **15:6** (One sins who then sees me / and does not comfort my affrighted soul), **8** (they sin who do not show compassion for me), **9** (*One sins*), **22:15** (one sins who ever comforts us).

sing [cantare] **12:10** (my excuse, which you must sing), **23:7** (these angels sang gloriously). See **melody, song.**

sleep [dormire] **3:3** (thinking of her, I was overcome by a sweet sleep), **4** (I seemed to see in his arms a person asleep), **3:6** (he appeared to waken her who slept), **7** (I could not sustain my fragile sleep), **9** (I wrote to them what I had seen in my sleep), **12** (my lady wrapped in a cloth asleep), **12:2** (I fell asleep like a beaten child in tears), **3** (almost in the middle of my sleep), **9** (having said these words, he disappeared, and my sleep was broken), **20:4** (Love as Lord and the heart as his mansion, / in which, sleeping, he rests), **21:1** (how he [Love] awakens where he sleeps), **23:12** ("Don't sleep any more"), **18** (One said: "Do not sleep"), **24:7** (I felt awakening in my heart / an amorous spirit that slept).

smile [sorriso] **4:4** (I regarded them smiling and said nothing), **21:4** (What she seems when she but smiles), **8** (her wonderful smile), **8** (memory cannot retain her smile), **24:7** (with each word he [Love] smiled), **25:2** (I also say of him that he smiled).

So gentle and so honest appears [*Tanto gentile e tanto onesta pare*] **26:5**.

song [sono, canto] **23:7** (the words I seemed to hear of their song). See **melody, sing.**

sonnet [sonetto] **3:9** (I resolved to compose a sonnet), **9** (I then began this sonnet), **13** (This sonnet divides into two parts), **14** (This sonnet was answered by many), **14** (one whom I call first among my friends, who then wrote a sonnet), **7:2** (I resolved to express a lamentation in a sonnet), **2** (my lady was the immediate cause of certain words in the sonnet), **2** (I then wrote this sonnet), **7** (This sonnet has two principal parts) **7** (another meaning that the last parts of the sonnet do not manifest), **8:3** (I wrote then these two sonnets), **7** (The first sonnet divides into three parts), **12** (This sonnet divides into four parts), **9:8** (I began this sonnet about the event), **13** (This sonnet has three parts), **13:7** (I then wrote this sonnet), **10** (This sonnet can be divided into four parts), **14:10** (I then wrote this sonnet), **13** (This sonnet I do not divide into parts), **14** (the occasion of this sonnet), **15:3** (I wrote this sonnet), **7** (This sonnet divides into two parts), **16:1** (This sonnet divides into four parts), **6** (Therefore I wrote this sonnet), **11**(This sonnet divides into four parts), **17:1** (After I wrote these three sonnets), **20:2** (I wrote this sonnet), **6** (This sonnet divides into two parts), **21:1** (I wrote this sonnet), **5** (This sonnet has three parts), **22:8** (I wrote two sonnets), **11** (This sonnet divides into two parts), **12** (Here following is the other sonnet), **17** (This sonnet has four parts), **24:6** (I wrote this sonnet), **10** (This sonnet has many parts) **26:4** (Then I wrote this sonnet), **8** (This sonnet is . . . open to understanding), **9** (I then wrote this other sonnet), **26:14** (This sonnet has three parts), **27:1** (in these two preceding sonnets), **2** (not believing that I could relate this in the brevity of a sonnet, I therefore began a canzone), **32:3** (I resolved to write a sonnet), **3** (Later, pondering the matter, I resolved to write a sonnet), **33:1** (After I had written this sonnet), **2** (before I gave him the sonnet), **3** (the sonnet transcribed above), **34:3** (I then wrote this sonnet), **4** (this sonnet has three parts), **6** (In this same way does the sonnet divide), **35:4** (Therefore I resolved to write a sonnet), **4** (The sonnet begins: *My eyes saw*), **36:3** (I wrote this sonnet), **37:3** (I resolved to write a sonnet), **3** (I wrote this sonnet), **38:4** (I wrote this sonnet), **5** (In this sonnet I make two parts of myself), **6** (in the preceding sonnet), **38:7** (This sonnet has three parts), **39:6** (I resolved to compose a sonnet), **7** (This sonnet I do not divide), **40:5** (I resolved to write a sonnet), **5** (I wrote this sonnet), **8** (This sonnet I do not divide), **41:1** (I then wrote a sonnet), **1** (I sent it to them accompanied by the previous sonnet), **2** (The sonnet that I then wrote), **9** (The sonnet could be divided more subtly), **42:1** (After this sonnet there appeared to me a wonderful vision).

sorrow [dolore] **7:2** (if of her departure I did not write somewhat sorrowfully), **7** (see if there be a sorrow like my sorrow), **8:5** (ladies invoke Pity, / showing bitter sorrow through their eyes), **22:2** (this lady was most bitterly filled with sorrow), **9** (with eyes lowered, showing sorrow), **23:27** (I became in my sorrow so humble), **31:1** (they [the eyes] could not relieve my sorrow), **1** (I would relieve it with some sorrowful verses), **3** (this somewhat sorrowful canzone), **3** (I address the canzone sorrowfully), **9** (left Love with me, sorrowing), **32:4** (I speak of my sorrowful condition), **35:5** (I bear through sorrow many times), **36:4** (gentle eyes or sorrowful tears), **39:10** (these sorrowful ones [sighs]), **40:3** ("the center of the sorrowful city"), **40:5** (so that it [sonnet] would appear all the more sorrowful), **9** (the center of the sorrowing city), **41:13** (the sorrowing heart).

soul [anima]:
— Beatrice: **16:28** (Blessed is the one, sweet soul, who sees you), **19:7** (a marvel in that act that comes forth / from a soul), **18** (I speak of the nobility of her soul), **18** (the effective powers that emanate from her soul), **23:8** (the body in which had dwelled that most noble and blessed soul), **10** ("Oh, most beautiful of souls"), **29:1** (her most noble soul departed), **31:11** (this gentle soul full of grace).
— Narrator-protagonist: **2:7** (Love ruled over my soul), **4:1** (my soul was wholly given to thoughts of this most gentle lady), **15:6** (my affrighted soul), **16:10** (a tremor / that . . . causes the soul to part), **23:21** (my soul became . . . lost), **27:4** (my frail soul feels / so much sweetness), **31:1** (pain had become the destroyer of my soul), **32:6** (in the name of the suffering soul), **33:5** ("My soul, why don't you go"), **35:8** (I said then in my sad soul), **38:7** (I tell how my soul, that is, my reason, speaks to my heart), **7** (*The soul says*), **9** (The soul says to the heart: "Who is this one"), **10** (The heart replies: "Oh, pensive soul"), **42:3** (may it please Him who is the Lord of courtesy that my soul may go to see the glory of his lady).
— Others: **3:9** (*To every captive soul*), **3:10** (To every captive soul and gentle heart), **8:1** (her body I saw lying soulless amid many ladies), **6** (where the gentle soul already dwelled).
— General: **31:12** (of every consolation the soul is stripped), **26:7** (that goes saying to the soul: Sigh).
— Principles: **20:3** (as much as rational soul without reason), **38:5** (appetite, I call heart; the other, that is, reason, I call soul), **5** (it is proper to call the heart "appetite" and the reason "soul"), **41:6** (our intellect is to those blessed souls just as a weak eye is to the sun).

speak [parlare]:

— Compositional: **5:4** (to speak of that most gentle Beatrice), **8:7** (I speak of a certain honor that Love paid this lady), **12** (speaking to her, I tell the cause that moves me to chide her), **12** (I turn to speak to a person undefined), **12:14** (of your servant speak what you will), **17** (the ballade is none other than these words that I speak), **13:10** (say "lady" as a scornful way of speaking), **17:1** (After I wrote these three sonnets in which I spoke to this lady), (thereafter I would keep silent in that I would not speak to her), **18:9** (I resolved to take as the subject of my speaking always and ever what would be in praise of this most gentle one), **9** (the desire to speak and the fear of beginning), **19:2** (my tongue spoke as if it moved by itself), **13** (Canzone, I know that you will go forth speaking), **16** (I wish to speak of my lady), **16** (why I wish to speak), **16** (I hope to speak about her), **16** (saying to whom I wish to speak), **16** (I tell the reason for speaking to them), **16** (*And I do not wish to speak*), **17** (I begin to speak about this lady), **18** (I speak of the nobility of her soul), **19** (I speak of some of the beauties), **19** (I speak of some beauties with reference to specific parts), **20** (I speak of her eyes), **20** (I speak of her mouth), **20:2** (words in which I would speak of Love), **6** (the first I speak of Love insofar as he is in potentiality; in the second I speak of him insofar as from potentiality he is reduced to act), **21:7** (I make it known to whom I intend to speak), **22:7** (I had a worthy reason to speak), **8** (*Are you he who has often spoken*), **17** (four manners of speaking were employed by the ladies), **23:29** (speaking to an unspecified person), **25:1** (I speak of Love as a thing in itself), **2** (I speak of him as if he were a body), **2** (I also say of him that he smiled, and also that he spoke), **7** (to them is granted a greater license to speak), **8** (have made them speak to each other), **8** (they have said of things non-existent that they speak), **8** (accidents speak as if they were substances), **9** (a goddess enemy of the Trojans, spoke to Aeolus, Lord of the winds), **9** (Through the same poet speaks an inanimate thing to things animate), **9** (Through Lucan a thing animate speaks to a thing inanimate), **9** (Through Horace one speaks to one's own poetic faculty), **10** (not only are they Horace's words, but he speaks them), **10** (Through Ovid, Love speaks), **26:1** (This most gentle lady, of whom it has been spoken in the preceding words), **1** (I seemed to have spoken imperfectly), **14** (I speak of those things that through her power she brought about in others), **27:1** (I had not spoken of what at that time she worked in me),

1 (I seemed to have spoken imperfectly), **29:3** (I speak by similitude), **31:1** (a canzone in which, weeping, I would speak about her), **3** (in the second I speak of her), **4** (I say to whom I want to speak), **4** (I speak about whom I want to write), **5** (when I say: *Gone has Beatrice*, I speak about her), **6** (I speak of my condition), **32:4** (I speak of my sorrowful condition), **33:2** (who examines them closely sees clearly that different persons speak), **34:4** (I speak about the effects of Love), **35:4** (a sonnet, in which I would speak to her), **37:4** (who it is that speaks this way), **38:5** (I call heart; the other, that is, reason, I call soul; and I tell how one speaks against the other), **6** (the one way of speaking is not contrary to the other), **40:5** (I resolved to write as if I were speaking to them), **41:7** (they are ladies to whom I speak), **8** (*I know that he speaks*).

— Conversation: **4:3** (I spoke of Love), **5:2** (it spoke, I understood, of the lady who had been intermediate), **7:5** (in a way I fear to speak of), **10:1** (too many spoke about it beyond the bounds of courtesy), **12:4** (I, reassuring myself, began to speak), **5** (I strove to speak), **5** ("you speak to me with such obscurity"), **6** (certain people who spoke of you), **8** (do not speak to her directly), **13:8** (All my thoughts speak of Love), **9** ([I] wish to speak but know not what to say), **10** (desiring to speak of Love), **18:2** (The lady who had called me was of a graceful way of speaking), **3** (others who spoke among themselves), **4** (I then spoke these words to them), **6** (they had spoken somewhat among themselves), **6** (the lady who had first spoken to me), **7** (the one who was speaking to me), **7** ("If you were speaking the truth to us"), **19:1** (speaking about her was not appropriate), **4** (I wish to speak with you of my lady), **5** (I would through speaking enamor the people), **6** (I do not wish to speak so loftily), **6** (I will speak of her gentle estate), **11** (one cannot end in evil who has spoken to her), **21:3** (every humble thought / is born in the heart of whoever hears her speak), **22:3** ([I] heard the words they spoke regarding this most gentle one), **5** ("Who can ever be happy among us, having heard this lady speak so piteously"), **13** (Are you he who has often spoken / of our lady, speaking only to us), **15** (in her cries we heard her speak), **23:13** (as they were speaking to me like this, my powerful fantasy ceased), **20** (my color / . . . made them speak of death), **31:8** (I must speak, dragging up woes), **9** (I remember that I spoke / of my lady), **9** (I wish to speak to no other / than the gentle heart that is in a lady), **11** (Who weeps not for her, when speaking of her, / has a heart of stone), **32:2** (I, aware that he spoke only of this blessed one), **2** (he dissembled his words in order to seem to speak of another lady), **37:2** (I cursed the vanity of my eyes and spoke to them in my mind), **3** (when I had thus spoken within myself to my eyes), **38:4** (it seemed necessary to speak to her), **40:2** (I do not believe that they have yet heard speak of this lady), **4** ("I would speak words that would make anyone weep").

— Figurative: **2:5** (speaking especially to the spirits of sight), **3-3** (in his words he [Love] spoke of many things), **9:6** (these words that I have spoken), **12:3** ([Love] seemed to call me, sighing, and spoke these words), **5** (I thought he had spoken most obscurely), **7** (I [Love], who am he, will gladly speak), **16:3** (a single thought that spoke to me of this lady), **8** (one live spirit / and remains because it speaks of you), **19:8** (God speaks, having my lady in mind), **23:26** (Then spoke Love), **24:3** (these words, which my heart spoke with the tongue of Love), **4** (Love seemed to speak in my heart), **27:4** (my spirits go speaking), **34:5** (all my sighs issued speaking), **37:4** (my heart spoke within me), **38:4** (the battle of thoughts was being won by those who spoke for her), **4** (*A gentle thought*; and I say "gentle" insofar as it spoke of a gentle lady), **7** (my soul, that is, my reason, speaks to my heart), **8** (A gentle thought that speaks of you), **8** ([thought] speaks of love so sweetly), **41:12** (I do not understand him [a spirit], so subtly does he speak), **12** (the sorrowing heart, which makes him speak), **13** (I know that he speaks of that gentle one).

— See **say**.

spirit [spirito]:

— Holy Spirit: **29:3** (the factor of miracles multiplied by itself is three, that is, Father, Son, and Holy Spirit). See **God**.

— Of love: **11:2** (a spirit of love), **19:12** (From her eyes . . . / issue spirits of love inflamed), **20:5** (it wakens the spirit of Love), **24:7** (I felt awakening in my heart / an amorous spirit that slept), **26:7** (from her lips moves / a spirit, soothing and full of love), **38:10** (this is a new little spirit of love).

— Of goodness: **31:11** (a heart of stone so wicked and base / that no good spirit can enter it).

— Of beauty: **33:8** great spiritual beauty / that throughout heaven spreads / light of love).

— Of life: **2:4** (the spirit of life, which dwells in the most secret chamber of the heart).

— Animal spirit: **2:5** (the animal spirit, which dwells in the upper chamber).

— Natural spirit: **2:6** (At that point the natural spirit), **4:1** (my natural spirit began to be hindered).

— Of the senses: **2:5** (the upper chamber to which all the spirits of the senses carry their perceptions), **11:2** (destroying all other spirits of the senses), **14:5** (At that moment my spirits were so destroyed), **6** (I grieved much for these little spirits), **8** (my dead spirits having resurrected), **8** (the outcasts [spirits] having returned to their possessions), **12** (he smites among my affrighted spirits), **14** (I say that Love slays all my spirits), **23:22** (so confounded were / my spirits that each wandered off), **27:4** (my spirits seem to flee), **4** ([Love] makes my spirits go speaking).

— Of sight: **2:5** (speaking especially to the spirits of sight), **11:2** (drove out the feeble spirits of sight), **14:5** (no spirits remained alive but those of sight), **14** (Love slays all my spirits, the visual ones remain alive but outside their own organs), **16:8** (there survives in me but one live spirit).

— Pilgrim spirit: **41:5** (I call it then "pilgrim spirit," since it ascends on high spiritually), **11** (the pilgrim spirit gazes upon her).

stanza [stanza, stanzia] **19:21** (I add a stanza about almost as a servant), **28:1** (I had completed the stanza transcribed above), **33:2** (I wrote two stanzas of a canzone), **4** (in the first stanza), **4** (in the other stanza).

star [stella] **2:2** (the heaven of fixed stars), **3:11** (the time in which to us every start shines), **23:5** (the stars appeared of a color that made me think they wept), **24** (I seemed to see, little by little, / the sun grow dim and the star appear).

stream [rivo] **19:1** (walking along a path beside which ran a very clear stream).

substance [sentenzia, sustanzia] **1:1** (if not all of them, at least their substance), **25:1** (I speak of Love as . . . a corporeal substance), **1** (Love is not in himself a substance), **1** (Love . . . is an accident inherent in a substance), **8** (many accidents speak as if they were substances) **39:6** (a sonnet in which I would express the substance of this account). See **meaning**.

sun [sole] **23:5** (I seemed to see the sun darken), **24** (the sun grow dim and

sight), **4** (seeing often / gentle eyes or sorrowful tears), **37:2** ("never . .
. should your tears have ceased"), **40:10** (in tears would you [pilgrims]
then depart from here). See **cry, weep**.

That which befalls me in my memory dies [*Ciò che m'incontra, ne
la mente more*] **15:4**.

The bitter weeping that you did [*L'amaro lagrimar che voi faceste*]
27:6.

think [pensare]:

— Narrator-protagonist: **3:2** (thinking upon this most courteous one), **3**
(thinking of her), **8** (immediately I began to think), **9** (Thinking upon
that which had appeared to me), **4:1** (my soul was wholly given to
thoughts of this most gentle lady), **5:3** (immediately I thought of
making this gentle lady a screen to the truth), **7:2** (thinking that if of her
departure I did not write), **12:3** (the aspect of one deep in thought), **5**
(thinking upon his words), **5** (I thought he had spoken most obscurely),
9 (thinking back, I realized that this vision had appeared to me at the
ninth hour), **13** (in your service has he been molded by every thought),
13:1 (many and diverse thoughts began to assail and try me), **1** (among
which thoughts four seemed most to disrupt my life's peace), **3** (The
next thought was), **6** (each thought assailed me), **6** (if I thought to look
for a way common to all of them), **7** (*All my thoughts*), **8** (All my
thoughts speak of Love), **10** (all my thoughts are of Love), **14:1** (After
the battle of the diverse thoughts), **3** (I, thinking to please this friend),
15:1 (there occurred to me an insistent thought), **2** (to this thought
responded another, a humble thought), **3** (I, moved by such thoughts),
16:1 (four more thoughts about my condition), **3** (a single thought that
spoke to me of this lady), **9** (I come to see you, thinking to be healed),
18:8 (I, thinking about these words), **9** (thinking much upon it), **19:1**
(I thought that speaking about her was not appropriate), **3** (These words .
. . thinking to use them for my opening), **3** (thinking for some days), **5**
(as I think of her worth), **16** (when I think upon her worth), **20:2**
(thinking that after that discourse it would be beautiful to treat Love
further), **2** (thinking that the friend should be served), **22:7** (I later,
thinking, resolved to write words), **23:2** (I was taken by a thought that
concerned my lady), **3** (when I had thought somewhat about her), **3**
(thinking about my enfeebled life), **5** (stars appeared of a color that made
me think that they wept), **21** (sighing I said in thought), **24:2** ("Think

about blessing the day I took you captive"), **2** (I thought it could not be my heart), **7** ("Now think indeed of paying me honor"), **11** (*"Now think"*), **31:1** (I thought I would relieve it with some sorrowful verses), **12** (one who sees in thought at times / what she was), **13** (when thought in the oppressed mind), **13** (many times, thinking of death), **33:1** (thinking who he was), **34:1** (in a place where, thinking of her), **2** (I was in thought), **3** (there came to me the thought of writing words in rhyme), **35:1** (I became pensive and with painful thoughts), **38:1** (I often thought of her), **1** (I thought of her in this way), **1** (often I thought more amorously), **2** (what thought is this), **2** ("lets me think of almost nothing else"), **3** (Then arose another thought), **4** (the battle of thoughts was being won by those who spoke for her), **4** (*A gentle thought*), **4** (the thought was extremely base), **5** (according as my thoughts were divided), **8** (A gentle thought that speaks of you), **10** ("it lets no other thought stay with us"), **39:2** (I then began to think about her), **2** (all my thoughts began to revert to their most gentle Beatrice), **3** (I began to think of her), **3** (one of my thoughts had within itself so much suffering), **8** (the thoughts that dwell in the heart), **10** (These thoughts, and the sighs I send forth), **40:2** (These pilgrims . . . thinking of them), **41:3** (I tell where my thought goes), **6** (my thought ascends, in contemplating the quality of her), **7** (that to which my thought takes me), **7** (all such thought is about my lady), **7** (I often hear her name in my thought).

— Beatrice: **14:11** (you do not think, lady, whence it comes).

— Others: **14:1** (a friend, who thought to do me a great favor), **18:4** ("the greeting of this lady, of whom you are perhaps thinking"), **19:9** (all their thoughts freeze and perish), **20** (to remove at this point every vicious thought), **21:3** (every humble thought / is born in the heart of whoever hears her speak), **35:6** (I realized that you were thinking), **40:2** (their thoughts are on other things than these here), **2** (they perhaps think about their distant friends) **5** (*Oh pilgrims, who go along in thought*), **9** (Oh pilgrims, who go along in thought).

— See **conceive, consider, pensive, ponder, reflect.**

three [tre]: **3:11** (Almost had passed a third of the hours), **8:7** (This first sonnet divides into three parts), **7** (in the third I speak of a certain honor that Love paid this lady), **7** (the third: *Hear*), **12** (in the third, I upbraid her), **12** (the third: *And if I want you*), **9:13** (This sonnet has three

degree), **7** (from that time forward, Love ruled over my soul), **8** (Many times he commanded that I seek to behold this youthful angel), **8** (many times in my childhood I sought her), **9** (at no time did it allow Love to rule me without the faithful counsel of reason), **3:2** (that was the first time that her words were moved to come to my ears), **9** (many who were famous troubadours at that time), **11** (the time in which to us every star shines), **6:1** (during that time when this lady was a screen), **9:4** (at times his eyes seemed to turn toward a river), **5** (her return will not take place for a long time), **10:1** (n a short time I made her my defense), **12:3** ("My son, it is time to end our fabrications"), **14:3** (he first time she would sit at the dining table in the house of her new bridegroom), **16:6** (*Oftentimes*), **7** (Oftentimes there come to mind), **18:5** (as when at times we see rain falling mixed with beautiful snow), **20:4** (sometimes a brief and sometimes a long season), **5** (so long it lasts sometimes therein / that it wakens the spirit of Love), **22:4** (some tears at times bathed my face), **23:14** (at times they asked me what I had feared), **21** (The time must come when my lady dies), **22** (they said to me time and again: —You will die), **24:3** (she was given the name *Primavera* [Springtime]), **25:4** (only a short time has passed), **4** (poetry written before the present time), **27:1** (what at that time she worked in me), **28:2** (at all times reprehensible to whoever does it), **3** (the number nine has many times occurred), **29:1** (the perfect number nine had been completed nine times in that century in which she had come into this world), **3** (three times three make nine), **31:1** (After my eyes had for some time wept), **12** (one who sees in thought at times / what she was), **13** (many times, thinking of death), **32:5** (many times more than I would desire), **33:4** (*Every time*), **5** (Every time, alas, I remember), **34:2** (they had been there some time before I noticed them), **35:1** (Some time afterwards), **1** (a place in which I remembered times past), **5** (the acts and state / that I bear through sorrow many times), **37:2** (time and again I cursed the vanity of my eyes), **39:2** (remembering her according to the order of time past), **3** (my sighs manifested this many times), **9** (oftentimes they cry so), **40:1** (at the time when many folk go to see that blessed image that Jesus Christ left to us).

— Moment [momento, punto] **2:4** (At that moment I say truly that the spirit of life . . . began to tremble), **12:15** (go forth at that moment when you may receive honor), **14:5** (At that moment my spirits were so destroyed), **34:8** (at the moment when her worth / led you to watch what I was doing).

— Hour [ora] **3:2** (The hour in which her most sweet greeting reached me was firmly the ninth), **8** (I found that the hour in which this vision had appeared to me had been the fourth hour of the night), **8** (the first of the nine last hours of the night), **11** (Almost had passed a third of the hours), **12:9** (this vision had appeared to me at the ninth hour of the day), **23:31** (saying at what hour they called me), **29:1** (the first hour of the ninth day of the month), **39:1** (at about the ninth hour).

— Day [die, dì, giorno]: **3:1** (After many days had passed), **1** (on the last of these days this marvelous lady appeared), **1** (her ineffable courtesy, which today is rewarded in life everlasting), **2** (The hour in which her most sweet greeting reached me was firmly the ninth of that day), **4** (who the day before had deigned to greet me), **5:1** (One day it happened that this most gentle one was seated), **5:3** (my secret had not been revealed to anyone on that day), **9:1** (A few days after the death of this lady), **7** (I rode that day deeply pensive), **8** (The next day, I began this sonnet), **9** (Riding the other day along a road), **12:9** (this vision had appeared to me at the ninth hour of the day), **14:3** (a gentle lady who had married that day), **18:9** (I tarried for some days with the desire to speak), **19:3** (thinking for some days), **22:1** (not many days later), **23:1** (A few days after that), **1** (continuously for nine days I suffered bitterest pain), **2** (on the ninth day, feeling myself in pain), **3** ("Beatrice one day will die"), **24:1** (it happened one day), **2** ("Think about blessing the day I took you captive), **4** ("She who comes first is called *Primavera* uniquely for this, today's coming"), **4** (on the day that Beatrice will show herself), **27:1** (I began to reflect one day about what I had said about my lady), **29:1** (the first hour of the ninth day of the month), **34:1** (On that day when a year was completed since this lady had become a citizen of life eternal), **11** ("today makes a year since to heaven you ascended"), **39:1** (Against this adversary of reason arose in me one day), **2** (for several days against the constancy of reason).

— Month [mese]: **5:4** (I concealed myself for some years and months), **29:1** (her most noble soul departed in the first hour of the ninth day of the month), **1** (she departed in the ninth month of the year), **1** (the first month is Tixryn the first).

— Year [anno]: **2:2** (at about the beginning of her ninth year did she appear

present whenever it is necessary"), **18:1** (each [lady] had been present at many of my defeats), **22:16** (She bears in her face pity so present), **25:3** (to the extent appropriate at present), **4** (we will not find poetry written before the present time), **28:2** (it is not part of the present purpose), **2** (supposing it did pertain to the present purpose), **38:6** (that seems contrary to what I say in the present), **40:9** (something not present to you).

Tixryn the first [Tisirin primo] **29:1** (the first month is Tixryn the first).

To every captive soul and gentle heart [*A ciascun'alma presa e gentil core*] **3:9**.

tongue [lingua] **8:8** (upbraiding you my tongue grows weary), **19:2** (my tongue spoke as if it moved by itself), **24:3** (my heart spoke with the tongue of Love), **26:5** (every tongue, trembling, becomes mute), **31:15** (there is not a tongue that knows how to tell it).

transcribe [scrivere] **1:1** (Beneath this rubric I find written the words that it is my intention to transcribe into this little book), **5:4** (I made for her certain small things in rhyme, which it is not my purpose to transcribe here), **7:2** (I resolved to express a lamentation in a sonnet, which I will transcribe), **13:1** (After the vision transcribed above), **28:1** (this canzone, of which I had completed the stanza transcribed above), **31:2** (I will divide it before I transcribe it), **33:2** (before I gave him the sonnet transcribed above), **3** (the sonnet transcribed above I gave to him).

transfiguration [trasfiguramento, trasfigurazione] **14:7** (these ladies, noting my transfiguration), **10** (I would express the cause of my transfiguration [see **14:12**: whence I change into someone else's semblance)], **15:1** (After the strange transfiguration).

tremble [tremore, tremare, tremoto] **2:4** (the spirit of life . . . began to tremble), **4** (and trembling it said these words), **11:2** (whoever wanted to know Love could do so by looking at the tremor of my eyes), **13:8** (trembling with the fear that is in my heart), **14:4** (I seems to feel the wondrous tremor commence in my breast's left side), **4** (I rested my body, to disguise my tremor), **4** (fearing lest one might notice my trembling, I raised my eyes), **15:5** (through the intoxication caused by great trembling), **16:10** (in my heart arises a tremor), **21:2** (whomever she greets trembles at heart), **22:10** (my heart trembles to see so much), **24:1** (I felt the beginning of a tremor), **10** (I felt the awakening of the wonted tremor in my heart), **26:5** (every tongue, trembling, becomes mute).

Trinity [Trinitade] **29:3**, (Father, Son, and Holy Spirit, who are three and one), **3** (a miracle, whose root . . . is solely the wondrous Trinity).

Trojans [Dardanide, Troiani] **25:9** (Juno, who is a goddess enemy of the Trojans), **9** (You hard Trojans).

troubadour [trovatore] **3:9** (I resolved to make it known to many who were famous troubadours).

truth [vero, verità, veritade, verace] **2:4** (I say truly that the spirit of life . . . began to tremble), **3:15** (The true meaning of the said dream), **5:3** (making this gentle lady a screen to the truth), **8:6**, (I saw him lament in his true form), **12:7** (your secret is in truth somewhat known to her), **13** (tell her to ask Love, who knows the truth), **14:3** (the truth is that they were gathered there), **14** (It is true that among the words), **14** (my written explanations would be in vain, or in truth superfluous), **18:7** ("If you were speaking the truth to us"), **19:22** (in truth I fear having communicated its meaning to too many people), **22:1** (to eternal glory passed truly), **2** (as many believe and is true), **13** (You seem in voice to be truly he [narrator]), **23:8** ("It is true that dead likes our lady."), **22** (to all knowledge and truth lost), **26** (with her she had true humility), **27** (I resemble you [Death] truly), **30** (I returned to my true condition), **24:4** (that John who preceded the true light), **25:1** (which, according to truth, is false), **8** (not only of true things but of things not true), **10** (in a way that would show their true reasoning), **29:2** (according to Ptolemy and according to Christian truth), **3** (according to infallible truth) **33:2** (one truly for him and the other for me), **38:6** (It is true), **42:2** (as she truly knows).

Tuus, o regina, quid optes explorare labor; michi iussa capessere fas est (Yours, o queen, is the task of examining your wishes; mine, the duty to carry out orders) **25:9**.

understand [intendere] **3:3** (he spoke of many things, of which I understood only a few), **3** (among his words I understood these), **5:2** (it spoke, I understood, of the lady who had been intermediate), **7:2** (as is clear to anyone who understands it), **8:3** (anyone who understands it), **12** (in my understanding this person is defined), **12:17** (it is not understood to whom my words are addressed), **19:2** (*Ladies who have understanding of love*), **4** (Ladies who have understanding of love), **15** (This canzone, to

unschooled individuals achieved fame for knowing how to versify is that they were almost the first to versify in the language of *sì*), **6** (it was difficult to understand Latin verses), **6** (versification was developed from the beginning in order to write of love), **7** (it is granted to vernacular versifiers), **27:2** (I therefore resolved to write verses), **31:1** (I would relieve it with some sorrowful verses), **41:1** (requesting that I send them some of my verses).

vice [vizi, vizioso, viziosamente] **10:2** (these excessive voices that appeared to defame me viciously), **2** (destroyer of vices and queen of virtues), **19:20** (to remove at this point every vicious thought).

"Vide cor tuum" ("Behold your heart") **3:5**.

Virgil [Virgilio] **25:9** (That poets have written as I have said above is evident in Vergil).

virtue [virtù, virtute] **3:1** (she greeted me with exceeding virtue), **8:10** (all that in a lady is praiseworthy virtue), **10:2** (that most gentle lady, who was destroyer of all vices and queen of virtues), **12:7** (by virtue of its long usage), **19:9** (I wish to have you know of her virtue), **21:6** (what, by her virtue, she then effects), **26:4** (wonderful operations proceeded from her virtuousness), **9** (how her virtue served the other ladies), **32:6** ([Beatrice] has gone / to the world worthy of her virtue).

vision [visione] **3:3** (there appeared to me a marvelous vision), **8** (the hour in which this vision had appeared), **9** (requesting them to judge my vision), **4:1** (From this vision onwards), **12:9** (this vision had appeared to me at the ninth hour of the day), **13:1** (After the vision transcribed above), **42:1** (After this sonnet there appeared to me a wonderful vision).

vita nova. See *Incipit vita nova*.

voice [voce] **10:2** (these excessive voices that appeared to defame me viciously), **22:13** (You seem in voice to be truly he[narrator]), **23:10** (I began to utter in my real voice), **13** (my voice was so broken by my weeping), **19** (My voice was so woeful), **30** (*My voice*), **24:4** ('I am the voice crying in the wilderness'), **33:7** (a voice of pity) **34:10** (with a voice that often calls up / tears).

weep [piangere, lagrimare]:
— Beatrice weeps: **22:3** (many ladies gathered where this Beatrice piteously wept), **3** (Surely she weeps so), **14** (Did you see her weep), **34:8** (that gentle lady for whom weeps Love).

weeping that you did"), **7** ("her for whom you wept"), **39:4** (was rekindled my alleviated weeping), **4** (my eyes appeared to be two things that desired only to weep), **4** (through long, incessant weeping), **9** (to weep and display suffering), **9** (oftentimes they cry so).

— Others: **8:1** (many ladies, who wept piteously), **3** (*Weep, lovers*), **4** (Weep, lovers), **7** (I call and urge Love's faithful to weep), **22:10** (I see your eyes, which have wept), **15** (Leave weeping to us), **16** (would in her presence have died weeping), **17** (*Leave weeping to us*), **23:5** (women roaming disheveled, crying along the way), **11** (with great fear began to cry), **17** (was moved by fear to bitter weeping), **18** (through her who with me wept), **23** (some weeping, some crying out their laments), **31:5** (I tell how the others wept), **11** (Who weeps not for her), **11** (no pain of weeping comes to it), **12** (to sigh and to die of weeping), **37:6** ("made other persons weep"), **38:10** (come from the eyes of that compassionate one / who became perturbed), **40:4** ("I would nevertheless make them weep"), **4** (I would speak words that would make anyone weep), **9** (weep not when you pass), **10** (the power to make one cry).

— See **tears**.

white [bianco] **3:1** (this marvelous appeared to me dressed in purest white), **12:3** (a young man dressed in whitest garments), **23:7** (angels . . . had before them a small cloud of purest white), **8** (women covered her— that is, her head— with a white veil).

wonder [maraviglia, mirabile] **3:3** (he appeared so happy in himself that it was a wondrous thing), **5:1** (wondering at my gazing), **6:2** (that which, as I composed it, wonderfully came to pass), **14:4** (a wondrous tremor commence in my breast's left side), **6** (we could stay and gaze at the wonder of this lady), **7** (these ladies, noting my transfiguration, began to wonder), **15:2** (I imagine her wondrous beauty), **21:8** (her wonderful smile), **23:5** (women roaming disheveled, crying along the way, wondrously sad), **6** ("Your wonderful lady has departed from this world"), **24:3** (I saw approaching the wondrous Beatrice), **9** (one after the other wonder), **26:4** (more wonderful operations proceeded from her virtuousness), **4** (her wondrous and excellent operations), **15** (she worked wondrously), **29:3** (the wondrous Trinity), **30:1** (no one may wonder why), **36:4** (Color of love and pity's semblance / never possessed so wondrously / the face of a lady), **41:7** (her wonderful quality), **42:1**

(there appeared to me a wonderful vision).

word [parola]:

— From Beatrice: **3:2** (the first time that her words were moved to come to my ears), **2** (my lady was the immediate cause of certain words in the sonnet), **28:1** (Mary, whose name was in greatest reverence in the words of this blessed Beatrice).

— From Love: **2:4** (trembling it said these words: *"Ecce deus fortior me* ["Behold a god more powerful than I"]), **3:3** (in his words he spoke of many things), **3** (among his words I understood these: *"Ego dominus tuus"* ["I am your Lord"]), **5** (he seemed to say to me these words: *"Vide cor tuum"* ["Behold your heart"]), **9:5** (Love called to me and said these words), **6** ("these words that I have spoken"), **7** (these words said, this image of mine disappeared), **12:3** (he seemed to call me, sighing, and spoke these words: *"Fili mi, tempus est ut pretermictantur simulacra nostra"* ["My son, it is time to end our fabrications"]), **4** (he seemed to me to be weeping piteously and seemed to await some word from me), **4** (he said these words to me: *"Ego tanquam centrum circuli"* ["I am like the center of a circle"]) **5** (Then, thinking upon his words), **7** (I want you to write certain words in rhyme), **7** (she will recognize the words of those who were deceived), **8** (Let these words be like an intermediary), **9** (having said these words, he disappeared), **24:3** (shortly after these words, which my heart spoke with the tongue of Love), **5** (after these words, Love also seemed to say: "And who wishes subtly to consider would call Beatrice Love for the great likeness she bears to me"), **7** (with each word he smiled).

— From memory: **1:1** (I find written the words that it is my intention to transcribe), **2:10** (I shall come to those words that are written in my memory), **19:3** (These words I stored in my memory).

— From narrator-protagonist: **2:5** (the animal spirit . . . speaking especially to the spirits of sight, it said these words: *"Apparuit iam beatitudo vestra"* ["Now has appeared your beatitude"]), **6** (the natural spirit, . . . weeping said these words), **3:10** (into whose regard shall come the present words), **12:5** (I said to him these words: "Why is it, Lord, that you speak to me with such obscurity"), **14:8** (I said to my friend these words: "I have set my feet in that part of life beyond which one cannot go with the intention of returning."), **18:4** (I then spoke these words to them: "Ladies, the end of my love was indeed the greeting of this lady"),

other than these words that I speak), **13:1** (words that Love had commanded me to say), **7** (caught by a desire to set words about it in rhyme), **14:10** (I resolved to write words in which, addressing her, I would express the cause of my transfiguration), **10** (I resolved to write these words in the hope that they would by chance come to her hearing), **14** (among the words that expound the occasion of this sonnet are written obscure words), **14** (the solution to the obscure words is clear), **15:3** (resolved to write certain words in which, asking her to excuse me from such criticism), **16:2** (additional words in which I would express four more thoughts about my condition), **18:8** ("beatitude lies in those words that praise my lady"), **8** ("why have other words been mine"), **19:15** (the first part is proem to my subsequent words), **15** (the third is almost a servant to the preceding words), **20:1** (having perhaps, through the words he heard, more hope in me than I deserved), **2** (I proposed to write words in which I would speak of Love), **21:1** (I felt a desire to say some words also in praise of this most gentle one), **22:7** (I later, thinking, resolved to write words), **24:6** (omitting certain words that seemed better left unsaid), **25:6** (the desire to make his words understandable to ladies, to whom it was difficult to understand Latin verses), **25:10** (could not unveil their words in a way that would show their true reasoning), **26:1** (This most gentle lady, of whom it has been spoken in preceding words), **4** (I resolved to write words in which I would make known her wondrous and excellent effects), **4** (know of her what words can make one understand), **9** (to write additional words in which it would be expressed), **28:3** (the number nine has many times occurred among the previous words), **30:2** (And if any one should want to blame me for not transcribing here the words that follow those quoted), **2** (the words that follow those that have been quoted are all in Latin), **34:3** (there came to me the thought of writing words in rhyme as for her anniversary), **5** (some were saying certain words different from the others), **36:3** (I felt the desire to write some words, addressing her), **38:4** (I wanted to write more words about it), **39:6** (no doubt about this could be inferred from the words in rhyme), **10** (of her death many words), **40:4** ("I would speak words that would make anyone weep who heard them"), **6** (I wrote "pilgrims" according to the broad signification of the word), **10** (the words that one may say of her).

wretched [*miser*, vile] **2:7** ("Wretched me, for often hereafter shall I be impeded"), **35:3** (fearing lest I display my wretched life), **6** (revealing with my eyes my wretchedness).

"Wretched me, for often hereafter shall I be impeded!" [*"Heu miser, quia frequenter impeditus ero deinceps!"*"] **2:7.**

write [dire, scrivere] **1:1** (I find written the words that it is my intention to transcribe into this little book), **2:10** (I shall come to those words that are written in my memory under the greater paragraphs), **3:9** (I wrote to them what I had seen in my sleep), **14** (one whom I call first among my friends, who then wrote a sonnet that begins: *You saw, in my opinion, all worth*), **5:4** (I shall write something that will clearly be in praise of her), **7:2** (if of her departure I did not write somewhat sorrowfully), **2** (I then wrote this sonnet), **8:2** (I resolved to write some words about her death), **3** (the words I wrote about it), **3** (I wrote then these two sonnets), **12:7** (I want you to write certain words in rhyme), **13:4** (names are consequent upon the things named, just as it is written), **7** (I then wrote this sonnet), **14:10** (I resolved to write words in which, addressing her, I would express the cause of my transfiguration), **10** (I resolved to write these words in the hope that they would by chance come to her hearing), **10** (I then wrote this sonnet), **14** (among the words that expound the occasion of this sonnet are written obscure words), **14** (my written explanations would be in vain), **15:3** (I, moved by such thoughts, resolved to write certain words), **3** (and I wrote this sonnet), **16:1** (After I had written this sonnet), **1** (the desire moved me to write additional words), **6** (Therefore I wrote this sonnet), **17:1** (After I wrote these three sonnets), **1** (I believed I should keep silent and write no more), **19:1** (I felt such a strong desire to write), **20** (above it is written that this lady's salutation), **20:2** (I proposed to write words in which I would speak of Love), **2** (so I wrote this sonnet), **21:1** (So I wrote this sonnet), **22:7** (I later, thinking, resolved to write words), **8** (I wrote two sonnets), **23:16** (I resolved to write verses about what had happened to me), **16** (I wrote this canzone about it), **24:6** (I resolved to write in rhyme to my best friend), **6** (I wrote this sonnet), **25:4** (we will not find poetry written before the present time by more than one hundred and fifty years), **6** (the first who began writing as a poet of the vernacular), **6** (versification was developed from the beginning in order to write of love), **7** (to poets is conceded greater license of expression than to prose writers) **7** (these writers in rhyme are none other than poets of the vernacular) **7** (to them is granted a greater license to speak than is granted to the other writers in the vernacular), **8** (worthy is the vernacular writer in rhyme to do the same, but not without a reason), **9** (That poets have written as I have said above is evident in Vergil), **10** (I say that neither Latin poets wrote in this manner without reason), **10** (nor vernacular poets should write like this without having any reasons), **10** (without having any reasons in mind for what they write), **26:4** (I resolved to write words), **4** (Then I wrote this sonnet), **9** (I . . . resolved to write additional words), **9** (I then wrote this other sonnet), **27:2** (I therefore resolved to write verses), **30:1** (I wrote to the princes of the earth somewhat about its condition), **2** (not to write anything but in the vernacular), **2** (it would be outside my intention if I wrote them), **3** (my first friend to whom I write), **3** (I would write to him only in the vernacular), **31:1** (I resolved to write a canzone), **4** (I tell why I am prompted to write), **4** (I speak about whom I want to write), **4** (*and I will write*), **9** (I will write of her as I weep), **32:1** (After I wrote this canzone), **2** (he requested that I write something for him), **3** (I resolved to write a sonnet), **3** (I then wrote this sonnet), **33:1** (After I had written this sonnet), **1** (I intended to give it as a poem written by him), **2** (I wrote two stanzas of a canzone), **2** (both appear written by the same person), **3** (telling him that I had written them for him alone), **34:3** (there came to me the thought of writing words in rhyme as for her anniversary), **3** (I then wrote this sonnet), **35:4** (I resolved to write a sonnet), **36:3** (I felt the desire to write some words), **3** (I wrote this sonnet), **37:3** (I resolved to write a sonnet), **3** (I wrote this sonnet), **38:4** (I wanted to write more words about it), **4** (I wrote this sonnet), **39:6** (the words in rhyme that I had written previously), **6** (I resolved to write a sonnet in which I would express the substance of this account), **6** (I wrote then), **6** (I wrote "alas" because I was ashamed that my eyes had so strayed), **40:5** (I resolved to write a sonnet), **5** (I resolved to write as if I were speaking to them), **5** (I wrote this sonnet), **6** (I wrote "pilgrims" according to the broad signification of the word), **41:1** (I resolved to send them some and to write something new), **1** (I then wrote a sonnet, which tells of my condition), **2** (The sonnet that I then wrote), **42:1** (I saw things that made me resolve to write no more of this blessed one).

writer [dicitore, dittatore, rimatore]:

— Of prose **25:7** (to poets is conceded greater license of expression than to prose writers).

— Of rhyme **25:7** (these writers in rhyme are none other than poets of the vernacular).

— Vernacular: **25:7** (the other writers in the vernacular), **8** (worthy is the vernacular writer in rhyme to do the same).

— See **verse**.

Wars against me, I see, wars are being prepared, he says [*Bella michi, video, bella parantur, ait*] **25:9**.

Weep, lovers, since Love weeps [*Piangete, amanti, poi che piange Amore*] **8:4**.

With the other ladies you mock my aspect [*Con l'altre donne mia vista gabbate*] **14:11**.

You saw, in my opinion, all worth [*Vedeste, al mio parere, onne valore*] **3:14**.

You who bear your aspect downcast [*Voi che portate la sembianza umile*) **22:9**.

Concordance and Glossary

- The purpose of this "Concordance and Glossary" is to list all occurrences of all the terms in the *Vita nuova*, and to help the reader understand archaic, poetic, or otherwise difficult words and expressions in the Italian text.
- A contemporary Italian word is provided within brackets when the term in the *Vita nuova* is either archaic, poetic, difficult, or is not easily found in college dictionaries.
- Synonyms are provided to help understand difficult terms and may be indicated in the masculine singular.
- Following original words within double quotation marks, translations are placed within single quotation marks.
- Irregular verbal forms are normally provided with the infinitive.
- Verbal endings for the imperfect indicative in the first and third person singular -*ea* and -*ia*, and for the third person plural -*eano* and -*iano*, do not contain the consonant -*v*- that contemporary Italian places between the two adjacent vowels to form, respectively, -*eva* /-*iva* and -*evano* /-*ivano*. The first person singular of the imperfect subjunctive normally ends in -*sse* instead of -*ssi* as in contemporary Italian.
- When brackets contain a colon, the word or words preceding it provide the infinitive of the verbal form and/or synonyms, while what follows the colon provides the contemporary term or grammatical explanations.
- Different meanings of the same term are separated by a semicolon.
- Forms of the definite and indefinite articles, simple and contracted prepositions, and relative pronouns have been included, but their place of occurrence has not been indicated because of their high frequency.
- Barbi's standard chapter and sentence divisions, placed along the margins of this edition, mark the location of each word. References to De Robertis are to his commentary of the *Vita nuova*.

A [prep.]
A' [ai]
Abbandona 16:8
Abbandonata 32:6
Abbandono 31:16
Abbia [avere] 30:1; 41:6
Abbiano 25:9
Abbisogna [bisognare] 26:8
Abitava 11:4
Abito 9:9
Abitudine [abito, relazione]
29:2
Accidente [ciò che non è
essenziale] 25:1
Accidenti 25:8
Acciò che [affinché; perché]
7:2; 8:7; 10:1; 14:14; 15:8;
19:15; 19:16; 19:20; 22:7; 25:10;
26:4; 28:3; 30:1; 31:2; 32:2;
32:3; 33:2; 37:3; 38:1; 40:5;
41:1; 41:5
Accolta [accogliere, radunare]
35:2
Accompagnarlo 6:1
Accompagnata 12:11; 29:3
Accompagnato 9:7; 41:1
Acconcino [preparare] 8:7
Accordano [concordare, essere
d'accordo] 13:8; 13:10
Accordanza [accordo] 13:9
Accordassero 13:6
Accordino 13:10
Accorgendomi 4:2; 32:2; 35:2
Accorgendosi 14:7
Accorgesse 34:2
Accorsero [accorgersi] 5:2;

23:12
Accorsi [accorgersi] 9:12; 35:6
Accorte [accorgersi] 7:2; 23:18
Accorto [accorgersi] 14:4
Acerba [doloroso] 31:16
Acqua 18:5
Ad [prep.]
Addivegna [avvenire] 25:3
Addivenia [avvenire]16:4
Addivenisse [avvenire] 25:3
Addivenne [avvenire] 6:2
Addivenuto [avvenire] 23:16
Addormentai 12:2
Adempiesse 41:1
Adirata 12:11
Adopera 21:6; 21:8
Adoperare 8:5; 26:2
Adoperava 26:9; 27:1
Adoperino 29:2
Adorna 19:11; 23:17
Adornare 12:8
Adornata 19:13
Adunaro [adunare: adunarono]
22:3
Adunate 14:1; 14:3; 18:1
Adunino 22:3
Affatica 8:8
Affaticati 31:1
Agghiaccia [gelarsi] 19:9
Aggie [avere: abbia] 12:14
Aggiungo 19:21
Ait [Lat.; defective vb. *aio, ais*:
'to say'] 25:9
Aiuta 12:2
Aiutatemi 21:2; 21:7
Aiutino 21:7

Aiuto 21:5
Al [prep.]
Alcun 7:3; 19:8; 19:10; 19:12
Alcuna 5:4; 7:2; 8:2; 8:3; 9:6;
10:2; 11:1; 11:1; 12:4; 12:6;
22:4; 23:1; 23:3; 24:1; 25:4;
25:7; 25:8; 25:9; 25:10; 26:8;
28:3; 28:3; 31:12; 32:2; 37:4;
40:3; 42:2
Alcuno 2:10; 3:15; 6:2; 8:7;
12:16; 15:8; 20:1; 23:6; 23:13;
25:10; 26:1; 26:3; 29:3; 30:2;
38:6; 39:3; 39:4; 39:6; 40:7; 41:3
Allegate [citare] 30:2; 30:2
Allegato 30:1
Allegranza [allegria] 7:6
Allegro 3:12; 24:7; 24:10;
Allevata 19:13
Allor 19:12; 21:2; 23:18; 23:26;
23:28; 27:4; 35:6
Allora 2:7; 3:1; 3:9; 3:14; 3:15;
5:3; 7:2; 8:2; 8:3; 9:12; 11:1;
11:3; 12:4; 12:5; 12:6; 12:17;
13:7; 14:2; 14:4; 14:5; 14:8;
14:10; 15:6; 18:4; 18:5; 18:7;
19:2; 19:5; 20:2; 21:1; 22:4;
23:6; 23:8; 23:15; 23:22; 24:2;
26:4; 26:9; 27:2; 31:1; 32:3;
34:3; 35:2; 35:3; 39:2; 39:3;
39:5; 39:6; 41:1; 41:2; 41:5
Allore [allora] 14:12
Alma [anima] 3:9; 3:10; 8:6;
15:6; 20:3
Almeno 1; 41:7
Alquante 8:2; 8:2; 19:19;
19:19; 22:3; 31:1; 38:4

Alquanti 5:4; 9:1; 18:9; 19:3;
25:5; 34:5; 39:2; 40:1; 42:2
Alquanto 3:6; 7:2; 10:3; 11:2;
12:2; 12:3; 12:7; 14:8; 18:6;
19:18; 19:18; 20:1; 20:2; 22:10;
23:3; 23:15; 24:10; 28:2; 30:1;
31:1; 31:11; 32:3; 34:2; 35:1;
40:4
Alta 2:5; 18:9
Altamente 19:6
Altissimo 6:2; 22:2; 34:7; 40:7
Alto 22:2; 23:28; 31:10; 31:11;
33:8
Altra 12:12; 18:1; 22:13; 23:20;
24:4; 24:8; 25:3; 25:6; 25:9;
32:2; 33:2; 33:2; 33:2; 33:4;
33:4; 38:5
Altre 13:5; 14:10; 14:11; 18:3;
18:3; 18:3; 19:15; 19:21; 22:6;
22:6; 23:12; 23:18; 26:9; 26:11;
31:10; 37:6; 40:2
Altri [sing. indef. pron.; indef.
pron. masc. plur.] 9:6; 11:2;
14:4; 14:6; 15:8; 24:3; 25:7;
26:2; 26:4; 30:1; 31:5; 34:2;
34:5; 35:2; 39:4
Altro 6:2; 7:7; 9:9; 12:17; 13:3;
13:4; 13:4; 13:8; 13:8; 13:8;
13:8; 14:6; 15:2; 16:3; 18:7;
18:8; 19:7; 20:3; 20:7; 21:8;
22:8; 22:8; 22:12; 23:7; 23:25;
25:7; 26:9; 28:2; 28:2; 29:3;
30:2; 34:3; 34:6; 34:6; 38:2;
38:3; 38:4; 38:5; 38:6; 38:9;
40:7; 41:1
Altrui 4:1; 5:3; 5:4; 14:10;

14:12; 15:8; 19:6; 21:8; 22:14;
23:20; 26:5; 26:14; 26:15; 31:9;
35:3; 40:10

Amanti [chi è preso d'amore,
innamorato] 8:3; 8:4

Amarissima 23:1

Amarissimamente 22:2

Amarissime 12:1

Amarissimo 3:7

Amaritudine [amarezza] 38:3

Amaro 8:5; 37:3; 37:6

Ami [amare] 18:3

Amica 14:1

Amici 3:14; 4:1; 22:2; 40:2

Amico 14:2; 14:3; 14:7; 14:8;
20:1; 20:2; 23:6; 24:3; 24:6;
25:10; 28:3; 29:2; 29:2; 30:3;
32:1; 32:3

Amistade [amicizia] 22:2; 32:1

Amistà [amicizia] 3:14

Ammonimento 23:13

Ammonisco 19:13

Amor 3:11; 3:12; 7:4; 7:7; 8:5;
8:6; 8:7; 8:9; 12:11; 12:13;
14:12; 16:7; 16:8; 16:11; 19:5;
19:11; 19:12; 19:13; 19:14;
19:18; 20:4; 23:21; 23:26; 24:9;
24:9; 24:11; 31:9; 33:8; 34:4;
34:9; 38:8; 39:10

Amore 2:7; 2:9; 2:9; 3:9; 3:10;
4:2; 4:2; 4:2; 4:3; 6:1; 7:3; 7:7;
7:7; 8:4; 8:7; 8:7; 9:5; 9:6; 9:7;
9:9; 9:13; 11:1; 11:2; 11:2; 11:3;
12:2; 12:10; 12:12; 13:1; 13:2;
13:3; 13:4; 13:5; 13:8; 13:10;
13:10; 14:5; 14:5; 14:14; 14:14;

15:4; 15:8; 16:2; 16:3; 16:4;
16:8; 16:11; 18:3; 18:4; 18:4;
19:2; 19:4; 19:9; 19:12; 19:20;
19:20; 20:1; 20:2; 20:2; 20:2;
20:3; 20:5; 21:1; 21:1; 21:2;
21:6; 21:6; 22:9; 23:8; 23:13;
23:19; 24:2; 24:3; 24:4; 24:5;
24:7; 24:10; 24:10; 25:1; 25:1;
25:2; 25:3; 25:3; 25:6; 25:9;
25:9; 26:7; 26:11; 26:13; 27:3;
27:4; 32:4; 33:6; 34:4; 34:4;
34:8; 35:3; 35:8; 36:1; 36:3;
36:4; 38:1; 38:3; 38:3; 38:10;
39:9; 41:10

Amorosa 8:10; 13:9; 20:4;
23:16; 25:6

Amorosamente 38:1

Amorose 19:6

Amoroso 7:5; 24:7

Ancella [ancella, serva] 19:21

Anche 15:3; 15:8; 16:1; 18:6;
19:16; 21:1; 22:4; 22:5; 24:4;
24:5; 25:2; 25:2; 26:9; 36:3;
38:6; 40:2

Ancide [uccidere: uccide] 14:12;
15:6

Ancor 19:10; 24:6; 31:16

Ancora 12:17; 14:5; 16:1; 16:1;
22:5; 23:3; 25:2; 25:3; 28:1;
28:2; 29:4; 30:1; 37:5; 38:4;
38:6; 41:9

Andai 2:8; 12:1

Andar 9:9; 12:11; 19:14; 22:9;
23:23; 26:11; 35:8

Andare 9:1; 9:2; 12:16; 13:6;
15:7; 22:15; 23:5; 23:8; 41:4

Andaro [andarono] 24:4

Andasse 7:1

Andate 11:2; 34:9; 40:5; 40:9

Andava 26:2; 36:2

Andavano 22:5; 40:2; 40:7

Andò 31:15

Angeli 8:1; 23:7; 23:7; 23:25; 26:2; 31:10; 33:8; 34:3

Angelo 19:7; 19:15; 19:17; 34:1

Angiola [angelo] 2:8

Angoscia 3:7; 9:2; 23:19; 31:6; 31:13; 31:15

Angosciosi 37:3; 39:10

Anima 2:7; 4:1; 8:1; 16:10; 19:7; 19:18; 19:18; 23:8; 23:10; 23:21; 23:28; 26:7; 27:4; 29:1; 31:1; 31:11; 31:12; 32:6; 33:5; 35:8; 38:5; 38:5; 38:7; 38:7; 38:9; 38:10; 42:3

Animale [spirito animale, anima sensitiva] 2:5

Animata [con anima razionale] 25:9; 25:9

Animate 25:9

Anime 41:6

Anni 3:1; 5:4; 25:4; 25:4; 29:1; 42:2

Anno 2:2; 29:1; 29:1; 34:1; 34:11

Annovale [anniversario] 34:3

Annunzi 12:14

Antica 8:8

Anticamente 25:3

Anzi 3:7; 8:2; 11:1; 14:9; 15:1; 25:3; 25:4; 26:2; 26:11; 40:2

Anzi che [prima che] 12:9; 33:2; 34:2; 40:4

Apersi [aprire] 23:13

Aperto 38:5

Apostolo 40:7

Appare 3:8; 7:2; 8:3; 11:4; 20:5; 20:7; 20:8; 25:2; 25:2; 25:2; 25:9; 26:9; 33:2; 33:4; 38:6; 39:5

Apparia [appariva] 2:4; 11:1

Apparimento [apparizione] 3:1

Apparir 23:24

Apparire 39:4

Appariro [apparirono] 25:4

Apparisse 24:10

Apparita [apparsa] 3:8; 12:9; 35:5; 38:1

Apparuit 2:5 [Lat.: preterite of *appareo,-es* 'to appear']

Apparuto [apparso] 3:9

Apparve 2:1; 2:2; 2:3; 3:1; 3:3; 3:11; 9:3; 23:24; 39:1; 42:1

Apparver [apparire: apparvero] 23:22

Apparvero 23:4; 23:4

Appena 24:7

Appetito [tendenza istintiva, inclinazione] 38:5; 38:5; 38:6; 38:6; 38:7

Appoia [appoggiare: appoggia] 15:5

Apporta [portare] 13:8

Appressarsi [avvicinarsi: si avvicinarono] 23:18

Appresso 2:1; 3:1; 3:7; 3:12; 5:2; 8:1; 9:1; 9:8; 10:1; 12:12;

13:1; 14:1; 15:1; 16:1; 18:1;
20:1; 20:2; 22:1; 22:6; 22:12;
23:1; 24:1; 24:4; 24:4; 24:8;
27:1; 30:1; 31:5; 42:1

Appropinquare [avvicinarsi]
16:4

Appunto [a punto, proprio] 3:1

Aprire 14:13; 19:22; 25:8

Arabia 29:1

Ardea [ardeva] 3:6

Ardendo 3:12

Ardesse 3:5

Ardia [ardiva] 18:9; 26:1

Ardimento 19:16

Ardire 12:11; 19:5

Ardiscon 26:5

Are [aria] 23:24

Aria 23:5

Armis [Lat.: dative plural of
arma, -orum 'arms' 'armaments']
25:9

Armonia 12:8

Arte 3:9

Artificiosamente [con arte]
19:15

Ascoltando 23:17

Ascoltarmi 8:7

Aspettando 18:3

Aspetto 3:3; 5:1; 8:1; 23:8

Assai 7:1; 8:1; 8:1; 12:4; 14:13;
17:1; 19:13; 22:17; 23:6; 23:17;
23:27; 35:4; 37:1; 38:5; 39:7;
40:8

Assale [assalire] 16:8

Assalia [assaliva] 16:3

Assalito 22:4

Assalivano 37:3

Assegnerò 28:3

Assembra [assemblare, radunare]
33:5

Assemplare [esemplare, ritrarre
da un esemplare, ricopiare] 1

Assicurandomi 5:3; 12:4

Astioso [invidioso] 33:6

Astrologa [astronomica] 29:2

Atare [aiutare] 16:9

Attende 19:8

Attendea [attendeva] 22:4

Attendere 18:3

Attendesse 12:4

Attendete 7:3

Attendite [Lat.: sec. pers. plur.
of the imperative of *attendo, -is*
'to wait') 7:7

Atterzate [from *terzo* 'a third':
to reach a third part of, or to
reduce to a third of something]
3:11

Atti 2:10; 21:8; 26:13; 26:15;
35:5

Atto 19:7; 20:6; 20:8; 21:5;
21:6; 22:9

Audesse [udire: udisse] 31:15

Audienza [udienza]14:10

Audir [udire] 7:3

Audire (udire) 7:7; 12:11; 19:22;
22:4; 40:10

Audite [udire: udite] 8:6; 8:7

Augelli [uccelli] 23:24

Autem [Lat.: 'however'] 12:4

Avante che [prima che] 12:14

Avanzata [mandare avanti]

19:13

Avea [aveva] 3:4; 3:9; 3:12;
3:14; 4:2; 7:1; 7:7; 8:2; 8:2;
12:3; 12:4; 12:9; 13:1; 14:2;
18:2; 18:3; 18:6; 22:7; 22:7;
23:10; 23:13; 23:15; 23:26;
23:26; 27:1; 27:1; 28:1; 33:3;
37:3; 37:3; 38:2; 39:2; 39:3;
39:6; 40:5

Aveamene [me ne aveva] 37:1

Avean [avevano] 23:25

Aveano [avevano] 22:4; 23:7;
29:2; 39:6

Avemo [abbiamo] 22:5; 22:6;
22:12

Avendo 13:1; 20:1; 25:10; 35:3;
38:4

Aver 8:11; 19:7; 19:11; 23:27

Averai [avrai] 12:12

Avere 9:5; 12:11; 15:8; 17:1;
18:9; 19:16; 19:22; 24:2; 27:1;
37:2

Averei [avrei] 22:7

Avesse 3:9; 9:10; 11:1; 11:1;
11:2; 12:5; 14:7; 22:6; 22:7;
22:16; 23:8; 23:14; 28:3; 40:5

Avesser 23:25

Avessero 18:1; 22:7; 22:8;
25:8; 25:10

Avessi 15:1; 32:3; 38:6

Avete 19:2; 19:3; 19:4

Avrei 6:2; 7:1

Avrestù [avresti tu] 15:1; 18:7

Avrò 19:13

Avuto 23:14; 23:15

Avvegna che [benché] 2:9;

8:12; 9:1; 14:6; 17:1; 23:13;
25:3; 28:2; 33:2; 38:6; 41:7

Avvene [avviene] 27:5

Avvenente [bello] 8:6

Avvenia [avveniva] 39:3; 39:4

Avvenisse 19:22

Avvenne 3:1; 5:1; 9:1; 12:3;
14:1; 19:1; 23:1; 24:1; 36:1; 40:1

Avventura [caso] 14:10

Avversario 39:1

Avvien 19:10

Avviene 16:7

Bagnandoli 23:6

Bagnar 22:9

Bagnare 12:1

Bagnati 23:25

Bagnava 22:4

Baldanza [confidenza] 2:9; 7:4;
14:12; 25:10

Ballata 12:9; 12:9; 12:9; 12:10;
12:11; 12:15; 12:16; 12:16;
12:17

Bassando [abbassare] 21:2

Bassi 22:9

Battaglia 14:1; 16:4; 16:4;
37:3; 38:4

Battuto 12:2

Beata 23:8; 28:1

Beati 19:8

Beatitudine 3:1; 5:1; 9:2; 10:2;
11:3; 11:4; 12:1; 18:4; 18:4;
18:6; 18:8

Beatitudo [Lat.; It. 'beatitudine']
2:5

Beato 23:10; 23:28

Beatrice 2:1; 5:2; 5:4; 12:6;
14:4; 22:1; 22:3; 23:3; 23:13;
23:13; 24:4; 24:4; 24:5; 28:1;
31:3; 31:5; 31:10; 31:14; 39:1;
39:2; 40:10; 41:13; 42:3
Bel [bello] 12:14
Bella [Lat. *bellum, -i* 'guerra']
25:9; 25:9
Bella [bello] 7:1; 15:4; 18:5;
23:24; 23:28; 26:10; 31:11; 35:2;
38:1
Belle 6:2
Bellezza 15:2; 33:8
Bellezze 14:1; 19:18; 19:19;
19:19
Bellissima 23:10; 40:1
Bellissimi 26:2
Bello 9:4; 20:2
Beltate [bellezza] 14:11
Ben servidore [perfetto
servitore] 12:13
Ben [bene] 19:11; 22:13; 23:21;
31:14; 31:16; 35:8; 41:13
Bene 9:6; 14:10; 14:12; 14:14;
18:1; 18:2; 19:22; 25:10; 33:2;
37:5
Benedetta 23:13; 28:1; 32:2;
40:1; 42:1; 42:3
Benedette 41:6
Benedetto 26:2
Benedicere [benedire] 24:2
Benedictus [Lat. 'benedetto']
42:3
Benegno [benigno] 31:11
Benignamente 26:6
Benignitate [benignità] 31:10

Bestemmiava [maledire] 37:2
Bianchissima 23:7
Bianchissime 12:3
Bianchissimo 3:1
Bianco 23:8
Biasimevole 28:2
Bice [familiar form of Beatrice]
24:8
Bieltade [bellezza] 24:3; 24:3;
24:6
Bieltate [bellezza] 12:12; 20:5;
20:7; 20:8; 26:11; 26:14; 33:8
Bieltà [bellezza] 19:11
Blasimarla [biasimare + la]
8:12
Blasmar [biasimare] 8:8
Bocca 19:20; 19:20; 21:5; 21:8
Bon [buono] 12:11
Bona [buona]12:14
Bono [buono] 22:2
Bontade [bontà] 22:2
Bontate [bontà] 7:4
Braccia 3:4; 3:7; 3:12; 12:16;
13:6
Brevitade [brevità] 27:2
Brieve [breve] 10:1
Brievemente [brevemente] 17:2
Buon 22:2; 22:2; 22:2; 22:2
Buona 13:2; 13:3; 14:7
Buono 25:3; 25:9

C' (relat. pron. & conj.: 'che')
Cader 23:24
Cadere 18:5
Cadessero 23:5
Cagion [cagione, causa] 8:4

Cagione [cagione, causa] 7:2;
8:7; 8:7; 8:12; 10:2; 12:6; 14:10;
14:13; 14:14; 15:7; 17:2; 19:16;
22:7; 25:5; 31:5; 37:7
Calore 31:10
Cambiato 9:7
Camera 2:4; 2:5; 3:3; 3:3; 12:2;
12:3; 12:9; 14:9; 23:10; 23:12
Cammino 9:4; 9:9; 10:1; 12:6;
13:6; 19:1
Campami [campare: mi
sopravvive] 16:8
Cangiare [cambiare] 12:12
Cangio [cambiare] 14:12
Canosciute [conoscere] 8:10
Cantassero 23:7
Cante [cantare] 12:10
Canto 23:7
Canzone 19:3; 19:3; 19:13;
19:15; 19:15; 19:21; 19:21;
19:22; 20:1; 23:16; 23:29; 27:2;
28:1; 31:1; 31:1; 31:2; 31:3;
31:3; 31:3; 31:7; 31:7; 31:17;
32:1; 33:2; 33:3; 33:4; 33:4
Capacitade [capacità] 11:4
Capessere [Lat. inf.: 'to take']
25:9
Capo 9:10
Care [caro] 41:7; 41:13
Caritade [carità] 11:1
Caro 33:4
Casa 40:6; 40:7
Cattivella [misero, doloroso]
31:3
Caunoscenza [conoscenza]
23:22

Cavalcai 9:7
Cavalcando 9:8; 9:9
Celai 5:4
Celan [celare] 7:6
Celar 22:14
Celare 4:1
Celata 7:1
Celate 22:10
Celo [celare] 23:26
Centinaio 29:1; 29:1
Cento 25:4
Centrum [Lat.; *centrum, -i*
'center') 12:4
Cercando 2:8
Cercare 10:1; 13:6; 15:2; 25:4
Cercasse 2:7
Cerchi 15:1
Certamente 32:2
Certe 5:4; 7:2; 12:6; 12:7: 15:3;
18:1; 18:3; 23:29; 23:30; 24:6;
24:10; 34:1; 34:5
Certi 8:12; 23:4; 23:4; 25:3
Certo 2:8; 18:3; 19:22; 22:3;
24:2; 36:2; 40:10
Cessò 23:13
Ch' [che]
Che [relative pron.; interrogative
adj. & pron.; conjunction]
Ché [conjunction: "perché,"
"poiché"] 12:11; 14:12; 16:9;
18:3; 18:4; 19:10; 19:13; 19:22;
23:10; 23:27; 24:4; 25:1; 25:4;
31:10; 32:5; 33:6; 33:6; 37:2;
37:2; 38:4; 40:2; 40:6
Ched [relative pron. "che"] 12:17
Cherer [chiedere] 13:8

Chesta [past part. of "chiedere":
chiesto] 12:12

Chi [indefinite. & interrogative
pron.] 3:3; 7:2; 8:3; 8:9; 8:11;
8:12; 11:1; 11:2; 12:17; 12:17;
14:14; 15:6; 19:10; 19:20; 19:22;
21:3; 22:5; 22:15; 23:28; 24:5;
25:9; 26:1; 26:7; 26:7; 26:9;
26:10; 28:2; 31:6; 31:6; 31:11;
31:12; 31:15; 33:1; 33:2; 33:2;
37:2; 37:4; 38:9; 40:6; 41:4

Chiama 12:7; 33:2

Chiamando 12:2; 21:7; 23:11;
23:18; 27:4; 33:7

Chiamandomi 18:3

Chiamano 40:7

Chiamansi [si chiamano] 40:7;
40:7; 40:7

Chiamar 13:9; 31:10; 32:6

Chiamare 2:1; 7:7; 8:1; 8:5;
13:6; 38:5

Chiamarla 24:4

Chiamaro [chiamare:
chiamarono] 23:31

Chiamasse 9:5; 12:3; 23:13

Chiamaste 23:28; 23:31

Chiamata 2:1; 24:3

Chiamato 12:4; 18:1; 18:2

Chiamava 12:4; 23:9; 23:17

Chiamerebbe 24:5

Chiami 13:10

Chiamo 3:14; 8:7; 8:12; 22:11;
31:14; 31:14; 32:4; 33:6; 38:5;
38:5; 40:7

Chiamoe [chiamare: chiamò]
28:1

Chiamolo [lo chiamo] 41:5

Chiamò 9:11

Chiarissimo 9:4

Chiaro 19:1

Chiave 7:3; 12:14

Chiede 19:7; 23:27

Chino [chinato, piegato] 9:10

Chiosatore [glossatore,
commentatore] 28:2

Chiunque 11:1; 33:6; 40:4;
40:6

Chiusamente [implicitamente]
23:31

Chiusi [chiudere] 23:4; 23:22

Ci [adv. of place: 'here'] 19:20

Ci [first pers. plur. pers. pron.:
'us'] 14:6; 31:10; 38:3

Ciascun 19:7; 19:12; 23:22;
34:9

Ciascun' 3:9; 3:10

Ciascuna 15:1; 18:1; 24:7;
26:12

Ciascuno 13:1; 13:6;

Ciel [cielo] 8:6; 31:9; 34:7;
34:11

Cieli 29:2; 29:2; 29:2; 31:10

Cielo 2:1; 2:2; 3:7; 19:7; 19:9;
19:17; 23:7; 23:10; 23:25; 26:2;
26:6; 31:10; 33:8

Cinquanta 25:4

Cinque 15:8; 15:8; 41:2

Cinta [cingere, avvolgere intorno
alla vita: past. part.] 2:3

Ciò 3:7; 3:9; 3:9; 3:9; 3:10;
3:14; 7:7; 8:2; 8:3; 8:5; 8:10;
9:8; 12:5; 12:7; 12:7; 12:9;

12:14; 13:4; 14:13; 14:14; 15:2;
15:3; 15:4; 15:8; 16:1; 18:1;
18:9; 19:10; 20:1; 21:2; 21:6;
22:1 22:2; 22:3; 22:7; 22:8; 23:1;
23:31; 25:1; 25:2; 25:6; 25:7;
26:2; 26:4; 26:9; 26:9; 26:9;
27:1; 27:2; 28:2; 28:2; 28:2;
29:2; 29:3; 29:3; 29:4; 30:2;
30:2; 30:3; 31:5; 32:2; 32:3;
34:3; 34:6; 35:1; 35:3; 35:4;
38:2; 38:5; 38:6; 39:3; 39:6;
40:5; 41:6; 41:6; 42:2

Cioè 3:10; 6:2; 10:2; 13:6;
13:6; 14:14; 15:8; 23:8; 24:4;
25:8; 25:9; 26:15; 27:1; 29:1;
29:3; 29:3; 29:3; 30:3; 33:4;
33:4; 34:3; 38:1; 38:5; 38:5;
38:7; 38:7; 39:3; 41:4; 41:5;
41:6; 41:6; 41:7; 41:7; 42:3

Circuli [Lat.: genit. sing. of
circulum, -i 'circle'] 12:4

Circumferentie (Lat.: genit.
sing. of *circumferentia, -ae*
'circumference') 12:4

Circundava [circondare] 14:4

Cittade [città] 6:2; 7:1; 8:1; 9:1;
14:3; 19:3; 22:3; 30:1; 30:1;
40:1; 40:3; 40:4

Cittadini [abitanti] 34:1

Città 40:9

Civilibus [Lat.: dat. pl. of
civilis, -e 'civil') 25:9

Civitas (Lat.: *civitas, -atis*
'city') 28:1; 30:1

Clama [chiamare] 19:7; 19:15;
19:17

Clamantis [Lat.: pres. part. of
clamo, -as 'chiamare'] 24:4

Co [con] 7:1; 39:1; 41:1

Colà 22:3

Colei 5:2; 37:7

Color [colore] 19:11

Color [coloro] 15:5; 31:13;
36:3; 36:4

Colore 2:3; 3:1; 3:3; 22:9;
23:5; 23:9; 23:20; 25:7; 25:10;
36:1; 36:1; 39:4

Coloro 7:6; 14:14; 15:8; 19:1
21:6; 22:2; 23:1; 25:6; 26:4;
38:4; 38:5; 41:7

Colui 12:7; 12:14; 13:6; 22:1;
22:2; 22:8; 22:13; 23:10; 25:10;
42:2; 42:3; 42:3

Com' [preposition 'come'; see
'come']

Comandava 2:8; 4:2

Comandi 12:13

Combattea [combatteva] 13:5

Combattere 13:1

Combattuto 38:4

Come 3:2; 5:2; 7:2; 7:6; 8:3;
9:3; 9:5; 9:10; 9:12; 9:13; 11:3;
12:2; 12:4; 12:7; 12:7; 12:11;
12:12; 13:4; 13:5; 13:6; 14:6;
15:2; 15:8; 16:5; 18:1; 18:5;
19:2; 19:11; 19:12; 19:14; 19:14;
19:16; 19:16; 19:21; 20:3; 20:3;
20:7; 20:7; 20:7; 20:8; 20:8;
20:8; 21:1; 21:1; 21:5; 21:6;
21:6; 21:8; 22:1; 22:2; 22:2;
22:3; 22:6; 22:6; 22:7; 22:8;
22:12; 23:29; 23:1; 23:3; 23:4;

23:10; 23:16; 23:21; 23:29;
23:29; 23:31; 24:1; 24:9; 24:10;
24:10; 24:10; 24:10; 25:1; 25:1;
25:1; 25:2; 25:2; 25:3; 25:6;
25:8; 25:8; 25:9; 25:9; 25:9;
26:1; 26:9; 26:9; 26:14; 26:15;
27:2; 27:2; 27:3; 28:2; 28:3;
29:3; 30:1; 31:5; 31:10; 31:12;
33:1; 33:2; 33:4; 33:4; 33:6;
35:3; 36:1; 36:4; 37:4; 37:6;
38:1; 38:2; 38:3; 38:5; 38:7;
38:7; 38:7; 39:3; 40:5; 40:9;
40:9; 41:5; 41:6; 41:6; 42:2
Comincia 3:9; 3:13; 3:14; 7:2;
7:7; 8:3; 8:7; 8:12; 9:8; 12:9;
12:12; 12:16; 13:7; 13:10; 14:10;
15:3; 15:7; 15:9; 16:6; 16:10;
16:11; 19:3; 19:15; 19:16; 20:2;
20:7; 20:7; 21:1; 21:5; 21:5;
21:6; 22:8; 22:11; 22:17; 23:30;
23:30; 23:31; 24:6; 24:10; 24:11;
26:4; 26:9; 26:14; 26:15; 27:2;
31:1; 31:3; 31:4; 31:5; 31:6;
32:3; 32:4; 33:4; 33:4; 34:3;
34:4; 34:6; 35:4; 36:3; 37:3;
37:4; 38:4; 38:7; 40:5; 41:1;
41:2; 41:8
Cominciai 3:8; 3:9; 9:8; 12:4;
12:6; 19:1; 19:3; 23:3; 23:4;
23:6; 27:1; 27:2; 31:1; 39:2; 39:3
Cominciamenti [inizio] 16:11;
34:3
Cominciamento [inizio] 19:3;
19:3; 30:1; 34:6; 34:7
Cominciando 23:5
Cominciandomi [cominciare:

cominciando] 23:15
Cominciare 18:9; 18:9; 24:1;
35:3
Cominciaro [cominciarono]
13:1; 14:7; 18:3; 18:5; 23:14;
37:1
Comincio 19:17; 38:7
Cominciò 2:4; 2:5; 2:6; 2:7;
4:1; 23:11; 25:6; 39:2
Compagnia 8:2; 8:11; 9:2;
12:16; 12:11; 14:3; 14:3; 14:3;
18:1; 26:14
Compassione 35:3
Compiea [compiere: compiva]
34:1
Compiere 23:10
Compiuta 28:1
Compiutamente 2:7
Compiuti 3:1
Compiuto 29:1
Componendola 6:2
Comprende 19:17; 19:17
Comprendeano
[comprendevano] 26:3
Comprendere 37:3; 41:6
Comprendesse 39:6
Comprendi 12:7
Compreso 18:1
Compuosi [comporre] 6:2
Comune 13:6; 29:2
Comunicato 5:3; 19:22
Con [preposition]
Conceduta [concedere: concesso]
25:7
Conceduto [concedere:
concesso] 25:7; 25:7

Conchiudesse [conchiudere, comprendere] 22:7; 35:4

Con ciò fosse cosa che ['since it was the case that,' 'since,' 'whereas']

Con ciò sia cosa che ['since it is the case that,' 'since,' 'whereas']

Condizione 4:1; 14:9; 18:7; 23:30; 24:2; 30:1; 31:6; 32:4; 37:2; 37:3; 38:1

Condotto [condurre] 14:1; 14:2

Condusse 23:1; 23:26

Conforta 15:6; 22:15; 31:14

Confortai 5:3

Confortarlo 23:14

Confortarmi 23:14

Confortato 23:20

Conforto 15:8

Confortola [la conforto] 12:16

Congiunta [legata] 23:12

Conobbi [conoscere] 3:4; 9:6

Conoscemo [conoscere: conosciamo] 40:2

Conoscere 11:2

Conoscerà 12:7

Conoscesse 12:4

Conoscia [conoscere: conoscevo] 24:7

Conosciuto 12:7; 23:15

Consentir 38:8

Consentito 38:2

Consentiva 38:1

Consequentia [Lat.: nom. pl. neuter of *consequens, -tis*]13:4

Considerare 24:4; 24:5

Consigliato 15:8

Consiglio 2:9; 2:9; 4:2

Consolar 31:12; 38:9

Consolare 38:2

Consoliam [consoliamo] 23:20

Consuetudine 12:7

Consuman [consumano] 36:5

Consumato 23:28

Contar [contare, raccontare, dire] 12:14

Continuamente 2:9; 15:1; 23:1

Continuare 39:4

Continuatamente [continuamente] 15:1

Contra [contro] 12:17; 14:12; 15:2; 25:6; 38:6; 39:1; 39:2

Contraria 12:6

Contrario 38:6; 38:6

Convene [conviene] 13:10; 19:11; 23:3

Convenemi [mi conviene] 13:9; 31:8

Convenesi [si conviene; conviene, bisogna] 8:9; 28:3

Convenevole 28:2

Convenia [conveniva] 2:7; 14:3; 19:1; 23:1; 34:1

Convenirsi 28:3

Convenisse 26:3; 38:4

Convenne 7:1; 9:1; 17:1

Converrebbe 19:22; 28:2; 28:2

Converrà 9:6; 23:21

Convertia [convertiva] 3:7

Conviene 13:3; 18:3

Cor [Lat.: 'heart'] 3:5

Cor [cuore] 8:8; 9:11; 16:10;
19:9; 19:12; 20:2; 20:3; 20:4;
22:10; 23:27; 24:2; 31:9; 31:11;
31:13; 32:5; 32:5; 33:5; 35:6;
36:4; 38:9; 39:10; 40:10; 41:12
Coralmente [con tutto il cuore;
accoratamente] 22:14
Core [cuore] 3:10; 3:12; 3:12;
7:4; 7:6; 8:5; 12:12; 12:13; 13:8;
15:5; 20:5; 21:2; 21:3; 22:9;
23:19; 23:21; 24:7; 26:7; 27:3;
31:1; 31:8; 31:11; 31:15; 34:9;
35:7; 37:8; 38:8; 39:8; 41:10
Corona 39:9
Coronata 26:2
Corpo 8:1; 11:3; 14:4; 19:18;
23:8; 25:2; 25:2; 25:2
Corpora [corpi] 23:10
Corporale 25:1
Correano [correvano] 26:1
Corrente [fluente, scorrevole]
9:4
Cortese [nobile, onesto] 19:14
Cortesemente [nobilmente,
onestamente] 12:11
Cortesia [nobiltà, onestà] 3:1;
8:10; 10:1; 12:2; 42:3
Cortesissima [nobile, cortese]
3:2
Cosa 3:3; 3:5; 3:6; 3:9; 5:4; 8:3;
9:1; 9:6; 11:1; 11:3; 12:7; 13:4;
14:13; 14:13; 18:1; 19:6; 19:9;
19:11; 19:11; 20:1; 20:3; 20:5;
22:2; 22:3; 23:16; 23:27; 25:1;
25:1; 25:2; 25:3; 25:6; 25:7;
25:9; 25:9; 25:9; 26:6; 26:12;

27:5; 28:2; 28:3; 29:2; 30:2;
31:10; 32:2; 35:1; 35:3; 36:4;
40:9; 41:1; 41:6
Cose 2:9; 2:10; 3:3; 13:2; 13:4;
13:4; 16:1; 16:11; 19:15; 23:23;
24:10; 25:2; 25:2; 25:3; 25:4;
25:8; 25:8; 25:8; 25:8; 25:9;
25:10; 26:4; 26:14; 39:4; 40:2;
42:1; 42:2
Cosette [diminutive of 'cosa']
5:4
Così 3:7; 4:2; 4:3; 7:4; 12:4;
12:4; 13:5; 13:9; 14:6; 14:6;
14:9; 15:1; 16:4; 16:9; 18:5;
18:9; 20:3; 22:5; 22:7; 23:5;
23:13; 24:1; 24:3; 24:4; 24:4;
25:9; 25:10; 25:10; 25:10; 27:3;
29:3; 33:1; 33:4; 34:6; 35:8;
36:4; 37:3; 37:4; 37:4; 37:6;
37:8; 38:1; 38:2; 38:3; 38:4;
39:6; 41:4
Cospetto [presenza] 3:10
Costanzia [costanza] 39:2
Costei 15:2; 21:7; 33:2; 38:6;
41:6
Costoro 13:6; 22:6; 34:3; 34:3;
40:5
Costui 5:2; 15:2; 20:5; 23:20;
33:2; 38:9
Costumato [abituare] 27:3
Cotale [tale] 2:9; 5:2; 14:14;
15:1; 15:3; 16:5; 18:3; 20:2;
22:2; 22:3; 23:6; 24:10; 25:3;
25:6; 25:10; 28:2; 28:3; 31:2;
39:2; 39:6; 41:7
Cotali [tale] 15:3

Cotanto [tanto] 18:6; 23:19;
28:3

Covrian [coprire: coprivano]
23:26

Covrissero [coprire: coprissero]
23:8

Creda 19:4

Crede 12:13; 22:2; 24:3; 27:5

Credendo 16:4; 16:9; 23:11;
23:12; 24:6; 27:2

Credendomi [credendo] 14:3;
17:1

Credendosi [credendo] 14:1

Credente 5:4

Credesse 26:1

Credo 12:11; 14:9; 14:9; 14:10;
19:16; 22:11; 40:2

Creduto 5:3; 7:1

Crescete [crescere, accrescere]
36:5

Cria [creare: si crea, nasce] 15:6

Cristiana 29:2

Cristiani 29:1

Cristo 40:1

Crucciati 23:22

Crucciava 37:1

Cruccioso [corrucciato, dolente]
8:9

Crudele 8:5

Crudelitate [crudeltà] 33:7

Cu' [cui] 19:16; 40:7

Cui [Lat.: dative sing. of relat.
pron.] 12:4

Cui [rel. pron. direct & indirect
obj.] 3:10; 3:11; 3:14; 4:3; 8:1;
12:16; 12:17; 13:5; 18:4; 19:13;

21:2; 21:6; 21:6; 21:7; 22:17;
26:1; 28:1; 29:1; 29:3; 30:3;
31:1; 31:4; 31:4; 31:17; 33:1;
34:8; 37:2; 37:7; 38:5; 39:2;
41:7; 42:2

Cuore 2:4; 9:2; 9:5; 13:5; 15:8;
18:1; 18:1; 23:8; 24:1; 24:2;
24:2; 24:3; 24:4; 24:6; 24:10;
24:10; 24:10; 26:1; 37:1; 37:4;
38:1; 38:5; 38:5; 38:6; 38:6;
38:7; 39:2; 39:3; 39:3

Cuori 21:6; 21:6; 21:8

D' [da; di]

Da [preposition]

Dà 3:11; 26:7

Da che [dacché, poiché] 12:12

Dal [contracted preposition 'da']

Dannomi [mi dànno] 31:6;
31:13

Dardanide [Lat. *Dardanidae*
'Trojans'] 25:9

Dare 10:3; 29:2; 29:3; 33:1;
41:7

Darlo [dare+lo] 32:3

Darmi [dare+mi] 27:4

Data 4:1; 8:8; 8:12

Dato 19:10

Dava 2:7

Davante [davanti] 12:10

Davanti 23:25; 36:4

De [di]

De' [contracted preposition 'di']

Dea 25:9

Debbo [devo] 33:5

Debes [Lat.: sec. sing. of prcs.

indic. of *debeo, -es* 'to owe'] 25:9

Debilitata [indebolita] 23:3

Debole 4:1; 41:6

Deboletti [dimin. of *debole*] 11:2;

Deboletto 3:7

Debolezza 23:1

Dee [dovere: deve] 3:13; 12:11; 22:5

Defettivamente [difettivamente] 27:1

Degli [contracted prep. 'di']

Degna 20:1; 25:1; 31:10

Degnamente 14:2; 22:7; 39:5; 42:1

Degnato [degnare, stimare degno] 3:4

Degno 12:8; 19:10; 25:7; 25:8; 31:11; 32:6; 38:5

Degnò 12:6

Deh 23:20; 40:5; 40:9

Dei [dovere: devi] 19:14; 23:9; 23:27; 23:27; 24:2

Deinceps [Lat.: temporal adv.] 2:7

Del [contracted prep. 'di']

Delle [contracted prep. 'di']

Dentro 3:3; 7:6; 20:4; 20:5; 24:7

Denudare [spogliare, levare] 25:10

Deo [dio] 2:8; 7:4; 38:2

Deono [dovere: devono] 25:10

Deserto [Lat.: sing. abl. of *desertum, -i*] 24:4

Desiderando 14:10

Desiderii 18:4; 19:20

Desiderio 15:2; 36:5; 38:6; 38:7; 39:2; 39:2; 39:6

Desidero 19:21

Desideroso 23:27

Desiri [desiderio] 38:10

Desolata 30:1

Desse [dare] 9:7

Dessi [dare] 26:4; 33:2

Destrutto [distrutto] 34:9

Detta 32:1; 33:2

Dette 9:7; 12:9; 13:1; 18:3; 18:7; 25:4; 39:6

Detti 29:2

Detto 3:15; 21:8; 22:7; 22:8; 23:13; 23:25; 25:8; 25:8; 25:9; 27:1; 27:1; 33:1; 34:2; 37:3; 38:6; 40:5; 42:2

Deus [Lat.: 'dio'] 2:4

Deven [diviene] 26:5

Di [preposition]

Dì [die, giorno] 18:9; 22:1; 23:1; 23:1; 24:1

Dì [dire: sec. pers. sing. of the imper.] 12:13; 12:14

Dic [Lat.; sec. pers. sing. of the imperative of *dicere*] 25:9

Dica 8:9; 12:7; 13:9; 25:2; 25:2; 31:16

Dicano 22:11

Dice 1; 15:4; 15:8; 19:7; 19:11; 19:18; 22:9; 24:10; 24:10; 24:10; 25:9; 30:1; 37:4; 37:8; 38:5; 38:7; 38:7; 38:9; 40:10; 41:6

Dicea [diceva] 3:3; 4:2; 4:3; 5:2; 11:2; 12:4; 12:5; 14:9; 15:2;

23:3; 23:9; 23:18; 23:18; 23:21; 23:27; 23:28; 32:2; 35:3; 35:8; 37:2; 38:2; 40:3; 40:4

Diceali [gli diceva] 12:5

Diceame [mi diceva] 38:3

Diceami [diceva] 12:3

Dicean [dicevano] 23:22

Diceanmi [mi dicevano] 23:12

Diceano [dicevano] 14:6; 22:3; 22:6; 23:4; 23:4; 23:14; 26:2; 26:2; 34:5; 39:3

Dicele [le dice] 25:9

Dicendo 12:2; 18:8; 22:6; 22:11; 23:11; 23:31; 24:4; 24:7; 24:10; 26:7; 33:3; 34:11

Dicendomi 23:24

Dicer [dire] 19:16; 21:4; 31:15; 42:2

Dicere [dire] 5:2; 8:2; 12:17; 22:3; 23:13; 26:4

Dicerò [dirò] 17:2; 28:3; 31:4; 31:9

Dicerollo [lo dirò] 23:20

Dicesse 3:5; 14:10; 16:1; 23:8; 23:8; 23:26; 24:2; 24:4; 24:5; 24:10; 27:2; 32:2

Dicessemi [mi dicesse] 9:5

Dicessi 9:6; 18:7

Diceva 23:26; 34:9

Dicevan 23:20

Diche [dici, dica] 19:13

Dichi [dici] 12:7; 18:6

Dichiarando 14:14

Dichiarare 12:17; 14:14; 25:1; 25:3

Dichiararle 25:1

Dicitore [poeta] 25:8

Dicitori [poeti] 25:3; 25:3; 25:7

Dico 2:4; 2:7; 6:1; 7:7; 8:7; 8:7; 8:12; 9:13; 9:13; 10:1; 11:1; 12:1; 12:16; 12:16; 12:16; 12:17; 13:10; 13:10; 13:10; 13:10; 13:10; 14:4; 14:7; 14:14; 15:7; 15:7; 15:8; 15:8; 15:8; 15:8; 16:7; 16:11; 19:2; 19:5; 19:9; 19:16; 19:16; 19:16; 19:16; 19:16; 19:16; 19:17; 19:17; 19:17; 19:18; 19:18; 19:19; 19:19; 19:20; 19:20; 19:21; 19:21; 19:22; 20:6; 20:6; 20:7; 20:7; 20:8; 20:8; 21:5; 21:5; 21:6; 21:6; 21:6; 21:7; 21:8; 21:8; 21:8; 22:8; 23:2; 23:29; 23:29; 23:30; 23:30; 23:31; 23:31; 23:31; 24:2; 24:11; 24:11; 25:1; 25:2; 25:2; 25:2; 25:3; 25:10; 26:3; 26:8; 26:14; 26:14; 26:14; 26:15; 26:15; 26:15; 29:1; 29:3; 30:1; 31:3; 31:4; 31:4; 31:4; 31:5; 31:5; 31:5; 31:6; 31:6; 31:6; 31:7; 31:14; 33:5; 33:6; 34:4; 34:4; 34:4; 34:4; 34:5; 34:5; 34:6; 34:6; 38:4; 38:5; 38:6; 38:6; 38:7; 38:7; 39:3; 41:3; 41:4; 41:5; 41:6; 41:7; 41:7

Dicono 7:7; 25:10

Die [giorno] 3:1; 3:1; 9:1; 12:9; 19:3; 24:1; 24:4; 39:1; 39:2

Diedi [dare] 33:3

Dietro 7:4

Difenda 13:9

Difende 19:8
Difendea [difendeva] 16:5
Difendesse 16:4
Difensione [difesa] 9:5
Difesa 7:1; 9:1; 9:5; 10:1
Difetto 19:7; 21:2
Diffinita [definita] 8:12
Dignitade [dignità] 30:1
Dignitate [dignità] 7:4
Dilettandosi 18:1
Dilettare 37:1
Dilettevole 17:2
Diletti [amati]19:8
Dille [dì+le] 9:6; 12:13
Dilloci [dì+lo+ci: diccelo] 18:3
Dilungava 9:2
Dimandare [domandare] 12:6;
22:8
Dimenticando 16:4
Dimenticarlo 37:2
Dimenticava 39:3
Dimora 2:4; 2:5; 2:6; 23:21
Dimorai 18:9
Dimorando 13:7; 22:5
Dimorar 38:8
Dimorava 3:7; 18:4
Dimoro 7:5
Dimostrando 15:6
Dimostrar 35:6
Dimostrate 40:9
Dinanzi 1; 3:4; 7:1; 18:2; 21:2;
22:12; 23:7; 23:30; 26:8; 28:3;
35:3; 35:7; 36:5; 38:3
Dintorno [intorno] 39:4
Dio 19:8; 19:10; 19:11; 26:10
Dipoi [poi] 22:6

Dir [dire] 3:10; 7:4; 7:5; 31:16
Dire 2:8; 3:9; 6:2; 13:1; 13:9;
13:10; 14:10; 14:10; 15:3; 16:1;
17:1; 17:1; 18:3; 18:9; 19:1;
19:4; 19:16; 19:16; 19:16; 20:1;
20:2; 21:1; 21:6; 22:7; 22:7;
22:7; 23:6; 23:10; 23:14; 23:14;
23:16; 24:4; 25:4; 25:4; 25:5;
25:6; 25:6; 26:9; 27:2; 28:3;
31:4; 31:4; 31:4; 32:2; 34:3;
35:4; 36:3; 38:4; 38:7; 40:4;
40:5; 40:10; 41:6; 42:1
Direi 15:2; 19:16; 21:6; 22:7;
22:7; 22:7; 38:7; 40:4
Dire'lo [lo direi]
Dirla 23:29
Diroe [dirò] 23:15
Dirà 19:8
Disbigottito [sbigottito] 9:4
Discacciati [scacciati]14:8
Discacciato [scacciato] 39:2
Discernea [discerneva] 3:3
Discernesse 9:6
Dischernevole [schernevole,
ridicolo] 15:1
Disciolte [con i capelli sciolti]
23:23
Discolorito [scolorito] 16:4
Disconfiggea [sconfiggeva]
16:5
Disconfortai [sconfortarsi] 7:1
Disconsolata [sconsolata]
31:17
Disconsolati [sconsolati] 32:4;
32:5
Discovrir [scoprire] 8:10

Discovrire [scoprire] 9:10
Disdegno [sdegno] 23:27
Disdegnoso [sdegnoso] 13:10
Disegnare 34:3
Disegnava 34:1
Disfogare [sfogare] 9:2; 31:1;
36:2
Disfogarla [sfogarla] 31:1
Disia [desiderava] 32:5
Disiata [desiderata] 19:9; 19:17
Disiderassero [desiderassero]
39:4
Disiderio [desiderio] 18:9
Disidero [desidero] 23:9
Disignandole [designandole,
indicando a lei] 31:7
Disio [desiderio] 20:5; 31:13
Disira [desidera] 41:11
Disire [desiderio] 31:10
Disiri [desideri] 33:7; 38:3; 39:9
Disnore [disonore] 12:11
Disparve [sparire: sparve] 9:7;
9:12; 12:9
Dispiace 19:22
Dispiacea [dispiaceva] 9:2
Dispogliata [spogliata] 30:1
Disponsata [sposata] 2:7
Disposata [sposata] 14:3
Disposto 27:2
Dispregiar [spregiare] 32:6
Disse 2:4; 2:5; 2:6; 3:14; 9:11;
14:2; 18:3; 18:6; 19:2; 24:3;
24:9; 24:11
Dissero 23:30; 23:30; 25:5
Dissi 7:2; 8:3; 8:3; 14:2; 14:8;
14:10; 15:3; 16:1; 16:6; 17:1;

18:4; 18:6; 20:2; 21:1; 23:15;
23:16; 23:20; 23:29; 23:31; 24:6;
26:4; 26:9; 32:2; 32:3; 33:2;
34:2; 34:3; 36:3; 37:3; 38:4;
39:6; 39:6; 40:2; 40:5; 40:6; 41:1
Dissine [ne dissi] 13:7
Distendersi [estendersi,
diffondersi] 14:4
Distinguere 16:11
Distinguo 22:17
Distretta [stretta] 33:1
Distretto [stretto] 32:1; 33:4
Distrugge 5:2; 15:2
Distruggendo 11:2
Distruggitore [distruttore] 31:1
Distruggitrice [distruttrice]
10:2
Distrutta 8:10; 15:8
Distrutti 14:5; 36:5
Distrutto 4:3; 39:6
Disturbasse 37:7
Disvegliasse [svegliasse] 3:6
Disvegliato [svegliato] 3:7
Ditelmi [ditemelo] 22:9
Diterminata [determinata]
19:19
Dittare [scrivere in poesia] 20:3
Dittatori [poeti] 25:7
Divenia [diveniva] 11:3; 23:27
Divenisse 19:6
Divenne 33:8
Divenni 4:1
Diventan 39:10
Divento 31:14
Divenuto 22:6; 22:9
Diverria [diverrebbe] 19:9

Diverse 3:14; 15:8; 33:2; 34:5

Diversi 13:1; 13:10; 14:1; 23:4

Diversitade [diversità] 13:10

Divide 3:13; 8:7; 8:12; 12:16;
15:7; 15:8; 16:11; 19:16; 19:18;
19:19; 19:20; 20:6; 20:7; 21:6;
22:11; 23:30; 24:11; 26:15; 31:4;
31:6; 34:5; 34:6

Dividere 13:10; 41:9

Dividerlo 36:3; 41:9

Dividerò 19:15; 31:2; 34:3;
35:4

Dividesi [si divide] 19:17

Divido 14:13; 39:7; 40:8

Diviene 15:3; 15:7

Divino 19:7

Divisa [dividere] 14:13; 41:9

Divisi 38:5

Divisione [suddivisione e
chiosa] 14:13; 14:13; 19:3;
23:16; 26:8; 26:9

Divisioni 19:21; 19:22; 19:22;
37:5

Diviso 31:13

Divolgata [divulgata] 20:1

Do [dare] 21:7

Dodici 2:2

Doglia [dolere: third pers. sing.
of pres. subj.] 15:6

Doglia [dolore] 31:11; 31:15

Dogliose [dolorose] 34:10

Doglioso [doloroso] 8:8

Dolce 7:4; 13:4; 13:4; 19:5;
23:27; 31:10; 33:6; 39:10

Dolcemente 38:8

Dolcezza 3:2; 11:3; 21:3; 21:5;

21:8; 26:3; 26:7; 26:13; 27:4

Dolcissima 23:9

Dolcissimo 3:2; 9:3; 10:2;
21:8

Dole [duole: third pers. sing. of
pres. indic. of *dolere*] 39:10

Dolea [doleva] 14:6; 16:2

Dolente [sofferente] 31:9; 32:6;
33:5; 34:9; 36:4; 40:9; 41:12

Dolenti [sofferenti] 31:1; 31:8

Dolere [soffrire] 23:2

Dolor [Lat.: 'suffering'] 7:7; 7:7

Dolor [dolore] 8:8; 23:27;
31:14; 32:5; 35:5

Dolore 7:3; 12:1; 22:2; 22:9;
23:11; 31:1; 31:8; 33:5; 39:3;
39:9

Dolorosa 22:14; 23:1; 23:19;
33:5; 37:2; 40:3

Dolorosamente 7:2; 39:2

Dolorose 31:1

Dolorosi 13:3; 23:10; 35:1;
36:4; 39:10

Doloroso, 22:2; 23:11

Dolze [dolce] 12:12; 12:16

Dolzore [dolcezza] 13:8

Domandai 18:2

Domandailo [verb. form
domandai with enclitic pron.
lo=gli] 12:6

Domandare 4:2; 22:8

Domandate 22:7; 22:7

Domandato 11:1; 15:1; 25:10

Domandatrice [colei che
domanda; 'she who asks'] 21:5

Domandava 32:2

Domandavano 4:3; 23:14

Domandi 12:13

Domando 3:13; 22:8; 22:11

Domandò 14:7

Domina [Lat.: signora; 'lady']
28:1

Dominabitur [Lat.: third pers.
sing. of fut. of *dominor,-aris*] 2:4

Domini [Lat.: genit. sing. of
dominus, -i] 24:4; 29:1

Dominus [Lat.] 3:3

Dona 16:7; 19:10

Donna 2:1; 3:1; 3:4; 3:7; 5:1;
5:2; 5:3; 5:3; 6:1; 6:1; 6:2; 6:2;
7:1; 7:2; 8:1; 8:1; 8:2; 8:5; 8:6;
8:7; 8:10; 8:10; 9:1; 9:1; 9:3;
9:5; 9:5; 10:1; 11:2; 12:2; 12:6;
13:5; 14:3; 14:5; 14:5; 14:6;
14:9; 14:11; 15:1; 15:7; 15:8;
16:3; 16:4; 17:1; 18:2; 18:2;
18:2; 18:3; 18:4; 18:6; 18:6;
18:8; 19:1; 19:4; 19:9; 19:11;
19:16; 19:17; 19:20; 20:5; 20:5;
20:8; 20:8; 21:2; 21:5; 22:2;
22:2; 22:5; 22:9; 22:13; 23:2;
23:6; 23:8; 23:8; 23:11; 23:16;
23:17; 23:18; 23:21; 23:24;
23:26; 23:27; 24:1; 24:2; 24:3;
24:3; 24:3; 25:6; 26:1; 26:5;
26:8; 26:10; 26:14; 27:1; 27:4;
29:3; 31:9; 31:9; 31:15; 31:16;
32:2; 32:5; 32:6; 33:2; 33:5;
33:7; 34:1; 34:4; 34:6; 34:7;
34:8; 35:2; 35:3; 35:8; 36:1;
36:1; 36:2; 36:4; 37:1; 37:2;
37:2; 37:8; 37:8; 38:1; 38:1;

38:3; 38:4; 38:6; 38:7; 40:1;
40:1; 40:2; 41:5; 41:7; 41:11;
42:3

Donne 3:1; 6:1; 6:2; 6:2; 8:1;
8:5; 13:5; 14:1; 14:1; 14:2; 14:3;
14:4; 14:7; 14:7; 14:10; 14:11;
18:1; 18:1; 18:3; 18:5; 19:1;
19:2; 19:3; 19:4; 19:6; 19:13;
19:14; 19:16; 21:2; 21:5; 21:7;
21:7; 22:3; 22:3; 22:3; 22:3;
22:4; 22:4; 22:5; 22:6; 22:7;
22:7; 22:9; 22:11; 22:17; 23:4;
23:4; 23:5; 23:8; 23:12; 23:13;
23:18; 23:20; 23:22; 23:23;
23:26; 23:29; 23:30; 23:30; 24:4;
26:10; 26:15; 26:15; 31:7; 31:9;
31:10; 31:16; 31:17; 41:1; 41:7;
41:7; 41:13

Donzelle [giovani donne] 19:6;
19:16; 31:17

Dopo 23:4; 23:25; 24:3; 24:4;
24:5; 31:2; 32:1; 37:2; 40:1

Dorme 21:1

Dormendo 3:12; 20:4

Dormia [dormiva] 3:6; 24:7

Dormire 3:4; 12:3; 23:12;
23:18

Dottanza [Provençal *doptansa*:
timore 'fear'] 7:5

Dov', Dove 9:1; 14:14; 22:3;
39:3; 41:11

Doverebbe [dovrebbe]15:8; 22:3

Dovesse 20:1

Dovessi 18:3; 32:2

Dovrebbero 37:2

Dovreste 37:8

Dovresti 12:11

Drappi 9:3

Drappo 3:4; 3:12

Dubbio 12:17; 14:14; 39:6

Dubbiosa [che causa dubbi]
12:17

Dubbiose [che causa dubbi]
14:14

Dubita 12:17; 25:9

Dubitare 25:1; 25:1

Dubitazione [dubito] 14:14;
25:1; 37:4

Dubitosamente
[timorosamente] 3:6

Dubitose [che causa dubbi]
14:14; 23:23

Due 3:1; 3:13; 7:7; 8:3; 15:7;
19:17; 19:18; 19:19; 19:20; 20:6;
20:7; 21:5; 21:8; 22:8; 22:11;
23:29; 23:30; 23:31; 24:11; 27:1;
31:5; 32:4; 33:2; 33:4; 33:4;
34:3; 34:5; 37:4; 38:5; 39:4;
39:9; 40:6; 41:1

Dunque 12:12; 25:8; 29:3

Duol [dolore] 8:5

Duolo [dolore] 23:28

Dura 20:5

Duramente 10:1

Durar 23:21

Durare 23:3

Duri [Lat.: nom. masc. plur. of
durus, -i 'hard'] 25:9

Duri [durare] 42:2

E [conjunction]

È [essere] 3:10; 3:15; 5:4; 7:3;

8:5; 8:10; 9:5; 12:5; 12:6; 12:8;
12:11; 12:11; 12:12; 12:12;
12:13; 12:14; 12:17; 13:2; 13:3;
13:4; 13:4; 13:5; 13:8; 14:10;
14:14; 14:14; 14;14; 14:14; 15:2;
15:4; 15:8; 16:2; 16:3; 16:4;
16:5; 17:2; 18:8; 18:8; 19:6;
19:8; 19:9; 19:11; 19:15; 19:15;
19:15; 19:17; 19:20; 19:20;
19:21; 19:22; 20:1; 20:4; 20:6;
21:1; 21:3; 21:4; 21:5; 21:5;
21:6; 21:6; 21:7; 21:8; 21:8;
22:2; 22:2; 22:6; 22:6; 22:7;
22:12; 23:6; 23:8; 23:10; 23:21;
23:24; 23:30; 24:4; 24:4; 24:4;
24:9; 25:1; 25:1; 25:1; 25:3;
25:3; 25:4; 25:4; 25:4; 25:5;
25:6; 25:7; 25:7; 25:7; 25:8;
25:9; 25:9; 26:1; 26:2; 26:2;
26:2; 26:8; 26:8; 26:11; 26:13;
26:15; 27:5; 28:2; 28:2; 28:2;
28:2; 28:2; 28:2; 28:2; 29:1;
29:1; 29:3; 29:3; 29:3; 29:3;
29:3; 29:4; 31:3; 31:3; 31:5;
31:9; 31:10; 31:11; 31:12; 31:15;
31:15; 31:16; 32:1; 32:6; 33:5;
33:8; 34:7; 35:4; 35:4; 35:8;
36:3; 37:4; 37:5; 37:8; 38:1;
38:2; 38:3; 38:3; 38:3; 38:5;
38:6; 38:6; 38:9; 38:9; 38:10;
40:1; 40:6; 40:6; 40:7; 40:9;
41:5; 41:7; 41:8; 41:11; 42:3

E' [egli; esso] 33:4; 33:7; 35:3;
38:7

E' [essi] 34:2

Ebbe [avere] 18:3; 28:3; 30:3

Ebbero 18:6; 22:17; 25:5; 31:1
Ebrietà 15:5; 15:9
Ecce [Lat.: 'ecco'] 2:4
Eccellenti 26:4
Ecco 15:1
Ed [conjunction 'e']
Effetti 34:4
Effettive ["vertudi effettive"
'virtuose operazioni'] 19:18
Effetto 41:3
Ego [Lat.: first person subject
pron.] 3:3; 12:4; 24:4
Ei [egli] 38:7; 38:10
Ei [ebbi] 23:3; 33:1
Ell', Ella 2:2; 2:8; 3:6; 3:8;
9:1; 11:1; 11:2; 12:7; 12:13;
12:14; 12:16; 14:10; 18:3; 19:12;
19:11; 21:1; 21:2; 21:2; 21:4;
21:6; 22:3; 22:3; 22:15; 22:17;
23:24; 26:1; 26:2; 26:2; 26:3;
26:5; 26:6; 26:8; 27:5; 29:1;
29:1; 29:1; 29:1; 29:3; 29:3;
31:12; 31:12; 40:10; 42:2
Elle 14:2; 22:7; 23:5; 23:12;
31:17
Elli [egli; esso; at times
pleonastic] 2:8; 3:6; 3:14; 7:3;
9:4; 9:12; 9:13; 11:2; 11:3;
12:12; 16:7; 19:22; 23:20; 23:24;
27:3; 41:6; 41:8; 41:11
Elli [essi] 34:2; 36:5; 39:10;
40:3; 40:4
Ello [esso] 37:3
Eneida [Eneide] 25:9; 25:9
Entrai 23:23
Entrar 31:11

Entrata [introduzione, inizio]
30:1
Entro [dentro] 34:8
Entrò [entrare] 23:13
Eo [io] 8:9; 12:13; 34:8; 36:5;
39:10
Eole [Lat.: vocative of *Aelos, -i,*
Aeolus, lord of the winds] 25:9
Eolo [Aeolus, lord of the winds]
25:9
Era 2:1; 2:2; 2:2; 2:9; 3:1; 3:2;
3:3; 3:4; 3:6; 3:8; 3:9; 3:14; 4:1;
4:2; 5:1; 5:2; 5:3; 6:1; 7:1; 8:6;
9:1; 9:1; 9:4; 9:5; 9:11; 13:6;
14:3; 11:3; 12:9; 13:2; 13:3;
13:4; 13:5; 15:1; 18:1; 18:2;
18:2; 18:4; 19:20; 20:2; 20:2;
22:1; 22:1; 22:4; 23:2; 23:3;
23:8; 23:10; 23:10; 23:11; 23:12;
23:13; 23:13; 23:16; 23:17;
23:19; 23:19; 23:20; 23:24;
23:28; 23:30; 24:3; 24:3; 24:3;
24:3; 24:8; 25:6; 26:2; 26:3;
26:8; 26:14; 27:3; 28:1; 29:1;
29:3; 31:1; 31:10; 32:1; 32:2;
32:2; 33:1; 34:1; 34:2; 34:3;
34:4; 34:6; 34:7; 34:8; 34:9;
35:5; 35:7; 38:4; 38:6; 39:3
Eran [erano] 3:11; 3:13
Erano 3:1; 3:1; 3:9; 14:1; 14:3;
18:1; 18:3; 18:3; 18:3; 23:12;
25:3; 25:3; 26:8; 31:1; 31:17;
34:2; 34:3; 38:5
Ero [Lat.: first pers. sing. of fut.
of *esse*] 2:7
Errando [errare, vagare,

smarrirsi] 23:22

Erranza [errore, smarrimento, incertezza] 13:9

Errare [vagare, smarrirsi] 23:4; 23:5

Erronea 23:8

Esce [uscire] 41:10

Escon [uscire: escono] 27:4

Escono 19:12

Escusandomi [scusando+mi] 15:3

Escusomene [me ne scuso] 30:2

Esperti [che ha esperienza] 26:1

Essa 3:7

Esse 2:10; 18:2; 41:1

Essemplo [esempio, esemplare, immagine] 2:10; 15:8; 19:11; 40:1

Essendo [essere] 23:15

Essenza 3:11

Esser [essere] 19:11; 19:14; 20:3; 22:5; 23:23; 23:27; 23:27

Essere 4:1; 12:2; 12:8; 19:14; 20:7; 23:9; 23:9; 25:2; 25:2; 25:2; 25:2; 25:9; 27:2; 28:2; 29:2; 35:3

Èssi [si è; si sta] 31:11

Esso 12:4; 16:11; 19:14; 22:6; 35:4

Est [Lat.: third pers. sing. of pres. indic. of *esse*] 7:7; 12:3; 25:9; 28:1; 42:3

Esta [questa] 31:10

Este [queste] 12:12

Esto [questo] 3:12

Estreme 7:7

Estremitade [estremità]14:2

Et [Lat.: conjunction 'e'] 7:7

Etade [età] 2:3; 3:1; 39:1

Etate [età] 23:16; 23:17

Eterna 34:1

Etternale [eterno] 22:1

Etterno [eterno] 31:10

Excelsis [Lat.: ablative plur. of *excelsus*; "in excelsis" 'in the highest'] 23:7

Explorare [Lat.: infinitve; It.: "esplorare" 'to explore'] 25:9

Fa [fare] 8:4; 12:8; 12:14; 13:8; 13:8; 14:13; 16:10; 19:5; 20:5; 21:1; 21:2; 21:2; 22:15; 26:12; 26:12; 27:4; 29:3; 29:3; 31:16; 34:11; 37:8; 41:4; 41:12

Fabuloso [favoloso, immaginario] 2:10

Faccendo [fare: facendo] 23:12; 34:3

Faccia [viso] 22:4; 23:8; 42:3

Faccio [fare: fo] 35:5

Face [fare: fa] 12:12; 15:6; 15:9; 20:5; 20:8; 26:11; 31:10; 33:8; 35:8; 38:8

Facea [faceva] 3:6; 9:5; 11:1; 13:6; 14:3; 16:2; 23:20; 34:2; 34:4; 36:1; 37:6; 39:4

Faceano [facevano] 4:2; 23:5; 35:1

Facesse 5:4; 19:1

Facessero 14:3

Faceste 37:6

Facia [fare: facevo] 34:8

Facta [Lat.: past partic. femin. of *facio,-is* 'to make'] 28:1

Fae [fare: fa] 21:6; 28:2

Fai [fare] 22:14; 23:24

Fallace [non vero] 23:15; 23:26

Fallar [fallo, torto] 8:9

Falle [le fa] 12:8; 12:13

Falli [li fa] 20:4; 20:7

Falsa 25:1

Fama 25:5

Famosa 24:3

Famosi 3:9

Fan [fare: fanno] 33:5

Fantasia 16:2; 23:4; 23:5; 23:6; 23:8; 23:13; 23:18; 23:29; 23:30

Far [fare] 7:6; 8:9; 19:11; 19:11; 40:10

Farà [idiom. *farà mestiere = sarà necessario*] 12:8

Fare 2:7; 3:9; 5:3; 5:4; 8:2; 11:2; 12:9; 12:16; 13:9; 14:1; 14:2; 14:3; 23:10; 23:12; 24:2; 25:6; 25:8; 26:4; 31:1; 32:2; 32:3; 34:1; 37:2; 37:3; 39:6; 40:5; 41:1; 41:9

Farebbero [fare] 40:4

Farei [fare] 19:5; 40:4

Faria [fare: farebbe]12:11

Farle 21:2

Farlo 3:9

Farmi 23:18; 24:7

Farne 7:2; 8:9

Farnetica 23:4

Farneticare 23:30

Farvi 19:9

Fas [Lat. 'fate,' 'divine will'] 25:9

Fate 37:2

Fatta 34:1

Fatte 19:22; 19:22

Fattele [fare: femin. past partic., *fatte*, + pron. *le*] 25:8

Fatti 39:9

Fatto 6:2; 31:1; 31:14; 32:3; 33:1; 33:3

Fattore 29:3; 29:3

Fé [fare: fece] 31:10

Fece 8:6; 8:7; 12:12; 23:4; 23:19

Fecer [fare: fecero] 23:18

Fecero 23:30; 42:1

Feci 5:4; 10:1; 12:9; 22:8; 41:2

Fede 12:13; 13:2; 13:3; 14:7; 23:27; 26:11

Fedele 2:9; 12:2; 13:3; 14:14; 24:4

Fedeli 3:9; 7:7; 8:7; 32:4

Fella [la fece] 31:10

Fellone [sleale] 37:7

Femmina [donna] 26:2

Femmine 19:1

Fere [ferire: ferisce] 14:12

Fermamente 3:2

Fermata [ferma, stabile] 12:13

Feron [ferire: feriscono] 19:12

Fiamma 11:1

Fiata [volta] 8:2

Fiate [volte] 2:1; 7:4; 10:1; 12:4; 13:8; 16:6; 16:7; 31:13; 32:5; 35:5; 36:1; 36:5

Fidandomi 14:2

Figlio 29:3

Figliuola 2:8; 19:13; 31:17

Figliuolo 22:2; 22:2

Figura 3:3; 14:11; 14:12;
22:13; 25:7; 25:10; 35:5; 40:1

Figure 34:3

Fili [Lat.: vocat. of *filius, -i*]
12:3

Filosofo 25:2; 41:6

Finalmente 16:5

Fine 2:2; 12:13; 14:4; 18:3;
18:3; 18:4; 18:4; 19:20; 19:20;
23:15; 31:2; 41:7

Finestra 35:2

Finir 19:10

Finire 19:4

Fioco 23:24

Fiso [fisso] 19:12; 31:14

Fiume 9:4

Fo [fare: fo, faccio] 19:15; 38:5;
38:6

Foco [fuoco] 23:23

Foe [fare: fo, faccio] 23:31; 31:5

Folle 13:8

For [fuori] 19:11; 27:4; 34:4;
34:10; 34:11

Fora [fuori] 23:22

Fore [fuori] 8:5; 14:12; 34:9;
35:1

Forma 8:6; 19:11; 20:7

Formata 23:27

Forse 12:11; 15:8; 18:4; 20:1;
25:3; 28:2; 29:4; 38:1; 40:2; 40:9

Forte [adv. & adj.] 14:6; 15:1;
16:3; 23:3; 23:4; 23:8; 23:10;
23:13; 23:17; 27:3; 31:13; 33:5;

36:4; 37:8; 39:1

Fortemente 2:4

Fortior [Lat.: comparative of
fortis] 2:4

Fortuna 12:16; 18:1

Forza 12:7; 14:5; 39:6; 39:8

Fosse 2:9; 2:9; 3:9; 9:1; 9:2;
11:2; 11:3; 12:6; 12:13; 12:17;
14:4; 14:14; 18:9; 20:1; 22:2;
22:2; 22:4; 22:7; 23:3; 23:5;
23:16; 24:1; 24:2; 25:1; 25:1;
25:2; 25:2; 25:6; 25:9; 26:1;
26:9; 28:2; 28:2; 29:2; 35:1;
35:1; 37:7

Fosser [fossero] 32:5

Fossero 16:1; 23:5; 23:7;
23:11; 25:8; 40:3

Fossi 12:11; 14:2; 14:6; 15:1;
15:2; 23:30

Fosti 12:7

Fra [preposition] 14:9; 18:8;
19:11; 23:3; 23:3; 35:3; 37:3;
38:2; 40:2; 40:3; 40:4; 40:5

Fraile [frale, fragile, debole] 4:1

Frale [frale, fragile, debole]
23:21; 27:4

Frate [fratello] 33:4

Frequenter [Lat.: adv.
'frequentemente'] 2:7

Fu [essere] 2:1; 2:7; 8:6; 12:13;
23:21; 33:7; 34:2; 34:7

Fue [essere: fu] 3:8; 3:14; 3:14;
3:14; 3:15; 5:2; 5:3; 6:2; 7:2;
8:1; 8:1; 10:2; 12:1; 12:2; 12:6;
12:6; 12:9; 18:4; 19:20; 20:1;
22:2; 23:8; 24:3; 24:10; 28:1;

28:3; 29:1; 29:1; 29:2; 29:3;
29:3; 30:1; 30:2; 31:5; 31:10;
31:12; 32:1; 32:1; 32:2; 40:7;
42:2

Fuggan [fuggire: fuggano] 27:4

Fugge 21:2

Fuggi 15:4

Fui [essere] 3:7; 14:1; 18:1;
18:2; 23:20; 23:29

Fuoco 3:3

Fuor [fuori] 7:6

Fuori 14:5; 14:6; 14:7; 14:14;
30:2; 36:2; 40:6; 41:5

Fuoro [essere: furono] 3:1;14:5;
17:1; 23:18; 25:5; 39:5

Furon [essere: furono] 23:22

Gabbare [deridere, beffare] 15:8

Gabbasse 14:9

Gabbate 14:11

Gabbavano 14:7

Gabbo [derisione, beffa] 15:6

Gaia [lieto, leggiadro] 8:6; 8:10

Galizia [region in Spain] 40:7

Gelo [ghiaccio, freddo] 19:9;
31:10

Generazione 29:2

Genitore 22:1

Gente 8:9; 9:10; 10:1; 19:5;
19:14; 22:13; 25:3; 26:14; 40:1;
40:9

Genti [plur. of "gente"] 3:2;
12:1; 20:1; 26:1; 31:14; 40:7

Gentil [gentile, nobile] 3:10;
8:5; 8:5; 8:6; 12:15; 12:16; 19:9;
20:2; 20:3; 21:2; 31:9; 31:10;

32:6; 34:7; 34:8; 38:3; 38:4; 38:8

Gentile [nobile] 5:1; 5:3; 6:1;
8:1; 8:1; 9:1; 14:3; 19:6; 21:4;
21:6; 22:9; 23:9; 23:11; 23:27;
24:3; 24:6; 26:3; 26:4; 26:5;
26:13; 31:11; 33:8; 35:2; 35:3;
38:1; 38:4; 38:4; 41:13

Gentilezza [nobiltà] 16:4;
26:11

Gentilezze 23:17

Gentili 3:1; 14:1; 18:1; 19:1;
31:9; 32:5; 36:4; 41:1

Gentilissima 3:1; 4:1; 5:1;
5:2; 5:4; 6:1; 8:2; 9:3; 10:2;
11:3; 12:6; 14:1; 14:4; 14:5;
14:7; 18:2; 18:9; 21:1; 22:3;
23:3; 23:15; 26:1; 28:1; 38:6;
39:2; 39:3; 40:1

Gentium [Lat.: genit. plur. of
gens, -tis] 28:1

Geremia [prophet Jeremiah] 7:7;
30:1

Gia [gire, andare: giva, andava]
2:1; 2:2; 9:4; 19:1

Già 3:9; 3:11; 3:13; 4:1; 7:4;
7:7; 8:2; 8:6; 12:4; 12:17; 13:1;
18:4; 23:9; 23:13; 24:3; 33:5;
33:5; 34:2; 34:4; 38:6

Giace [giacere] 23:8; 23:26

Giacea [giacere: giaceva] 12:3

Giacere 8:1

Giano [gire, andare: givano,
andavano] 22:4

Gio [gire, andare: gì, andò] 22:1

Gioia [gioire: gioiva] 15:4

Giorno 3:2; 3:4; 5:1; 5:3; 9:7;

9:8; 14:3; 23:2; 27:1; 29:1; 34:1

Giovane 8:1; 12:3; 19:13; 23:11; 35:2; 38:1; 39:1

Giovanissima 2:3; 2:8

Giovanna 24:3; 24:4

Giovanni 24:4

Gioventudine [gioventù, giovinezza] 2:10

Gioventute [gioventù, giovinezza] 8:10

Gir [gire, andare] 3:12; 19:13; 27:4

Gira [girare] 21:2; 41:10

Girai 19:13

Girazione [giro, moto circolare] 2:1

Gire [andare] 12:11; 12:16; 15:7; 42:3

Gisse [gire, andare: andasse] 3:7

Gita [gire, andare: andata] 31:9; 32:6

Gitta [gettare: getta] 19:9

Gitto [gettare: getto] 39:10

Giù 31:10

Giudicare 23:5

Giudicassero 3:9

Giudicio [giudizio] 3:15; 8:8

Giugne [giungere: giunge] 15:2; 15:8

Giugnea [giungere: giungeva] 11:1

Giugnemi [mi giunge] 31:14

Giugnerebbe [giungere: giungerebbe] 14:10

Giugni [giungere: giungi] 19:13

Giungea [giungere: giungeva]

26:1; 26:1

Giunse [giungere: pret.] 3:2; 12:1; 13:7; 15:1; 19:1; 22:8; 23:1; 23:2; 23:4; 23:9; 24:2; 31:10; 35:6

Giunta [giungere: past partic. femin.] 23:19; 33:7

Giunto [giungere: past partic. masc.]18:2; 41:8; 41:11

Giura [giurare] 19:11

Giuso [giù] 29:2

Giustizia 28:1

Giva [gire, andare: andava] 23:22

Gli [defin. artic. masc. plur.] 34:4; 34:5

Gloria 5:1; 8:1; 22:1; 26:2; 42:3

Gloriare [essere nella gloria celeste] 28:1

Gloriosa 2:1; 31:11; 32:1; 33:1; 37:2; 39:1

Gloriosamente 23:7; 40:1; 42:3

Glorioso 22:1

Governato 4:2

Gradi 32:1

Grado 2:2; 14:14; 22:2; 22:2; 41:6

Gran [grande] 9:5; 9:12; 13:8; 15:5; 31:10

Grande 3:1; 3:7; 14:1; 19:3; 23:11; 25:10; 33:8

Grandissima 9:7; 28:1

Grandissimi 23:5; 37:3

Gravati [aggravati, appesantiti] 23:22

Grave 7:3; 31:13
Gravi [grave] 13:3
Gravitate [gravità, afflizione]
40:9
Gravoso [pesante, duro] 8:8
Grazia 8:9; 8:12; 12:14; 19:10;
26:1; 26:8; 26:10; 31:11
Graziosa 8:1; 26:14
Grecia 25:3
Grida [gridare, chiedere] 19:7
Gridavan [gridare: gridavano]
23:25
Gridin [gridare: gridino]15:5
Grossa [rozzo] 25:10
Grossi [rozzo] 25:5
Guai [guaio, lamento] 14:12;
23:23; 31:8
Guarda 20:7; 33:2
Guardando 23:28; 24:4; 24:8
Guardare 12:12; 16:10; 23:7;
23:10; 26:5; 28:2
Guardasse 3:3; 39:5
Guardaste 35:5
Guardate 7:3
Guardato 12:3
Guardava 4:3; 9:4
Guardavano18:3
Guastando [rovinare] 8:5
Guati [guardare: guardi] 19:12
Guerire [guarire] 16:9
Guiderdonati [premiare:
premiati] 39:5
Guiderdone [premio] 8:2
Guisa [modo, maniera] 2:3; 7:5;
12:6; 25:10; 39:4

Ha [avere] 4:3; 7:7; 8:5; 9:13;
12:12; 12:13; 14:13; 18:4; 19:10;
19:10; 21:5; 22:16; 22:17; 22:17;
23:29; 24:5; 24:9; 24:10; 25:9;
26:14; 27:3; 28:3; 31:3; 31:9;
31:10; 31:11; 31:13; 32:4; 33:4;
34:3; 34:4; 38:7; 40:10; 41:2
Habent [Lat.: third pers. plur.
pres. indic. of *habeo, -es*] 12:4
Hae [avere: ha] 37:4; 38:3
Hai [avere] 8:8; 8:10; 8:10; 8:12;
9:6; 18:7; 22:8; 22:13; 23:20
Hanno 13:8; 13:10; 15:6; 22:10;
25:8; 25:8; 31:8; 31:10; 36:5;
39:8; 39:10; 40:10
Have [avere: ha] 7:4; 19:7
Heu [Lat.: interjection used to
express sorrow] 2:7
Ho [avere] 7:5; 9:5; 9:6; 19:13
Hoe [avere: ho] 7:7; 23:15

I [ivi, lì, in quel posto] 31:11
I' [io] 12:9; 12:10; 15:4; 15:4;
19:4; 23:15; 31:8; 31:14; 37:7
Iacopo [Giacomo] 40:6; 40:7
Iam 2:5 [Lat.: adv., It. *già*]
Ier [ieri] 9:9
Iesu [Gesù] 40:1
Il [defin. artic.] 8:15; 13:8; 19:5;
20:3; 21:2; 22:9; 23:13; 23:18;
23:19; 24:8
Il [lo: pers. & demonstr. pron.]
24:7; 31:16
Imaginai [immaginare] 23:6
Imaginando 23:22
Imaginar 23:26; 31:11

Imaginare 16:2; 23:4; 23:15; 23:23

Imaginate 7:3

Imaginava 23:7

Imaginazione [immaginazione] 2:7; 9:3; 9:7; 23:6; 23:9; 23:10; 23:31; 23:31; 24:1; 24:2; 24:4; 39:1

Imagine [immagine] 2:9; 8:6; 40:1

Imagino [immaginare] 15:2

Immediata 7:2

Immediatamente 12:8; 32:1

Impedito [rendere difficoltoso, impossibile, ostacolare] 4:1; 19:16

Impeditus 2:7 (Lat.: past participle of *impedio,-is* 'impedito']

Imponitore [colui che impone, dà] 24:4

Impossibile 13:4; 14:14

Imposte [imporre: past part. femin. plur.] 13:1

Imposto [imporre: past part.] 12:9; 24:3

Impresa 18:9

In [preposition]

In [Lat.: preposition] 24:4

Inanimata [senza anima razionale] 11:3; 25:9

Inanimate 25:8

Incipit [Lat.: *Incipio,-is* 'to begin'] 1

Incominciai 23:10

Incominciamento [inizio] 23:4

Incominciare 14:4

Incontanente [adv.: sùbito] 22:4

Incontastabile [incontrastabile] 8:8

Incontra [incontrare] 15:3; 15:14

Indarno [invano] 14:14; 37:5

Indefensibilemente [senza possibilità di difesa] 13:1

Indiffinita [non definita] 8:12; 23:29

Indizione [era, epoca] 29:1

Inducere [indurre] 21:6; 39:6

Inebriato 3:2

Ineffabiie 3:1

Infallibile 29:3

Infamasse [dare fama] 10:2

Infermitade [infermità] 23:1; 23:11; 23:16

Inferno 19:8

Infino [fino, sino] 23:15; 42:1

Inflammati [infiammati] 19:12

Infolgorasse [fulminare] 14:6

Infrascritta [scritta sotto] 23:16

Ingannati 12:7

Ingannato 14:7; 23:13

Ingegnati [ingegnarsi: sec. pers. sing. imperat.: adòperati, fa in modo] 19:14

Ingegno 3:6; 19:22; 31:11

Ingentilite [ingentilire: past partic. femin. plur.: diventate gentili, nobili] 22:11

Ingombrassero [impedire] 13:1

Inimica [nemica] 13:6; 13:10

Innamorar 19:5

Innanzi 2:7; 4:1; 8:9; 22:16; 31:2; 38:10; 39:3; 39:5; 39:6

Insegna [stendardo, bandiera] 28:1

Insegnatemi [inseganre] 19:13

Insegne [insegna, segno] 4:2

Insieme 25:8; 29:2; 29:2

Intelletto 19:2; 19:4; 19:7; 33:8; 34:11; 41:6; 41:6

Intelligente 25:1

Intelligenza 41:8; 41:10

Intenda [intendere, capire] 12:17; 19:16

Intendano 32:4

Intende 7:2; 8:3; 19:8; 40:6

Intendea [intendere: intendeva] 3:3; 3:3; 33:1

Intender 26:7; 32:3; 32:5; 41:1

Intendere 10:3; 12:16; 19:21; 19:22; 21:7; 23:13; 25:3; 25:6; 25:6; 26:4; 26:4; 26:8; 29:2; 29:3; 40:6; 41:6; 41:7; 41:7; 41:9

Intendesse 40:4

Intendesser [intendessero] 40:9

Intendete 18:4

Intendiate 12:12

Intendimento 1; 5:4; 7:7; 8:12; 13:2; 14:8; 18:7; 19:22; 19:22; 25:10; 28:2; 30:2; 30:2; 39:5

Intendo 7:7; 12:17; 29:3; 38:6; 41:7; 41:12; 41:13

Intentivamente [attentamente] 3:4

Intento [1. past partic.: inteso, voluto; 2. noun: proposito] 19:15

Intenzione 21:7; 30:3

Intesa [intendere: past partic. femin. sing.] 19:15

Intese [intendere: past partic. femin. plur.] 12:8

Intesi [intendere: first pers. sing. of pret.] 5:2; 23:19

Inteso [intendere: past partic. masc. sing.] 22:7

Intima [ìntimo: adj.] 22:2

Intollerabile 11:3

Intollerabilmente 23:2

Intorno 23:31; 31:5; 33:5

Intra [tra, fra] 21:5

Intrametto [intramettersi: intromettersi, preoccuparsi] 16:11; 22:17; 41:9

Inver [verso, in direzione di] 24:8

Invidia 4:1; 26:11

Involta [involgere, avvolgere: past partic. femin.] 3:4; 3:12

Io 1; 2:2; 2:7; 2:8; 3:1; 3:3; 3:3; 3:4; 3:7; 3:9; 3:9; 3:9; 3:9; 3:14; 3:14; 4:1; 4:1; 4:2; 4:2; 4:3; 5:1; 5:2; 6:2; 7:1; 7:1; 7:2; 7:2; 7:3; 7:4; 7:5; 7:7; 8:1; 8:3; 8:6; 8:8; 8:9; 8:12; 8:12; 9:2; 9:2; 9:4; 9:5; 9:5; 9:5; 9:6; 9:11; 9:13; 12:2; 12:3; 12:4; 12:4; 12:5; 12:6; 12:7; 12:7; 12:8; 12:9; 12:9; 12:9; 12:11; 12:17; 12:17; 13:6; 13:9; 13:9; 13:10; 13:10; 14:1; 14:2; 14:2; 14:3; 14:4; 14:6; 14:7; 14:7; 14:8; 14:8; 14:9; 14:10; 14:10; 14:11; 14:12;

14:12; 15:2; 15:2; 15:2; 15:2;
15:3; 15:4; 15:4; 15:7; 16:1;
16:1; 16:2; 16:4; 16:7; 16:10;
16:11; 18:1; 18:2; 18:3; 18:6;
18:8; 19:1; 19:1; 19:1; 19:1;
19:3; 19:4; 19:5; 19:5; 19:6;
19:6; 19:8; 19: 13; 19:13; 19:13;
19:13; 19:15; 19:16; 19:16;
19:16; 19:16; 19:16; 19:16;
19:16; 19:16; 19:16; 19:20;
19:21; 19:22; 20:1; 20:2; 20:2;
21:1; 22:3; 22:4; 22:4; 22:4;
22:4; 22:4; 22:7; 22:7; 22:7;
22:8; 22:9; 22:10; 22:11; 23:1;
23:2; 23:3; 23:5; 23:5; 23:7;
23:8; 23:9; 23:9; 23:10; 23:11;
23:12; 23:12; 23:13; 23:13;
23:13; 23:13; 23:14; 23:15;
23:17; 23:19; 23:20; 23:21;
23:22; 23:22; 23:23; 23:26;
23:26; 23:27; 23:27; 23:27;
23:28; 23:29; 23:29; 23:30;
23:30; 23:30; 23:31; 23:31; 24:1;
24:1; 24:1; 24:2; 24:3; 24:4;
24:6; 24:6; 24:6; 24:7; 24:8;
24:8; 24:10; 24:10; 24:11; 24:11;
25:1; 25:2; 25:2; 25:2; 25:10;
26:3; 26:4; 26:4; 26:9; 27:1;
27:2; 28:1; 29:1; 29:4; 30:1;
30:1; 30:2; 30:3; 30:3; 31:2;
31:3; 31:4; 31:4; 31:4; 31:8;
31:9; 31:14; 31:14; 31:14; 31:16;
31:16; 31:16; 31:16; 31:16;
31:16; 32:2; 32:2; 32:5; 33:2;
33:3; 33:4; 33:5; 33:5; 33:5;
33:6; 34:1; 34:1; 34:2; 34:2;

35:1; 35:2; 35:3; 35:4; 35:5;
35:8; 36:2; 36:4; 37:1; 37:2;
37:3; 37:7; 37:7; 37:8; 38:2;
38:2; 38:4; 38:6; 38:6; 39:1;
39:3; 39:3; 39:6; 39:6; 39:6;
40:2; 40:3; 40:4; 40:4; 40:4;
40:5; 40:5; 40:5; 40:7; 41:1;
41:1; 41:2; 41:6; 41:7; 41:7;
41:7; 41:8; 41:12; 41:13; 41:13;
42:1; 42:1; 42:2; 42:2

Ira 21:2
Ire [ire, gire, andare] 9:1; 14:8
Isfogar [sfogare] 19:4
Istrumenti [strumenti] 14:5
Isvegliarmi [svegliarsi] 23:12
Ita [ire, gire, andare: past particp.
femin.] 31:3; 31:5; 31:10
Iuno [Giunone] 25:9
Iussa [Lat.: accusat. plur. of
iussum, -i 'comando'] 25:9
Ivi [lì, in quel luogo] 29:1; 38:6

'l [il: pers. & demonstr. pron.;
defin. artic.]
L' [lo, la, le: demonstr. & pers.
pron.; defin. artic.]
La [demonstr. & pers. pron.;
defin. artic.]
Là 2:9; 7:7; 9:4; 12:2; 12:3;
13:6; 14:1; 14:8; 19:8; 19:12;
19:13; 19:14; 21:1; 21:1; 21:6;
23:17; 24:8; 36:1; 39:3; 40:7;
40:7; 41:4; 41:5; 41:5; 41:7;
41:11
Labbia [plur. of *labbro*: faccia,
volto, aspetto] 26:7; 31:16; 36:4

Labor [Lat.: nom. sing. of *labor, -is*] 25:9

Lagrima 22:4

Lagrimando [lagrimare, piangere] 12:2; 23:23; 30:1; 40:10

Lagrimar 31:8; 36:5; 37:3; 37:6; 37:6

Lagrimare 12:2; 35:3; 36:2; 39:4; 39:9

Lagrimato 31:1

Lagrime 8:2; 12:1; 14:9; 22:4; 23:6; 34:10; 35:7; 36:2; 37:2

Lamenta 33:4; 33:4

Lamentano 33:4

Lamentanza [lamento] 7:2

Lamentare 8:6

Lamentarmi 12:2

Lamentasse 32:3

Lamentava 22:3

Lamentavano 14:6

Lamento 31:14; 33:4

Larga 40:6; 41:10

Largita [largire, dare: past. partic.] 25:7

Largo 40:6; 40:6

Lascerò 5:4

Lascia 19:22; 22:15; 22:17; 38:2; 38:9

Lasciai 23:30

Lasciato 31:9; 39:2

Lascio 28:2

Lasciò 40:1

Lassai [lasciare: lasciai] 23:18

Lassando [lasciando] 26:8

Lassate [lasciate] 31:10

Lasso [exclamation: 'alas'] 16:7; 32:5; 33:5; 39:6; 39:6; 39:8

Latina 25:3

Latine 30:2

Latini 25:6

Latino 25:4

Lato [parte] 37:7

Laudabili [lodevoli] 2:8

Laudare [lodare] 8:5; 26:6

Laudata [lodata] 26:8

Laudate [lodate] 26:8

Laudato [lodato] 21:3

Laudatore [lodatore] 28:2

Laude [lode] 19:4; 19:13

Le [defin. artic. femin. plur.]

Le [direct pers. & demonstr. pron. femin. plur.: 'them']

Le [indir. pers. pron. femin. sing.: 'to her']

Lei 2:8; 3:2; 3:12; 5:1; 5:1; 5:4; 5:4; 8:12; 9:5; 12:7; 12:7; 12:8; 12:8; 12:10; 12:14; 12:16; 12:16; 14:10; 15:1; 15:1; 15:3; 15:3; 15:7; 17:1; 18:6; 19:1; 19:6; 19:7; 19:8; 19:9; 19:10; 19:11; 19:11; 19:14; 19:16; 19:17; 19:17; 19:18; 19:18; 19:18; 21:1; 21:2; 21:2; 22:3; 22:4; 22:4; 22:7; 22:10; 22:11; 22:11; 22:14; 22:16; 23:3; 23:9; 23:12; 23:18; 23:27; 24:4; 26:1; 26:3; 26:4; 26:4; 26:8; 26:9; 26:10; 26:12; 26:15; 28:3; 29:2; 29:2; 31:1; 31:3; 31:5; 31:9; 31:11; 31:16; 32:5; 33:4; 33:7; 34:1; 35:2; 35:4; 36:3; 38:1; 38:4; 38:4;

38:7; 39:2; 39:2; 39:3; 40:10;
42:1; 42:2

Legge [leggere] 19:20

Leggeramente [leggermente]
3:4; 9:3; 12:11; 13:5; 19:6

Leggere 1

Leggiadria ['manifestazione
visibile della condizione amorosa':
De Robertis] 8:10

Leggiadro [adj. of *leggiadria*]
7:4; 18:2

Leggier [leggero] 9:9

Leggiero [leggero] 23:3; 23:21;
38:6

Le ne [gliene] 12:7; 14:9

Letizia 3:3; 3:7; 19:3; 26:1;
31:17

Letto ['bed'] 23:11

Levai 14:4; 34:2; 35:2

Levare 15:2; 26:1

Levato 23:29

Levava 23:25

Levo 16:10; 16:11

Levoe [levare: levò] 39:1

Li [pron. of third person masc.
sing. *gli* 'to him']

Li [demonstr. pron. third person
masc. pl.: 'them']

Li le [glielo] 12:7

Libello [libro, piccolo libro] 1;
12:17; 25:9; 28:2

Libera 15:1

Libero 15:2

Libro 25:9; 25:9

Licenza [permesso] 25:7

Licenzia [licenza] 25:7

Licenzio [licenziare: dò licenza,
congedo] 12:16

Lien [gliene] 39:10

Lieta 22:5

Lietamente 24:2

Lieto 24:2

Lieve [facile] 19:21

Lievi [third pers. sing. of pres.
subj.: levare: levi] 19:20

Linea 5:1; 5:2

Lingua 8:8; 19:2; 24:3; 25:3;
25:3; 25:4; 25:5; 26:5; 28:2;
31:15

Litterati ["litterati poete": poeti
che scrivono in latino] 25:3

Lo [person. & demonstr. pron.
masc. sing.]

Locale [adj.: di luogo] 25:2

Localmente [adv. of "locale":
per quanto concerne il luogo, lo
spazio] 25:2

Locata [locare, situare: past
partic. femin. sing.] 8:6

Loco [luogo] 23:23; 24:8; 31:11

Loda [lode] 5:4; 18:9; 21:1; 26:4

Lodano [lodare] 18:6; 18:8

Lontana 9:11; 40:2; 40:7; 40:9

Lontani 40:2

Lontano 7:1; 9:1

Lor [loro] 3:10; 7:6; 13:8;
13:10; 15:6; 19:9; 23:19; 32:6;
36:5; 39:10

Loro 1; 2:5; 3:9; 4:2; 4:3; 8:7;
9:6; 11:2; 11:2; 13:10; 14:1;
14:4; 14:5; 14:5; 14:8; 14:14;
16:11; 18:1; 18:1; 18:2; 18:2;

18:3; 18:3; 18:4; 18:5; 18:5;
18:6; 18:8; 19:16; 21:6; 22:3;
22:5; 22:8; 22:8; 22:11; 22:17;
23:7; 23:7; 23:13; 23:14; 23:15;
23:15; 23:29; 23:29; 23:31; 25:7;
25:10; 26:3; 26:15; 26:15; 29:2;
31:7; 31:10; 33:8; 34:2; 35:3;
37:2; 39:2; 39:3; 39:4; 39:5;
39:5; 40:2; 40:2; 40:2; 40:5;
41:1; 41:1; 41:1; 41:1; 41:1; 41:1
Lucano [Roman poet Lucan, 30-
65 A.D.] 25:9
Luce 2:1; 24:4; 31:10; 33:8;
41:11
Lucente [risplendere: pres.
partic.] 3:11
Lui 2:7; 3:14; 8:4; 9:12; 12:6;
12:6; 12:7; 12:10; 12:11; 12:11;
12:12; 14:2; 14:9; 15:2; 19:14;
20:6; 20:6; 21:8; 22:13; 25:2;
25:2; 25:2; 25:2; 26:8; 32:3;
33:1; 33:3; 33:3; 38:1; 38:8;
39:3; 41:10
Lunga 3:1; 9:5; 12:7; 20:4;
24:10; 37:6
Lungi [adv.; da lungi: da
lontano] 24:7
Lungiamente [adv.:
lungamente] 27:2; 27:3
Lungo 9:4; 12:3; 19:1; 23:11;
34:1; 39:4
Luogo [adj. & prepos.] 3:2; 5:1;
5:2; 11:2; 14:5; 14:6; 22:4; 22:5;
28:3; 28:3; 28:3

M' [see "mi"]

Ma 2:8; 3:15; 7:4; 8:9; 9:6;
11:3; 12:8; 12:11; 14:12; 16:5;
18:3; 18:4; 19:1; 19:4; 19:6;
19:22; 21:1; 22:13; 23:6; 25:1;
25:1; 25:3; 25:8; 25:8; 25:8;
25:9; 26:4; 26:8; 26:12; 26:15;
26:15; 29:3; 29:4; 31:6; 31:10;
31:12; 31:16; 33:2; 34:6; 34:11;
36:5; 37:2; 37:5; 38:6; 41:9
Madonna 3:12; 12:10; 12:12;
12:13; 13:9; 13:10; 13:10; 19:8;
19:9; 19:17; 23:26; 39:10
Madonne 18:4
Madre 8:8
Maggior 19:10; 34:11
Maggiore 22:4; 25:7; 25:7;
38:6
Maggiori 2:10
Maginar [immaginare] 31:14
Magione [casa] 14:3; 14:4; 20:4
Mai 8:11; 12:13; 18:9; 22:5;
22:15; 33:5; 36:4; 37:2; 37:8;
42:2
Mal [adv.: male] 19:8; 19:10
Maladetti [maledetti] 37:2
Malagevole [non facile] 25:6
Malvagio 4:2; 31:11; 39:2;
39:6
Mancanza 7:6
Manda 12:12
Manda'lo [lo mandai] 41:1
Mandare 12:8; 41:1
Mandaro [mandare: mandarono]
41:1
Mandasse 41:1; 41:1
Mandata [mandare: past. partic.

femin. sing.] 19:13

Mandato 3:14

Mangiare 3:6

Mangiava 3:6

Mani 3:5; 22:4

Manifesta 14:14; 23:16; 39:7; 40:8

Manifestamente [chiaramente] 3:8; 8:3; 11:4; 29:3; 33:2

Manifestando 37:4

Manifestare 26:9

Manifestasse 40:5

Manifestate 16:1

Manifestato 17:1

Manifestavano 39:3

Manifesti [adj.: chiari] 22:17

Manifestissimo [chiarissimo] 3:15

Manifesto [chiaro] 14:13; 14:14; 15:8; 22:2; 25:9; 35:4; 37:5; 38:5

Manna 23:25

Mano 3:6; 3:12; 14:7

Mantenente [adv.: sùbito] 3:8; 5:3

Maravigli [meravigliare] 30:1

Maraviglia [meraviglia] 14:6; 19:7; 22:1; 24:8; 26:2

Maravigliandomi [meravigliandomi] 23:6

Maravigliandosi [meravigliandosi] 5:1

Maravigliar [meravigliare] 31:10; 33:8

Maravigliare [meravigliare] 2:5; 14:7

Maravigliosa [meravigliosa] 3:3

Maravigliosamente [meravigliosamente] 6:2; 23:5

Maria 28:1; 34:7

Martìri [plur. of *martirio*: sofferenze] 38:10; 39:9

Martirio [sofferenza] 39:4

Matera [materia] 8:8; 13:9; 13:10; 17:1; 17:2; 18:9; 18:9; 22:7; 25:6

Materia 20:7; 30:1

Me [Lat.: abl. of *ego*] 2:4

Me 2:2; 2:7; 2:9; 3:1; 3:1; 3:3; 3:9; 3:14; 4:1; 5:1; 5:2; 5:3; 7:1; 9:1; 9:5; 10:3; 11:3; 12:1; 12:3; 12:3; 12:4; 12:8; 12:11; 12:17; 13:6; 14:1; 14:7; 14:9; 14:12; 14:14; 15:1; 15:6; 15:8; 16:1; 16:3; 17:1; 17:1;18:3;18:4; 18:6; 18:8; 18:9; 19:1; 19:8; 19:16; 19:16; 19:22; 20:1; 20:1; 22:4; 22:5; 22:6; 22:7; 23:1; 23:2; 23:3; 23:3; 23:4; 23:7; 23:9; 23:9; 23:11; 23:12; 23:12; 23:12; 23:18; 24:2; 24:2; 24:3; 24:4; 24:10; 26:1; 27:1; 27:2; 27:2; 27:4; 28:2; 28:2; 28:2; 30:2; 31:4; 31:9; 31:14; 32:1; 32:1; 33:2; 33:6; 34:1; 34:2; 34:2; 34:3; 35:3; 37:1; 37:3; 37:4; 38:2; 38:2; 38:4; 38:5; 38:10; 39:1; 40:2; 40:3; 40:4; 40:5; 41:1; 42:1

Meco [con me] 2:9; 9:5; 15:1; 22:10; 23:12; 23:18; 24:5; 24:8;

24:10; 31:9; 32:2; 34:2; 37:3;
38:8

Medesima 25:9; 29:3

Medesime 26:15

Medesimo 2:1; 3:9; 7:1; 18:18;
21:5; 21:8; 22:5; 23:3; 25:9;
28:2; 29:3; 29:3; 29:3; 34:6;
35:3; 37:3; 37:4; 38:2; 38:4;
40:2; 40:3; 40:4; 40:5

Meglio 19:15

Membrandovi [rimembrandovi,
ricordandovi] 37:7

Membrar [rimembrare, ricordare]
3:11

Memoria 1; 2:10; 15:2; 16:2;
21:8; 34:4; 34:6

Mena [menare, condurre] 31:8;
34:10

Menato [menare, condurre] 14:2;
18:1

Menava [menare, condurre] 14:1

Mendica ["povera, priva di
grazia, sgradita"; De Robertis] 8:9

Menimi [minimi, più piccoli]
2:4

Meno 7:1; 15:8; 18:4; 22:6

Mensa [tavola] 14:3

Mente 2:1; 5:2; 15:4; 16:7;
19:3; 19:4; 21:4; 22:14; 24:9;
26:13; 31:13; 33:5; 34:7; 34:8;
34:9; 36:4; 38:9

Mentr', Mentre 19:20; 23:21;
23:30; 23:31; 31:9; 31:14; 34:1

Menzione [riferimento,
citazione] 6:2

Meo [mio] 3:12; 37:8

Meritata 3:1

Merranno [meneranno] 19:14

Merta [meritare: merita] 8:11;
8:12

Merzede [mercede, pietà, grazia,
bontà] 18:4; 19:7; 23:28; 26:10;
31:16

Meschino [povero, misero,
avvilito] 9:10

Mese 29:1; 29:1; 29:1

Mesi 5:4

Messo [messaggero] 12:13

Mestiere [far mestiere: esser
necessario]12:8; 14:13

Mestieri [plur.; from Lat.
ministerium: ufficio, dovere]
23:10

Metafisica 41:6

Metta 12:16

Mette 41:10

Mettermi 13:6

Meus [Lat.: nom. sing. poss.
adj.] 7:7

Mezzo 3:1; 5:1; 5:2; 8:1; 9:9;
11:3; 12:3; 12:8; 40:1; 40:3; 40:9

Mi [Lat.: vocat. of *meus*]] 12:3

Mi 2:8; 2:9; 2:10; 3:1; 3:2; 3:2;
3:3; 3:3; 3:4; 3:4; 3:5; 3:5;
3:7; 3:8; 3:9; 3:10; 3:11; 3:11;
3:12; 4:2; 4:2; 4:2; 4:3; 5:1; 5:2;
5:3; 5:3; 6:1; 7:1; 7:3; 7:4; 7:4;
7:5; 7:7; 7:7; 8:2; 8:12; 8:12;
9:2; 9:2; 9:4; 9:4; 9:5; 9:7; 9:7;
9:9; 9:10; 9:11; 9:11; 9:12; 9:13;
10:1; 10:1; 10:1; 10:1; 10:2;
10:2; 11:1; 11:1; 11:1; 11:1;

12:1; 12:1; 12:2; 12:2; 12:3;
12:3; 12:3; 12:4; 12:4; 12:4;
12:4; 12:5; 12:5; 12:5; 12:5;
12:5; 12:6; 12:6; 12:9; 12:9;
12:12; 12:12; 12:13; 13:1; 13:1;
13:1; 13:4; 13:6; 13:6; 13:7;
13:8; 13:8; 13:8; 13:9; 13:9;
13:9; 14:1; 14:2; 14:4; 14:6;
14:7; 14:7; 14:9; 14:12; 14:12;
15:1; 15:1; 15:2; 15:2; 15:3;
15:3; 15:4; 15:6; 15:7; 15:7;
15:8; 15:8; 15:8; 15:8; 16:1;
16:1; 16:2; 16:2; 16:3; 16:4;
16:4; 16:4; 16:4; 16:5; 16:7;
16:8; 16:8; 16:9; 16:9; 16:10;
16:11; 16:11; 17:1; 18:2;
18:3;18:3; 18:4; 18:5; 18:6;
18:6;18:7; 18:7; 18:8; 19:5;
19:21; 19:22; 21:7; 22:4; 22:4;
22:4; 22:7; 22:7; 22:8; 22:8;
22:9; 22:10; 22:10; 22:11; 22:17;
23:1; 23:1; 23:4; 23:4; 23:4;
23:4; 23:5; 23:5; 23:5; 23:6;
23:7; 23:7; 23:8; 23:8; 23:8;
23:8; 23:9; 23:9; 23:10; 23:10;
23:13; 23:13; 23:13; 23:14;
23:14; 23:14; 23:16; 23:16;
23:19; 23:22; 23:22; 23:23;
23:24; 23:26; 23:28; 23:28;
23:30; 23:31; 23:31; 24:1; 24:2;
24:2; 24:2; 24:3; 24:4; 24:5;
24:5; 24:6; 24:7; 24:9; 24:9;
24:9; 24:10; 24:10; 24:10; 24:10;
24:11; 26:1; 27:3; 27:3; 27:3;
27:4; 27:5; 27:5; 29:4; 31:4;
31:8; 31:13; 31:13; 31:13; 31:14;

31:14; 31:14; 31:15; 31:15;
31:15; 31:16; 31:16; 32:2; 32:2;
32:3; 32:4; 32:5; 33:1; 33:4;
33:5; 33:5; 33:5; 34:1; 34:2;
34:3; 34:4; 35:1; 35:1; 35:2;
35:2; 35:3; 35:6; 35:6; 35:8;
36:1; 36:1; 36:3; 36:4; 37:3;
37:7; 37:8; 38:1; 38:2; 38:2;
38:4; 38:5; 39:1; 39:6; 39:6;
40:2; 40:2; 40:10; 41:7; 41:9;
41:12; 42:1

Mia 1; 2:8; 2:10; 3:3; 3:3; 3:9;
4:1; 5:1; 5:3; 6:1; 6:2; 6:2; 7:1;
7:2; 7:4; 7:5; 8:2; 9:1; 9:2; 9:3;
9:7; 9:7; 10:1; 10:1; 10:2; 11:1;
11:4; 11:4; 12:1; 12:2; 12:3;
12:10; 12:14; 12:14; 12:15; 13:9;
13:10; 14:4; 14:7; 14:9; 14:9;
14:11; 15:2; 16:2; 16:5; 18:1;
18:2; 18:3; 18:4; 18:6; 18:8;
19:2; 19:4; 19:16; 19:21; 21:2;
21:7; 22:4; 23:1; 23:2; 23:3;
23:4; 23:5; 23:10; 23:10; 23:11;
23:13; 23:18; 23:19; 23:21;
23:21; 23:21; 23:27; 23:30;
23:30; 23:31; 24:2; 26:5; 26:8;
26:10; 27:1; 27:4; 27:4; 28:2;
31:1; 31:1; 31:3; 31:6; 31:7;
31:9; 31:15; 31:15; 31:16; 31:16;
31:17; 32:4; 32:5; 32:6; 33:5;
33:7; 34:3; 34:4; 34:6; 34:7;
34:8; 35:3; 35:6; 35:6; 36:1;
36:2; 36:4; 38:1; 38:6; 40:1;
40:5; 41:7; 42:2; 42:3

Michi [mediev. Lat. for *mihi*,
dat. of *ego*, pers. pron] 2:4; 25:9;

25:9; 25:9
Mie 15:2; 18:1; 23:11; 31:16;
41:1; 41:7; 41:13
Miei 3:2; 3:14; 5:2; 11:2; 12:4;
13:7; 13:8; 13:10; 14:5; 14:8;
14:12; 14:14; 18:4; 19:8; 19:20;
22:4; 23:17; 23:22; 23:25; 27:4;
31:1; 32:3; 32:5; 33:4; 33:7;
33:7; 34:5; 35:3; 35:4; 35:5;
36:2; 37:1; 37:2; 37:3; 37:4;
37:6; 38:5; 39:1; 39:2; 39:4; 39:6
Ministra [ministrare,
somministrare, provvedere] 2:6
Minute [piccole] 19:22
Mio 1; 3:7; 3:9; 3:14; 4:1; 5:1;
5:3; 5:3; 5:4; 7:2; 7:3; 8:12; 9:1;
9:11; 10:1; 10:1; 11:3; 12:3;
12:9; 12:9; 12:10; 12:17; 14:4;
14:4; 14:4; 14:4; 14:8; 14:10;
14:14; 16:1; 17:1; 18:1; 18:1;
18:4; 18:4; 18:8; 18:9; 19:3;
23:11; 23:11; 23:13; 23:19;
23:19; 23:20; 24:2; 24:2; 24:3;
24:6; 24:8; 24:10; 24:10; 25:9;
25:10; 27:1; 28:2; 30:2; 30:2;
30:3; 31:14; 32:3; 33:4; 33:6;
34:10; 35:2; 37:1; 37:2; 37:4;
37:7; 38:6; 38:7; 39:2; 41:1;
41:3; 41:6; 41:6; 41:7; 41:10
Mira [mirare, guardare] 21:2;
26:7; 33:2; 37:2; 37:2; 37:8;
41:11; 42:3
Mirabile [che causa meraviglia,
miracoloso] 3:1; 3:2; 3:3; 11:1;
14:4; 14:5; 15:2; 21:8; 23:6;
24:4; 26:1; 26:14; 29:3; 41:7;

42:1
Mirabilemente 21:1; 26:2;
26:15
Mirabili 26:4; 26:4
Mirabilmente 36:4
Miracol [miracolo] 26:6
Miracoli 29:3
Miracolo 21:4; 29:3; 29:3
Mirando [mirare] 11:2; 14:4
Mirare 22:16; 26:3; 39:5
Mirarla 19:12
Mirasse 22:3; 24:6
Mirava 5:1
Miravano 26:3
Miri 39:8
Mischiata [mischiare] 18:5
Mischiate 18:5
Miser [Lat.: nom. & voc. sing.]
2:7
Misera 32:4
Miseri 35:3
Miseria 23:3
Misericordia 12:2
Misero 37:3
Misi [mettere] 10:1
Misimi [mi misi] 12:2
Miso [mettere: past partic. masc.
sing.; messo] 8:5
Misura 19:11
Mobile 25:2
Mobili 29:2
Modi 22:17; 40:6; 40:7
Modo 9:6; 12:17; 13:10; 19:1;
19:3; 22:7; 22:8; 23:4; 25:6;
25:9; 31:2; 34:6; 38:2; 40:6
Modo [Lat.: ablat. sing. of

modus] 12:4

Moia [morire: muoia] 12:13;
15:5; 15:5

Molta 14:9; 24:5; 40:1

Molte 2:8; 2:10; 3:3; 8:1; 10:1;
11:3; 11:4; 14:1; 14:7; 16:2;
18:1; 18:1; 18:3; 22:3; 23:14;
23:23; 24:10; 26:8; 28:3; 32:5;
35:5; 36:1; 36:2; 37:1; 38:1;
38:1; 39:3; 39:3; 39:10; 40:7

Molti 2:1; 3:9; 3:14; 4:1; 4:1;
5:2; 6:1; 9:2; 9:7; 13:1 19:22;
22:1; 22:2; 25:8; 26:1; 26:2;
39:6; 39:8

Moltitudine 23:7

Molto 2:5; 3:1; 3:1; 3:4; 5:1;
5:3; 7:1; 9:7; 12:3; 12:5; 13:6;
14:6; 18:2; 18:9; 19:1; 23:6;
23:9; 23:13; 24:3; 25:4; 28:3;
35:1; 35:2; 37:2; 40:2

Mondo 8:5; 19:7; 29:1

Monna [madonna, signora] 24:8;
24:8

Mora [morire: muoia] 23:21

More [morire: muore] 15:4; 33:6

Morio [morire: morì] 40:1

Morir 31:12

Morire 22:3

Morrai 23:4

Morra'ti [tu morrai] 23:22;
23:22

Morrei 32:5

Morria [morire: morrebbe] 19:9

Morta 8:6; 15:6; 22:16; 23:8;
23:8; 23:24; 23:26; 31:14; 32:2;
32:2; 37:8

Mortale 2:8; 19:11

Morte 8:2; 8:3; 8:5; 8:8; 8:12;
9:1; 15:6; 22:1 23:9; 23:9; 23:11;
23:17; 23:20; 23:27; 31:8; 31:13;
33:6; 33:7; 37:2; 37:8; 39:10

Morti 14:8; 23:5; 23:10

Morto 23:4; 23:14

Mossa [muovere: past partic.
femin. sing.] 19:2

Mosse [muovere: third pers. sing
of preter.] 16:1; 20:1; 23:17;
25:6; 38:10

Mossero [muovere: third pers.
plur. of preter.] 3:2

Mossi [muovere: first pers. sing
of preter.] 24:4

Mosso [muovere] 2:2; 15:3;
38:2; 38:3

Mosterrà [mostrare: mostrerà]
24:4

Mostra 15:5; 15:8; 15:9

Mostrai 5:3

Mostrando 8:5; 22:9; 26:2

Mostrano 7:7

Mostrar 39:9

Mostrare 9:6; 26:6; 35:3

Mostrasi [si mostra] 26:7

Mostrasse 21:1

Mostrata 38:3

Mostrato 9:6

Mostrava 26:3; 36:1

Mostravano 14:1; 23:5

Mostrino 7:7

Mostro [mostrare] 7:6

Mostrò 23:8

Moto 25:2

Mova [muovere: muova) 14:11; 19:12; 26:7

Movea [muovere: muoveva] 5:2; 7:5; 11:3; 16:4

Movean [muovere: muovevano] 35:7

Movesse 16:2

Movi [muovere, partire: muovi] 12:14

Movimento 12:16

'mpronto [aphaeresis of "impronto": improntato, disposto] 12:13

Multum [Lat.: 'molto'] 25:9

Muoia [morire] 23:3

Muova 13:5

Muovere 23:1; **31**

Muovo 8:12; 31:4

Muovono 29:2; 35:3

Musa [Lat.: vocat. of *musa*] 25:9

Muta [adj.: muto] 26:5

Mutò [mutare]12:12

'n [in]

N' [indefin. pron. *ne*]

Nacque [nascere] 40:1

Nanque [Lat. conj.: *namque*] 25:9

Narra 26:9; 41:1

Narrando 19:18; 19:18

Narrare 22:17; 27:2

Narrate 16:11

Narrato 22:12; 26:8; 35:4

Narratori 17:1

Narrazioni 15:8

Narro 7:7; 8:7; 13:10; 32:4

Nasce [nascere] 20:5; 21:3

Nascimento [nascita] 2:1

Nascon [nascono] 39:8

Nascondere 7:2

Nascono 2:10

Nascoso [nascosto] 8:9; 22:4

Nati 19:8

Natura 19:11; 20:4; 20:7

Naturale 2:6; 4:1

'ncerchia [incerchiare, cerchiare, circondare] 39:9

'ncrescerebbe [rincrescere, dispiacere] 31:15

Ne [indef. pron.; pers. pron: a noi, per noi, etc.] 3:7; 3:11; 3:12; 5:3; 5:4; 6:2; 7:1; 8:3; 9:6; 10:1; 12:14; 13:6; 14:5; 14:10; 18:3; 18:6; 18:7; 18:7; 19:7; 19:15;19:16; 22:1; 22:2; 22:4; 22:13; 22:15; 23:16; 25:10; 25:10; 26:1; 26:4; 26:11; 27:4; 28:1; 28:3; 29:4; 31:3; 31:5; 31:5; 31:7; 31:9; 31:10; 31:11; 31:12; 31:15; 31:16; 32:6; 34:2; 34:11; 37:1; 38:1; 38:3; 38:4; 38:6; 40:2; 40:9; 40:10; 42:3

Ne [preposition "in"]

Né [adv. of negation] 21:4; 22:6; 22:6; 25:10; 25:10; 26:1; 26:3; 31:10; 36:2

Nebula [Latinism: nuvola] 3:3

Nebuletta [diminutive of "nebula" 'nuvoletta'] 23:7

Necessitade [necessità] 23:3

Neente [niente] 40:2; 40:9

Negarlo 18:4

Negata 12:1; 12:6
Negoe [negare: negò] 22:1
Negò 10:2
Nei [contracted preposition *in*]
Nel [contracted preposition *in*]
Nemica 8:8; 13:9; 25:9
Nemico 11:1
Nessun [nessuno] 26:13
Neve 18:5
'nfin [preposition: infino, fino a]
19:7
No [adv. of negation: non] 12:8;
26:5; 26:7; 26:7; 31:11; 31:11;
31:11; 41:6; 41:12
Nobil [nobile] 19:9
Nobile 17:1; 34:11
Nobili 2:8
Nobilissima 2:8; 21:5; 21:5;
22:1; 23:8; 29:1; 36:1
Nobilissimo 2:3; 14:5; 35:3
Nobilitade [nobiltà] 19:18;
19:18; 41:1
Nobiltade [nobiltà] 12:4
Nobiltate [nobiltà] 7:4
Noi 14:2; 14:6; 18:6; 22:5;
22:6; 22:15; 22:17; 25:3; 25:4;
25:8; 28:2; 29:1; 39:3; 40:1; 40:2
Noia [molestia, danno alla
reputazione] 12:6; 12:13; 15:4
Noie [plur. of *noia*] 12:6
Noiosa [adj. derived from
noia] 12:6; 31:10
Noioso [adj. derived from *noia*]
33:5
Nol [non lo; non gli] 22:10;
23:26; 26:3; 27:5

Nollo [non lo] 35:4
Nome 6:1; 6:1; 6:2; 9:6; 9:11;
13:4; 18:3; 23:13; 23:15; 23:18;
23:19; 24:3; 24:3; 24:4; 24:4;
24:4; 24:9; 25:9; 28:1; 39:3;
39:10; 41:3; 41:7
Nomi 6:1; 6:2; 6:2; 8:12; 13:4
Nomina [Lat.: nomin. plur. of
nomen, -is 'nome']13:4
Nominai [nominare] 12:6
Nominandola 5:2
Nominandolo 41:3
Nominata 10:1; 24:4
Nominate 13:4
Nominollami [me la nominò]
9:6
Non [adv. of negation]
Non [Lat.: adv. of negation]
Nona [nono] 3:2; 12:9; 39:1
Nono 2:2; 2:2; 23:2; 29:1; 29:1
Nostra 12:6; 19:8; 22:9; 22:13;
23:8; 23:26; 29:1; 29:1; 33:8;
38:9
Nostra [Lat.: nomin. neuter
plur.] 12:3
Nostri 14:6; 38:10
Nostro 2:6; 14:6; 41:6
Nota [suono] 12:14
Notificando [rendere noto,
narrare] 18:7
Notrica [notricare, nutrire] 8:9
Notte 3:8; 3:8
Nova [nuova, strana,
straordinaria] 14:11; 19:11; 23:18;
41:8; 41:10
Nova [Lat.: 'nuova,' 'rinnovata']

1

Nove [number nine] 2:1; 3:1; 3:8; 6:2; 23:1; 28:3; 29:1; 29:2; 29:2; 29:3; 29:3; 29:3; 29:3; 29:3; 29:3

Novella [adj.: giovane] 23:16; 23:17

Novella [noun: notizia] 23:24

Novello [adj.: sposato da poco] 14:3

Novissimo [straordinario, mai sentito] 18:3

Novo [nuovo, strano, straordinario] 9:11; 21:4; 31:15; 38:10

'ntenda [intendere: intenda] 19:11

'ntender [intendere] 26:7

'ntendesser [intendere: intendessero] 40:9

'ntendo [intendere: intendo] 41:13

Nuda 3:4

Nudo 33:1

Nui [noi] 22:13; 38:9

Nulla [adj. femin. of "nullo": nessuna] 2:9; 22:2; 26:2; 26:11

Nulla [pronoun: nulla, niente] 4:3

Nullo [adj.: nessuno] 11:1; 32:1

Numero 6:2; 25:4; 28:3; 28:3; 28:3; 29:1; 29:2; 29:2; 29:3; 29:3; 29:3; 29:3

Nuova [nuova, strana, straordinaria] 15:1; 17:1; 17:2; 24:2; 30:1; 38:1; 41:1

Nutrimento [cibo] 2:6

Nuvoletta [dimin. of *nuvola*] 23:25

'nvilita [invilire, avvilire, prostrare: past. partic. femin. sing.] 31:16

O [interj. used to address someone and to show strong emotions] 7:2; 7:3; 19:8; 23:13; 23:13

O [Lat.: same meaning as above] 7:7; 25:9

O [conj.: oppure, ovvero] 12:17; 14:14 19:9; 19:14; 25:7; 25:10; 36:4; 40:6

Oblia [dimenticare: dimentica] 19:10

Obliare [dimenticare] 37:8

Obliereste [dimenticare: dimentichereste] 37:7

Obumbrare [Latinism: velare d'ombra, impedire] 11:3

Occhi 2:1; 5:2; 8:5; 9:4; 11:2; 14:4; 15:6; 15:8; 16:10; 18:3; 19:12; 19:12; 19:19; 19:20; 20:5; 21:1; 21:2; 21:5; 22:4; 22:9; 22:10; 23:4; 23:6; 23:13; 23:17; 23:22; 23:25; 26:1; 26:5; 26:7; 31:1; 31:1; 31:8; 32:5; 34:1; 34:10; 35:2; 35:3; 35:3; 35:4; 35:5; 35:6; 36:2; 36:4; 36:5; 37:1; 37:2; 37:3; 37:4; 37:6; 38:3; 38:6; 38:10; 39:1; 39:4; 39:6; 39:8

Occhio 41:6

Oco [Provençal: sì; lingua d'oc]

25:4

Offesa 19:10

Offeso [offendere: past. partic.]
11:1

Oggi 3:1; 24:4; 34:11

Ogn' [ogni] 21:2; 31:16

Ogne 21:3; 21:3; 21:5; 21:8;
23:28; 26:5; 31:14; 37:7

Ogni 7:3; 12:14; 19:1; 19:10;
19:20; 21:2; 30:1

Oi [interj. used to address
someone and to show strong
emotions] 23:10; 32:5; 34:11;
37:6; 38:10

Oltre [adv. & prepos.: più in là,
di là da] 10:1; 20:1; 41:2; 41:10

Oltremare [oltre + mare:
Palestina]] 40:7

Om' [uomo, uno, gente] 21:2;
31:16; 40:10

Omai [ormai] 23:27; 31:8

Omero [Greek poet] 2:8; 25:9

Omnes [Lat.: vocat. plur. of
omnis, -e] 7:7

Omnia [Lat.: accus. plur. of
omnis, -e] 42:3

Omo [uomo] 19:14; 20:5; 23:24

Ond', Onde [adv. & conj.: da
dove, da cui, perché, cosicché]
2:8; 2:10; 3:7; 4:1; 5:2; 7:5; 8:8;
10:1; 12:4; 12:6; 12:7; 12:9;
13:6; 13:9; 13:10; 14:2; 14:7;
14:11; 14:12; 14:13; 15:3; 16:11;
18:8; 19:3; 20:2; 21:3; 22:2;
22:3; 22:4; 22:4; 22:7; 22:9;
23:1; 23:3; 23:12; 23:12; 23:14;

23:15; 23:16; 24:6; 24:8; 25:2;
25:7; 25:7; 26:1; 26:4; 26:9;
28:3; 28:3; 30:1; 30:2; 32:2;
32:3; 33:5; 33:6; 34:3; 35:2;
35:3; 36:1; 37:1; 37:2; 38:4;
38:6; 39:5; 39:6; 40:2; 40:5;
40:7; 41:1

Onesta [nobile, cortese] 26:3;
26:5

Onestade [nobiltà, cortesia] 26:1

Onesto [nobile, cortese] 2:3

Onne [ogni] 3:11; 3:14; 12:13;
15:8; 16:9; 19:9; 25:1; 26:9;
26:10; 26:12; 31:12

Onni [ogni] 8:9

Onorare 11:2; 21:7

Onorata 26:8; 41:5

Onorate 26:8

Onore 8:5; 8:7; 12:14; 21:2;
24:7; 26:12; 34:1; 41:11

Onorevolemente 41:1

Opera [lavoro] 34:3

Operando [fare, realizzare] 21:1

Operate [adoperare, dire: past
partic. femin. plur.] 18:7

Operava [fare, realizzare] 10:3;
26:14; 26:15; 26:15; 26:15; 27:2

Operazione [atto dell'operare]
4:1; 13:4; 15:8; 21:8; 27:2

Operazioni [operazione] 19:20;
26:4

Oppinione [opinione] 29:2

Opporre [obiettare] 12:17; 12:17

Optes [Lat.: sec. pers. sing.
pres. subj.: *opto, -as*] 25:9

Or [ora: adv.] 7:5; 19:8; 19:9;

19:13; 23:6; 23:9; 24:7; 24:10; 31:14; 31:17; 37:2; 38:3

Ora 3:2; 3:8; 3:8; 3:15; 12:1; 12:9; 23:31; 27:3; 29:1; 31:8; 37:2; 37:7; 39:1

Orazio [Latin poet; 65-8 B.C.] 25:9; 25:9

Ordinata 19:3; 23:16

Ordine 23:31; 39:2

Ore 3:8; 3:11

Orecchi 3:2

Oriente 2:2

Ornata 2:3

Orranza [onoranza, onore] 8:6

Orribile 37:3

Orribili 23:4

Orribilmente 2:4

Orrore 3:11

Osa [osare, potere: può] 20:3

Osanna 23:7; 23:25

Oscura 35:6

Oscuramente 12:5

Oscurare 23:5

Oscure 16:7

Oscuritade [oscurità] 12:5

Ostale [ostello, albergo, luogo] 7:3

Ottobre 29:1

Ov', Ove [dove] 2:6; 2:9; 3:1; 5:1; 6:2; 7:7; 8:6; 9:4; 9:11; 12:2; 12:3; 12:8; 12:16; 14:1; 14:1; 18:6; 19:13; 19:14; 21:1; 21:1; 21:2; 21:6; 21:6; 23:5; 23:8; 23:17; 23:21; 23:23; 24:2; 24:8; 31:10; 34:7; 40:1; 40:7; 41:3; 41:7

Ovidio [Latin poet: 43 B.C.-17 A.D.] 25:9

Ovunque 15:5; 27:5; 31:15; 36:1

Pace 12:14; 19:8; 23:8; 23:26; 31:10

Padre 22:2; 22:2; 22:2; 29:3

Paese 7:1; 40:3

Paia [parere: third pers. sing. pres. subj.] 31:2; 33:2

Paion [paiono] 39:9

Paiono [parere: third pers. plur. pres. indic.] 25:2; 40:2

Palese 19:14

Palido [pallido] 36:1

Palma 40:7

Palmieri [pellegrini che portano le palme dalla Terra Santa] 40:7

Par [parere, sembrare: pare] 15:5; 21:4; 22:9; 22:13; 26:6; 26:7; 27:4; 31:16; 37:7; 40:9

Paragrafi 2:10

Parantur [Lat.: third pers. plur. passive pres. indic.: *paro, -as*] 25:9

Parate [Lat.: sec. pers. plur. imper.: *paro, -as*] 24:4

Pare [parere, sembrare] 2:10; 5:4; 13:4; 13:10; 15:8; 19:16; 22:6; 23:14; 26:5; 28:3; 28:3; 28:3; 37:2; 38:6

Parea [pareva] 2:8; 3:3; 3:4; 3:4; 3:5; 3:7; 5:1; 9:4; 9:4; 9:13; 10:2; 12:4; 12:4; 12:5; 13:1; 16:1; 17:1; 18:5; 23:5; 23:7;

23:7; 23:7; 23:8; 23:8; 23:8;
23:10; 23:10; 23:16; 23:23;
23:26; 24:2; 24:2; 24:10; 24:10;
26:14; 27:2; 33:1; 35:2; 36:2;
38:6

Pareami [mi pareva] 3:3; 3:5;
3:6; 12:3; 12:3; 18:9; 23:5; 23:5;
23:7; 23:8; 23:8; 24:2; 27:1; 39:1

Parean [parevano] 23:25

Pareano [parevano] 24:6; 39:4

Parer [parere] 26:12

Parere [opinione] 3:14; 23:13

Parere [sembrare] 19:9; 35:1

Paresse 32:2; 32:3; 39:6; 40:5

Pargoletto [fanciullo] 12:2

Pari [plur. noun: uguali, della
stessa condizione] 14:6

Parla 19:8; 25:9; 25:9; 25:9;
25:9; 37:4; 38:8; 41:8; 41:12;
41:13

Parlai 17:1; 31:9

Parlan [parlano] 13:8

Parlando 2:5; 8:12; 14:10;
19:5; 19:13; 22:13; 23:29; 27:4;
34:5; 36:3

Parlandomi 23:13

Parlano 25:8; 25:8; 33:2

Parlar 19:6; 19:16; 21:3; 31:8;
31:9

Parlare 2:10; 8:12; 10:1; 12:4;
12:5; 12:17; 13:10; 14:14; 18:2;
18:5; 18:8; 18:9; 19:1; 21:7;
21:8; 22:5; 22:15; 22:17; 25:6;
25:7; 25:7; 25:8; 25:10; 38:4;
40:2; 41:12

Parlarne 19:6

Parlasse 7:2; 19:1; 24:4; 35:4

Parlato 12:5; 18:6; 18:6; 19:10;
25:8; 25:9; 27:1; 40:5

Parlatori [scrittori] 25:7

Parlava 16:3; 18:7; 25:2; 37:4

Parlavano 18:3; 25:10; 38:4

Parli 12:5; 12:8

Parlo 8:7; 12:17; 31:3; 31:7;
37:4; 41:7

Parloe [parlò] 25:9

Parlò 19:2

Parola 2:8; 12:4; 24:7

Parole 1; 2:4; 2:5; 2:6; 2:10;
3:2; 3:3; 3:5; 3:9; 5:1; 7:2; 7:7;
8:2; 8:3; 9:5; 9:6; 9:7; 12:3;
12:4; 12:5; 12:5; 12:5; 12:7;
12:7; 12:8; 12:9; 12:12; 12:17;
13:1; 13:7; 14:8; 14:10; 14:14;
14:14; 14:14; 15:3; 16:1; 18:3;
18:3; 18:4; 18:5; 18:6; 18:6;
18:7; 18:8; 18:8; 19:3; 19:15;
19:15; 20:1; 20:2; 21:1; 22:3;
22:3; 22:5; 22:7; 22:7; 22:7;
23:7; 23:11; 23:11; 23:14; 23:16;
23:17; 24:3; 24:5; 24:6; 25:6;
25:9; 25:10; 26:1; 26:4; 26:4;
26:9; 27:2; 28:1; 28:3; 30:2;
30:2; 31:1; 32:2; 34:3; 34:5;
36:3; 38:4; 39:6; 39:10; 40:4;
40:10; 41:1

Parrebbero 40:3

Parte [parte, luogo, regione,
direzione] 1; 2:2; 2:6; 3:1; 3:13;
3:13; 5:1; 6:1; 7:7; 8:3; 8:7; 9:7;
9:11; 9:12; 9:13; 10:2; 11:1;
12:1; 12:8; 12:16; 12:17; 13:10;

13:10; 14:1; 14:1; 14:4; 14:8;
15:7; 15:8; 15:9; 16:11; 19:8;
19:15; 19:16; 19:17; 19:18;
19:18; 19:18; 19:19; 19:19;
19:20; 19:21; 21:5; 21:5; 21:5;
21:6; 21:8; 22:4; 23:1; 23:9;
23:30; 23:30; 23:31; 24:1; 24:2;
24:8; 24:10; 24:10; 24:11; 25:9;
26:14; 26:15; 31:3; 31:4; 31:5;
31:6; 31:14; 31:14; 34:1; 34:5;
34:6; 35:1; 37:4; 38:3; 38:5;
38:6; 38:7; 40:2; 41:7; 41:8

Partendo [separando] 33:8

Partendomi [allontanandomi]
5:2

Partes [Lat.: nomin. plur.: *pars,
-tis*] 12:4

Parti [parte: plur.] 2:2; 3:13;
7:7; 7:7; 8:7; 8:12; 9:1; 9:13;
12:11; 12:16; 12:16; 13:10; 14:4;
14:13; 15:7; 16:11; 16:11; 19:15;
20:6; 21:5; 21:5; 22:11; 22:17;
22:17; 23:29; 23:31; 24:10;
26:14; 31:3; 31:5; 32:4; 33:4;
34:4; 37:4; 38:5; 38:7; 41:2

Partia [partiva] 15:1; 23:28;
34:9

Partiano [partivano] 22:4

Particella [piccola parte] 21:5

Partio [partì] 3:2; 18:8; 29:1;
29:1; 29:1; 35:3; 39:3

Partir 23:18

Partire 8:1; 9:1; 16:10; 22:2;
23:12

Partirò 2:10

Partisse 7:1

Partissi 31:5; 31:11

Partita [partenza, morte] 7:2;
28:2; 28:3; 28:3; 31:5

Partita [trans. use of *partire*:
allontanata] 8:10

Partita [partire: past partic.]
23:6; 30:1

Partiti 34:3

Partito 12:1

Partitomi [allontanatomi] 14:9

Parve [parere: third pers. sing. of
preter.] 3:1; 9:5; 9:7; 12:3; 14:4;
23:24; 24:2; 24:4; 24:5; 24:10;
38:4; 39:1; 40:2

Parvemi [mi parve] 12:4

Parvente [parere, giudizio] 3:10

Pascea [pascere: nutriva, faceva
mangiare] 3:12

Passa [passare, muoversi] 21:2;
21:6; 41:10

Passan [passano, penetrano]
19:12

Passando 3:1; 10:2; 18:1; 19:1;
22:7; 40:3

Passare 13:3 [attraversare,
sopportare]; 41:9 ["lasciar
correre," "passar per buono"; De
Robertis]

Passaro [passarono] 22:5; 22:6

Passata [passare, andare] 17:1;
26:2

Passate 7:3; 15:2; 40:9

Passati 3:1; 22:1; 25:4; 40:5

Passato 35:1; 39:2

Passava 11:4; 26:1

Passavano 40:1

Passioni [sensazioni, sofferenza]
2:10; 15:2
Passò 31:10
Patria 40:6; 40:7; 41:5
Paura 13:8; 18:9; 23:11; 23:14;
23:17; 33:5; 35:6
Paurosi 14:12
Pauroso 3:1; 3:3
Paventando [aver paura, temere]
23:6
Paventosa [impaurita, esitante]
3:12
Pecca [peccare] 15:8
Peccato 15:6; 15:9; 22:15
Pena 23:1; 31:8; 31:14; 34:11
Pensa 24:2; 24:7; 24:10
Pensai 5:3; 19:1; 31:1
Pensamenti [pensieri] 13:1;
13:1; 15:3; 35:1; 39:2
Pensamento [pensiero] 15:1
Pensando 3:3; 3:9; 7:2; 12:3;
12:5; 18:8; 18:9; 19:3; 19:3;
19:5; 20:2; 20:2; 22:7; 23:3;
26:4; 29:3; 31:13; 32:3; 40:2;
41:1
Pensandomi [pensando fra me]
33:1
Pensano 40:2
Pensare 3:2; 3:8; 4:1; 19:1;
27:1; 37:8; 38:2; 39:2; 39:3; 41:7
Pensate 14:11
Pensatel [pensate+lo] 12:12
Pensato 23:3
Pensava 10:1; 13:6; 23:21;
23:30; 23:31; 34:2; 38:1; 38:1;
38:1

Pensavate 35:6
Penser [pensiero, pensieri] 13:7;
13:8; 38:9; 39:8
Penseri [pensieri] 39:10; 40:2
Pensero [pensiero] 12:13; 15:2;
16:3; 19:9; 21:3; 23:2; 23:21;
27:1; 31:12; 31:13; 34:3; 37:2;
38:2; 38:3; 38:4; 38:8; 39:3;
41:3; 41:6; 41:7; 41:7
Pensieri 13:10; 14:1; 38:4;
38:5
Pensiero 19:20
Penso 19:16
Pensosa 38:10
Pensosi 40:2; 40:5; 40:9
Pensoso [doloroso, addolorato,
afflitto] 8:8; 9:7; 9:9; 9:10; 24:1;
33:5; 35:1
Pentere [pentirsi] 39:2
Per [prepos.]
Per [Lat.: prepos.: It. *per*] 7:7;
42:3
Percezioni 2:5
Perch', Perché 8:5; 12:4;
12:12; 14:2; 15:1; 15:8; 16:8;
18:8; 19:4; 19:13; 19:16; 22:9;
22:14; 22:17; 23:18; 29:2; 30:1;
31:4; 31:4; 31:9; 31:10; 33:8;
38:3; 41:4
Perder 19:8
Perdessi 15:2; 19:5; 19:16
Perdona 12:14
Perdonare 11:1; 12:13
Perduta 7:5; 40:10
Perduto 7:7; 9:10
Pere [perire, morire: perisce,

muore] 19:9

Peregrini [pellegrini] 40:1; 40:2; 40:2; 40:5; 40:6; 40:6; 40:7; 40:7; 40:9

Peregrino [pellegrino] 9:3; 9:9; 40:6; 40:6; 41:5; 41:5; 41:11

Perfettamente 26:9; 26:10

Perfettissimamente 29:2

Perfetto 29:1

Pericolo 12:16

Perir 15:4

Perle 19:11

Però [perciò, poiché] 2:10; 3:2; 4:1; 4:2; 5:4; 8:9; 9:2; 9:3; 9:5; 12:4; 12:6; 12:6; 12:11; 12:16; 12:17; 12:17; 13:2; 13:3; 14:3; 14:5; 14:13; 14:14; 15:2; 16:6; 16:11; 17:1; 17:1; 17:2; 18:1; 18:9; 19:15; 19:21; 21:8; 22:4; 22:5; 22:7; 22:11; 22:17; 22:17; 23:4; 23:9; 23:16; 23:16; 24:2; 24:4; 25:2; 25:6; 25:10; 26:8; 27:1; 27:4; 28:2; 28:3; 29:1; 29:3; 30:2; 31:1; 31:11; 31:16; 32:5; 33:2; 34:2; 34:3; 34:4; 35:3; 35:4; 35:4; 36:3; 37:5; 37:5; 38:4; 38:4; 38:6; 38:6; 38:6; 39:3; 39:7; 39:10; 40:4; 40:7; 40:7; 40:8; 41:7; 41:9; 41:13

Persona 3:4; 5:2; 8:12; 12:6; 12:17; 14:1; 14:2; 14:4; 14:9; 16:7; 19:1; 19:19; 19:19; 23:1; 23:4; 23:29; 25:1; 25:9; 25:9; 25:10; 29:4; 31:11; 32:6; 33:1; 33:2; 38:1; 39:5; 39:8

Persone 5:3; 7:2; 12:6; 18:1; 26:1; 26:15; 33:2; 33:4; 37:6; 40:9

Pertiene [pertenere: si pertiene = spetta, tocca] 12:16

Pervieni [pervenire] 15:1

Pesa [pesare: rincresce, duole] 37:2

Pesava [pesare, rincrescere] 4:1

Petto 14:4; 34:10

Piaccia [piacere] 12:12; 42:3

Piacciavi [vi piaccia] 22:10

Piace 12:14; 19:8; 20:5; 29:4; 38:5

Piacente [che piace e suscita amore] 20:5; 26:7; 26:12

Piacere [used only as a noun: piacere, volontà] 8:1; 9:11; 14:1; 14:3; 33:8; 42:2

Piacerebbe 28:2

Piaceri [piacere: beneplacito, volontà] 2:7; 26:3

Piacesse 18:2; 38:1

Piacevole 5:1

Piacque [piacere: third pers. sing. pret.] 18:4; 22:1

Piana ["mansueta, sommessa, soave, affabile"; De Robertis] 19:13

Piange 8:4; 8:7; 8:7; 22:3; 22:6; 31:5; 31:6; 31:6; 31:11; 34:8

Piangea [piangeva] 22:3; 23:6; 23:6; 23:12

Piangeano [piangevano] 8:1

Piangendo 2:6; 3:7; 3:12; 8:2;

14:9; 22:16; 23:5; 23:10; 31:1;
31:9; 31:14; 31:17; 32:5; 34:4;
34:10; 35:8; 41:10

Pianger [piangere] 13:8; 22:14;
23:17; 23:24; 31:11; 31:15; 32:5;
36:5

Piangere 2:6; 8:7; 22:15;
22:17; 23:3; 23:6; 23:11; 23:11;
23:13; 35:3; 37:2; 37:2; 39:4;
40:4; 40:4; 40:10

Piangesse 12:4

Piangessero 23:5

Piangeste 37:7

Piangete 8:3; 8:4; 40:9

Piangi 12:4; 22:14; 22:17

Piangia [piangere: piangeva]
23:18

Piangon [piangono] 39:9

Piano [facile] 26:8; 36:3

Piansemi [mi pianse; "Piansemi
Amor nel core" 'Amor mi pianse
nel cuore'] 23:21

Pianti 23:25; 36:4

Pianto 3:7; 14:10; 22:9; 22:10;
22:15; 23:11; 23:12; 23:19;
31:12; 39:4

Picciolo [piccolo, poco] 4:1;
25:4

Piedi 14:8

Pien [pieno] 23:17; 26:7

Piena 22:2; 26:3; 31:11

Pieni 4:1

Pietà 13:9; 14:10; 15:6; 15:8;
15:8; 15:8; 15:9; 16:7; 19:8;
22:9; 22:14; 22:16; 31:1; 31:8;
32:5; 35:2; 36:4

Pietade [pietà] 13:10; 14:9;
22:3; 35:3

Pietate [pietà] 12:12; 13:8;
14:12; 22:10; 23:17; 23:27; 33:7;
35:5; 37:6

Pietosa [che mostra dolore e
suscita pietà] 15:8; 15:8; 23:16;
23:17; 31:3; 31:7; 31:17; 35:3;
36:1; 36:2; 38:3; 38:10

Pietosamente 8:1; 12:4; 22:3;
22:5; 23:6; 31:3; 35:2

Pietoso [che mostra dolore e
suscita pietà] 40:5

Pietra 31:11

Pietre 15:5

Pietà 8:5; 8:8; 12:14; 13:6

Pigli [pigliare, prendere] 13:6;
13:10; 25:10

Pigliando, 22:8; 30:1

Pigliare 13:10

Pinge [spinge] 14:12

Pingea [spingeva] 11:2

Pinto [dipinto, raffigurato] 19:12

Pintura [pittura] 14:4

Pioggia 23:25

Più 3:1; 3:15; 5:3; 5:4; 6:2; 7:1;
7:2; 8:7; 8:10; 10:1; 12:6; 12:16;
12:17; 13:1; 13:3; 13:3; 13:4;
14:5; 14:8; 14:12; 17:1; 17:1;
17:2; 19:15;19:21; 19:22; 19:22;
22:6; 23:12; 23:26; 26:4; 26:14;
27:4; 29:3; 29:4; 29:4; 29:4;
31:2; 32:1; 32:5; 35:3; 37:2;
37:5; 38:1; 38:4; 40:5; 40:7;
41:1; 41:9; 41:9; 41:9; 41:10;
42:1; 42:1

Pistola [componimento] 6:2
Plena [Lat.: nomin. femin. adj.:
plenus] 28:1
Plorare [piangere] 8:4
Ploro [piangere: piango] 7:6
Pò [può] 15:5; 19:10; 19:11;
19:11; 21:4; 40:10
Poca 7:4; 16:5; 20:4
Poche 3:3
Pochi 23:1
Poco 1; 3:7; 5:3; 10:1; 15:1;
21:4; 23:20; 23:24; 23:24; 24:3;
24:8; 24:10; 31:8;31:8
Poeta 2:8; 25:6; 25:9
Poete [poeti] 25:3; 25:3; 25:4;
25:7; 25:7; 25:7; 25:8; 25:9;
25:10
Poetria [Horace's Ars poetica
'Arte poetica'] 25:9
Poggiai [appoggiare: appoggiai]
14:4
Poi 3:12; 4:1; 7:3; 12:9; 12:10;
17:1; 19:1; 19:3; 19:11; 20:8;
21:6; 22:7; 23:4; 23:16; 23:23;
23:24; 23:28; 24:6; 24:7; 25:8;
27:4; 28:3; 32:3; 34:2; 35:1;
35:3; 36:1; 37:8; 38:3; 40:3;
40:4; 41:1; 42:3
Poi che [dopo che; poiché] 3:1;
8:4; 8:8; 8:12; 12:1; 12:2; 17:1;
18:3; 18:3; 18:4; 18:6; 18:18;
19:1; 23:27; 23:30; 24:10; 26:2;
30:1; 31:1; 32:1; 32:2; 33:1; 36:1
Polsi [pulsazioni, vene] 2:4;
16:10; 18:8
Pone [porre] 20:3

Ponendo 15:1
Ponesse 15:3
Ponga 25:2; 25:2
Populo [Lat.: ablat. of populus,
-i] 28:1
Poria [potrebbe] 14:12
Porre 22:4
Porta [portare] 13:3; 21:1; 21:2
Portamenti [comportamenti,
modi] 2:8
Portano 2:5
Portar [portare] 31:17
Portate 22:8; 22:9
Portava 4:2
Porterai 33:5
Porto [portare] 23:9
Portolo [lo porto] 9:5
Poscia [poi] 15:1; 16:9; 16:11;
19:17; 19:21; 20:8; 21:1; 21:7;
21:8; 23:22; 23:31; 25:10; 31:5;
31:7; 31:14; 31:15; 35:8
Pose [porre] 7:4
Possa [potere] 19:22; 31:11;
41:7; 42:3
Possedere 39:2
Possente [forte, capace] 38:9
Possessioni [possesso,
possedimento, luogo proprio]
14:8
Possibile 25:8
Posso 36:5; 41:6; 42:2
Possono 23:1; 26:4; 40:6
Posta [porre: past. partic. femin.
sing.] 29:1; 34:7
Posto [porre: past partic.] 5:2;
7:7; 18:4; 28:2; 28:2

Postutto ["al postutto" 'del tutto', 'assolutamente'] 28:2
Pote [può] 19:12
Potea [poteva] 2:8; 4:2; 11:2; 12:2
Poteano [potevano] 9:2; 26:4; 31:1
Potei 19:20
Potendo 36:2
Potenzia [philosophical term: potenza, potenzialità] 20:6; 20:6; 20:7; 20:7; 20:8; 21:1; 21:5; 21:6
Poteo [potere: poté, potéi]] 3:7; 8:2
Potere 27:2
Potero [potere: poterono] 39:5
Potesse 11:3; 15:2; 26:3; 39:5; 40:4; 42:1
Potessero 12:8; 19:22; 39:6
Potessi 15:2
Potestate [podestà, potere] 13:8
Potete 37:2
Potrebbe 1; 12:17; 25:1; 25:1; 29:2; 37:5
Potrebbero 2:10; 26:1
Potrebbesi [si potrebbe] 41:9
Potremmo 14:6
Potrò 17:2
Pottero [potere: poterono] 23:13
Pover [povero] 7:5
Povero 33:1
Precede 28:2
Precedente 21:5; 36:3; 37:5; 38:6; 41:1
Precedenti 19:15; 26:1; 27:1
Precedette [precedere] 24:4

Pregando 19:13; 41:1
Pregandoli 3:9
Pregare 7:7; 20:1
Pregava 23:20
Preghero [preghiera] 12:13
Preghiamo 18:6
Pregiar [apprezzare, stimare] 8:10
Prego [pregare] 7:3; 22:11
Prego [preghiera] 12:14; 32:2
Pregoe [pregare: pregò] 32:2
Prenda 13:9
Prende 14:12; 27:4
Prendere 2:7; 18:9
Prenderle 19:3
Presa [prendere: past partic. femin. sing.: presa d'amore, innamorata] 3:9; 3:10
Prese [prendere] 14:5; 14:7
Presente 3:10; 10:3; 24:1; 25:3; 25:4; 27:1; 28:2; 28:2; 28:2; 38:6; 40:9
Presenza 18:3
Presenzia [presenza] 26:15
Preser [prendere: presero] 36:4; 36:4
Presi 3:2; 6:2; 9:12; 22:7; 23:22; 24:2
Preso [prendere: past partic.] 28:3
Presso [adv. & prepos.: vicino] 14:12; 15:1; 15:3; 15:4; 15:7; 15:7; 15:7; 15:8; 18:1; 22:5; 24:4; 26:1; 32:1
Pretermictantur [Lat. : third pers. plur. passive of

pretermittere, praetermittere:
praetermittantur] 12:3

Pria [prima] 12:11; 27:3

Prieghi [pregare: preghi] 12:7

Prieghi [preghiere] 41:1

Prima [adv. & adj.] 2:1; 3:2;
3:8; 3:13; 7:7; 8:7; 8:12; 9:13;
12:16; 13:10; 14:6; 15:7; 15:8;
16:2; 18:6; 19:15; 19:15; 19:16;
19:16; 19:17; 19:18; 19:19; 20:6;
20:7; 20:7; 20:8; 21:3; 21:5;
21:6; 21:6; 21:8; 22:11; 23:29;
23:30; 23:30; 23:31; 24:4; 24:4;
24:4; 24:10; 24:11; 25:3; 25:4;
26:14; 26:15; 28:2; 29:1; 31:2;
31:3; 31:4; 31:4; 31:5; 31:6;
32:4; 33:4; 34:4; 34:6; 37:4;
38:7; 39:1; 39:1; 41:3

Primavera 24:3; 24:4; 24:4;
24:6; 24:9

Primi [primo] 25:5

Primo 3:14; 8:3; 8:7; 14:3;
22:8; 24:3; 24:4; 24:6; 25:6;
25:9; 25:10; 29:1; 30:3; 32:1;
34:4; 34:6

Principali 7:7

Principi [plur. of "prìncipe"]
30:1

Principio 2:2; 3:14; 19:20;
23:8; 23:15; 25:6; 25:9; 26:3;
30:2

Procacciavano [procurarsi,
adoperarsi] 4:1

Proccuriamo [procurare,
cercare: procuriamo, cerchiamo]
23:14

Procede 19:7; 26:11

Procedeano [procedevano]
19:18; 26:4

Produtti [produrre: prodotti]
20:7

Proemio 19:15; 28:2; 31:3

Profeta 7:7; 30:1

Promisi [promettere] 23:29

Propietà [proprietà, qualità]
8:10

Propinqua [Latinism: vicina a]
11:2

Propinquissima [vicinissima]
23:12

Propinquitade [vicinanza] 14:5

Propinquo [vicino] 40:3

Proponimento [proposito]
14:4; 28:1

Proporre 42:1

Proporzione 25:4

Proposito 10:3; 12:1; 28:2;
28:2; 28:3

Propri 8:12

Propria 2:1; 13:4

Propriamente 40:7

Proprie 25:2

Propuosi [proporre] 3:9; 3:9;
7:2; 8:2; 12:9; 14:3; 14:10; 15:3;
18:9; 20:2; 22:7; 23:16; 24:6;
26:4; 26:9; 27:1; 31:1; 32:3;
35:4; 37:3; 39:6; 40:5; 40:5; 41:1

Propuosile ["propuosile di
dire" 'proposi di dirle,' i.e., 'di
dire le parole'] 14:10

Prosa 25:8

Prosaici ["prosaici dittatori"

'scrittori in prosa'] 25:7

Prova [prova, resistenza] 14:12

Prova [provare, conoscere per esperienza] 19:10; 19:11; 26:7

Puerizia 2:8; 12:7

Pugnava [pugnare, combattere] 16:4

Pui [poi] 20:5; 31:9; 40:10

Pui [potere: puoi] 22:14

Punti [plur. of "punto"] 13:3

Punto [luogo, momento] 2:1; 2:4; 2:5; 2:6; 12:14; 22:15; 23:13; 34:8

Può 13:10; 26:7; 26:13

Puoi 18:3; 19:14

Puosimi [mi posi, mi misi] 3:2

Puote [può] 14:8; 18:4; 21:8; 25:9; 31:11; 35:3; 41:6

Puotesi [si può] 41:9

Pur [pure, anche] 15:1; 19:22; 23:4; 23:22; 24:7; 26:4; 31:16; 37:2; 37:3; 39:4; 40:4; 41:10

Pura [perfetta] 19:11

Pure [soltanto] 19:1

Purpureo 39:4

Qua giù [quaggù: in terra] 19:2

Qua giuso [quaggiù: in terra] 29:2

Qua su [quassù: in cielo] 19:7

Quai [quali: rel. pron. plur.] 32:4; 32:5

Qual [rel. & interrog. pron.]

Qual che [chiunque] 19:12; [qualunque cosa] 22:10

Quale [rel. & interrog. pron.]

Qualitade [qualità] 41:6; 41:6; 41:7

Qualità 16:7; 31:10; 35:6

Qualora 36:4

Quand', Quando 2:1; 3:6; 3:11; 3:14; 4:3; 9:11; 11:1; 11:2; 11:3; 12:3; 12:12; 12:12; 12:14; 12:16; 14:11; 14:12; 14:14; 15:1; 15:4; 15:4; 15:7;15:8; 16:2; 16:4; 18:2; 19:9; 19:10; 19:13; 19:16;19:17; 19:21; 20:4; 20:8; 21:4; 21:7; 21:8; 23:3; 23:10; 23:13; 23:14; 23:20; 23:26; 23:28; 23:31; 26:1; 26:1; 26:5; 27:4; 28:1; 31:5; 31:7; 31:11; 31:13; 31:14; 33:7; 34:2; 34:6; 35:3; 35:5; 37:3; 38:2; 40:9; 41:8; 41:11; 41:12

Quanta 22:1; 35:5

Quanto 2:1; 3:3; 5:4; 6:1; 7:3; 8:6; 8:12; 9:1; 9:2; 12:3; 13:3; 14:1; 15:1; 17:2; 18:9; 19:8; 19:18; 20:6; 20:6; 21:6; 23:30; 24:4; 25:4; 35:2; 37:2; 37:2; 38:4; 39:6; 39:6; 40:6; 40:7; 40:7; 40:7; 42:2

Quantunque ["quantunque volte": quante mai volte] 33:4; 33:5

Quarta 3:8; 8:12; 8:12; 13:10; 13:10; 15:8; 15:9; 16:5; 16:11; 19:16; 19:16; 22:17; 41:6; 41:8

Quarto 13:5

Quasi [circa, forse, come] 2:1; 2:2; 2:2; 3:11; 3:14; 7:1; 9:2; 9:7; 11:3; 12:3; 12:8; 13:6;

13:10; 14:2; 16:4; 16:8; 17:1;
18:8; 19:2; 19:15; 19:21; 21:5;
22:11; 25:5; 25:9; 28:1; 30:1;
30:1; 33:1; 34:3; 35:3; 36:1;
38:2; 39:1; 39:3; 40:1

Quattro 8:12; 13:1; 13:10;
16:1; 16:11; 16:11; 19:16; 22:17;
22:17; 23:2

Que' [quei, quegli: demonstr.
pron. masc. sing.] 16:8

Quei [quegli: demonstr. pron.
masc. sing.] 19:10; 34:6; 34:11

Quel [demonstr. adj. & pron]
9:7; 12:14; 21:4; 31:16; 34:8;
34:8; 39:10

Quell', Quella [demonstr. adj.
& pron. femin.] 1; 3:1; 3:2; 3:6;
5:4; 6:1; 8:2; 9:5; 10:2; 12:6;
12:11; 14:8; 19:13; 23:8; 23:18;
24:2; 24:4; 24:5; 24:8; 24:9;
24:9; 25:4; 28:1; 29:4; 31:13;
34:8; 35:3; 35:8; 38:1; 38:3;
38:6; 38:10; 34:8; 39:3; 40:1;
41:13; 42:3

Quelle [demonstr. adj. femin.
plur.] 2:10; 7:7; 9:1; 18:6; 18:7;
18:8; 22:4; 26:10; 26:14; 26:14;
30:2; 30:2; 39:1; 40:9; 41:6

Quelli [demonstr. pron. masc.
sing.: quegli, colui] 3:14; 3:14;
4:2; 12:4; 12:5; 12:7; 12:12;
14:2; 15:8

Quelli [demonstr. pron. masc.
plur.: quelli, coloro] 25:10;
25:10; 26:3

Quello [demonstr. adj. & pron.]

2:4; 3:2; 3:9; 4:1; 6:2; 9:5; 9:13;
10:3; 15:3; 15:7; 15:8; 16:4;
18:4; 18:4; 18:9; 19:21; 21:6;
21:8; 22:8; 23:5; 23:13; 23:15;
23:15; 23:30; 23:30; 24:4; 24:11;
24:11; 25:10; 26:1; 26:4; 26:8;
26:15; 26:15; 27:1; 27:1; 28:2;
29:1; 29:1; 30:1; 34:1; 34:2;
34:4; 35:8; 38:6; 39:3; 40:1;
41:5; 42:2

Questa [demonstr. adj. & pron.]
2:2; 2:8; 3:1; 3:1; 3:2; 3:6; 3:7;
3:8; 4:1; 4:1; 5:1; 5:3; 5:4; 6:1;
6:1; 8:1; 8:1; 8:7; 9:1; 9:6; 9:7;
10:1; 10:2; 10:2; 11:3; 12:6;
12:6; 12:9; 12:9; 12:9; 12:16;
13:1; 13:6; 14:1; 14:4; 14:6;
14:7; 14:9; 15:1; 15:7; 15:7;
15:8; 15:8; 15:8; 16:3; 16:4;
16:4; 16:4; 17:1; 18:3; 18:4;
18:6; 18:6; 18:7; 18:9; 19:15;
19:17;19:17; 19:18; 19:19;
19:20; 19:20; 19:21; 19:21;
19:22; 20:1; 20:7; 20:7; 20:8;
21:1; 21:5; 21:5; 22:1; 22:1;
22:2; 22:2; 22:3; 22:3; 22:5;
23:8; 23:9; 23:12; 23:15; 23:16;
23:16; 23:29; 23:30; 23:31;
23:31; 23:31; 24:1; 24:1; 24:3;
24:4; 24:6; 26:1; 26:2; 26:2;
26:8; 26:14; 26:15; 28:1; 28:1;
28:1; 28:1; 29:2; 29:3; 29:3;
29:4; 30:1; 31:2; 31:3; 31:5;
31:6; 31:7; 32:1; 32:1; 32:2;
32:6; 33:1; 33:3; 33:4; 34:1;
34:4; 34:5; 34:6; 35:3; 35:4;

35:4; 36:1; 36:2; 37:1; 37:2;
37:3; 37:3; 37:4; 38:1; 38:7;
39:1; 39:6; 40:1; 40:2; 40:4;
41:7; 41:9; 42:1

Queste [demonstr. adj. & pron.]
2:4; 2:5; 2:6; 2:10; 3:3; 3:5; 6:2;
9:5; 9:6; 9:7; 12:3; 12:4; 12:5;
12:8; 12:9; 12:17; 14:2; 14:7;
14:7; 14:8; 18:1; 18:3; 18:3;
18:4; 18:5; 18:6; 18:8; 19:3;
19:22; 19:22; 21:5; 22:4; 22:5;
22:7; 22:7; 22:11; 23:4; 23:7;
23:11; 23:13; 23:30; 24:3; 24:4;
24:5; 25:3; 26:4; 40:2; 41:1

Questi [dem. adj. pl.] 3:1; 8:3;
14:6; 17:1; 23:7; 25:4; 25:7;
27:1; 39:10; 40:2

Questi [dem. pron. masc. sing.]
3:5; 7:4; 14:6; 22:6; 22:6; 23:14;
24:10; 32:1; 32:2; 33:1; 38:10

Questi [dem. pron. masc. plur.]
14:5; 40:7

Questo [demonstr. adj. & pron.]
3:9; 3:13; 3:14; 3:14; 4:2; 4:3;
5:2; 6:1; 7:2; 7:7; 8:7; 8:12; 9:4;
9:8; 9:13; 12:2; 12:7; 12:17;
12:17; 12:17; 13:2; 13:3; 13:4;
13:5; 13:7; 13:7; 13:10; 14:3;
14:8; 14:10; 14:10; 14:13; 14:14;
14:14; 15:3; 15:7; 16:1; 16:6;
16:11; 19:3; 20:2; 20:6; 20:7;
21:1; 21:1; 21:5; 21:5; 21:6;
21:8; 22:7; 22:11; 22:17; 23:4;
23:6; 23:8; 23:13; 23:16; 23:30;
24:3; 24:6; 24:10; 25:6; 25:9;
25:9; 25:9; 25:9; 25:10; 26:1;

26:4; 26:8; 26:9; 26:14; 27:5;
28:2; 28:3; 29:1; 29:2; 29:2;
29:3; 29:3; 30:1; 30:1; 30:3;
32:3; 32:3; 33:1; 33:2; 33:3;
33:4; 34:3; 34:4; 34:6; 36:3;
37:3; 38:2; 38:3; 38:4; 38:5;
38:7; 39:1; 39:2; 39:4; 39:7;
40:5; 40:8; 41:7; 42:1

Qui [adv. of place] 5:4; 12:12;
12:17; 12:17; 12:17; 22:6; 22:10;
22:12; 25:1; 28:2; 30:2; 31:2;
40:2

Qui [Lat.: rel. pron.] 2:4; 7:7;
42:3

Quia [Lat. conj.: 'perché,'
'poiché'] 2:7

Quid [Lat.: interrog. pron.] 25:9

Quinci [adv. of place: da qui, da
questo passo] 19:20

Quindi [conj.: perciò] 28:3

Quinta 15:9; 41:7; 41:7; 41:8

Quivi [adv. of place: ivi, in quel
luogo] 3:13; 7:7; 8:7; 8:7; 8:12;
8:12; 8:12; 12:2; 12:16; 12:16;
13:10; 13:10; 13:10; 14:3; 15:7;
15:9; 15:9; 16:11; 16:11; 16:11;
19:15; 19:15; 19:16; 19:16;
19:17; 19:18; 19:19; 20:7; 20:7;
20:8; 21:5; 21:5; 21:6; 21:6;
22:11; 22:17; 23:10; 23:30;
23:30; 23:31; 24:10; 24:10;
24:11; 25:9; 25:9; 25:9; 25:9;
25:9; 25:9; 26:14; 26:14; 26:15;
26:15; 31:3; 31:3; 31:4; 31:4;
31:5; 31:6; 31:6; 32:4; 34:4;
34:4; 34:6; 37:4; 38:7; 38:7;

41:8; 41:8; 41:8; 41:8

Quomodo [Lat.: adv.] 28:1;
30:1

Raccendimento
[riaccendimento, atto del
riaccendere] 39:4
Raccese [riaccendere: third pers.
sing. pret.] 39:4
Raccoglie [raccogliere] 33:4;
33:7
Raccomandami [raccomandarsi]
19:14
Raccomandando
[raccomandarsi] 12:16
Radice 29:3; 29:3
Ragion [ragione, causa] 12:14
Ragiona [ragionare, discorrere,
parlare] 12:14; 13:8; 16:8; 31:11;
38:8
Ragionamento [conversazione,
discorso] 15:1; 25:10
Ragionando [ragionare] 12:6;
14:7; 22:5
Ragionar [ragionare] 19:4;
23:20
Ragionare [ragionare, discorrere,
parlare] 12:6; 32:2; 38:1
Ragionassi 31:1
Ragionata 14:13
Ragionate 9:6; 16:11
Ragionato 26:1
Ragionava 10:1; 38:4; 39:3
Ragionavano 5:3
Ragione [facoltà di pensare,
causa, motivo] 2:9; 4:2; 15:8;

20:3; 25:8; 25:8; 25:8; 25:10;
28:3; 28:3; 29:2; 29:3; 29:4;
38:2; 38:5; 38:5; 38:7; 39:1; 39:2
Ragione [esposizione,
spiegazione, ragionamento in
prosa; Prov. *razo*] 35:4; 35:4;
36:3; 37:5; 39:6; 39:7; 40:8
Ragionerò 12:7
Ragionevole 25:7
Ragioni [ragionare] 12:10
Ragioni [ragione: plur.] 28:2
Ragiono 31:3; 31:5
Rassembri [sembrare, parere]
14:11
Rassicurandomi 18:2
Razional [razionale, provvista di
ragione] 20:3
Reame [regno] 31:10
Reca [recare] 31:13; 38:3; 38:10
Recano 40:7
Recare 26:13
Recitando [riferire, citare] 25:9
Recolo [lo reco] 9:11
Reduce [ridurre, portare, mutare]
21:6
Redundava [ridondare, superare]
11:4
Reggesse [governare,
signoreggiare] 2:9
Reggimento [governo,
signoria] 11:3
Regina 5:1; 10:2; 28:1
Regina [Lat.: vocat. of *regina,
-ae*] 25:9
Regno 23:28
Reguarda [guardare, guardare di

nuovo] 19:11

Reguardin [guardare: guardino] 36:5

Rei [masc. plur. of "reo" 'debitori, obbligati (e inadempienti)'; De Robertis] 32:5

Reman [rimanere: rimani] 12:14

Remane [rimanere: rimane] 14:12

Remasi [past. partic. masc. plur. of "rimanere": rimasti] 31:8

Remedio ["Libro di Remedio d'Amore" *'Remedies of Love'*] 25:9

Render [rendere] 26:10

Rerum [Lat.: genit. plur. of *res, rei* 'cosa'] 13:4

Rescrivan [riscrivere, rispondere: third pers. plur. of pres. subj.] 3:10

Respetto [rispetto a, in confronto con] 19:6

Restar [sostare, soffermarsi] 22:10

Restare 19:14

Restaste 40:10

Restate [aver restato, cessato] 37:2

Resurressiti [risuscitati, risorti] 14:8

Retrova [ritrova] 12:11; 19:12

Retta [diretta] 5:1; 5:2

Rettorico [retorico] 25:7; 25:10

Reverenzia [riverenza] 28:1

Riceva [ricevere] 39:4

Riceve 26:12; 41:11

Ricevea [riceveva] 12:6

Ricevere 19:20; 37:5

Ricogliea [raccogliere: raccoglieva] 3:7

Riconfortato [rianimato] 23:15

Ricopria [ricopriva] 22:4

Ricorda 31:4; 31:9; 41:13

Ricordandomi 8:2; 12:9; 34:1; 39:2

Ricordandosi 26:15

Ricordare 6:1

Ricordarmi 38:6

Ricordava 35:1; 36:1

Ricordisi [ricordarsi: third pers. sing. of imper.] 19:20

Ricorsi [ricorrere, rifugiarsi] 3:2

Ricovrai [ricoverare, ricuperare] 38:1

Ricovrire [coprire, nascondere] 4:2

Ridea [rideva] 25:2

Rideano [ridevano] 18:3

Ridia [rideva] 24:7

Ridice [ripete, riferisce] 24:9; 41:12

Ridicendo [dicendo di nuovo] 19:16

Ridicere [ridire, esprimere] 26:3

Riduce [ridurre, portare, mutare] 20:6; 20:8; 20:8; 20:8; 21:5

Riede [redire, ritornare: ritorna] 40:6

Riguardando [guardando] 3:4

Riguardandolo [guardandolo] 12:4

Riguardar [guardare] 34:8; 39:8

Riguardava [guardava] 8:6;
12:3; 35:2

Riguardavano [guardavano]
34:2

Riguardo [guardare: guardo]
14:11

Rilevava [rilevarsi, levarsi] 38:3

Rima 3:9; 5:4; 12:7; 21:1; 24:6;
25:4; 25:7; 25:8

Riman [rimane, resta] 16:8

Rimanea [rimaneva] 11:1; 11:2;
16:3

Rimanere 31:2

Rimanesse 37:3

Rimangono 14:14; 22:2

Rimano [scrivere in rima, in
poesia] 25:6; 25:10; 25:10

Rimase [rimanere] 30:1

Rimasero 14:5; 14:5

Rimasi 22:4

Rimasse [scrivere in rima, in
poesia] 25:10

Rimate [per, in rima] 13:7;
39:6; 41:1

Rimatori [poeti] 25:7

Rimembra [rimembrare,
ricordare] 33:5

Rimembrerò 37:2

Rimuovo [levare, allontanare]
37:4

Ringrazio 23:31

Ripensando 24:6

Ripensava 38:2

Ripigliare [riprendere] 17:1;
26:4

Riposa 20:4

Riposato 14:8

Riposi [riposare: third pers.
sing. of pres. subj.] 38:1

Riposo [noun] 13:1; 33:6

Riprendea [riprendeva] 15:1

Riprendere 30:2

Riprensione [rimprovero,
biasimo] 15:3; 22:7

Ripuosi [riporre, porre: first
pers. sing. of pret.] 19:3

Riscotendomi [riscuotersi,
risvegliarsi, riaversi] 23:13

Riscuoto ["torno in me, torno
alla realtà"; De Robertis] 31:11

Risibile ["essere capace di
ridere"; De Robertis] 25:2

Riso 21:8

Risomigli [rassomigliare,
sembrare] 22:13

Risplende 19:7

Risponde 38:7; 38:7; 38:10

Rispondea [rispondeva] 4:2;
15:2

Rispondendo 18:6; 22:8

Rispondere 3:13; 15:1; 15:2;
26:1

Rispondessi [rispondere] 15:1

Risponditore [colui che
risponde] 3:14

Rispondo 22:17

Risponsione [risposta] 3:13;
11:1; 18:3; 22:8

Risposto 3:14; 12:6; 22:7

Rispuose 18:7; 25:9

Rispuosi 23:15

Ritenere [tenere, conservare]

21:8

Ritornai 14:9; 23:3

Ritornaimi [mi ritornai, ritornai] 34:3

Ritornare 14:8; 22:3

Ritornata [ritorno] 10:1

Ritornato 19:3

Ritraggono [ritrarre, distogliere, trattenere] 15:2

Ritrarre [distogliere, trattenere] 38:3

Ritrovi [cercare, trovare] 12:10

Ritruova [ritrova, ritorna da] 31:17

Rivenire [ritornare] 9:5

Rivenuti [ritornati] 14:8

Rivo [fiume] 19:1

Rivolsero [rivolgersi, volgersi di nuovo: third pers. plur. of pret.] 39:2

Rivolsi [rivolgersi: third pers. sing of pret.] 23:13

Roma 40:7

Roma [Lat.: vocat. of *Roma, -ae*] 25:9

Romei [pellegrini che andavano a Roma] 40:7

Rotta [rompere: past partic. femin. sing.] 23:13; 23:19

Rotto [rompere: past partic. masc. sing.] 12:9

Rubrica [titolo scritto in rosso] 1; 1

Ruppe [rompere: third pers. sing. of pret.] 3:7

S' [se; si]

Sa [sapere] 12:7; 12:13; 13:6; 13:6

Sa' [santo] 40:6; 40:7

Sae [sapere: sa] 26:2; 42:2

Saettavan [saettare, lanciare: saettavano] 23:23

Saggia 20:5

Saggio 20:3

Sai [sapere] 23:6; 23:24

Sale 41:6

Salisti 34:11

Saluta [salutare] 21:2; 21:6; 26:5; 33:8

Salutai 18:2

Salutando 34:2

Salutare 3:2; 3:4; 10:2; 10:3; 11:2; 12:6

Salutasse 3:9;

Salutava 11:3

Salute [saluto, salvezza] 3:4; 3:10; 8:11; 8:12; 11:1; 11:3; 11:4; 12:6; 19:10; 26:9; 26:10; 27:4; 31:10; 32:6

Saluto 3:13; 18:4; 19:20; 26:1

Salutoe [salutare: salutò] 3:1

Salvo [eccetto] 3:4; 5:4; 9:4; 14:14; 21:8; 24:3; 34:6

Sana [sano] 23:3

Sanato [sanare] 23:16

Sanguigne [color sangue] 39:1

Sanguigno 2:3; 3:4

Sanguinitade [consanguineità] 23:12; 32:1

Sanno [sapere] 36:5; 40:2

Santo 19:7; 29:3

Sanz', Sanza [senza] 2:9; 8:1;
12:2; 12:8; 12:11; 12:11; 12:16;
20:3; 20:3; 22:9; 25:8; 25:10;
28:3; 29:3; 36:3
Sapea [sapere: sapeva] 23:5
Sapeano [sapere: sapevano] 2:1;
18:1; 26:3
Sapemo [sapere: sappiamo]
25:10
Sapere 4:1; 5:3; 25:5; 40:7
Sapesse 12:17; 14:9; 25:10;
31:15
Sappiano 26:4
Sappiendo [sapere: sapiendo]
14:2
Saprei 31:16
Saprà 12:14
Saputa 14:10; 37:3
Sarebbe [essere] 11:1; 14:14;
15:8; 22:16; 25:10; 28:2; 30:2
Sarebber 32:5
Sarebbero 7:2
Sarei 22:4
Sariano [essere: sarebbero] 37:5
Sarà 9:5; 9:5; 42:2
Sarò 12:8
Savere [sapere] 19:9
Saveste [sapere: sapeste] 14:12
Savia [saggio] 38:1
Sbigottimento 35:1
Sbigottita 15:6
Sbigottito 7:1;
Scacciati 14:12
Scapigliate 23:4; 23:5
Schermo [riparo, difesa,
impedimento] 5:3; 6:1

Schianti [schiantare, spezzare]
36:4
Scienzia [scienza] 25:9
Scolorito [pallido, smorto]
23:24
Sconfitte [sconfitta] 18:1
Sconfortare [perdere coraggio,
perdersi d'animo] 23:12
Sconforte [sconfortare:
sconforti] 23:18
Scorta [scorgere: past partic.]
22:16; [visibile, manifesto] 23:26
Scrissi [scrivere] 3:9; 30:1
Scritte 1; 2:10
Scritto 13:4; 19:20; 39:10
Scriva 31:2
Scrivere 5:4; 24:6; 30:2; 34:3
Scriverne 13:7
Scriverò 5:4; 6:2; 7:2
Scrivessi 30:2; 30:3
Scrivo 30:2; 30:3
Scrivono 14:14
Scusa [noun] 12:10; 12:12
Sdonnei [sec. pers. sing. pres.
indic. of *sdonneare*: to conclude an
amorous conversation with a lady,
the opposite of *donneare*, from
Provençal *domneiar*] 12:14
Se' [essere: sei] 12:12; 15:1;
22:8; 22:13; 23:4; 23:9; 31:14;
31:17; 38:3
Se, S' [conj.] 5:4; 7:2; 7:3; 7:3;
8:9; 9:6; 12:11; 12:11; 12:13;
12:14; 12:16; 13:6; 13:9; 13:10;
14:6; 14:9; 14:12; 14:13; 15:2;
15:4; 15:6; 16:3; 16:10; 16:11;

16:11; 18:7; 19:1; 19:5; 19:14;
19:14; 19:16; 19:22; 19:22; 22:4;
22:6; 22:7; 22:7; 22:10; 22:11;
22:11; 23:25; 24:1; 24:4; 25:1;
25:2; 25:2: 25:4; 25:7; 25:8;
25:8; 25:8; 25:9; 28:2; 29:3;
30:2; 30:2; 31:8; 31:9; 32:5;
35:2; 35:3; 37:2; 37:2; 37:7;
37:8; 40:3; 40:4; 40:5; 40:6;
40:10; 42:2
Se, Sé [pron.] 3:3; 9:7; 13:6;
19:2; 19:11; 22:1; 22:1; 22:2;
22:4; 23:27; 25:1; 25:1; 25:2;
26:12; 29:3; 29:3; 29:3; 31:7;
31:10; 33:8; 35:3; 39:3; 41:2;
42:3
Se [Lat.: pron.] 12:4
Seco [con sé] 23:26; 26:11
Secol [vita terrena; "secol
degno," "secol novo" 'vita
eterna'] 31:15; 32:6; 33:5
Secolo [vita terrena; "grande
secolo" 'vita eterna'] 3:1; 8:10;
23:6; 30:1
Seconda [adj.] 3:13; 3:13; 7:7;
7:7; 8:7; 8:7; 8:12; 8:12; 9:13;
12:16; 12:16; 12:17; 13:10;
13:10; 15:7; 15:8; 15:8; 15:8;
15:9; 16:3; 16:11; 19:1; 19:15;
19:15; 19:16; 19:16; 19:17;
19:18; 19:18; 19:19; 19:19;
19:20; 19:20; 20:6; 20:6; 20:7;
20:7; 20:7; 21:6; 21:6; 22:11;
22:11; 22:17; 23:29; 23:30;
23:30; 23:31; 24:10; 24:10;
24:11; 24:11; 26:14; 26:14;

26:15; 26:15; 28:2; 31:3; 31:3;
31:4; 31:4; 31:6; 31:6; 32:4;
32:4; 33:4; 34:4; 34:4; 34:5;
34:6; 37:4; 38:7; 38:7; 41:4; 41:8
Secondo [adj.] 8:3
Secondo [prep.] 4:2; 14:3; 15:8;
16:11; 19:19; 19:19; 21:5; 21:5;
21:8; 22:3; 22:17; 23:13; 24:3;
25:1; 25:2; 25:3; 25:4; 29:1;
29:1; 29:1; 29:2; 29:2; 29:2;
29:2; 29:3; 32:1; 34:2; 34:3;
34:3; 34:4; 34:6; 34:7; 38:5;
39:2; 40:2; 40:6; 41:6
Secretissima [segretissima] 2:4
Secreto [segreto] 5:3; 5:3; 12:7;
18:1
Secula [Lat.: accus. plur. of
seculum, -i] 42:3
Securamente [sicuramente]
12:11
Securtate [sicurezza, coraggio,
ardire] 14:12
Sed [conj. *se*] 12:12; 12:13
Sedea [sedere: sedeva] 5:1; 5:1;
34:1
Sedendo 24:1
Sedere 12:3; 14:3
Sedet [Lat.: third pers. sing.
pres. indic.: *sedeo, -es*] 28:1; 30:1
Segno 25:4
Segnor [signore] 3:10; 19:7
Segnore [signore] 3:3; 8:1; 8:7;
9:3; 10:1; 10:1; 12:4; 12:5; 12:9;
12:10; 18:4; 24:8; 25:9; 25:9;
26:2; 28:1
Segnoreggiare [signoreggiare,

dominare] 2:9

Segnoreggiava [signoreggiare: signoreggiava] 9:3

Segnoreggiò [signoreggiare] 2:7

Segnoria [signoria, dominio] 9:10; 27:3

Seguitano [seguitare, venire dopo] 30:2; 30:2

Seguitasse [seguitare, eseguire, compiere] 12:9

Seguitino [seguitare, seguire, essere conseguenza di] 13:4

Sembiante [aspetto, volto] 12:14

Sembianti [aspetto, volto] 36:4

Sembianza [aspetto] 8:6; 9:10; 22:8; 22:9

Sembrava 3:12

Semo [essere: siamo] 14:2

Semplici 3:15;

Sempre 17:1; 18:9

Sen [se ne] 9:4; 19:1; 38:8

Sensibilemente [con i sensi, gli occhi] 26:4

Sensitivi [dei sensi, sensoriali] 2:5; 11:2

Senso [facoltà percettiva] 25:8

Senta [sentire] 14:12

Sente 8:5; 8:7; 21:3; 27:4

Sentendo 12:7; 35:7

Sentendome [sentendomi] 23:2

Sentendosi 26:6

Sentenzia [sentenza, sostanza] 1; 14:13; 22:17; 39:6

Sentenzie [sentenza, significato] 3:14

Senti' [sentire: sentìi] 24:6; 24:7; 24:10; 35:3

Sentia [sentire: sentiva] 7:4; 9:2; 34:9; 37:3

Sentio [sentire: sentìi] 5:2; 24:1

Sentire 3:9; 14:4; 19:5; 23:18

Sentirà 12:7

Sento 15:4; 31:14; 41:7

Sepultura [sepolcro, tomba] 40:7

Seppe [sapere] 3:14

Sequente [seguente] 21:5

Sequenti [seguenti] 19:15

Serventese [sirventese, componimento poetico] 6:2

Servidore [servitore] 12:13

Servigio [servizio) 14:3; 33:1; 40:7

Servir [servire] 9:11; 12:13

Servire 20:2

Servite 14:2

Serviziale [al servizio di, ancella] 19:15

Servo 12:14; 33:4

Sessanta 6:2

Sfigurate [alterate, sconvolte] 22:10

Sfogar [sfogare] 31:8

Sfogasser [sfogassero] 32:5

Sforzava [sforzare, forzare] 3:6; 12:5

Sforzo 16:9; 16:11

Sgradia [sgradire, non essere gradevole: gradiva] 9:9

Sguardare [guardare] 5:1

Si [Lat.: conj.] 7:7

Si [reflex. or pleonastic pron.]
2:3; 2:5; 2:6; 2:8; 2:10; 3:2; 3:6;
3:7; 3:13; 3:13; 4:1; 4:2; 5:1;
5:2; 7:1; 7:5; 8:7; 8:7; 8:8; 8:9;
8:12; 8:12; 9:4; 9:6; 11:2; 11:4;
12:16; 12:16; 12:16; 13:5; 13:6;
13:8; 13:10; 13:10; 13:10; 14:4;
14:6; 14:7; 14:7; 14:8; 14:11;
14:13; 14:14; 14:14; 15:1; 15:2;
15:5;15:6; 15:7; 15:8; 16:2; 16:3;
16:4; 16:5; 16:11; 18:1; 18:3;
19:1; 19:3; 19:5; 19:7; 19:8;
19:9; 19:11; 19:16; 19:18; 19:17;
19:17; 19:19; 19:20; 19:20;
19:22; 20:4; 20:6; 20:6; 20:7;
20:8; 20:8; 20:8; 21:1; 21:1;
21:2; 21:2; 21:4; 21:5; 21:6;
22:1; 22:2; 22:3; 22:3; 22:3;
22:4; 22:11; 23:1; 23:3; 23:5;
23:10; 23:12; 23:12; 23:17;
23:18; 23:30; 24:4; 24:11; 25:6;
26:2; 26:3; 26:6; 26:7; 26:13;
26:15; 27:5; 28:2; 28:2; 28:2;
29:1; 29:1; 29:1; 29:2; 29:2;
29:4; 30:1; 31:4; 31:5; 31:6;
31:9; 31:16; 32:2; 32:6; 33:4;
33:4; 33:4; 33:4; 33:7; 33:7;
34:1; 34:1; 34:5; 34:6; 34:9;
34:9; 35:3; 35:7; 36:1; 36:1;
36:4; 36:5; 38:1; 38:3; 38:3;
38:4; 38:7; 38:10; 39:1; 39:2;
39:3; 39:3; 39:4; 39:4; 40:6;
40:6; 40:7; 41:6

Sì [adv.: "lingua di *sì*" 'volgare
italiano'] 25:4; 25:5

Sì [adv. & conj., often
pleonastic: così; a tal punto] 2:2;
2:4; 2:5; 2:7; 2:8; 2:9; 3:7; 3:8;
4:1; 6:1; 7:2; 7:4; 7:6; 8:3; 8:6;
9:2; 9:6; 9:12; 9:13; 11:3; 12:5;
12:8; 12:9; 12:10; 12:11; 12:11;
12:13; 12:13; 13:4; 13:4; 13:8;
14:2; 14:3; 14:5; 14:7; 14:11;
14:12; 14:12; 14:12; 15:2; 15:2;
15:8; 16:3; 16:7; 16:8; 18:1;
18:2; 18:5; 18:9; 19:5; 19:6;
19:10; 19:11; 19:11; 19:12;
19:14; 20:3; 20:5; 20:7; 21:2;
21:4; 21:5; 21:6; 22:1; 22:2;
22:2; 22:3; 22:8; 22:10; 22:12;
22:14; 22:16; 23:3; 23:4; 23:4;
23:5; 23:8; 23:10; 23:13; 23:13;
23:16; 23:18; 23:19; 23:19;
23:21; 23:22; 23:24; 23:27;
23:27; 24:2; 24:7; 24:9; 24:9;
25:1; 25:1; 25:2; 25:3; 25:6;
25:8; 25:8; 25:9; 25:9; 26:1;
26:2; 26:2; 26:3; 26:3; 26:7;
26:8; 26:9; 26:14; 27:2; 27:3;
27:3; 27:4; 27:5; 29:3; 31:8;
31:10; 31:10; 31:11; 31:11;
31:14; 31:15; 31:16; 31:16; 32:1;
32:2; 32:5; 33:2; 33:2; 33:5;
33:8; 35:2; 35:4; 35:6; 36:1;
36:4; 36:5; 37:4; 37:7; 37:8;
38:1; 38:1; 38:2; 38:8; 39:2;
39:2; 39:2; 39:3; 39:5; 39:5;
39:6; 39:9; 39:10; 39:10; 40:9;
41:5; 41:6; 41:11; 41:12; 41:13;
42:2; 42:2

Sia [essere] 5:4; 8:9; 8:10; 8:12;

10:1; 12:6; 12:7; 12:7; 13:4;
13:4; 14:13; 14:13; 18:1; 18:3;
19:8; 19:10; 19:14; 19:15; 19:16;
20:7; 22:2; 22:2; 22:2; 22:3;
22:10; 25:2; 25:2; 25:4; 25:6;
25:7; 25:7; 25:7; 25:8; 26:2;
26:6; 28:3; 29:2;30:2; 31:9;
31:16; 35:3; 35:3; 38:5; 38:5;
41:6

Siano [essere] 12:8; 14:2; 20:7;
25:7; 29:2; 30:2

Sic [Lat.: adv.] 12:4

Sicura 12:16

Sicuramente 12:16

Sicurtade [sicurezza, coraggio,
libertà, ardire] 2:7; 15:8

Sicut [Lat.: adv.] 7:7

Sie [essere: sia] 23:13

Significasse 14:10

Significato 26:9

Significazione [signifcato]
40:6

Significo 3:13

Signore 34:7

Signoria [dominio] 2:7; 13:2;
13:3

Simiglianza [somiglianza] 24:5

Simil [simile, similmente] 20:5;
20:8

Simile 14:14; 15:8; 22:9; 30:3;
36:1; 39:1; 39:5

Simili [Lat.: ablat. sing.:
similis, -e] 12:4

Similitudine 29:3

Simulacra [Lat.: nom. plur.:
simulacrum, -i] 12:3

Simulatamente 14:4

Simulato 9:6

Simulava 32:2

Singulto [singhiozzo] 23:11;
23:13

Sinistra 14:4

Sire [signore] 6:2; 19:7; 20:4;
22:1; 31:10; 42:3

Siria 29:1

Smagati [smagare, indebolire,
venir meno] 23:22

Smagato [smagare, indebolire,
venir meno] 12:13

Smarrimento 23:4; 23:22

Smarrita 23:21

Smore [smorire, divenire pallido,
smorto] 21:2; 27:4

Smorto [pallido] 16:9

So [sapere] 9:5; 13:9; 13:9;
13:10; 13:10; 14:10; 19:13;
19:15; 19:21; 23:23; 30:3; 40:3;
41:8; 41:13

So' [essere: sono] 19:13

Soave 3:3; 7:4; 12:8; 12:14;
26:3; 26:7; 27:3; 31:13; 33:6

Sofferiate [soffrire: soffriate]
7:3

Sofferino [soffrire: soffrino] 7:7

Sofferite [soffrire: soffrite] 19:8

Sofferse [soffrire: soffrì] 2:9;
6:2

Soffersi [soffrire: soffrìi] 23:1

Sofferta [soffrire] 31:8

Soffrisse 19:9

Sognasse 23:12

Sogno 3:15

Sol [adj. & adv.: solo] 7:3; 13:8; 13:10; 15:6; 22:13; 31:14; 31:15

Sola 19:8; 23:30; 26:12; 30:1

Sola [Lat.: femin. of *solus, -a*] 28:1

Solamente 11:1; 16:5; 16:8; 18:3; 19:1; 21:1; 22:17; 23:6; 23:11; 25:1; 25:2; 25:8; 25:9; 26:8; 26:15; 26:15; 29:3; 30:3; 32:2

Solavate [solere, esser soliti: solevate] 37:2

Sole [noun] 23:5; 23:24; 41:6

Solete [solere, esser soliti] 37:2

Solinga [isolato, appartato] 12:1

Solingo 3:2

Sollenato [sollevare, alleviare] 12:2; 39:4

Sollicito [sollecitare: sollecito] 8:7

Solo [adj. & adv.] 14:12; 19:14; 23:19; 23:28; 24:4; 31:10; 33:3

Solvere 12:17; 14:14

Solverebbe 14:14

Somiglia 24:9

Somigliante 25:8

Somiglio 23:27

Sommo 19:9

Sommosso [sommuovere, commuovere: commosso] 35:7

Son [essere: sono] 7:3; 12:7;15:4; 15:7; 19:13; 26:10; 31:8; 39:8; 39:8; 39:9

Sonetto 3:9; 3:9; 3:13; 3:14; 3:14; 7:2; 7:2; 7:2; 7:7; 7:7; 8:7; 8:12; 9:8; 9:13; 13:7; 13:10;

14:10; 14:13; 14:14; 15:3; 15:7; 16:1; 16:6; 16:11; 20:2; 20:6; 21:1; 21:5; 22:11; 22:12; 22:17; 24:6; 24:10; 26:4; 26:8; 26:9; 26:14; 27:2; 32:3; 32:3; 33:1; 33:2; 33:3; 34:3; 34:4; 35:4; 35:4; 36:3; 37:3; 37:3; 38:4; 38:5; 38:6; 38:7; 39:6; 39:7; 40:5; 40:5; 40:8; 41:1; 41:1; 41:2; 42:1

Sonetti 8:3; 17:1; 22:8; 27:1

Sonni 12:4

Sonno 3:3; 3:7; 3:9; 12:9

Sono [essere] 2:10; 7:2; 13:10; 13:10; 14:14; 15:8; 16:11; 16:11; 19:1; 19:1; 19:19; 19:19; 19:20; 19:22; 19:22; 20:3; 22:2; 22:17; 23:8; 23:26; 25:8; 25:9; 29:3; 30:2; 31:16; 33:6; 40:2; 41:7

Sono [noun: suono] 12:12; 12:16; 25:9; 33:7

Soperchio [troppo, superfluo] 14:14

Soppongo [supporre: suppongo] 13:10

Sopra 2:7; 5:1; 12:7; 16:1; 16:11; 19:15;19:20; 22:17; 25:6; 27:1; 30:1; 34:1

Sopradetta 7:1; 8:1; 9:1; 14:3; 19:3; 22:3; 30:1

Sopragiunse [sopraggiungere] 3:3

Soprascritta 13:1; 21:1; 28:1

Soprascritto 3:1; 33:2; 33:3

Soprastare [soffermarsi, trattenersi] 2:10

Sorelle 31:17
Sorride 21:4
Sorridendo 4:3
Sospir [sospiro: sospiri] 39:10
Sospira 21:2; 26:7; 37:8
Sospirando 9:10; 12:3; 23:3; 23:21
Sospirar 31:15
Sospirare 26:3; 31:12
Sospiri 9:2; 9:7; 10:1; 12:6; 18:5; 26:13; 31:13; 32:3; 32:5; 33:7; 34:5; 34:9; 37:3; 39:3; 39:4; 39:6; 39:8; 40:10
Sospiro 41:10
Sostenea [sostenere: sosteneva] 3:7
Sostenere 3:7; 8:2; 18:3
Sottile 29:4; 29:4; 33:8; 41:12
Sottilmente 24:5; 29:3; 33:2; 33:2; 41:9; 41:9
Sotto 1; 2:10; 6:2; 11:3; 19:3; 25:10; 28:1
Sovente [spesso] 8:6; 16:7; 22:8; 22:13; 23:20; 32:6; 34:10; 36:4; 38:8
Soverchievole [molto, eccessivo] 10:2
Soverchio [molto, eccessivo] 11:3
Sovra [sopra] 8:5; 8:6
Spande [spandere, versare] 33:8
Spaventami [mi spaventa] 37:8
Spene [speranza] 19:8
Spera [sfera] 41:2; 41:10
Sperando 13:8
Speranza 11:1; 19:8; 20:1

Speri 8:11
Spero 31:16; 42:2
Spesse [frequente] 5:1; 7:4; 13:8; 16:3; 16:6; 16:7; 31:13; 36:5; 39:9; 41:7
Spesso 22:4; 23:17; 37:2; 39:4; 41:7; 41:13
Spezialmente [specialmente] 2:5; 6:1; 25:2
Spiramento [ispirazione, suggerimento] 38:3
Spiral [spirituale] 33:8
Spiritel [piccolo spirito] 38:10
Spiritelli [piccoli spiriti] 14:6;
Spiriti 2:5; 2:5; 11:2; 11:2; 14:5; 14:5; 14:8; 14:12; 14:14; 27:4; 27:4
Spirito 2:4; 2:5; 2:6; 4:1; 11:2; 20:5; 24:7; 26:7; 29:3; 31:11; 41:5; 41:11
Spiritualmente 41:5
Spirti [spiriti] 19:12; 23:22
Spirto [spirito] 16:8
Splendore 41:11
Spoglia [privo] 31:12
Sposo 14:3
Sta 18:6; 27:3; 31:10
Stae [stare: sta] 41:5
Stagione 20:4; 37:6
Stando 14:10; 24:8; 24:10
Stanno 14:6
Stanza [strofa] 19:21
Stanzia [stanza, strofa] 28:1; 33:4; 33:4
Stanzie [stanze, strofe] 33:2
Star [stare] 31:17; 38:9

Stare 6:2; 13:6; 14:3; 14:5;
14:6; 19:22; 23:1
Starla [stare + la] 19:9
Stata [essere: past partic.] 2:2;
3:8; 5:2; 9:1; 9:5; 11:1; 18:1;
22:7; 23:8; 23:9; 23:27; 31:15
Stati [essere: past partic.] 22:2;
34:2
Stato [essere: past partic.] 3:6;
12:13; 15:8; 18:8; 22:1; 24:1;
24:10; 38:3
Stato [noun] 13:7; 15:8; 16:1;
17:1; 19:6; 41:1
Statura [stato, condizione] 35:5
Stava [stare] 2:9; 10:2; 24:2;
35:1
Steasi [si stia] 31:7
Stella 3:11; 23:24
Stellato [delle stelle; "cielo
stellato" 'il cielo ottavo,' 'lo
Zodiaco'] 2:2
Stelle 23:5
Stessa 19:2
Stessi 35:3
Stesso 14:9; 19:11; 19:16; 23:3
Stilo [stile, modo, maniera] 26:4
Stoltamente 25:10
Stretto 40:6; 40:6
Stringe [legare, cingere,
avvincere] 13:5
Strugge [distruggere, uccidere]
31:15
Struggo [consumarsi, logorarsi]
7:6
Strumenti 14:14
Studio [studiarsi, adoperarsi]

42:2
Su [prepos. & adv.] 6:2; 19:7;
41:10
Sua 2:1; 2:3; 2:9; 3:1; 3:7; 4:1;
7:2; 7:4; 8:1; 8:2; 8:11; 12:3;
13:4; 13:8; 14:3; 14:10; 14:13;
15:2; 15:8; 16:4; 18:3; 18:4;
19:3; 19:4; 19:9; 19:10; 19:18;
19:18; 19:20; 20:4; 21:5; 21:8;
21:8; 23:8; 23:8; 24:2; 24:3;
24:7; 25:9; 26:4; 26:7; 26:9;
26:9; 26:11; 26:12; 26:14; 26:14;
26:15; 26:15; 27:2; 27:2; 27:3;
28:2; 28:3; 28:3; 29:1; 29:2;
30:1; 31:5; 31:5; 31:10; 31:10;
31:11; 32:6; 32:6; 33:2; 33:7;
33:8; 36:2; 36:3; 38:9; 38:10;
39:7; 39:10; 40:1; 40:6; 40:7;
40:8; 40:9; 40:10; 41:5; 41:7;
42:3
Subitamente [d'improvviso]
3:11; 9:7; 31:9
Subitanamente [d'improvviso]
16:8
Subito 14:4; 16:3
Sue 3:3; 3:4; 3:7; 8:10; 11:4;
12:5; 19:18; 19:18; 25:6; 25:10;
26:4; 32:2
Sufficiente 28:2
Suggetto [soggetto] 20:7; 20:7
Sunt [Lat.: third pers. sing. plur.
pres. indic.: *esse*] 13:4
Suo 2:2; 3:1; 3:10; 8:5; 9:5;
10:2; 10:3; 11:3; 12:7; 12:13;
13:2; 13:3; 13:5; 13:6; 13:8;
14:2; 14:3; 19:5; 19:6; 19:7;

19:16; 19:18; 19:22; 20:3 21:2;
21:8; 21:8; 22:2; 22:9; 22:15;
23:3; 23:21; 24:4; 24:4; 24:4;
24:6; 26:1; 31:2; 32:2; 34:7;
34:8; 38:1; 38:10; 40:9; 41:3;
41:7; 41:11

Suoi 2:7; 8:12; 9:4; 12:16;
18:3; 19:12; 19:19; 21:5; 26:13;
38:10

Suole [solere] 39:4

Superbia 21:2

Suso [su] 23:7; 23:25; 41:4;
41:5; 41:5

Sustanzia [sostanza] 25:1; 25:1;
25:1; 25:1

Sustanzie [sostanze] 25:8

Sveglia [svegliare, destare] 21:1;
21:1

Svegliar 20:5; 24:6; 24:7

Svegliare 24:10

Svegliato 34:9

Svegliava 3:12

T' [ti] 4:3; 9:6; 15:4; 19:13;
19:13; 19:13; 31:16; 33:5

Tacendo 23:15

Tacendomi [tacendo] 24:6

Tacere 17:1; 24:6

Tacesse 17:1

Tal [tale] 11:3; 20:4; 20:4; 22:6;
23:9; 41:8; 41:12

Tale 11:3; 23:20; 41:6; 41:6

Talora 9:4; 18:5; 20:5; 22:4;
23:14; 32:6

Tamen [Lat.: adv] 25:9

Tanquam [Lat.: adv.] 12:4

Tanta 2:7; 2:7; 2:10; 3:2; 3:3;
12:5; 14:5; 14:12; 15:2; 16:4;
18:8; 19:1; 22:1; 22:4; 22:7;
22:10; 23:1; 23:3; 23:9; 23:27;
26:1; 26:1; 26:8; 26:11; 27:4;
27:4; 31:10; 31:10; 31:14; 38:3;
38:3

Tante 4:2; 14:1

Tanti 3:1

Tanto 2:2; 3:1; 3:6; 5:2; 5:3;
6:1; 7:1; 9:1; 10:1; 12:1; 13:3;
13:5; 15:2; 19:22; 20:5; 21:6;
22:10; 23:8; 23:8; 23:22; 24:4;
25:4; 26:3; 26:4; 26:5; 26:5;
26:13; 29:2; 31:1; 31:1; 31:13;
32:1; 33:5; 33:5; 33:6; 35:1;
37:1; 38:1; 38:3; 38:9; 39:3; 42:1

Tavolette [piccole tavole,
pannelli] 34:1

Te [pron.] 8:8; 12:6; 12:6; 12:7;
22:14; 23:27; 23:28; 38:3

Tegno [tenere: tengo] 12:7;
23:27

Tema [timore, paura] 9:13

Temendo 12:6; 14:4; 35:3

Temenza [timore, paura] 19:6

Temo 19:22; 36:4; 37:8

Tempi 9:5

Tempo 2:2; 3:9; 3:11; 4:1; 5:3;
6:1; 7:1; 10:1; 25:4; 25:4; 27:1;
31:1; 35:1; 35:1; 39:2; 40:1

Tempus [Lat.: nom. sing. of
tempus, -oris] 12:3

Ten [te ne] 33:5

Tenendo 3:12

Tener 14:12; 36:5

Tenere 21:4; 40:4
Tenesse 3:5; 19:1
Tengo 12:7; 15:7
Tenni [tenere] 14:8
Tentare [mettere alla prova] 13:1
Tentazione 39:6
Tenute [tenere: tenuto] 26:10
Tenuto 27:3
Terminasse 5:1
Terminava 5:2
Termine [fine, punto estremo]
9:1
Termini [fine, punto estremo;
parola, locuzione] 3:1; 10:1
Terra 9:4; 12:1; 19:17; 23:24;
26:6; 30:1
Terribile 35:1
Terrò [tenere] 31:2
Terza 8:7; 8:7; 8:12; 8:12;
12:16; 12:16; 13:10; 13:10; 15:8;
15:9; 16:4; 16:11; 19:15; 19:15;
19:16; 19:16; 21:5; 21:5; 21:6;
21:6; 22:17; 24:10; 24:10; 24:11;
26:14; 26:14; 26:15; 26:15; 28:2;
31:3; 31:3; 31:4; 31:4; 31:6;
31:6; 34:4; 34:4; 38:7; 38:7;
41:5; 41:8
Terzo 25:9
Terzodecimo [tredicesimo] 29:1
Tesoro 7:5
Testa 23:8
Testimoniare [essere
testimone] 26:1
Testimonio [testimone] 12:7
Testé [poco fa, or ora] 34:2
Ti 8:9; 9:5; 9:6; 12:6; 12:6;

12:11; 12:11; 12:13; 12:14; 13:5;
18:6; 19:14; 23:9; 23:10; 23:12;
23:18; 23:22; 23:22; 23:26;
23:27; 23:27; 24:2
Tibi [Lat.: dat. sing. of pers.
pron. *tu*] 25:9
Tira [tirare, portare] 41:10
Tirasse 36:2
Tisirin [It. rendition of Lat.
Tisrim, the month of October, as
Dante learned from Alfraganus'
*Liber de aggregatione scientiae
stellarum*; CV 2:5.16; 2:13:11]
29:1
Toccai [toccare, fare cenno a] 8:3
Tolle [Latinism; togliere: toglie]
27:4
Tolomeo [Alexandrian
astronomer: sec. cent. A.D.] 29:2
Tolse [togliere] 31:10
Tolsimi [mi tolsi] 35:7
Tolta [togliere: past partic.]
31:5; 31:12
Tormenti 33:5
Tormento 7:3
Tormentosi [tormentati,
affannati] 14:12
Tornando 12:1
Tornano 22:11
Tornar 22:10
Tornare 23:10
Tornassero 23:7
Tornato 23:30; 2:1
Tornavan 23:25
Torto [colpa] 8:9
Tortoso [colpevole] 8:9

Tostamente che [tosto, sùbito da, fin da] 12:7

Tostana [breve, spedita] 19:14

Tosto [sùbito] 2:7; 7:2; 12:13; 15:2; 15:2; 35:3

Tra 3:3; 3:14; 3:14; 6:2; 13:1; 14:4; 14:14; 18:3; 18:3; 18:3; 18:5; 18:6; 20:1; 22:3; 22:5; 23:14; 25:3; 25:3; 26:10; 26:14; 28:3

Trae [trarre] 13:2; 15:8; 41:7

Traendo 23:23; 31:8

Traendomi [trarre] 14:7

Tramortendo [tramortire, perdere i sensi, venir meno] 15:5

Tramortisce 39:10

Tramortita 31:16

Tramuta [tramutare, mutare] 31:13

Transitis [Lat.: sec. pers. plur. pres. indic. of *transeo, -is*] 7:7

Trapassando [passare oltre, tralasciare] 2:10

Trapassaro [trapassare: trapassarono] 22:4

Trarre 2:10; 39:5

Trasfiguramento [trasformazione, mutamento] 14:10

Trasfigurazione [trasformazione, mutamento] 14:7; 15:1

Trasse [trarre] 34:8

Trassero [trarre] 23:12

Trattai 21:1

Trattando 28:2

Trattare 5:4; 19:17; 20:2; 28:2; 28:2; 28:2; 42:1

Trattarne 28:2

Trattassi 20:2

Trattato [past partic. of *trattare*; esposto, discusso; noun: trattazione, discussione] 19:15; 20:2; 22:8; 22:13; 28:2

Trattavano 25:3

Tratterò 19:6

Travagliar [soffrire] 31:16

Travagliare [soffrire] 23:4; 35:2

Travaglio ["non mi travaglio di" 'non mi do pena di,' 'non perdo tempo in'] 19:21

Tre 8:7; 9:13; 12:16; 17:1; 19:15; 21:5; 21:6; 25:2; 26:14; 26:15; 28:2; 29:3; 29:3; 29:3; 29:3; 29:3; 29:3; 31:3; 31:4; 31:6; 34:4; 38:7; 40:7

Tremando 2:4; 13:8; 26:5

Tremar 21:2

Tremare 2:4; 11:2; 14:4; 23:24

Tremore [tremito] 14:4; 15:5; 24:10

Tremoto [tremore, tremito] 16:10

Tremuoti [terremoti] 23:5

Tremuoto [tremore, tremito] 24:1

Tribulazione [tribolazione, sofferenza] 38:3; 40:1

Triema [tremare: trema] 22:10

Trinitade [Trinità] 29:3

Trista [triste] 35:8

Triste 22:15; 23:5
Tristi 34:10
Tristizia 22:3; 22:4; 23:23; 31:1; 31:6; 31:12; 31:17; 36:2
Troiani 25:9
Troppa 10:1
Troppi 19:22
Troppo 18:9; 37:1; 38:1
Trova [trovare] 1; 14:12; 19:10
Trovai 3:8; 9:9; 9:13; 12:9
Trovato [escogitare, inventare] 25:6
Trovatori [poeti; Provençal *trobador* 'troubadour'] 3:9
Troverai 19:14
Troviamo 25:4
Trovo 1; 31:15
Tu 9:6; 12:4; 12:7; 12:7; 12:7; 12:7; 12:8; 12:10; 12:10; 12:11; 12:11; 12:11; 12:14; 12:14; 15:1; 15:1; 15:1; 15:1; 15:1; 18:3; 18:3; 18:6; 18:7; 18:7; 19:13; 19:13; 19:14; 19:14; 19:21; 22:8; 22:13; 22:13; 22:14; 22:14; 23:4; 23:4; 23:9; 23:9; 23:13; 23:20; 23:27; 23:27; 24:2; 31:14; 31:17; 33:5; 38:3; 38:3; 38:3
Tu [Lat.: subject pron.] 12:4
Tua 9:5; 9:5; 12:6; 12:7; 12:7; 15:1; 18:3; 18:6; 18:7; 23:6; 23:24
Tue 31:17
Tuo 8:9; 9:11; 12:2; 12:7; 12:14; 12:14; 23:9
Tuoi 23:27
Turbar [oscurarsi] 23:24

Turbati [preoccupati, inquieti] 40:3
Turbava ["si turbava" 'si commoveva, si affliggeva, provava pietà'; De Robertis] 38:10
Tutta 3:5; 4:1; 7:5; 9:7; 10:2; 18:4; 19:19; 23:19; 30:1; 35:2
Tuttavia 2:9; 9:6; 19:22; 23:13; 28:3; 33:7; 36:1
Tutte 1; 5:4; 12:6; 12:8; 12:11; 13:2; 14:4; 18:3; 26:15; 30:2; 42:2
Tutti 2:5; 2:7; 3:1; 3:9; 10:2; 11:2; 13:6; 13:7; 13:8; 13:9; 13:10; 13:10; 13:10; 14:14; 18:4; 21:6; 23:10; 23:25; 26:3; 29:2; 33:7; 34:5; 36:5; 39:2; 39:3
Tutto 4:1; 9:2; 11:3; 16:4; 17:1; 21:2; 21:6; 22:7; 23:13; 35:4; 38:7; 38:10; 39:3; 41:7 ["tutto che," "con tutto che" 'sebbene']
Tuum [Lat.: accus. neuter of possessive adj. *tuus, tua, tuum*] 3:5
Tuus [Lat.: nomin. masc. of possessive adj. *tuus, tua, tuum*] 3:3; 25:9

Ubidir [ubbidire] 12:13
Uccelli 23:5
Uccide 14:14; 15:2
Udendo 8:4; 8:7
Udia [udire: udiva] 26:2
Udiano [udire: udivano] 5:1
Udimmo 22:15

Udio [udire: udìi; udì] 12:6;
22:3; 22:3; 22:7; 22:8; 24:10;
24:11

Udire 2:9; 13:4; 17:2; 18:5;
23:7; 23:7; 23:16

Udirete 32:6

Udisse 20:1

Udissero 40:2

Udita 22:5

Udite 20:1

Udito 12:2

Ultima 8:3; 15:8; 19:21; 26:15

Ultime 3:8

Ultimo 3:1; 21:8

Umana 25:9

Umane 23:17

Umil [umile] 12:13; 27:5

Umile 2:3; 15:2; 21:3; 22:8;
22:9; 23:27; 26:12

Umilemente [umilmente] 23:20

Umilia [umiliare] 19:10

Umilitade [umiltà] 11:1; 23:8;
23:9; 26:2

Umilitate [umiltà] 31:10

Umilità [umiltà] 23:26

Umilmente 3:12

Umiltate [umiltà] 34:7

Umiltà 23:27; 26:6

Un [indefinite article]

Un' [indefinite article]

Una [indefinite artic.; indefinite
pron.]

Uno [indefinite artic.; indefinite
pron.]

Uomini 22:3; 22:3; 25:8; 34:1

Uomo [uomo; persona; uno] 2:8;

12:17; 20:8; 25:2; 25:2; 25:2;
25:9

Usano 23:10

Usanza 14:3; 22:3; 29:1; 29:1;
29:1

Usare 19:22

Usata [solita, consueta] 14:12

Usate [solite, consuete] 31:17

Usato 24:10

Uscendo 10:3; 22:1

Uscian [uscivano] 34:11

Uscire 18:5;18:5; 39:3

Uscireste 40:10

Uscisse 12:9

Uscissero 40:4

Uscivan 34:4; 34:10

Uscivano 34:5

Ut [Lat.: conj.] 12:3

Utile 2:9; 12:6

V' [adv. "vi"] 18:3; 18:3

V' [pron. "vi"] 33:8; 40:9

'v' [adv. "ove"] 19:8; 23:17;
24:8; 33:8

Va [andare] 19:9; 22:2; 26:6;
26:7; 31:17; 33:7; 40:1; 40:6;
41:3; 41:4; 41:5

Vada 12:16; 12:16; 13:6; 19:9;
31:7

Vade [andare: vada] 12:10

Vado 8:8

Vai 12:11; 33:5

Valente [degno] 20:5

Valor 16:9

Valore 3:14; 13:8; 19:5; 19:16;
23:20; 27:4; 34:7; 34:8; 38:10;

39:8
Vana 19:14; 23:29; 24:1; 39:6
Vane 23:17
Vaneggiato [vaneggiare,
perdersi dietro a cose vane] 39:6
Vanitade [vanità, incostanza]
37:2; 39:5
Vanità 37:8
Vanna [proper name, diminutive
of "Giovanna"] 24:8
Vanno 26:10; 26:14; 32:5; 40:7;
40:7; 40:7; 40:7
Vano 23:23
Varietate [varietà, differenza]
13:8
Vatten [andare: vattene] 31:17
've [ove, dove] 19:12; 19:13
Vede 19:7; 21:6; 21:6; 23:10;
23:28; 26:9; 26:10; 26:10; 27:5;
31:12; 31:16; 33:2; 40:1; 41:6;
41:11
Vedea [vedeva] 3:12; 5:1; 22:1
23:21; 23:25; 23:26; 26:2; 26:9;
31:10; 36:1; 37:2
Vedeala [la vedevo] 2:8
Vedeano [vedevano] 23:12
Vedela [la vede] 41:8; 41:12
Vedemo [vediamo] 18:5; 25:8;
29:3
Veder 9:10; 12:3; 14:12; 15:4;
19:10; 23:20; 23:23; 23:26;
23:26; 33:5; 36:4; 40:1
Vedere 2:8; 3:1; 3:3; 3:4; 14:5;
14:6; 15:1; 16:4; 19:9; 23:4;
23:5; 23:5; 23:7; 23:8; 23:8;
23:9; 23:24; 26:1; 26:4; 35:2;

36:2; 38:6; 39:1; 42:3
Vederebbe [vedrebbe] 29:4
Vederebbono [vedrebbero] 15:8
Vederla 15:2; 37:1
Vederlo 24:2
Vederne 22:10
Vedervi 16:9
Vedesse 35:2
Vedeste 3:14; 22:9; 37:6
Vedestù [vedesti] 22:14; 23:20
Vedete 19:12
Vedetevi [vi vedete] 36:4
Vedi 5:2; 22:6; 23:9; 23:27;
38:3
Vedova 30:1; 31:2
Vedrassi [si vedrà] 12:13
Vedrà 19:3
Veduta 8:2; 8:2; 14:7; 15:2;
16:4; 16:5; 22:6; 33:8; 40:5
Veduto 3:9; 3:9; 3:15; 23:10;
23:15
Veggendo [vedere: vedendo]
22:3; 23:3; 23:17; 23:27; 26:9;
27:1; 31:16
Veggendosi [vedere: vedendosi]
14:5
Veggio [vedere: vedo] 22:9;
22:10; 29:4
Veggiono [vedere: vedono] 35:3
Veggiovi [vedere: vi vedo]
22:10
Vegno [venire: vegno] 9:5; 9:11;
15:4; 16:9; 23:27
Vegnonmi [venire: mi vengono]
16:7
Vegnono [venire: vengono]

22:11

Velo 23:8; 23:26

Ven [venire: viene] 3:10; 7:5;
31:6; 31:11; 31:12; 31:14; 36:4;
37:7

Vene [venire: viene] 30:1; 38:8;
38:9

Venemene [me ne viene] 31:13

Venia [venire: venivo, veniva]
9:10; 18:8; 24:8

Venian [venivano] 34:11

Veniano [venivano] 22:6

Veniens [Lat.; pres. part. of
venio, -is] 2:4

Venir 24:6; 24:8

Venire 3:2; 18:4; 21:1; 22:14;
24:2; 24:3; 24:4; 25:2; 25:2;
31:10; 42:2

Venisse 23:6; 23:11

Venissero 14:10

Venite 22:9; 22:10; 22:11;
32:3; 32:5; 40:9; 41:1

Venmene [me ne viene] 16:7

Venne 6:1; 14:1; 26:1; 26:8;
32:1; 34:3; 36:3

Vennemi [mi venne] 21:1

Venni 23:5; 37:1

Venti 25:9

Venuta [verb; noun] 7:1; 24:4;
26:6; 34:3; 34:6; 34:7; 34:8

Venuti 14:2; 34:3

Ver [prep.: verso] 8:6; 12:11;
21:2

Vera 8:6

Verace [vero] 3:15; 23:10;
23:26; 23:30; 24:4; 25:10

Veracemente [veramente] 12:7;
22:1; 33:2; 42:2

Veramente 2:4

Vere 23:6; 25:8; 25:8

Vergogna 7:6; 25:10; 31:14

Vergognandomi 14:9

Vergognasse 23:13

Vergognava 39:6

Vergognosa 23:19

Vergognoso 18:8; 39:3

Veritade [verità] 5:3; 29:2; 29:3

Verità 23:22

Veritate [verità] 25:1

Vero 12:13; 14:3; 14:14; 18:7;
22:2; 23:8; 38:6

Verrebbe 14:9

Verrà 24:4; 24:4

Verrò, 2

Versi [noun] 25:4; 25:6

Verso [prep.] 2:2; 3:1; 3:7; 9:1;
13:6; 18:3; 23:7; 23:10; 23:12;
23:19; 23:28; 24:3; 38:7; 40:6;
40:6

Vertude [virtù] 15:1; 15:2; 26:9;
27:2

Vertudi [virtù] 15:2; 19:18

Vertuosamente [virtuosamente]
10:3; 26:14

Vertute [virtù] 8:10; 19:10;
26:11; 27:4; 31:10; 32:6

Vertù [virtù] 2:7; 2:9; 9:3; 38:9;
40:10

Vesta [veste, ornamento] 25:10;
25:10

Vestimenta [vesti, vestiti]
12:3; 39:1

Vestita 2:3; 3:1; 26:2
Vestito 9:3; 11:1; 12:3
Vestra [Lat.; poss. adj.: *vester,
vestra, vestrum*] 2:5
Vestuta [vestita] 26:6
Vestute [vestite] 26:11
Vi [adv.] 5:2; 14:14
Vi [pron.] 12:12; 15:4; 15:7;
18:3; 18:3; 22:9; 23:15; 31:16;
34:8; 37:2; 37:8; 39:10; 41:5
Via [noun; adv.] 3:1; 7:2; 7:3;
9:9; 13:6; 13:6; 13:6; 19:9;
19:14; 23:5; 23:18; 23:23; 26:1;
27:4; 29:3; 32:5; 40:1
Viam [Lat.; accus. sing.: *via,
-ae*] 7:7; 24:4
Vide [Lat.: sec. pers. sing. of
imper.: *video, -es*] 3:5
Vide [vedere] 9:11; 15:6; 21:3;
41:5
Video [Lat.: first pers. sing.
pres. indic.: *video, -es*] 25:9
Videro [vedere: third pers. plur.
of pret.] 23:14; 35:4; 35:5
Videte [Lat.; sec. pers. plur.
imper. of *video, -es*] 7:7
Vidi 2:2; 8:1; 8:6; 14:4; 18:2;
19:8; 23:13; 23:23; 24:3; 24:4;
24:7; 24:8; 24:10; 24:11; 25:2;
33:1; 34:1; 34:2; 35:2; 39:1; 42:1
Vidua [Lat.; *viduus*] 28:1
Viene 15:8
Vieni 23:9; 23:9; 23:26; 23:27;
33:6
Vile [di poco valore, virtù,
coraggio] 19:6; 22:9; 31:11;

35:3; 37:1; 38:2
Vili 9:3; 13:2
Vilissimo 38:4
Villan [villano: senza gentilezza,
senza intelletto d'amore] 31:11
Villana [villano] 8:3; 8:5; 8:8;
19:14; 23:9
Villani [villano] 19:9
Vilmente 23:22; 39:2
Viltate [viltà] 35:6
Viltà 19:16
Vinceano [vincevano] 38:4
Vinti 31:8; 39:8
Virgilio [Latin poet: 70-19
B.C.] 25:9
Virgo [Latinism: vergine] 28:1
Virtuosamente 3:1; 21:6;
21:6; 26:4
Virtù 19:9
Virtudi [virtù] 10:2
Virum [Lat.; accus. sing.: *vir,
viri*] 25:9
Visi [viso] 23:4; 23:4; 23:22
Visione 3:3; 3:8; 3:9; 4:1;
12:9; 13:1; 42:1
Visivi [della vista] 14:14
Viso 2:5; 4:2; 11:1; 11:2; 14:5;
15:5; 15:8; 15:9; 19:12; 21:2;
22:9; 22:16; 22:17; 23:19; 27:4;
31:13; 36:4; 37:8
Vista 4:1; 5:3; 9:2; 9:7; 12:3;
12:12; 14:11; 15:1; 15:6; 18:1;
18:3; 23:19; 26:12; 26:15; 35:1;
35:2; 35:7; 36:1; 36:2; 37:1;
38:1; 40:3
Vita 1; 2:2; 2:4; 7:4; 13:1; 14:2;

14:5; 14:8; 14:14; 16:3; 16:5;
16:8; 22:1; 23:3; 23:21; 31:10;
31:15; 31:16; 32:6; 34:1; 35:3;
35:6; 38:1; 38:10; 42:2
Vitupero [vituperare, offendere]
8:12
Vivette [vivere: visse] 40:1
Vivia [vivere: viveva] 31:9
Vivo [adj.] 16:8
Vivono 42:2
Vizi 10:2
Viziosamente 10:2
Vizioso 19:20
Vo' [voglio] 19:4; 19:6
Vo [andare] 33:5
Vocabulo [parola, termine] 40:6
Voce [fama, diceria; voce, suono]
10:2; 22:13; 23:10; 23:13; 23:19;
23:30; 34:10
Vogli [vuoi] 24:4
Voglia [desiderio] 15:6; 22:8;
31:6; 31:12; 36:5
Vogliate 37:2
Voglio 10:3; 12:7; 13:10;
19:16; 19:16; 31:4; 31:4; 31:8
Voi [pron.] 7:2; 7:3; 12:12;
12:13; 14:12; 15:4; 16:8; 16:9;
18:4; 19:4; 19:12; 22:8; 22:9;
22:9; 23:25; 23:28; 23:31; 31:10;
32:6; 35:6; 35:7; 36:4; 36:5;
36:5; 36:5; 37:2; 37:2; 37:6;
37:6; 37:7; 37:7; 37:8; 40:9;
40:9; 40:10
Voi [volere: voglio] 8:9; 8:10;
12:9; 12:10; 13:9; 19:4; 19:6;
19:9; 19:16; 31:9

Vol [volere: vuole] 12:12
Volando 23:5; 23:24
Vole [volere: vuole] 12:12
Volea [voleva] 4:1; 14:5; 23:13
Volemo [volere: vogliamo]
25:4; 28:2
Volendo 7:6; 13:10; 26:4; 26:9;
39:6
Volentier [volentieri] 31:9
Volentieri 12:7; 22:7
Voler 13:8
Volere 6:1; 9:11; 13:6; 21:1;
31:1; 35:3
Volerlo 40:10
Volesse 12:17; 24:5; 30:2;
31:16
Volgare [in vernacolo, in
italiano] 25:3; 25:4; 25:6; 30:2;
30:3
Volgari [in vernacolo, in
italiano] 12:5; 25:3; 25:4; 25:7;
25:7
Volge 38:7
Volgendo 18:3
Volgere 23:19
Volgessero 9:4
Volgo 8:12
Volle [volere] 25:6
Volli [volere] 38:4
Volontade [volontà] 4:2; 6:1;
7:1; 12:7; 13:7; 16:1; 19:1; 20:1;
21:1; 36:3; 38:1
Volontate [volontà] 36:5
Volse [volgere] 3:1
Volser [volgere: volsero] 33:7
Volsi [volgere] 34:1

Volta [noun] 2:9; 3:2; 20:4;
23:3; 31:12
Volte [noun: volta] 2:8; 5:1;
11:3; 11:4; 12:8; 16:2; 16:3;
28:3; 29:1; 33:4; 33:5; 36:2;
37:1; 37:2; 38:1; 38:1; 38:4;
39:3; 39:3; 39:9; 40:7
Voluta [volere] 22:16
Voluto 11:2
Vorrei 13:9
Vorria [volere: vorrei] 32:5
Vos [Lat.: pers. pron.] 7:7
Vostra 11:2; 12:12; 14:11;
19:8; 23:28; 35:5; 35:7; 37:2;
37:8; 37:8
Vostre 37:2
Vostri 22:10
Vostro 12:13; 15:6; 22:9; 36:4
Voto [vuoto] 16:9
Vox [Lat.; nom. sing.: *vox,*
vocis] 24:4
Vui [Sicilianism: voi] 12:12;
14:12; 19:6; 23:20; 31:9; 38:8
Vuoi 12:14
Vuol 19:9
Vuole 12:16; 12:16; 13:6; 38:2
Vuoli [volere: vuoi] 12:11;
19:13; 38:3

Appendix 1
The Manuscript Tradition
&
Barbi's Divisions of the *Vita nuova* into Chapters

Barbi (*La vita nuova di Dante Alighieri*. Edizione critica per cura di Michele Barbi. Firenze: Bemporad, 1932) classifies the manuscript tradition of the *Vita nuova* according to two families, which he calls "alpha" and "beta" and which each gives rise to two principal groups of manuscripts ("Capitolo IV, Classificazione dei testi"). We have excerpted from Barbi's description of these manuscripts all those passages that describe the *Vita nuova*'s division into chapters ("Capitolo II, Manoscritti"). When Barbi, in describing a manuscript, makes no comments concerning the manuscript's presence or absence of divisions into chapters, we have nevertheless listed the manuscript.

1. Vaticano Chigiano L, VIII, 305 (K)

"Le rime sono scritte a mo' di prosa, distinguendo i versi con lineette trasversali, non sempre però regolarmente. La *Vita nuova* è senza titolo ed *explicit*: non ha distinzioni di paragrafi, ma soltanto dopo la fine delle narrazioni si viene a capo per trascrivere la poesia e s'ha l'iniziale colorata, e col segno del paragrafo e l'iniziale colorata si torna ugualmente a capo per la divisione: ove dopo la divisione riprende la narrazione, fra l'una e l'altra non è fatta nessuna distinzione" (Barbi XXI).

2. Vaticano Chigiano L, V, 176 (K^2)

"La *Vita nuova* ha le divisioni in margine, come nella copia fatta dal Boccaccio (cfr. p. xvi), e reca in fatti a c. 13^a la nota giustificativa del Boccaccio stesso per aver tolto le divisioni dalla loro sede naturale: *Marauiglieannosi molti per quello che io aduisi,* ecc. La distinzione dell'opera in paragrafi, col mezzo sia di lettere miniate e capoverso, sia di sole iniziali miniate, corrisponde a qella da noi seguita, eccetto il § II e III, il cui principio non ha alcun segno di distinzione. Le rime sono scritte a mo' di prosa" (Barbi XXIV).

3. Vaticano Capponiano 262 (C)

"La *Vita nuova* ha le divisioni nel testo e senza alterazioni, e i versi scritti di

seguito a mo' di prosa. Da principio non si fa, ordinariamente, capoverso se
non per le poesie, che han per di più anche l'iniziale miniata, e la divisione
stessa è distinta dalla fine dei versi con una sola lineetta obliqua (al contrario
troviamo il capoverso nel § XII dopo ciascuna delle due citazioni latine!); ma
in seguito si distingue con capoverso anche la narrazione e, quando non è
indivisibile da questa, pur la divisione" (Barbi XXVI).

4. Biblioteca dei Lincei 44, E, 34, già Corsiniano 1085 (Co)
"Capoversi nel testo non mancano, ma non sono così frequenti come in altri
manoscritti e nelle moderne edizioni: c'è al § III (non è ben chiaro se anche al
VI, VII e IX), ai §§ XIII-XV, XVII, XVIII, XX, XXII-XXVII, XXVIII (tanto
per la rubrica come pel seguito), allla divisione del XXXI, e, naturalmente, al
§ XXXII e ai seguenti sino alla fine" (Barbi XXVII).

5. Codice Martelli (M)
"La *Vita nuova* è intera, con le divisioni al loro posto. Ha il titolo: *Incipit
uita noua*, e porta infine: *Explicit liber. Deo gratias. Amen.* Quanto alla
distinzione in paragrafi, si torna a capo, oltre che per il principio delle poesie
e per il riprendere poi della prosa, anche dopo il termine poi delle divisioni, e
vi si appone altresì il segno del paragrafo. A capo si torna pure a principio del
§ XXVI (sebbene il segno del paragrafo sia stato omesso) e del § XXXI:
nessuna distinzione al principio dei nostri §§ II, III, IV (c'è bensì a III 14), V,
VI, VII, XI, XII (c'è invece il segno del paragrafo, senza tornare a capo, a
XXVIII 3) e XXX" (Barbi XXVIII).

6. Laurenziano XL, 31.
"Mancano le divisioni. Si ha il capoverso, oltre che per le poesie e al
riprender via via della prosa dopo ciascuna di esse, ai § XIII, XXVI e XXXI, e
anche a metà del § XXIX ([L]o numero . . .) e a metà del XXX ([S]e alcuno .
. .)" (Barbi XXVII).

7. Laurenziano XL, 42.
"È mancante delle divisioni. L'iniziale dell'opera è in oro. . . . e miniate sono
pure le iniziali sia delle poesie che delle prose che seguono. . . . e segnata
intanto in carattere minuto la lettera da miniare, in principio dei nostri § IV,
VI, VII e XVII" (Barbi XXIX).

8. Laurenziano XC sup. 136
"La *Vita nuova* ha dunque le divisioni nei margini. . . . La distinzione dei
capoversi corrisponde a quella di K^2" (Barbi XXXI).

9. Laurenziano XC sip. 137
"Le divisioni della *Vita nuova*, in inchiostro rosso, sono nel testo, ma sempre

dopo le poesie, e colle modificazioni introdotte dal Boccaccio" (Barbi XXXI).

10. Laurenziano Ashburnhamiano 679

"Alla *Vita nuova* mancano le divisioni" (Barbi XXXII).

11. Laurenziano Ashburnhamiano 843 (A)

"Le divisioni della *Vita nuova* sono al loro posto. Si fa capoverso al principio dei §§ V, VIII-X, XIII, XIV, XVI, XVII, XX, XXXI, e naturalmente, di tutti i seguenti" (Barbi XXXIII).

12. Laurenziano Acquisti e doni 224 (O)

13. Bibl. Nazionale di Firenze, Magliabechiano VI, 30 (Mgl)

14. Bibl. Nazionale di Firenze, Magliabechiano VI, 143

"Oltre la grande iniziale in rosso con rabeschi violacei a principio dell'opera, ha iniziali miniate, più piccole, ordinariamente ai capoversi delle poesie e al riprendere della prosa, sia divisione o narrazione. Tra la divisione e il riprendere della narrazione, nella prima parte dell'opera, non c'è distinzione se non al § XIII, che comincia, facendo capoverso con lettera miniata; al § XXIII, che, pure a capoverso, ha un'iniziale maiuscoletta . . .; al § XXV con un semplice ritorno a capo e una maiuscoletta in nero; al § XXVII con un ritorno a capo e l'iniziale miniata; e così pure, terminata l'allegazione del passo di Geremia *Quomodo sedet* nel § XXVIII, al ricominciare del volgare, e, senza ragione, anche in fine della narrazione del § XXXIII, alle parole *Questa canzone e questo soprascritto sonetto*, ecc." (Barbi XXXVI).

15. Bibl. Nazionale di Firenze, Magliabechiano VI, 187

"La *Vita nuova* è priva delle divisioni. Ha iniziale miniata grande oltre che al principio d'ogni poesia e al riprender della prosa, anche al § XII e al § XXVI; il principio del § XVIII è distinto col capoverso e coll'iniziale colorata piccola . . .; al § XXVIII la citazione latina ha l'iniziale colorata piccola, le parole volgari che seguono (*Io era nel proponimento . . .*) la grande" (Barbi XXXVII).

16. Bibl. Nazionale di Firenze, Magliabechiano VI, 1103

". . . le divisioni nei margini. . . . Ha iniziali colorate a principio dei capoversi, i quali sono però in questo codice assai più rari che in altri, e basti notare che manca ogni segno di distinzione in principio dei §§ II, III, V, VI, VII, XI, XII, XVIII e XIX" (Barbi XXXVIII-XXXIX).

17. Bibl. Nazionale di Firenze, Palatino 204 (Pal)

18. Bibl. Nazionale di Firenze, Palatino 561

"Nella *Vita nuova* mancano le divisioni. Iniziali miniate si hanno non solo ad ogni poesia e al riprendere della prosa, ma anche a quegli altri punti che dal

Torri in poi si considerano come principii di paragrafi, fatta eccezione per il §
II e III che non hanno nel nostro codice, come in K^2, alcun segno di
distinzione" (Barbi XXXIX).

19. Bibl. Nazionale di Firenze, Panciatichiano 9
"La distinzione dei paragrafi è segnata da uno spazio bianco lasciato per la
lettera iniziale, che doveva essere miniata, e non fu: ma fuori del principio
delle rime e del riprender della prosa quel segno è raro, e manca, ad es., al § II,
III, IV, VI, VII, XII, XVIII, XIX, e c'è invece a metà del XVIII [A]*llora mi
rispuose quella che mi parlava*, dove logicamente non può stare" (Barbi XL).

20. Bibl. Nazionale di Firenze, Panciatichiano 10

21. Bibl. Nazionale di Firenze, Conv. B, 2, 1267

22. Riccardiano 1050
"La *Vita nuova* è senza divisioni. Iniziale colorata al principio di ogni poesia,
e al ricominciare della prosa; maiuscolette vergate di rosso spesso anche a
mezzo dei paragrafi; e iniziali grandi colorate, per distinguere pure i paragrafi,
al § XVIII, al § XIX e al § XXVI; ma anche queste sono talvolta dove
paragrafo nuovo non può cominciare" (Barbi XLIII).

23. Riccardiano 1118

24. Riccardiano 1054

25. Frammento dell'Archivio di Stato fiorentino

26. Braidense AG, XI, 5

27. Trivulziano 1058 (T)

28. Trivulziano 1050

29. Ambrosiano R 95 sup. (Am)
"Quanto alla distinzione dei paragrafi, si trova apposito segno in principio dei
nostri III, IV, VIII, IX, XIII-XVII, XXI-XXIV, XXVI e XXVII; e oltre a ciò
cominciano a nuova linea i § II, XX e XXVIII (e anche le parole che seguono
quivi stesso alla rubrica latina), e, naturalmente, tutti i paragrafi che vengon
dopo a quelli che terminano con una poesia" (Barbi LIII).

30. Biblioteca capitolare di Verona 445 (V)
"Il codice non ha segni speciali, e neppure iniziali colorate, per una
distinzione del testo in paragrafi. L'amanuense fa capoverso, oltre che al
principio delle poesie, a III 15 e al principio dei §§ VIII, XIII, XXIV, XXV e
XXVII" (Barbi LIV).

31. Marciano ital. X, 26 (Mc)
"La *Vita nuova* ha le divisioni colle modificazioni introdotte nella copia del
Boccaccio; non però nei margini, ma rimesse nel testo, sempre dopo le

poesie, anche nella parte delle rime dolorose, nonostante la dichiarazione di Dante al § XXXI 2: 'Ed acciò che questa canzone. . . .' Quanto alla divisione in paragrafi, soltanto al principio del § II e III non si ha né il capoverso né altro segno di distinzione" (Barbi LV).

32. Marciano ital. IX, 191

33. Marciano ital. IX, 491

34. Codice Pesarese, oggi Maiocchi (P)

35. Biblioteca Nazionale di Napoli XIII, C, 9 (N)

36. Biblioteca universitaria e territoriale di Strasburgo, L ital. 7 (W)

"Nella *Vita nuova* si ha il capoverso ai §§ II, XV, XVI, XVII (anzi a questo paragrafo è lasciato il posto per l'iniziale miniata e segnato il *p* nel margine), XX, XXII, XXIII, XXIV, XXV, XXVI, XXVIII, XXX e XXXI, e naturalmente a tutti i successivi: talvolta, pur cominciando il paragrafo a principio di riga, la cosa è incerta perché la linea precedente è piena, e a principio della nova non si ha spazio bianco né iniziale distinta" (Barbi LXII).

37. Codice Altemps

38. Biblioteca capitolare di Toledo: cajon 104, num. 6, Zelada (To)

"Le divisioni della *Vita nuova* sono nei margini e colle modificazioni introdotte dal Boccaccio; e il codice è infatti, come mostrai sin dall'edizione del 1907 . . . ed è ora generalmente ammesso, della mano di lui" (Barbi LXV).

39. Bibl. Bodleiana d'Oxford, Canonici Ital. 114

"Quanto alle divisioni della *Vita nuova* e alla distinzione in paragrafi, tutto è come in Marc. ital. X, 26" (Barbi LXI).

40. Biblioteca dell'Università Cornell di Ithaca, New York. Mss. D. 51

41. Estratto del § VIII

"A questi manoscritti che contengono della *Vita nuova* così la parte prosastica come quella poetica, sono da aggiungere, come dicemmo, altri [Mss. 42-80, Barbi LXXII-LXXXVIII] che contengono tutte o in parte le rime con evidenti indizi di essere estratte da testi completi dell'opera" (Barbi LXXI).

Appendix 2
Barbi's General Comments on Chapter Divisions
of the *Vita nuova*

On a few occasions Barbi makes general observations concerning the division of the *Vita nuova* into chapters: "Occasione a divergenze fra gli editori e i commentatori della *Vita nuova* ha dato anche la divisione dell'opera in paragrafi. Una vera distinzione di tal genere Dante non fece, tanto più che per ogni poesia pause spontanee s'avevano, ordinariamente, alla fine sia della narrazione, sia dei versi, sia delle divisioni; ma dove pure il racconto si svolge senza riferimento di poesie, pause e capoversi doverono all'autor venir fatti, anche se non ebbe una premeditata disposizione della materia. Un'edizione moderna non può far a meno di una più accurata distinzione in paragrafi e sottoparagrafi, e, sebbene sia cosa esteriore, deve adattarsi quanto più strettamente è possibile allo svolgimento del trattato: onde l'opportunità di attendere alle divisioni date dai vari testi e di verificare se ci sia una tradizione costante" (XVIII).

In concluding his analysis of the manuscripts, Barbi notes: "Abbiamo visto, nel descrivere i manoscritti, che una vera e propria distinzione in capitoli, che si mantenga uguale in tutti i testi non esiste, ma che capoversi e segni paragrafali qua e là tuttavia non mancano. Io non avrei voluto quindi introdurre nel testo una distinzione marcata di capitoli con la relativa numerazione fra l'uno e l'altro; ma non si può ormai, pel comodo delle citazioni, rinunziare a tale distinzione e numerazione. Pel numero di questi capoversi o paragrafi, poiché la disparità dei manoscritti mi lasciava libero di farne più o meno, ho cercato di discostarmi meno che fosse possibile dalle due divisioni più in uso, del Torri e del Casini. Bene sarebbe stato che quella del Torri si fosse mantenuta costante in tutte le edizioni successive, anche se difettosa (il vantaggio vero di queste numerazioni è che rimangono fisse: cfr. p. CXXII); ma ormai che l'accordo è rotto, ho cercato d'evitare gl'inconvenienti tanto della divisione Torri (distinzione del § XXVI in due paragrafi) quanto di quella del Casini (mancanza di numero per il proemio, distinzione del § III in due paragrafi). Così la mia numerazione concorda con quella del Torri sino al § XXVI e dopo rimane inferiore d'una unità, e concorda con quella del Casini dal § III in poi. Se non che pei bisogni dello studioso la divisione del testo in paragrafi non basta: ne occorre una più minuta in commi che dia modo di trovare alla prima un dato passo o una data voce, e che possa mantenersi inalterata in tutte le edizioni. Si doveva in questa suddistinzione tener conto soprattutto del senso, ma aver altresì riguardo da una parte al vantaggio dello studioso, che non vuol commi troppo lunghi, e dall'altra al gusto tipografico, che non vuol numerazioni troppo fitte e troppo irregolari. . . . io raccomando ai futuri editori queste mie suddivisioni, come anche quelle in paragrafi, perché siano accettate e tramandate quali sono: mutino pure nel mio testo quello che a loro parrà meno sicuro; ma non impediscano che una citazione fatta su questa o quella edizione possa valere per qualsiasi altra" (CCCVIII-CCCIX).

* * *

The following recapitulation can be made from Barbi's descriptions of the manuscripts and from his general comments concerning the text's divisions into chapters and commas: 1) In describing the manuscripts, Barbi normally employs the term "paragraph." Dante himself uses the same term in *Vita nuova* 2:10. It would seem, therefore, that the term "chapter" — *pace* Witte — should be avoided. 2) Barbi recognizes that the text's divisions are present here and there ("qua e là," "Introduzione" CCCVIII), and thus most divisions present in his critical edition do find some justification in some manuscript or other. 3) Precisely on the basis of the manuscript tradition, Barbi would have preferred no marked distinction into paragraphs and no numbering between them ("Io non avrei voluto quindi introdurre nel testo una distinzione marcata di capitoli con la relativa numerazione fra l'uno e l'altro" CCCVIII). However, for the sake of quotations ("pel comodo delle citazioni") Barbi divides the text into forty-two paragraphs and separates each paragraph from the following one by leaving ample space and placing at its head the number of the paragraph in Roman numerals, followed by square brackets enclosing the Witte/Casini numbering in small capitals when these differ from his own. 4) Barbi opted also for a more detailed division of each paragraph into *commi* ('commas'), for which, needless to say, the manuscript tradition offers no justification. One must note, however, that Barbi's edition sets the numbering of these *commi* not in the text itself (as the numbering of the paragraphs) but along the margins of the text and thus arguably outside the text. In Barbi's view, these *commi*, which cluster together several sentences, should be based primarily on meaning ("Si doveva in questa suddistinzione tener conto soprattutto del senso") — a fundamental principle to be fully endorsed. Barbi adds, however, that one should also be concerned with facilitating the scholars' needs and preserving typographical taste ("gusto tipografico"). In so doing, Barbi further demonstrates his concern not so much for reproducing a text as closely as possible to the author's original intention but rather for contemporary scholarship and print technology.

Barbi's critical edition incorporates further typographical arrangements of the text, most of which concern the alleged special status of the *divisioni*, the divisions of poems that Barbi views as different from the narrative:

1) Barbi's edition separates the poems' *divisioni* from the previous or following prose text and indents the initial line of the *divisione* at: *VN* 3:13; 7:7; 8:7; 8:12; 9:13; 12:16; 15:7; 16:11; 19:15; 20:6; 21:5; 22:11; 22:17; 23:29; 24:10; 26:14; 31:3 (first indented *divisione* before the poem); 33:4 (second indented *divisione* before the poem); 34:4 (third indented *divisione* before the poem); 38:7 (fourth indented *divisione* before the poem); 41:2-8 (fifth and last indented *divisione* before the poem).

2) By contrast, the following *divisioni* before the poems are not indented: *VN* 32:4 ; 37:4-5.

3) Although not a *divisione*, the line is indented at: *VN* 3:14 (after the *divisione*), 12:17 (after the *divisione*), and VN 22:12, which announces a sonnet and follows a *divisione*.

4) Several other instances with analogous characteristics are treated differently, and the initial line is indented in some cases while in others it is not: 14:13 (indented; right after the poem; the narrator offers justification for not dividing the poem); 19:22 (not indented; whereas 12:17, which has the same characteristics, has an indented line); 26:8 (indented; right after the poem; the narrator justifies not dividing the poem and continues the narrative); 38:5-6 (indented, although not a *divisione* but an explanation and justification of certain practices in the following sonnet; it is in fact followed by the *divisione*, which is indented); 35:4 (not indented; before the poem; the narrator states that the poem is obvious and thus needs no *divisione*); 36:3 (not indented; before the poem; the narrator states that the poem is obvious and thus needs no *divisione*); 40:5-7 (not indented; an explanation of certain terms employed in the following sonnet, it is not indented, although it shares

similar purposes with 38:5-6, which is indented); 32:4 and 37:4 (not indented, although here the same principle obtains as in 39:7, which is indented: "Questo sonetto non divido, però che assai lo manifesta la sua ragione," and 40:8, which is also indented: "Questo sonetto non divido, però che assai lo manifesta la sua ragione").

Appendix 3
Incipits and Explicits of the Paragraphs according to Barbi's Edition and Adopted Criteria

- The sign ¶ indicates paragraphs as entered in this edition. Each ¶ may include one or more of Barbi's chapter divisions.
- The two principal criteria for either maintaining or changing Barbi's divisions into chapters are: The presence, at the beginning of a paragraph, of temporal markers that clearly indicate the passing of time; the nature of the quasi-event. To be paragraphed, the quasi-event must be sufficiently self-contained to be read as a discrete narrative unit. Each quasi-event and quasi-story is linked with the preceding and following quasi-events and quasi-stories, which together constitute the totality of the event presented in the *Vita nuova*.
- When both criteria obtain and our proposed paragraph division corresponds with Barbi's, no explanation is usually needed.
- Notes discuss the reasons of our proposed changes of paragraphs.
- These revisions of the print structure of the *Vita nuova* should not be considered absolute. They represent, rather, decisions grounded on the manuscript tradition and the text's temporality and narrativity, and are therefore open to further consideration.

***

¶1) **I.** In quella parte del libro de la mia memoria dinanzi a la quale poco si potrebbe leggere, si trova una rubrica la quale dice: *Incipit vita nova.*[1] Sotto

---

[1] The formula *Incipit . . .* is a standard beginning of medieval books, and the title of the *libello* is thus *Vita nova: The new Life.* Many manuscripts use the following, or similar inscriptions to begin and end the work: "Et comincia la sua vita nuova. . . . Qui finiscie la vita nuova di Dante Alighieri di Firençe" (Barbi MS 2 [with reference to the manuscripts analyzed by Barbi, for which see Appendix 1].

la quale rubrica io trovo scritte le parole le quali è mio intendimento d'assemplare in questo libello; e se non tutte, almeno la loro sentenzia.

¶2) II. Nove fiate già appresso lo mio nascimento era tornato lo cielo de la luce quasi a uno medesimo punto. . . . e trapassando molte cose le quali si potrebbero trarre de l'essemplo onde nascono queste, verrò a quelle parole le quali sono scritte ne la mia memoria sotto maggiori paragrafi.

¶3) III. Poi che fuoro passati tanti die, che appunto erano compiuti li nove anni appresso l'apparimento soprascritto di questa gentilissima. . . . Lo verace giudicio del detto sogno non fue veduto allora per alcuno ma ora è manifestissimo a li più semplici. IV.[2] Da questa visione innanzi cominciò lo mio spirito naturale ad essere impedito ne la sua operazione. . . . E quando mi domandavano: "Per cui t'ha così distrutto questo Amore?", ed io sorridendo li guardava, e nulla dicea loro.

¶4) V.[3] Uno giorno avvenne che questa gentilissima sedea ove s'udiano parole de la regina de la gloria. . . . Con questa donna mi celai alquanti anni e mesi; e per più fare credere altrui, feci per lei certe cosette per rima, le quali non è mio intendimento di scrivere qui, se non in quanto facesse a trattare di quella gentilissima Beatrice; e però le lascerò tutte, salvo che alcuna cosa ne scriverò che pare che sia loda di lei. VI.[4] Dico che in questo tempo che questa

---

"Qui Incomincia la vita nuova. . . . Qui finiscie la vita nuova del poeta Dante fiorentino . . ." (Barbi MS 4).

[2] Here we propose not to employ a paragraph break, since "Da questa visione innanzi" does not mark the passing of time but rather the continuation of an existing situation, thus making this narrative a *continuum* with the preceding narrative. Barbi's *Vita nuova* 2-4, in fact, presents the text's first quasi-event, focused on the chronotope of the encounter: first, the twofold encounter, both physical and spiritual, with Beatrice, and, second, the poetic encounter with other poets and primarily with the "primo de li miei amici" (*VN* 3:14).

[3] Barbi's *VN* 5-7 presents the account of the screen lady, which is distinct from the previous and following narrative. In fact, this account contains no temporal phrases after the initial "Uno giorno avvenne che" and it displays no clearly marked chronological development (see next note). Insofar as it presents one single quasi-event marked by temporal continuity, *VN* 5-7 is placed under one single paragraph.

[4] The introductory formula "Dico che" cannot by itself justify creating a new paragraph: a) It has a high frequency, mostly in the middle of the narrative, with the purpose not of introducing a different quasi-event or quasi-story but of foregrounding the narrator-protagonist's presence (*VN* 2:7; 6:1; 7:7; 8:7; 10:1; 11:1; 12:1; 12:17; 13:10; 14:4; 14:7; 14:14; 15:8; 16:11; 19:2; 19:5; 19:17; 19:17; 23:2; 24:2; 25:2; 25:10; 26:8; 31:3; 34:4; 34:5; 34:5; 38:6; 39:3). Nor

donna era schermo di tanto amore. . . . E presi li nomi di sessanta le più belle donne de la cittade ove la mia donna fue posta da l'altissimo sire, e compuosi una pistola sotto forma di serventese, la quale io non scriverò se non n'avrei fatto menzione, se non per dire quello che componendola, maravigliosamente addivenne, cioè che in alcuno altro numero non sofferse lo nome de la mia donna stare, se non in su lo nove, tra li nomi di queste donne. **VII.**[5] La donna co la quale io avea tanto tempo celata la mia volontade, convenne che si partisse de la sopradetta cittade. . . . Questo sonetto ha due parti principali; che ne la prima intendo chiamare li fedeli d'Amore per quelle parole di Geremia profeta che dicono: "O vos omnes qui transitis per viam, attendite et videte si est dolor sicut dolor meus", e pregare che mi sofferino d'audire; ne la seconda narro là ove Amore m'avea posto, con altro intendimento che l'estreme parti del sonetto non mostrano, e dico che io hoe ciò perduto. La seconda parte comincia quivi: *Amor, non già.*

5¶) **VIII.** Appresso lo partire di questa gentile donna fue piacere del segnore de li angeli. . . . La seconda comincia quivi: *poi che hai data*; la terza quivi: *E s'io di grazia*; la quarta quivi: *Chi non merta salute.*

6¶) **IX.** Appresso la morte di questa donna alquanti die avvenne cosa per la quale me convenne partire de la sopradetta cittade. . . . La seconda comincia quivi: *Quando mi vide*; la terza: *Allora presi.*

7¶) **X.**[6] Appresso la mia ritornata mi misi a cercare di questa donna. . . . E uscendo alquanto del proposito presente, voglio dare a intendere quello che lo

---

do the temporal phrase "in questo tempo" and the imperfect tense "era" mark the passing of time; rather, they present another aspect of a situation already in existence. The perfect tense of the principal clause ("sì mi venne una volontade") introduces at an unspecified time an occurrence ("una volontade di volere ricordare lo nome") situated within the boundaries of the "donna schermo" narrative.

[5] The reasons presented above (*VN* 5-6) obtain also here. That *VN* 7 should not be separated from the previous one is implicitly demonstrated by De Robertis is his commentary to the *Vita nuova*: "il capitolo sesto costituisce una parentesi illustrativa di quanto accennato sul finire del V circa 'certe cosette per rima' scritte per la donna-schermo, e da non trascrivere nel 'libello'. Ora, al termine praticamente di quegli 'alquanti anni e mesi' di finzione, riprende il filo del racconto richiamandosi testualmente all'inizio di V, 4, e perciò senza ricorrere a particolare collegamenti" (*ad loc.*). The temporal phrase "tanto tempo" ("for such a long time"), furthermore, points up not so much the passing of time as the past time viewed by the narrator-protagonist as an extended duration.

[6] Barbi's *VN* 10-12 forms one quasi-event and one quasi-story, which needs be read as a continuous narrative (see below for further reasons).

suo salutare in me vertuosamente operava. **XI.**[7] Dico che quando ella apparia
da parte alcuna. . . . Sì che appare manifestamente che ne le sue salute abitava
la mia beatitudine, la quale molte volte passava e redundava la mia capacitade.
XII.[8] Ora, tornando al proposito, dico che poi che la mia beatitudine mi fue
negata, mi giunse tanto dolore, che, partito me da le genti, in solinga parte
andai a bagnare la terra d'amarissime lagrime. . . . Potrebbe già l'uomo
opporre contra me e dicere che non sapesse a cui fosse lo mio parlare in
seconda persona, però che la ballata non è altro che queste parole ched io
parlo: e però dico che questo dubbio io lo intendo solvere e dichiarare in
questo libello ancora in parte più dubbiosa, e allora intenda qui chi qui dubita,
o chi qui volesse opporre in questo modo.

8¶) XIII. Appresso di questa soprascritta visione. . . . Questo sonetto in
quattro parti si può dividere. . . . la quarta quivi: *Ond'io non so.*

9¶) XIV. Appresso la battaglia de li diversi pensieri avvenne che questa
gentilissima. . . . Vero è che tra le parole dove si manifesta la cagione di
questo sonetto, si scrivono dubbiose parole, cioè quando dico che Amore
uccide tutti li miei spiriti, e li visivi rimangono in vita, salvo che fuori de li
strumenti loro. E questo dubbio è impossibile a solvere a chi non fosse in
simile grado fedele d'Amore; e a coloro che vi sono è manifesto ciò che
solverebbe le dubitose parole: e però non è bene a me di dichiarare cotale
dubitazione, acciò che lo mio parlare dichiarando sarebbe indarno, o vero di
soperchio.

10¶) XV. Appresso la nuova trasfigurazione mi giunse uno pensamento
forte. . . . La seconda parte comincia quivi: *Lo viso mostra*; la terza quivi: *e
per la ebrietà*; la quarta: *Peccato face*; la quinta: *per la pietà.*

11¶) XVI. Appresso ciò che io dissi questo sonetto, mi mosse una
volontade. . . . Questo sonetto si divide in quattro parti, secondo che quattro
cose sono in esso narrate; e però che sono di sopra ragionate, non
m'intrametto se non di distinguere le parti per li loro cominciamenti: onde

---

[7] *VN* 11 needs be read in close conjunction with *VN* 10, since here the narrator
fully explains the effects of Beatrice's greeting, whose denial is simply stated in
VN 10 while the consequences of this denial upon the protagonist are then
described in *VN* 12. As expounded above, the metaliterary formula "Dico che"
cannot by itself justify breaking the narrative.

[8] Barbi's *VN* 12 is thematically and temporally linked with *VN* 10 by means of the
phrase "tornando al proposito" 'returning to my purpose' (the one narrated at *VN*
10:1-2) and the metaliterary "dico che" 'I say that.'

dico che la seconda parte comincia quivi: *ch'Amor*; la terza quivi: *Poscia mi sforzo*; la quarta quivi: *e se io levo*.

12¶) XVII. Poi che dissi questi tre sonetti. . . . E però che la cagione de la nuova matera è dilettevole a udire, la dicerò, quanto potrò più brievemente. **XVIII.**[9] Con ciò sia cosa che per la vista mia molte persone avessero compreso lo secreto del mio cuore. . . . E però propuosi di prendere per matera de lo mio parlare sempre mai quello che fosse loda di questa gentilissima; e pensando molto a ciò, pareami avere impresa troppo alta materia quanto a me, sì che non ardia di cominciare; e cosi dimorai alquanti dì con desiderio di dire e con paura di cominciare.

13¶) XIX.[10] Avvenne poi che passando per uno cammino lungo lo quale sen gia uno rivo chiaro molto, a me giunse tanta volontade di dire. . . . Dico bene che, a più aprire lo intendimento di questa canzone, si converrebbe usare di più minute divisioni; ma tuttavia chi non è di tanto ingegno che per queste che sono fatte la possa intendere, a me non dispiace se la mi lascia stare, ché certo io temo d'avere a troppi comunicato lo suo intendimento pur per queste divisioni che fatte sono, s'elli avenisse che molti le potessero audire.

14¶) XX. Appresso che questa canzone fue alquanto divolgata tra le genti. . . . Poscia quando dico: *Bieltate appare*, dico come questa potenzia si riduce in atto; e prima come si riduce in uomo, poi come si riduce in donna, quivi: *E simil face in donna*.

15¶) XXI. Poscia che trattai d'Amore ne la soprascritta rima, vennemi volontade. . . . Poscia quando dico: *Ogne dolcezza*, dico quello medesimo che detto è ne la prima parte, secondo due atti de la sua bocca; l'uno de li quali è lo suo dolcissimo parlare, e l'altro lo suo mirabile riso; salvo che non dico di

---

[9] *VN* 18 is connected, on the basis of time and content, with *VN* 17, which announces the new "subject matter" (*VN* 17:1; 17:2) that *VN* 18 explicates (*VN* 18:8). Notice also the brevity of *VN* 17, which consists of only two complex sentences, which in fact introduce "la cagione de la nuova matera": namely, *VN* 18.

[10] Although closely linked with *VN* 17-18, *VN* 19's beginning, which echoes the beginning of many Gospel chapters ("Factum est"; De Robertis 114), emphasizes the passing of time ("Avvenne poi"), announces the remote source of poetic inspiration ("passando per uno cammino lungo lo quale sen gia uno rivo chiaro molto") and also the manner to begin the poetic composition ("lo modo ch'io tenesse"). This volume's curators have decided to keep *VN* 19 separate from *VN* 17-18; they nevertheless cannot totally dismiss reasons for considering *VN* 17-19 as a unified event.

questo ultimo come adopera ne li cuori altrui, però che la memoria non puote ritenere lui né la sua operazione.

16¶) XXII. Appresso ciò non molti dì passati, sì come piacque al glorioso sire lo quale non negoe la morte a sé. . . . Questo sonetto ha quattro parti, secondo che quattro modi di parlare ebbero in loro le donne per cui rispondo; e però che sono di sopra assai manifesti, non m'intrametto di narrare la sentenzia de le parti, e però le distinguo solamente. La seconda comincia quivi: *E perché piangi*; la terza: *Lascia piangere noi*; la quarta: *Ell'ha nel viso*.

17¶) XXIII. Appresso ciò per pochi dì avvenne che in alcuna parte de la mia persona mi giunse una dolorosa infermitade. . . . Poscia quando dico: *Mentr'io pensava*, dico come io dissi loro questa mia imaginazione. Ed intorno a ciò foe due parti: ne la prima dico per ordine questa imaginazione; ne la seconda, dicendo a che ora mi chiamaro, le ringrazio chiusamente; e comincia quivi questa parte: *Voi mi chiamaste*.

18¶) XXIV. Appresso questa vana imaginazione, avvenne uno die. . . . La terza parte si divide in due: ne la prima dico quello che io vidi; ne la seconda dico quello che io udio. La seconda comincia quivi: *Amor mi disse*. **XXV.**[11]

---

[11] The adverb of place "qui" links the discussion on love's personification with the previous division, which also deals with Love's personified appearance to the protagonist. The close connection between the previous division and the following discussion supports the argument in favor of combining *VN* 24 and 25, which Marti proposes (in his essay, "'. . . l'una appresso de l'altra maraviglia'") on several grounds: 1) in *VN* 25, the text repeatedly refers to *VN* 24 ("I speak of Love" 25:1; "I speak of him" 25:2; "I say that I saw him approach" 25:2; "I also say of him that he smiled, and also that he spoke" 25:2), thereby evincing textual and thematic unity; 2) the conclusion of *VN* 25 ("And this best friend of mine and I myself know well some who rhyme so shamelessly" 25:9) links itself directly with the narrator's decision, in the previous paragraph, "to write in rhyme to *his* best friend" (24:6); 3) a similar argument could be made from the beginning of *VN* 26 ("This most gentle lady, of whom it has been spoken in the preceding words"), since the narrator speaks of Beatrice not in *VN* 25 but in *VN* 24; and, finally, 4) a similar strategy is also at work in *VN* 12, where, right after the division of the ballade (12:16), the glossator raises the possibility of someone's questioning his poetic practice ("One could indeed oppose me") and then defers to *VN* 25 for a clarification of his poetics ("I say that this doubt I intend to solve and explain in this little book in a passage still more questionable" 12:17). The same argument could also be made from the long division in 19:15-22 as well as from that in 38:5-7 (where the narrator explains such terms as heart and soul), in 40:6-7, and in 41:2-9. Marti, therefore, argues — and we wholly concur with him — that *VN* 25 should not be considered a digression, however precious and useful, but rather a harmonious element in the *Vita nuova*'s structure, which follows this pattern:

Potrebbe qui dubitare persona degna da dichiararle onne dubitazione. . . . E
questo mio primo amico e io ne sapemo bene di quelli che così rimano
stoltamente.

19¶) XXVI.[12] Questa gentilissima donna, di cui ragionato è ne le
precedenti parole, venne in tanta grazia de le genti. . . . La seconda comincia
quivi: *La vista sua*; la terza quivi: *Ed è ne li atti.*

20¶) XXVII.[13] Appresso ciò, cominciai a pensare uno giorno sopra quello
che detto avea de la mia donna. . . . / Questo m'avvene / ovunque ella mi
vede,/ e sì è cosa umil, che nol si crede./

21¶) XXVIII.[14] *Quomodo sedet sola civitas plena populo! facta est quasi
vidua domina gentium.* . . . Onde prima dicerò come ebbe luogo ne la sua
partita, e poi n'assegnerò alcuna ragione, per che questo numero fue a lei
cotanto amico. **XXIX.**[15] Io dico che, secondo l'usanza d'Arabia, l'anima sua

---

prose account, poetry, and division, before Beatrice's death; and, after Beatrice's
death, prose account, division, and poetry.

[12] Although linked with *VN* 24-25, *VN* 26 is paragraphed separately because what
it presents is not chronologically connected with either what precedes or follows
it: the condition Beatrice attained on earth among her contemporaries ("venne in
tanta grazie delle genti").

[13] *VN* 27 is introduced by a temporal marker and differs from *VN* 26, which
presents Beatrice among her people, in that it deals with the effects of Beatrice on
the narrator-protagonist. He decides to describe such effects with a canzone.

[14] *Vita nuova* 28 and 29 deal with the announcement, gloss, and effects of the
death of Beatrice, thus presenting a single event and therefore a single narrative
account. The narrative break between *VN* 27 and *VN* 28-29 is implemented by the
sudden interruption of the canzone through the quotation of the prophet Jeremiah.
The sentence that follows Jeremiah's quotation explains why the poet-protagonist
interrupted one event (the composition of the canzone) in order to present another
event, Beatrice's death ("*Io era* nel proponimento ancora di questa canzone, e
compiuta n'avea questa soprascritta stanzia, *quando* lo segnore de la giustizia
chiamoe" "*I was* still intent on this canzone, of which *I had completed* the stanza
transcribed above, *when* the Lord of justice called"). For these reasons (but see
also below at *VN* 29) we propose to read *VN* 28-29 as a single narrative, under one
paragraph heading.

[15] The narrator-protagonist continues the kind of explanatory discourse focused
on Beatrice that he has just announced in the previous sentence (*VN* 28:3). This
narrative continuity is emphasized by the repetition of the verb used in the
previous sentence: "Io dicerò" 'I will say' (*VN* 28:3) and "Io dico che" 'I say that'
(*VN* 29:1). As in all other instances, the expression "Io dico" ("I say") plays a
metaliterary function, since its present tense refers not to the time of the story,
narrated in the past, but to that of the narrator's writing. For these reasons, we
propose not to separate *VN* 29 from *VN* 28.

nobilissima si partio ne la prima ora del nono giorno del mese. . . . Forse ancora per più sottile persona si vederebbe in ciò più sottile ragione; ma questa è quella ch'io ne veggio, e che più mi piace.

22¶) XXX.[16] Poi che fue partita da questo secolo, rimase tutta la sopradetta cittade quasi vedova. . . . E simile intenzione so ch'ebbe questo mio primo amico a cui io ciò scrivo, cioè ch'io li scrivessi solamente volgare.

23¶) XXXI. Poi che li miei occhi ebbero per alquanto tempo lagrimato. . . . / e tu, che se' figliuola di tristizia,/ vatten disconsolata a star con elle./

24¶) XXXII. Poi che detta fue questa canzone, sì venne a me uno. . . . / in persona de l'anima dolente / abbandonata de la sua salute./ **XXXIII.**[17] Poi che detto èi questo sonetto, pensandomi chi questi era a cui lo intendea dare quasi come per lui fatto, vidi che. . . . / e lo intelletto loro alto, sottile / face maravigliar, sì v'è gentile./

25¶) XXXIV. In quello giorno nel quale si compiea l'anno che questa donna era fatta de li cittadini di vita eterna. . . . / venian dicendo: "Oi nobile intelletto,/ oggi fa l'anno che nel ciel salisti"./

26¶) XXXV.[18] Poi per alquanto tempo, con ciò fosse cosa che io fosse in

---

[16] Kept as is, *VN* 30 is striking for its brevity. Although linked with the previous quasi-event, *Vn* 30 possesses a specific identity; namely, the narrator-protagonist wrote, at the time of Beatrice's death, to "the princes of the earth" a letter that cannot become part of the text because it was in Latin. This brief paragraph's content is noteworthy: precisely in connection with Beatrice's death and entrance into the eternal life, the narrator-protagonist feels compelled to say that he has employed Latin but also that he has excluded it from his present writing in order to use the vernacular.

[17] The principle of temporality, expressed through the sentence "Poi che detto èi questo sonetto," would require keeping *VN* 33 as is; the analysis of the content, however, suggests that *VN* 33 is closely linked with *VN* 32 as to constitute a single quasi-event and quasi-story: heeding the friend's request to write a poetic composition for a dead person. In addition to words and phrases linking *VN* 33 with *VN* 32 ("chi questi era"; "questo soprascritto sonetto"), the friend's request is heeded in *VN* 33:3, "Questa canzone e questo soprascritto sonetto li diedi, dicendo io lui che per lui solo fatto l'avea."

[18] That *VN* 35 introduces a story different from *VN* 33-34 is clear not so much from the weak temporal marker at its beginning ("Poi") or from the vague temporal indication that follows ("per alquanto tempo") but rather from the new subject matter: the story of the compassionate lady. According to the current division of the *Vita nuova*, the "gentile donna" event spans *VN* 35-38, since it is at *VN* 38 that this event comes to an end. In *VN* 39, in fact, her influence over the narrator-protagonist is broken by Beatrice's raising in the protagonist's mind a "powerful imagining" of herself in the same crimson garments as she first appeared to him

parte ne la quale mi ricordava del passato tempo. . . . / Io dicea poscia ne
l'anima trista:/ "Ben è con quella donna quello Amore / lo qual mi face andar
così piangendo." **XXXVI.**[19] Avvenne poi che là ovunque questa donna mi
vedea, sì si facea d'una vista pietosa e d'un colore palido quasi come d'amore;
. . . . / e voi crescete si lor volontate,/ che de la voglia si consuman tutti;/ ma
lagrimar dinanzi a voi non sanno./ **XXXVII.**[20] Io venni a tanto per la vista
di questa donna, che li miei occhi si cominciaro a dilettare troppo di vederla. .
. . / Voi non dovreste mai, se non per morte,/ la vostra donna, ch'è morta,
obliare". / Così dice 'l meo core, e poi sospira./ **XXXVIII.**[21] Ricovrai la
vista di quella donna in sì nuova condizione, che molte volte ne pensava. . . .
/ e la sua vita, e tutto 'l suo valore,/ mosse de li occhi di quella pietosa / che

---

(*VN* 2). In order to emphasize the narrative and thematic unity of this account, and
also to contrast it with the image of the glorious Beatrice that precedes and
follows it, this edition's curators propose eliminating the story's current division
into four chapters (*VN* 35-38) in favor of one single paragraph. Not only the
story's thematic unity but also the criterion of temporality, a fundamental concept
for restructuring *VN*'s current forty-two chapters, supports reducing the present
four chapters into one paragraph. The proposed concept of temporality is
appropriately expressed by the narrator-protagonist's "remembering her
[Beatrice] according to the order of time past" precisely when he breaks away from
the influence of the "gentile donna" (*VN* 39:2). The temporal adverb "poi" in *VN*
36:1, because of its indeterminacy and weakness as a temporal marker, does not
seem to justify creating a break within the story itself, which is sufficiently
structured by the four sonnets contained therein.

[19] The temporal adverb "poi" is the weakest temporal marker to be found at the
beginning of the current paragraphs. (By contrast, the temporal phrase "Poi che,"
or "Poscia che," which is followed by a complete, dependent clause and is found at
the beginning of eight of the current paragraphs [*VN* 3; 17; 21; 30; 31; 32; 33],
marks the passing of time and justifies the narrative break that a paragraph
suggests.) Furthermore, the narrative that follows does not constitute an event
different from the protagonist's first encounter with the compassionate lady but
its direct continuation, since the protagonist's words to himself before deciding to
write a sonnet (*VN* 35:3), as well as the sonnet's last dystich, call for this kind of
narrative unfolding. Whatever break might seem necessary between these two
moments of the same event is provided by the sonnet; in fact, three more sonnets
mark the additional three stages of the unfolding event, which calls for no other
break until *VN* 39.

[20] This edition's curators propose not to break the narrative with a paragraph at
this juncture, since current *VN* 37 is closely related to what precedes and follows
and no temporal marker indicating the passing of time marks its beginning or
unfolding.

[21] See the previous note.

si turbava de' nostri martiri"./

27¶) XXXIX.[22] Contra questo avversario de la ragione si levoe un die, quasi ne l'ora de la nona, una forte imaginazione in me. . . . / però ch'elli hanno in lor li dolorosi / quel dolce nome di madonna scritto,/ e de la morte sua molte parole./

28¶) XL.[23] Dopo questa tribulazione avvenne, in quello tempo che molta gente va per vedere quella imagine benedetta. . . . / Ell'ha perduta la sua beatrice;/ e le parole ch'om di lei pò dire / hanno vertù di far piangere altrui./

29¶) XLI.[24] Poi mandaro due donne gentili a me pregando che io mandasse loro di queste mie parole rimate. . . . / So io che parla di quella gentile,/ però che spesso ricorda Beatrice,/ si ch'io lo 'ntendo ben, donne mie care.

30¶) XLII.[25] Appresso questo sonetto apparve a me una mirabile visione. .

---

[22] *VN* 39 constitutes a quasi-story on the basis of both temporality and new content, since it brings to conclusion the narrative of the "compassionate lady" and brings the narrator-protagonist back to Beatrice's remembrance.

[23] The temporal marker and the new content justify the creation of a new paragraph.

[24] Several reasons would seem to justify both keeping *VN* 41 separate and uniting it with *VN* 40 (as well as *VN* 42).

Reasons for uniting it with *VN* 40: 1) the notion of the pilgrimage on earth, which is the focus of *VN* 40, is also central here as well as in *VN* 42, for it develops into a spiritual and intellectual pilgrimage (*VN* 41:5, "spirito pellegrino" 'pilgrim spirit'; 41:9, v. 8, "lo peregrino" 'the pilgrim'); 2) the temporal adverb "Poi" ("Then") at the beginning of the passage is the weakest temporal marker among all those employed in the *Vita nuova*; 3) several elements link this passage directly to the previous one: the demonstrative adjective at *VN* 41:1, "*queste* mie parole rimate" ("*these* verses of mine"); "mio stato" ("my condition"), with reference to "questa tribulazione" ("this tribulation") of 40:1; "co lo precedente sonetto accompagnato" ("accompanied by the previous sonnet").

Reasons for keeping *VN* 41 separate from *VN* 40: The presence of the temporal marker, however weak it may be, at its beginning, and also of elements in the story differentiating it from the previous one: the two gentle ladies; the request of a poetic composition; and the spiritual and intellectual nature of the journey. In fact, unlike the pilgrims' voyage to the earthly Rome, such a movement is upward (41:5, "va là suso" 'he ascends on high') and intellectual (4:3, "ove va lo mio pensero" 'where my thought goes'; etc.); the earthly Rome is substituted by the spiritual Rome; finally, the pilgrim spirit's goal is to see not the "blessed image" that Christ left here on earth (*VN* 40:1), but "una donna onorata là suso" ("a lady honored up above" 41:5; 41:11, v. 6-7), a vision that he cannot understand (41:6; 41:12, v. 10).

For these reasons we have opted for keeping *VN* 41 as is.

[25] As we have noted above (*VN* 40 and 41), the theme of pilgrimage spans the

. . quella benedetta Beatrice, la quale gloriosamente mira ne la faccia di colui *qui est per omnia saecula benedictus.*

---

narrative from *VN* 40 to *VN* 42. In *VN* 40 the focus is on a pilgrimage on earth, and it involves several Christians, by extension the entire Christian community. Then the theme develops into a spiritual pilgrimage in *VN* 41, in which the protagonist's pilgrim spirit ascends momentarily to the Empyrean. Finally, in *VN* 42 the narrator-protagonist looks ahead to his own existence, viewing its remaining time as a lifelong pilgrimage ("che la mia vita duri per alquanti anni" 'that my life may last for some years'; "che la mia anima se ne possa gire" 'that my soul may go'; also, "E di venire a ciò" 'And to arrive at that'), animated by a twofold goal: first, here on earth, to be able to say of Beatrice what has never been said of anyone, and the promise of a lifelong dedication to studying and writing; and second, in heaven, to be allowed to contemplate the glory of Beatrice, who gazes upon God. The *libello*, therefore, is interrupted with this twofold anticipation.

While pointing out the continuity of the theme of the pilgrimage through *VN* 40-42, this edition's curators have decided to keep *VN* 42 separate to emphasize the highest vision announced and *VN* 42's function as the entire event's conclusion.

Appendix 4
Incipits of the Poems in the *Vita nuova*

"A ciascun'alma presa e gentil core."
> Sonnet. *VN* 3:10-12. Rhyme scheme: ABBA ABBA CDC CDC.

"Amore e 'l cor gentil sono una cosa."
> Sonnet. *VN* 20:3-5. Rhyme scheme: ABAB ABAB CDE CDE.

"Ballata, i' voi che tu ritrovi Amore."
> Ballade. *VN* 12:10-15. Rhyme scheme: XYYX AbC AbC CDDX.

"Cavalcando l'altr'ier per un cammino."
> Sonnet. *VN* 9:9-12. Rhyme scheme: ABBA ABBA CDE EDC.

"Ciò che m'incontra, ne la mente more."
> Sonnet. *VN* 15:4-6. Rhyme scheme: ABAB ABAB CDE CDE.

"Color d'amore e di pietà sembianti."
> Sonnet. *VN* 36:4-5. ABBA ABBA CDE DCE.

"Con l'altre donne mia vista gabbate."
> Sonnet. *VN* 14:11-12. Rhyme scheme: ABBA ABBA CDE EDC.

"Deh peregrini che pensosi andate."
> Sonnet. *VN* 40:9-10. ABBA ABBA CDE DCE.

"Donna pietosa e di novella etate."
> Canzone. *VN* 23:17-28. Rhyme scheme: ABC ABC CDdE eCDD.

"Donne ch'avete intelletto d'amore."
> Canzone. *VN* 19:4-14. Rhyme scheme: ABBC ABBC CDD CEE.

"Era venuta ne la mente mia."
> Sonnet (1st beginning). *VN* 34:7. ABBA. "Era venuta ne la mente mia."
> (2nd beginning). *VN* 34:8-11. ABBA ABBA CDE DCE.

"Gentil pensero che parla di vui."
> Sonnet. *VN* 38:8-10. ABBA ABBA CDE DCE.

"Io mi senti' svegliar dentro a lo core."
> Sonnet. *VN* 24:7-9. Rhyme scheme: ABAB ABAB CDE CDE.

"L'amaro lagrimar che voi faceste."
> Sonnet. *VN* 37:6-8. Rhyme scheme: ABBA ABBA CDE DCE.

"Lasso! per forza di molti sospiri."
> Sonnet. *VN* 39:8-10. ABBA ABBA CDE DCE.

"Li occhi dolenti per pietà del core."

Canzone. *VN* 31:8-17. Rhyme scheme: ABC ABC, CDEeDEFF; envoi: XYyZZY.

"Morte villana, di pietà nemica."

   Sonnet *doppio* or *rinterzato*. *VN* 8:8-11. Rhyme scheme: AaBBbA AaBBbA CDdC CDdC.

"Ne li occhi porta."

   Sonnet. *VN* 21:2-4. Rhyme scheme: ABBA ABBA CDE EDC.

"Oltre la spera che più larga gira."

   Sonnet. *VN* 41:10-13. ABBA ABBA CDE DCE.

"O voi che per la via d'Amor passate."

   Sonnet *doppio* or *rinterzato*. *VN* 7:3-6. Rhyme scheme: AaBAaB AaBAaB, CDdC DCcD.

"Piangete, amanti, poi che piange Amore."

   Sonnet. *VN* 8:4-6. Rhyme scheme: ABBA ABBA CDE EDC.

"Quantunque volte, lasso!, mi rimembra."

   Canzone of two stanzas. *VN* 33:5-8. Rhyme scheme: AbC AcB, BDEeDFF.

"Se' tu colui c'hai trattato sovente."

   Sonnet. *VN* 22:13-16. Rhyme scheme: ABBA ABBA CDC DCD.

"Sì lungiamente m'ha tenuto Amore."

   Sonnet, or stanza of a canzone. *VN* 27:3-5. Rhyme scheme: ABBA ABBA (a) CDdCEE.

"Spesse fiate vegnonmi a la mente."

   Sonnet. *VN* 16:7-10. Rhyme scheme: ABAB ABAB CDE CDE.

"Tanto gentile e tanto onesta pare."

   Sonnet. *VN* 26:5-7. ABBA ABBA CDE EDC.

"Tutti li miei penser parlan d'Amore."

   Sonnet. *VN* 13:8-9. Rhyme scheme: ABBA ABBA CDE EDC.

"Vede perfettamente onne salute."

   Sonnet. *VN* 26:10-13. Rhyme scheme: ABAB ABAB CDE CDE.

"Venite a intender li sospiri miei."

   Sonnet. *VN* 32:5-6. Rhyme scheme: ABBA ABBA CDE DCE.

"Videro li occhi miei quanta pietate."

   Sonnet. *VN* 35:5-8. Rhyme scheme: ABBA ABBA CDE EDC.

"Voi che portate la sembianza umile."

   Sonnet. *VN* 22:9-10. Rhyme scheme: ABBA ABBA CDC DCD.

Works Cited & Selected Bibliography

Primary Works Cited

Alighieri, Dante. *La commedia secondo l'antica vulgata*. Ed. G. Petrocchi. 4 vols. Milano: Mondadori, 1966-67.

_____. *Opere minori*. Vol. 5, tome 1, part 1. *Vita nuova*. Ed. Domenico De Robertis. *Il fiore*. *Il detto d'amore*. Ed. Gianfranco Contini. Milano: Ricciardi, 1984.

_____. *Opere minori. Convivio*. Vol. 5, tome 1, part 2. *Convivio*. Ed. Cesare Vasoli & Domenico De Robertis. Milano: Ricciardi, 1988.

_____. *Opere minori*. Vol. 5, tome 2. *De vulgari Eloquentia*. Ed. Pier Vincenzo Mengaldo. *Monarchia*. Ed. Bruno Nardi. *Epistole*. Ed. Arsenio Frugoni & Giorgio Brugnoli. *Egloge*. Ed. Enzo Cecchini. *Questio de Aqua et Terra*. Ed. Francesco Mazzoni. Milano: Ricciardi, 1979.

Selected Italian, French, and German Editions

(For this information see: Barbi 1932; E. Esposito. *Enciclopedia dantesca*. Vol. 6. 1978; E. Esposito. *Bibliografia*. 4 vols. 1990. *The National Union Catalog*.)

1527. Giunta. Firenze. [Rhimes only]

1576. Stamperia Bartolomeo Sermartelli. Firenze.

1723. MS. Anton Maria Biscioni. By G. G. Tartini and S. Franchi. Firenze.

1741. Ms. Anton Maria Biscioni. By G. B. Pasquali. Venezia. [1741; 1751; 1772]

1758. Ms. Anton Maria Biscioni. By A. Zatta. Venezia. [1758; 1760]

1793. MS. Anton Maria Biscioni. By P. Gatti. Venezia.

1810. [Zatta; Pasquali] Ed. G. C. Keil. Chemnitz: Carlo Maucke.

1827. Ed. G. G. Trivulzio, V. Monti, and A. M. Maggi. Milano: Pogliani.

1829. Ed. L. C. Ferrucci and Odoardo Machirelli. Pesaro: Nobili. [Reprints: 1839. Napoli: Tramater. 1855. Napoli: Francesco Rossi-Romano.]

1839. Ed. P. J. Fraticelli. Firenze: Allegrini and Mazzoni.

1841. Ed. L. Ciardetti and G. Molini. Firenze.

1843. *Vita nuova di Dante Alighieri.* Edizione 16.a corretta lezione ridotta mediante il riscontro di codici inediti e con illustrazioni e note di diversi per cura di Alessandro Torri. Livorno: Coi Tipi di Paolo Vannini.

1846. [Fraticelli 1839] Ed. Joseph Garrrow. Firenze: Le Monnier.

1855. Ed. P. Fraticelli. Napoli: F. Rossi Romano.

1855. Ed. A. Gotti. Firenze: Le Monnier. [Also 1856; 1859]

1855. Ed. B. Sermartelli. Firenze: A. Volpato.

1856. [P. J. Fraticelli.] Ed. Francesco Prudenzano. Napoli: Belle Arti.

1857. Ed. P. Fraticelli. Barbèra.

1861. Ed. P. Fraticelli. Barbèra.

1863. Ed. G. B. Giuliani. Firenze: Barbèra.

1864. M. Guigoni. Biblioteca delle famiglie. [Also: 1882]

1865. Ed. Ludovico Pizzo. Venezia: Antonelli.

1868. Ed. G. Giuliani. Firenze: Le Monnier. [Also: 1879; 1885]

1872. Ed. A. D'Ancona. Pisa: Nistri. [Also 1884]

1876. Ed. K. Witte. Leipzig: Brockhaus.

1878. Milano: Sonzogno.

1878. Ed. Giuseppe Romanelli. Viterbo: Monarchi.

1883. Ed. A. Fassini. Roma: Paravia.

1883. Ed. Ed. P. Fraticelli. Barbèra.

1883. Ed. Giovanni Fioretto. Padova: A. Draghi.

1883. Ed. G. Giuliani. Firenze: Le Monnier.

1883. Ed. A. Luciani. Roma: E. Botta.

1884. Ed. Ed. Alessandro D'Ancona. Pisa: Galileo già ff. Nistri.

1884. Roma: Biblioteca nova, E. Perino.

1885. Ed. T. Casini. Firenze: Sansoni.

1885. Ed. P. Fraticelli. Firenze: Barbèra.

1887. Roma: E. Perino.

1889. Milano, Biblioteca delle famiglie: Guigoni.

1890. Ed. T. Casini. Firenze: Sansoni.

1890. Ed. A. Gotti. Firenze: G. Civelli.

1890. Napoli: Fratelli Tornese.

1891. Napoli: D. de Feo.

1892. Roma: E. Perino.

1894. Ed. E. Moore. Oxford.

1896. Ed. F. Beck. München: Piloty and Loehle.

1897. Ed. G. L. Passerini. Torino: Paravia. [1920]

1897. Ed. F. Wulff. Stockholm.

1898. Ed. G. L. Passerini and Leo S. Olschki. Firenze: Franceschini. [1899]

1899. Ed. P. Fraticelli. Firenze: Barbèra. [Also 1906]

1900. Ed. F. Biondolillo. Roma: Edizioni dell'Ateneo.

1900. Ed. G. Canevazzi. Milano: Albrighi, Segati.

1900. Ed. Ed. G. L. Passerini. Firenze: Sansoni.

1902. Ed. T. Casini: Firenze: Sansoni.

1902. Ed. Ill. D. G. Rossetti. Torino: Roux e Viarengo. [Also 1903]

1904. Ed. T. Casini. Firenze: Sansoni. [Also 1905; 1913]

1905. Ed. G. Melodia. Milano: Vallardi. [Also 1911; 1925]

1906. *La vita nuova secondo la lezione del cod. strozziano VI, 143*. Trascritta
       e illustrata da A. Razzolini. [With the trans. of D. G. Rossetti] Firenze:
       Tipografia domenicana.

1907. Trans. and ed. Henry Cochin. Paris: Champion. [Also: 1914; 1916]

1907. Ed. Michele Barbi. Società Dantesca Italiana. Milano: Hoepli.

1909. Ed. H. Cochin. Paris: Champion. [Also 1914]

1909. Ed. F. Flamini. Livorno: Giusti.

1910. Ill. Luigi Guerrini Fiorentino. Firenze: G. Giannini & figlio.

1910. Ed. G. Federzoni and G. Carducci. Bologna: Zanichelli.

1911. Ed. M. Scherillo. Milano: Hoepli. [Also 1921]

1911. Ill. D. G. Rossetti. Torino: UTET. [Also 1918; 1921]

1914. Ed. G. A. Cesareo. Messina: Principato.

1920. Ed. G. L. Passerini. Torino: Paravia.

1921. Ed. M. Barbi. Bergamo: Istituto italiano delle arti grafiche.

1921. Ed. M. Barbi. Firenze: Bemporad.

1921. Ed. D. Guerri. Firenze: Perella.

1923. Ed. M. Barbi. Comm. G. L. Passerini. Palermo: Sandron.

1925. Ed. M. Barbi. Pref. B. Croce. Montagnola.

1928. Ed. L. Di Benedetto. Torino: UTET.

1928. Ed. G. Manacorda. Firenze: Rinascimento del libro.

1931. Ed. N. Sapegno. Firenze: Vallecchi. [Also 1949]

1932. Ed. Michele Barbi. *Edizione nazionale delle opere di Dante*. Società
       Dantesca Italiana, 1. Firenze: Bemporad. [Second ed. 1960]

1932. Ed. T. Casini. Per cura di L. Pietrobono. Firenze: Sansoni. [Also 1938; 1946]

1933. Parigi: Pichon.

1934. Ed. T. L. Rizzo. Palermo: Andò.

1936. Ed. D. Mattalia. Torino: Paravia.

1938. Ed. G. A. Ceriello. Milano: Signorelli.

1938. Ed. D. Mattalia. Torino: Paravia.

1938. Ed. A. Polvara. Torino: SEI.

1943. Ed. N. Sapegno. Firenze: Vallecchi. [Also 1949]

1944. Ed. Luigi Di Benedetto. Torino: UTET.

1949. Ed. F. Biondolillo. Roma: Ateneo. [Also 1950; 1951]

1952. Ed. L. Magugliani. Milano: Rizzoli.

1953. Ed. A. Fusai. Palermo: Palumbo.

1953. Ed. A. Pézard. Paris: UNESCO.

1954. Ed. A. Vallone. Roma: Ausonia.

1956. Ed. L. Russo. Messina: D'Anna.

1957. Ed. *Neues Leben*. Trans. Sophie Hildenbrandt. Köln: Böhlau.

1958. Ed. Erwin Laaths. It. and Ger. on opposite pages. Berlin: Tempel-Verlag, 1963.

1960. Ed. A. Del Monte. Milano: Rizzoli.

1964. Ed. U. Leo. Frankfurt a. M.: Fischer.

1965. Ed. F. Chiappelli. Milano: Mursia.

1965. Ed. F. Chiappelli. Firenze: Sansoni.

1965. Ed. E. Sanguineti. Milano: Lerici.

1965. Ed. L. Blasucci. Firenze: Sansoni.

1966. Ed. M. Porena and M. Pazzaglia. Bologna: Zanichelli.

1966. Ed. A. Vallone. Torino: Caula.

1968. Ed. G. R. Ciriello. Milano: Signorelli.

1970. Ed. G. Contini. Firenze: Sansoni.

1971. Ed. G. Davico Bonino. Milano: Club degli Editori.

1974. Trans. and introd. Louis-Paul Guigues. Paris: Gallimard.

1977. Ed. E. Sanguineti. Milano: Garzanti. [Second ed. 1979]

1980. Ed. D. De Robertis. Milano: Ricciardi.

1984. *Vita nuova*. Ed. Domenico De Robertis. *Opere minori*. Ed. Domenico De Robertis and Gianfranco Contini. La letteratura italiana, Storia e testi. Vol. 5, tome 1, part 1. Milano: R. Ricciardi.

1984. Ed. Marcello Ciccuto. Introd. Giorgio Petrocchi. Milano: Rizzoli.

1985. Ed. G. Davico Bonino. Milano: Mondadori.

1992. Ed. Michele Barbi. Notes Pietro Manera. Milano: Hoepli.

1993. Ed. Manuela Colombo. Milano: Feltrinelli.

1994. Ed. Jennifer Petrie & June Salmons. Dublin: Belfield Italian Library.

Selected Editions of the Vita nuova in English

1842. *The Poems of the Vita nuova and Convito.* Trans. Charles Lyell. London: C. F. Molini. [Preface v-ix; notes and essays xi-cclxxxviii; It. text and trans. of poems of the *Vita nuova* 1-85; It. text and trans. of the canzoni of the *Convivio* 87-115; appendix 117-37]

1846. *The Early Life of Dante Alighieri together with the Original in Parallel Pages.* Ed. Joseph Garrow. Firenze: Le Monnier.

1859. *The New Life of Dante.* Trans. and essay Eliot Norton. Boston: Phillips, Sampson.

1859. *The New Life of Dante.* Trans. and essay Eliot Norton. Cambridge: Riverside Press. Printed by H. O. Houghton.

1862. *The Vita nuova of Dante.* Trans. and introd. Theodore Martin. London: Parker.

1864. *The Vita nuova of Dante.* Trans. Theodore Martin. Edinburgh: W. Blackwood. [Introd. vii-lviii; English Trans. 1-74; notes and ill. 75-120] [Also 1893; 1902]

1866. *Notes on the Vita nuova and Minor Poems of Dante, together with the New Life and many of the Poems, by the Author of "Remarks on the Sonnets of Shakespeare, etc."* New York. [Trans. of the *Vita nuova* by D. G. Rossetti]

1867. *The New Life.* Trans. Charles E. Norton. Boston: Houghton, Mifflin, and Co. [Also 1892; 1889; 1892; 1895; 1896; 1898; 1899; 1902] [English trans., 1-92; essays: "On the New Life" 93-105; "The *Convivio* and the *Vita nuova*" 106-28; "On the Structure of the *Vita nuova*" 129-36; notes 137-68]

1871. *The vita nuova of Dante.* Trans. Theodore Martin. Sec. ed. Edinburgh: W. Blackwood. [Introd. vii-liv; trans. 1-81; notes and ill. 83-127]

1890. *The Vita nuova and its Author.* Trans., notes, and introd. Charles Stuart Boswell.

1892. *The vita nuova of Dante*. London: Chiswick Press, 1892. [Text and notes on parallel pages]

1893. *La vita nuova di Dante Alighieri with notes and commentary in English*. Ed. N. Perini. London: Hachette.

1895. *The Vita nuova and Its Author*. Trans. Charles Stuart Boswell. London: Kegan Paul, Trench, Trübner. [Introd. 1-97; English trans. 99-201; notes 202-28]

1896. *The New Life of Dante Alighieri*. Trans. D. G. Rossetti. Portland: Mosher. [Also 1900; 1905; 1912]

1899. *The New Life*. Trans. D. G. Rossetti. London: Ellis and Elvey. [Also 1901; 1903; 1905]

1902. *The Vita nuova or New Life*. Trans. Frances De Meÿ. London: G. Bell and Sons. [English trans., 3-114; note by trans., 117; essay, 118-20; contents, indices 121-30]

1903. *The New Life*. Ed. and trans. Luigi Ricci. London: K. Paul Trench, Trübner. [It. and Engl. on opposite pages]

1906. *The Vita nuova and Canzoniere*. Trans. Thomas Okey and Philip H. Wicksteed. The Temple Classics. London: Dent. [It. text and Engl. trans. 2-153; *Canzoniere* 155-323; Notes 324-53; Appendix 354-57]

1906. *La vita nuova (The New Life) secondo la lezione del cod. strozziano VI, 143 trascritta e illustrata da A. Razzolini*. Firenze: Tipografia domenicana. [Engl. trans. and text on opposite pages]

1908. *Dante's Vita nuova with Rossetti's Version*. Trans. D. M. Rossetti. Ed. H. Oelsner. The King's Classics. London: Chatto and Windus. [Preface by H. Oelsner ix-lix; It. text and trans. 1-203; notes 205-37; appendix 239-74]

1909. *The Vita nuova or New Life of Dante Alighieri*. Trans. Frances de Meÿ. London: G. Bell.

1908. *Dante's Vita nuova together with the Version of D. G. Rossetti*. Ed. H. Oelsner.

1922. *La vita nuova di Dante Alighieri*. Ed., introd., notes and vocabulary by Kenneth McKenzie. Heath's Modern Language Series. Boston: Heath.

1930. *Boethius and Dante*. Trans. D. G. Rossetti. 2 vols. Boston: Bibliophile Society.

1947. *Vita nuova. The Portable Dante*. Trans. D. G. Rossetti. [Several reprints] [Trans. of the *Vita nuova* and notes 545-618]

1956. *An English Translation of the* Vita nuova *of Dante Alighieri by Mark*

Musa. Translator's B.A. Thesis. New Brunswick, 1956.

1957. *The Vita nuova.* Trans. Mark Musa. New Brunswick: Rutgers UP.

1960. *Vita nuova.* Trans. Ralph Waldo Emerson. Ed. and notes J. Chesley Mathews. Chapel Hill: U of N. Carolina.

1962. *The Vita nuova.* Trans. Mark Musa. Bloomington: Indiana UP. [Introd. vii-xxii; English trans. 3-86]

1964. *The New Life.* Trans. William Anderson. Baltimore: Penguin.

1965. *Vita Nuova.* Trans. R. W. Emerson. Ed. and notes J. Ch. Mathews. New York: Johnson Reprint. [Rpt. of 1960]

1966. *La vita nuova.* Trans. Mark Musa. Gloucester, MA: P. Smith.

1969. *La vita nuova (Poems of Youth).* Trans. Barbara Reynolds. Middlesex, England: Penguin. [Introd. 11-25; translator's note 27; Trans. 29-99; Note on the structure 101; Notes on the text 103-20; Dante's chronology 121-22; Index of first lines of poems in Engl. trans. 123]

1972. *The Vita nuova.* Trans., introd. and notes Th. Martin. Freeport, N.Y.: Books for Libraries Press. [Rpt. of 1862]

1973. *Dante's Vita nuova.* Trans. Mark Musa. Bloomington: Indiana UP. [Preface ix-xii; translator's note xiii-xiv; English trans. 1-86; essay 87-174; notes to the essay 175-210]

1992. *Vita nuova.* Trans., introd. and notes Mark Musa. New York: Oxford UP.

1995. *The Portable Dante.* Ed. and trans. with introd., bibl. and notes Mark Musa. New York: Penguin.

Selected Studies for This Volume

Ahern, John. "The New Life of the Book: The Implied Reader of the *Vita Nuova, Dante Studies* 110 (1992): 1-16.

_____. "The Reader on the Piazza: Verbal Duels in Dante's *Vita nuova,*" *Texas Studies in Language and Literature* 32 (1970): 18-39.

Alighieri, Dante. *Dante's Lyric Poetry.* Ed. K. Foster and P. Boyde. 2 vols. Oxford: Oxford UP, 1967.

Alinei Mario. *Spogli elettronici dell'italiano delle origini e del duecento. II: Forme: 8: Dante Alighieri, La vita nuova.* Ed. M. Barbi. *A Linguistic Inventory of Thirteenth-Century Italian, II 8.* Bologna: Il Mulino, 1971.

_____. *Spogli elettronici dell'italiano delle origini e del duecento. II: Forme: 11: Dante Alighieri, Rime.* Ed. M. Barbi, F. Maggini, V. Pernicone. *A Linguistic Inventory of Thirteenth-Century Italian. II 11.* Bologna: Il Mulino, 1972.

Anderson,William. *Dante the Maker.* London: Routlege and Kegan Paul, 1979.

Augustine, Saint. *St. Augustine's Confessions.* Trans. William Watts [1631]. 2 vols. Cambridge: Harvard, 1960.

Bakhtin, M. M. *The Dialogic Imagination. Four Essays.* Ed. Michael Holquist. Trans. Caryl Emerson and Michael Holquist. Austin: U of Texas P, 1981.

Bargellini, Piero. *Florence the Magnificent: A History.* Vol 1. Florence: Vallecchi, 1980.

Barolini, Teodolinda. *Dante's Poets: Textuality and Truth in the* Comedy. Princeton: Princeton UP, 1984.

_____. *The Undivine Comedy: Detheologizing Dante.* Princeton: Princeton UP, 1992.

Benveniste, Emile. "Le Langage et l'expérience humaine." *Problèmes de linguistique générale.* 2 vols. Paris: Gallimard, 1974. 2:67-78.

Biblia sacra iuxta Vulgatam Clementinam. Biblioteca de autores cristianos: Madrid, 1982.

Boyde, Patrick. *Dante, Philomythes and Philosopher: Man in the Cosmos.* Cambridge: Cambridge UP, 1981.

Bruner, Jerome and Susan Weisser. "The Invention of Self: Autobiography and Its Forms." *Literacy and Orality.* Ed. David R. Olson and Nancy Torrance. Cambridge: Cambridge UP, 1991. 129-48.

Brambilla Ageno, Franca. *L'edizione dei testi volgari.* Sec. ed. Medioevo e Umanesimo, 22. Padova: Antenore, 1984.

Carruthers, Mary J. *The Book of Memory: A Study of Memory in Medieval Culture.* Cambridge: Cambridge UP, 1990.

Cervigni, Dino S. *Dante's Poetry of Dreams.* Firenze: Olschki, 1986.

_____ and Edward Vasta. "From Manuscript to Print: The Case of Dante's *Vita nuova. Dante Now: Current Trends in Dante Studies.* Notre Dame: U of Notre Dame P, 1995.

Charity, Alan Clifford. *Events and Their Afterlife.* Cambridge: Cambridge UP, 1966.

Clanchy, M. T. *From Memory to Written Record: England, 1066-1307.*

Cambridge: Harvard UP, 1979.

Conti, Maria. *Percossi dell'invenzione: il linguaggio poetico e Dante.* Torino: Einaudi, 1993.

Curtius, Ernst. *European Literature in the Latin Middle Ages.* Trans. Willard R. Trask. Princeton: Princeton UP, 1953.

D'Andrea, Antonio. *Il nome della storia. Studi e ricerche di storia e letteratura.* Napoli: Liguore, 1982.

De Robertis, Domenico. *Il libro della* Vita nuova. Firenze: Sansoni, 1970.

Duby, Georges. *The Three Orders: Feudal Society Imagined.* Trans. Arthur Goldhammer. Chicago: U of Chicago P, 1980.

Durling, Robert M. and Ronald L. Martinez. *Time and the Crystal: Studies in Dante's* Rime petrose. Berkeley: U of California P, 1990.

Eisenstein, Elizabeth. *The Printing Press as an Agent of Change: Communications and Cultural Transformations in Early-Modern Europe.* 2 vols. New York: Cambridge UP, 1979.

Enciclopedia dantesca. 6 vols. Roma: Istituto della Enciclopedia Italiana fondata da Giovanni Treccani, 1970-78.

Esposito, Enzo. *Gli studi danteschi dal 1950 al 1164.* Roma: Centro editoriale internazionale, 1965.

_____. *L'opera di Dante nel mondo: edizioni e traduzioni nel Novecento.* Ravenna: Longo, 1992.

Fiore, Quentin and Marshall McLuhan.*The Medium Is the Massage.* New York: Bantam, 1967.

Foley, John Miles. "Oral Literature: Premises and Problems." *Choice* 18 (1980): 487-96.

Giovannetti, Luciana. *Dante in America. Bibliografia 1965-1980.* Ravenna: Longo, 1987.

Gorni, Guglielmo. *Lettera nome numero. L'ordine delle cose in Dante.* Bologna: Il Mulino, 1990.

_____. *Il nodo della lingua e il verbo d'amore: studi su Dante e altri duecentisti.* Saggi di "Lettere Italiane" 29. Firenze: Olschki, 1981.

_____. "Per il testo della *Vita nuova.*" *Studi di filologia italiana.* 51 (1994): 5-37.

Harrison, Robert Pogue. *The Body of Beatrice.* Baltimore: Johns Hopkins UP, 1988.

Kelber, Werner. *The Oral and the Written Gospel: The Hermeneutics of Speaking and Writing in the Synoptic Tradition, Mark, Paul and Q.*

Philadelphia: Fortress, 1983.

Kermode, Frank. *The Sense of an Ending: Studies in the Theory of Fiction.* 1966. London: Oxford UP, 1968.

La letteratura italiana. Ed. Alberto Asor Rosa. 15 vols. Torino: Einaudi, 1982-94.

Marti, Mario. "'. . . l'una appresso de l'altra maraviglia' (Dante, *Vita nuova*, XXIV)." *Giornale storico della letteratura italiana* 158.544 (1991): 481-503.

————. *"Stil nuovo. Enciclopedia Dantesca.*

————. *Storia dello stil nuovo .* 2 vols. Lecce: Milella, 1973.

Mazzotta, Giuseppe. *Dante's Vision and the Circle of Knowledge.* Princeton: Princeton UP, 1993.

————. "The Language of Poetry in the *Vita nuova." Rivista di studi italiani* 1.1 (1983): 3-14.

McLuhan, Marshall. *The Gutenberg Galaxy: The Making of Typographic Man .* Toronto: U of Toronto P, 1962).

———— and Quentin Fiore. *The Medium Is the Massage.* New York: Bantam, 1967.

Nelson, William. "From 'Listen, Lordings' to 'Dear Reader.'" *University of Toronto Quarterly* 46 (1976-77): 111-24.

Ong, Walter. *Orality and Literacy: The Technologizing of the Word.* London: Methuen, 1982.

Pampaloni, Guido *"Bianche e neri." Enciclopedia Dantesca.*

Parry, Milman. *L'Epithète traditionelle dans Homère.* Paris: Société Éditrice Les Belles Lettres, 1928.

Pazzaglia, Mario. *"Vita nuova." Enciclopedia Dantesca.*

Petrocchi, Georgio. "Biografia." *Enciclopedia Dantesca.*

————. ————. "Guelfi e Ghibellini." *Enciclopedia Dantesca.*

————. *Vita di Dante.* Bari: Laterza, 1983.

Picone, Michelangelo. *Dante e le forme dell'allegoresi.* Ravenna: Longo, 1987.

————. *Vita nuova e tradizione romanza.* Padova: Livinia editrice, 1979.

Riché Pierre and Guy Lobrichon. *Le Moyen Age et la bible.* La Collection Bible de tous les temps. Paris: Beauchesne, 1984.

Ricoeur, Paul. "Narrative Time." *Critical Inquiry* (Fall 1980): 169-90.

————. *A Ricoeur Reader : Reflection and Imagination.* Toronto: U of Toronto P, 1991.

_____. *Time and Narrative.* 1983-1985. Vol. 1. Trans. Kathleen Blamey and David Pellauer. Vols. 2-3. Trans. Kathleen McLaughlin and David Pellauer. Chicago: U of Chicago P, 1984-1988.

Rouse, Richard H. and Mary A. Rouse. "*Statim invenire*: Schools, Preachers, and New Attitudes to the Page." *Renaissance and Renewal in the Twelfth Century.* Ed. Robert L. Benson and Giles Constable with Carol D. Lanham. Cambridge: Harvard UP, 1982. 201-25.

Singleton, Charles. 1949. *An Essay on the* Vita nuova. 2nd. ed. Baltimore: Johns Hopkins UP, 1977.

Speculum. 65.1 (1990).

Steiner, George. *Language and Silence: Essays on Language, Literature, and the Inhuman.* New York: Athenaeum, 1967.

Stillinger, Thomas C. *The Song of Troilus: Lyric Authority in the Medieval Book.* Philadelphia: U of Pennsylvania P, 1992.

Stock, Brian. *The Implications of Literacy.* Princeton: Princeton U P, 1983).

Took, J. F. *Dante: Lyric Poet and Philosopher. An Introduction to the Minor Works.* Oxford: Clarendon, 1990.

Vallone, Aldo. "*Beatrice.*" *Enciclopedia Dantesca.*

_____. *Dante.* 2nd. ed. Padova: F. Vallardi, 1981.

_____. *La prosa della* Vita nuova. Firenze: Le Monnier, 1963.

Vasta, Edward and Dino S. Cervigni. "From Manuscript to Print: The Case of Dante's *Vita nuova. Dante Now: Current Trends in Dante Studies.* Notre Dame: U of Notre Dame P, 1995.

Weisser, Susan and Jerome Bruner. "The Invention of Self: Autobiography and Its Forms." *Literacy and Orality.* Ed. David R. Olson and Nancy Torrance. Cambridge: Cambridge UP, 1991. 129-48.